<u>Demonic</u>
Book I of the Soul Trade Saga

E. Y. Bluestein

DEDICATION

Dedicated to the twelve hundred innocent souls taken by demons, and the brave heroes who rode into hell after them.

ACKNOWLEDGMENTS

To Adi, my love. Thanks for suffering me through all these years.

To Mom, for swooping in and saving the day.

To Amit. For being an officer, a gentleman and a true friend. Thanks buddy!

For Ilan. Thanks for being an anchor in a storm.

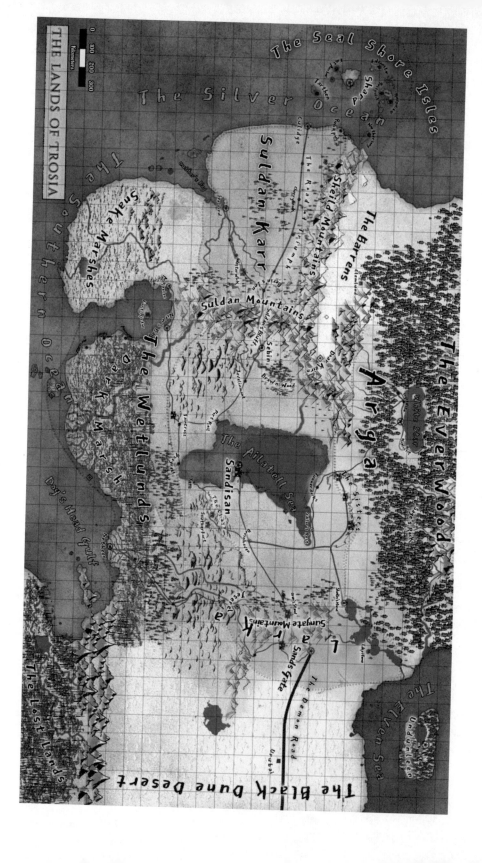

PROLOGUE

Let me offer you a trade. A story for a story and a song for a song. A fable for a fable.

The phrase is ancient. So ancient that one forgets that there was an age before it was uttered. It's been recanted for thousands of years in many tongues and on many tongues. It opens the ear and the mind and welcomes the wisdom in the tale.

But when all is said and done, it is still a trade at its heart. A transaction from a time that mortals needed stories to shape their young world. The mortal condition, with all its wonder, is fleeting. The currency of memory is that of the tale and the myth. And while you may balk at my words, know with no uncertainty that mortals need *their* trade as much as the gods need theirs.

But you my friend haven't come to hear of trade or economics. You came to hear about how the journey began. Before Sebin or the Library of Diam. Before the Demonic war and before the Shadow Altar. The bit of the tale that few know and fewer yet recant. Have no fear: we shall not leave out the good parts. The ones you have probably heard before in taverns or beside campfires, or perhaps at your mother's teat. The best stories live a thousand lives and differ slightly in each telling. Like autumn leaves falling from the same tree. They look alike yet are slightly different. Each a version of the others.

The one I shall tell isn't the best or the worst. And I wouldn't impose on you the arrogance of claiming it was the truth, as all tales are true in their own way. The only claim I will make is that this account is what actually happened in my own memory. And my memory is endless.

So how does it begin? That question is as pointless as following a single drop of rain in a stream. Instead, let us ask *where* it begins. And as I am the teller of this story, I choose to begin it at a lonely crossroad.

Indulge me the god's-eye perspective and the cliché of beginning this tale with a crow on a branch.

1 HANGING MEN

A crow cawed loudly as it perched on the gray branches of the large sycamore tree at the crossroad. It must have been the first of its peers to spot the feast that humans had recently left out for it. Three figures hung motionless from the tree's bare branches. The middle one was a full-grown human. Blood from a chest wound had already congealed on his clothes and stopped dripping into the pool that had formed, drying on the grass beneath his limp feet. This one had been dead when they'd strung him up. The other two figures, both lads in their teens, had died on the rope, apparent from their open bulging eyes.

The crow skipped down to a lower branch, eyeing the open eyes with hunger. Before it could approach the bodies, a rock hit the branch it was on and sent it flapping and squawking away in a flurry of feathers.

Three men stood in the clearing, solemnly staring at the grizzly sight. The one who had thrown the rock stood a head above the others. His skin was sun-bronzed, and a black stripe of coarse hair, cut low and centered on his scalp, ended in a long braid that reached the middle of his back. He was muscular, and while his hands were no strangers to the curved saber at his side, it was rather a golden half-sun medallion that they clutched.

To his right stood a sandy-haired man. He turned to the first man and raised an eyebrow but said nothing.

It was the third man who sighed and finally spoke: "So, I guess we're cutting them down."

"We're cutting them down," the taller man confirmed grimly.

The second man walked over to the macabre vestige and drew a long, thin rapier. The blade would have been an uncommon sight in the wild lands of Suldan-Karr and much more common on the streets of one of the bigger Heartland cities such as Sandisan. It spoke volumes about the young man's origins.

With a quick slash, he cut the body down, dropping him like a wet sack, and then he did the same to the two younger lads. Now that they were on the ground, he took a better look at the three. The two boys must have been the man's sons, as they had the same matted black hair. Their purple faces hinted at the terrifying and painful end they must have met.

"How old would you say they are?" asked the third man. Small, pointed ears poked through his shoulder-long auburn hair, suggesting an elven heritage.

"Thirteen. Maybe fifteen, that one," said the man with the rapier. He removed a circle-shaped copper badge from the man and turned it in his hand. The two boys had similar badges. He dropped it to the ground in disgust.

He knelt by the man who had been marked as the father and removed a paper note that was stuffed in the folds of his coat.

"'*Let them be a feast for the wolves or share their fate*,'" he read the note, which was written in the blood of its host.

"Perfect," said the half-elf. He looked over to the tall man with the braid. The man shook his head in response.

"I don't know who wrote that, but we'll deal with it. Every soul deserves proper passage to his maker." His accent, coupled with his hairstyle and cloak of seal fur unmistakably marked the man as *Tundrial*—a Seal Shore Barbarian, as they were called on the mainland.

"We don't know who they were, Bunda, or why they were up there," said the kneeling man.

"Nick. What could this man and his boys have possibly done to deserve such a fate?" answered Bunda.

Nick sighed and rose to his feet. Bunda was a devout follower of Seirn, Lord of Light. There was no changing his mind about showing respect for the dead. A week ago, two men who had shared their camp tried to kill them during the night and steal their belongings. While they had made short work of the thieves, Bunda insisted on burying the two assassins despite his companions' objections.

"Well, let's look for some rocks." The ground would have been too hard to dig without shovels, and his slim blade would be useless.

"Are you going to help?" he asked the third man, who had been silent during the discussion. The half-elf looked at the setting sun to the west. He was clearly measuring the time it would take for his companions to build a cairn with or without his help.

"It would be a mistake to be out here at night," he said carefully. Nick knew he was thinking of the pack of wolves that had been tracking them over the past two days. The wolves had come close the night before, but Nick had felled one with an arrow and they since kept their distance. Hunger would soon revitalize their boldness if they were still tracking them. It was apparent from the occasional howl they hadn't found any easier prey yet and would eventually prefer to risk a human blade than starvation.

"Where is Dorkah?" he asked the half-elf.

"I've sent her away," he said, giving a meaningful glance at the tiny village resting at the end of the path that forked off from the main road. Even calling it a main road was an exaggeration. They had chosen this path before entering the mountains rather than the dwarven paved Road of Triumph, which led most of the traffic from the western coast to Sebin.

These days, the lands of Suldan-Karr had become lawless and crawling with brigands, marauding bands of Orcs, and other wilderness beasties. Taking a less trodden path seemed safer. Bunda, being a member of the warlike inhabitants of the Seal Shore Islands, seemed to be fearless. He had never ventured this far east. Besides, most folks knew not to trifle with a Tundrial. The other two, who had made the Suldan-Karr towns dotting the Triumph Road from Culidge to Sebin their homes over the past few years, knew that if they wanted to travel these mountain passes this close to winter, caution was the better part of valor. The two of them had convinced the stubborn barbarian to take the detour.

The small village, which wasn't on any map of Nemir, was called Suldan's Bluff according to the faded wooden sign pitched at the crossroad. Nick vaguely remembered passing through it years ago when he first entered these lands. He couldn't recall why he hadn't stopped here. At the time, he had been traveling as a hired blade with a small caravan and hadn't bothered asking questions. The caravan master had been guarded regarding his cargo, which must not have been very respectable—not that Nick had minded, but it was probably the reason he chose this back road and why he had chosen to skirt by the town. At the time, Nick wouldn't have wanted to stop either.

"Are you going to help?" Bunda's deep voice split his reverie. He had finished blessing the dead in accordance with his god's rites and was carrying a large rock in his calloused hands.

Nick nodded, and the trio began piling rocks over the dead to protect their remains from scavengers.

One good deed in a bad land.

***

The village was little more than a hamlet in the middle of nowhere, with a smattering of houses and a few hides of land. Nick assumed the residents lived mostly from basic farming, hunting, and gathering. There were a few mountain streams nearby, so perhaps they also fished.

The ten buildings comprising the settlement were situated in a semi-circle surrounding a large green patch of grass, with the village well found near the central building. The central building, which was the only building made of stone, must have been the closest thing to an inn Suldan's Bluff had to offer.

The inn's name was *The Miner's Lodge*.

"These folks are miners?" asked Bunda, looking at the sign.

"Maybe once. Not anymore," answered the half-elf.

"Why do you say so, Tadok?" he asked.

"If an active mine existed, we'd see more people here. Ten homes would hardly house a retinue of miners. And let's not forget that this place isn't on maps. At least none I've ever seen. Finally, if any metal or other ore were being drawn from these mountains, we would have seen deep wagon grooves on the path to carry them west, which we didn't."

Nick thought about how Tadok didn't miss much. The half-elf never spoke of his origins...none of them did. But his accent placed him from the northlands of *Arga*, where the council of Freelan had carved out an independent state, breaking away from the Empire twenty-five years ago.

Tadok was a pale man, paler than other half-elves Nick had known. His green eyes often had a haunted look, which only abated when his unusual companion, Dorkah, was around. As for weaponry, Tadok had a simple, functional crossbow slung over his back and a curved sickle with an extended grip hanging from his belt. The latter

7

would have made a poor melee weapon and must have originally been a plowing instrument. Both had a sad backstory, suspected Nick, but like the rest of his past, Tadok hadn't shared that with them. It was impossible to know his age as elven blood brought on longevity.

As they entered the inn, a small bell above the door rang dully. The common room was empty. It wasn't a large inn, with only two round candlelit tables that could seat up to five people and one long table near the bar. The aroma of mouth-watering cooking came from a door behind the well-polished bar, and a narrow staircase led up to the second floor. A large stone hearth washed the room with warmth and a soft glowing light, pushing the evening shadows back.

They could overhear low voices from the kitchen in argument.

"Not with winter comin'," said a man's voice.

"And if they don't?" retorted a woman's voice harshly. "What could we possibly have to give next time?"

"Well," began the man solemnly, "when a man's got na' to give, he's got na' to lose."

"You mind yer tongue, Marven Darvey! Yer too old for talk like that, and ye groan every time you climb our steps."

"Hanged men donna' suffer from stiff knees, Ody," jested Marven in response.

The woman clicked her tongue. "Trin have yer eyes, man. Yer jests are as barren as your scalp."

The two must not have heard the entrance bell, and feeling embarrassed at eavesdropping on the intimate exchange, Nick cleared his throat, cutting their conversation short. The clatter of cutlery and the curses was evidence that Nick had startled them. A moment later an aging, potbellied man holding a skillet burst out of the kitchen. While he may have been cooking with it, as was apparent by the greasy sauce dripping from its edge, he now gripped it tightly, ready to turn pan into club if the situation warranted.

He eyed them suspiciously for a few moments, his wife peeking fearfully around the doorpost at the three well-armed, dusty figures.

The members of the trio each realized that they needed to look less menacing. Nick raised his hands and spread his fingers, smiling. Bunda grinned a toothy grin—which actually may have been worse— and Tadok simply waved.

"I am Nick Cartright; this is Bunda of the Jams and Tadok

Starkin. We mean you no harm and would rather *have* dinner than be bashed with it," said Nick, motioning to the skillet.

Marven's eyes remained fixed on Bunda.

It wasn't a surprise. Bunda's people had warranted their fearsome reputation. Since Shard had overthrown the Empire over two decades ago, they had ravaged the lands between the coast and the Suldan mountains repeatedly. They had looted, pillaged, burned, and raped their way east and had only been held off at the gates of Sebin. Luckily for the people of Suldan-Karr, the Tundrial had no interest in occupying and returned to their stormy islands come winter. Less luckily for the people of Suldan-Karr, they repeated their actions again come spring. The only reason the raids had abated and stayed closer to the coast these days was because the fragmented Tundrial tribes and clans warred amongst themselves more than with anyone else. The Lord Mayors of Culidge and Seaview exploited this by paying one tribe or another for their protection from the others. But this didn't stop barbarian raiding parties from attacking the coastal settlements from time to time, even venturing into the mainland when the coastal pickings were slim.

But Bunda was the opposite of the Tundrial stereotype.

Fiercely devoted to Seirn, he had adopted the Doctrine of Light, which he followed to the letter. He was terrifying in battle, calling upon his Lord's favor to crush his enemies, yet his demeanor became gentle when he used his master's healing touch in the aftermath.

"We have coin," offered Tadok. Either that statement or the sight of the Seirn medallion hanging from Bunda's neck seemed to ease the innkeeper, and his demeanor altered magically.

"In that case, welcome to the Miner's Lodge travelers. My name's Marven Darvey. How about you rest yer weary feet by the fire while me wife, Odetta, fetches you some tea."

Nick wasn't really in the mood for tea, but the fire beckoned to him seductively and he nodded, leading them to the nearest table.

Odetta was a petite woman with gray hair which was gathered in a tight bun. She laid three steaming mugs in front of them, and the scent of cinnamon, apples, and other spices changed his mind about the tea, which he sipped eagerly.

"What about some food, man? Or is that skillet only a weapon?" asked Tadok.

Marven looked puzzled for a moment, then he looked at the

frying pan still in hand and laughed a hearty laugh. "This? No, no. We have food, ale, mead, and cider. If you want room and board, it'll be three sorins per night."

Nick's eyes widened comically. "Three silver sorins!" He feigned shock. "I thought the brigands infested the roads, not the inns in these parts, Tadok."

A grave, fearful look passed over Marven's eyes, and thinking of the three they had buried earlier, Nick regretted the words as they fled his mouth. But the dread disappeared from the innkeeper's face as soon as it had come, and he resumed playing the game.

"You offend me, sir! In days past, a room in this fine establishment would fetch a full corin, it would!"

"Three sorins will do. Just fetch us some food," Tadok cut in. The half-elf was clearly hungry and in no mood for the haggling ceremony.

The innkeeper bobbed his head up and down once and went to carry out the order.

Nick was halfway through his bowl of stew when the door burst open, and an angry-looking dwarf with bushy black eyebrows barged into the room.

"Darvey, you silly old fool! You did it, didn't you?"

Marven, who was carrying a tray full of ceramic mugs, scowled at the four-foot-tall intruder.

"What in King Nem's name are ye on about, man?" He looked at the floor and added, "And I told you a thousand times to wipe yer muddy boots before stomping in here!"

The dwarf paused and looked at the trail left in his wake, but it didn't set him back for long.

"We talked about it. Do you think I *didn't* want to cut them down? Or Hanlan or Mendel? He was a brother to me as much as to you lot. Do you think Hayek will care that you did it on your own council?"

Both men stared at each other for a moment. But while the dwarf was enraged, Marven was confused. He then shot a glance over the dwarf to the window facing the hangman tree, realization dawning.

The dwarf's eyes narrowed under his bushy gray eyebrows. "It wasn't you, was it? Who then? Ren? Mendel?"

Marven scratched his balding pate. "Haven't seen Ren in three days, and Mendel's got a family to fret for."

Both men swiveled slowly to look at the three men dining.

"Here it comes..." muttered Tadok under his breath.

It was Bunda who spoke. His voice was calm as he wiped his chin from the stew with his sleeve. "The man and two boys hanging from the tree? Yes. We cut them down and gave blessing." He looked back at his bowl, trying to track down another chunk of chicken, and said, "I don't know what they did, but every soul deserves passage to his maker."

The two men stood there with a mixture of shock and fear in their eyes. Odetta, who had entered during the commotion, looked at the newcomers with a sense of admiration but shifted her eyes away when her husband shot a glance at her.

"You don't understand..." began the dwarf when the door burst open a second time. This time a brawny man with a tattoo of an anvil and another with a round belly and red beard were at the door.

"I thought we agreed *not* to," said the bearded man.

"T'wasn't him, Mendel" cut in the dwarf gloomily.

"Then who, Swegan?" asked the tattooed man.

In response, Swegan the dwarf nodded towards the three travelers, and the inn's newcomers seemed to notice them for the first time.

Nick wondered at the mixture of emotions passing over both villager's faces. Surprise, outrage, fear, then...shame?

"Please, we are not looking for trouble. We're just traveling on our way to Sebin," he began, trying to diffuse the situation, but Tadok interrupted.

"I think, good sirs, it's time you explained what this is about. Who were they? What was their crime, and who carried out their sentence? To the best of my knowledge, only lords and nobles kill by hanging. The sheriff would have used the sword. Why didn't he?"

"Because he *was* the sheriff," said Marven with a sigh, shutting his eyes tiredly.

The rest of the locals looked at their feet or at each other. Odetta blinked back tears.

"Then who did this deed?" asked Bunda, the tall barbarian's eyes darkening.

"I will tell you. But first, Hanlan," he said to the tattooed man, "fetch the others. We have to decide what to do now when Dell Hayek returns."

Nick, once the boy who grew up on the streets of Sandisan,

surviving by avoiding the gangs of Shadder's Street, assessed the local gang forming here. While Mendel and Marven were clearly not warriors, the dwarf had a soldier's look about him. And the man with the anvil on his muscular shoulder looked like he could do some damage. He wondered who the 'others' were. He was quick with a sword or knife, and Bunda would be useful in a fight. But the true advantage they would possess over the locals was unseen. If Tadok chose to summon Dorkah, she would make short work of the locals. Nick shot a glance over to his traveling companion. He was calm and composed, so Nick calmed as well.

Marven poured himself a drink into a ceramic mug as he stood behind the bar. "Suldan's Bluff was founded 'bout fifty years ago when me grandfather discovered a silver vein in the mountains. He then set the well above an old water pit and set his house right near it. First house in the Bluff." He beamed proudly.

Swegan rolled his eyes. Apparently, the Darvey foundation story of Suldan's Bluff wasn't very important for the story of the hangings, but Swegan and Mendel humored him nonetheless. It didn't stop the dwarf from reaching over and pouring a drink for himself too.

"At the time, caravans from Sebin and from Berin's Inn would roll in empty and leave heavy with ore. When his back was bent from the mines, he opened this inn." He smiled at the room with pride, then continued: "The mine was important enough that the empire built a tower here to protect it from orc raiders."

To this, the dwarf spat. He quickly wiped the spittle off the floor with his boot when Odetta gave him a stern glare.

"Then the war came. When the lands east fell to the Seal Shore barbarians, the garrison at the tower was recalled fer the defendin' of Sebin."

Nick glanced over to his own Seal Shore Barbarian companion, but if Bunda took offense, it never registered.

"With no other choice, me parents and myself, along with the rest of the village, fled to the mines. Be it pure luck or Trin's blessin', the barbarians never came this way, and after they retreated west, we returned to our homes."

Nick had heard many stories of the great civil war that had fractured the empire of Nemir a few years before his birth. Stories of bravery, treachery, and great battles. But the bards who made coin from those stories never seemed to sing of the hardship of the churls and peasants who made up the common folk of society. Those who had lost everything as armies from five nations swept back and forth over the land.

"The garrison never returned. Suldan's Bluff was no longer part of Nemir, and we were forced to fend for ourselves. See, the mines had dried up by then, and with nothing here of worth aside from an old well, the road became empty."

He trailed off, sinking into nostalgia. Mendel and Swegan were apparently residing in the same memory since none of them spoke or prodded the innkeeper to continue the story. After a moment, he cleared his head with a sip of his drink and continued: "T'wasn't so bad. We had each other, game was plentiful, and apples, barley, and potatoes grow easy here. Come spring, Mendel, our baerstmann, would take his cart to Sebin with his boys and would bring back whatever goods we needed. Aldeira kept us healthy, Father Okum kept us moral until he passed, and the Church of the Four sent us Father Sheilagh. Folk here took care of one another.

"Brigands usually didn't pass here as the road had slim pickins' for 'em. The few that did were usually chased off by Sheriff Murley, Onlan, and Ren."

He swallowed hard. After the long exposition, he was finally coming to the important part of the tale.

"I guess it started when Onlan—Jenathy Murley's best friend from the war—went missin'. We searched and searched the hills and forests, thinking he got bit by a snake or taken by wolves."

"Wolves would never have taken that half-orc beast," interjected Swegan. He turned to the companions and opened his arms wide. "Large as an ox that one"—he then brought his hands together until his fingers almost touched—"and a brain that don't match."

"Whatever the cause, we don't know. Maybe only the gods do. But three days ago, Ren O' the River, our village hunter, also disappeared. A day later, Dell Hayek and his men rode into town," said Marven darkly.

The story was cut short when Hanlan returned with a retinue Nick decided these must be 'the Others' Marven had spoken of.

With him was a young boy not much older than the ones they'd buried. By the prominent nose and the gray eyes, it was clear that he must have been Hanlan's son. Following in stride was a weathered man, thin as a rake with red blurry eyes and a veiny nose. Behind him was a young man with premature gray in his red hair and a close-cropped beard. The last of the retinue was a three-foot-tall gnome which Nick originally mistook for a child, wearing a dirty smock and a sooty cap.

They all eyed the newcomers and mumbled to themselves, but Odetta raised a finger to her lips and they all hushed. Marven Darvey continued his tale.

"Hayek and his men rode horses. There must have been at least thirty of them. They came into the inn demanding food and drink. We served them the best we could, but as the night went on and spirits lifted, they began acting less and less honorably. Odetta sent young Mara back home to her Ma through the back door as some of the men started looking at her all funny."

Odetta nodded quietly.

"I knew they were going to pay no coin and dinna press the point. They were bandits, and I simply prayed they would move on come mornin' when they figured there was nothing here for them.

"The leader of the band, a brute, hailed as Dell Hayek by his men, suddenly rose and hushed the room. 'This town is now under the guard of the Shadow Hands, and ye best pay for our service,' he said."

Shadow Hands. *Marven must have misheard*, Nick thought. He knew of another band of thieves with a similar name. Ice crept into his stomach.

"At this point, Jen Murley walked in. Without his two deputies, Ren and Onlan, he had brought his two eldest boys, John and Dreith. John was fifteen, and Dreith was a year behind him. They were scared but drew off their Da's courage." Marven paused as he choked back a lump in his throat.

"Courage or foolishness," muttered Tadok under his breath.

Marven looked up at the three of them, and Nick could see fresh tears trickling down the wrinkled grooves in the old man's face.

"I'd known them boys all their lives…"

When he couldn't go on, it was Mendel who continued.

"Murley, his sheriff's badge clearly visible on his breast, called out to Hayek, 'You've had your fill and now you must go. No charge for the drink and food—that's on our hospitality. But Suldan's Bluff has nothing more to offer you folk. So be on your way with Trin's blessing.'

"At first, Dell nodded, and it looked as if he would honor the sheriff's request. But then he walked up to Jen and, with no warning, plunged his sword into his chest fast as a cat while his men grabbed the two boys."

His voice shook as he continued.

"They dragged poor Murley and his boys out all the way to the sycamore tree and, as we all watched helplessly, they hanged the lads and their dying father by their necks until their crying faces turned purple. When Aldeira, the boys' mother wailed and tried to stop them, one of them struck her in her face as the others laughed.

"Hayek then turned to the rest of us and said, 'We will return in a week, and you will pay your tribute. You will pay in gold, in women, or in blood.' He then commanded us to leave the bodies hanging for the crows, so all would see and think twice before raising sword or ax. Then he rode off east with his men."

The inn fell into silence. Bunda finally broke it. "When did this sad tale take place?" he asked, his expression grim.

Marven took the lead back from Mendel. "The night before last."

"So that leaves you with four, maybe five more days until he returns," summarized Tadok. "Why are you not packed and on your way to Berin's Inn?"

The dwarf grumbled something unintelligible, and Mendel answered, "Berin's Inn is two weeks' travel by foot. We have young with us, and the snow will come quickly, as will the wolves."

Odetta quietly added, "And there's little Christopher."

"And who is little Christopher?" asked Bunda.

"He's Aldeira Murley's last surviving son. A boy of only eight. He ran the night his father and brothers were slain, and we haven't found the boy since."

The man with the veiny nose scowled. "Boy's dead. If it wasn't Dell Hayek's men, it was them wolves that got 'im."

Odetta spun on him with fury, and it was clear he regretted opening his toothless mouth.

"You shut yer drunken yappin' gob, Yorgen Kooly! Have you seen the boy's body? Until you do, you keep searchin', and may the Divine Father protect ye if I hear you blabber those words to Aldeira!" She then turned to the three travelers, as if looking for confirmation for the logic born out of her grief and hope. "He's all poor Aldeira's got left."

Yorgen knew better than to argue. Noticing his bloodshot eyes, Nick was pretty sure that the reason had less to do with sparing Aldeira or Odetta's feelings and more about the threat of being cut off from the drink which was probably coursing daily through his veins. Every village needed a drunk.

It was the gnome who spoke then. His voice was high—almost squeaky. Nick didn't know many gnomes and couldn't tell if this one was typical. Growing up on Shadder Street didn't put one in contact with the Wee Scholars, as they were often called.

"But you can help!" the gnome said excitedly.

Tadok snorted mirthlessly. "If you think we're taking on thirty brigands, you're drunker than that one," he said, pointing to Yorgen, who scowled in indignation, then shrugged as if conceding to the truth and went back to his ale.

"Thank you for the drink and food, Darvey, but we'll pay for our beds in coin and be off tomorrow," he said, rising to his feet.

"Wait, no—that's not what I mean." The gnome raised his hands quickly to halt Tadok. "You wouldn't hold a chance against Hayek and his men. No offense, of course."

"None taken," said Nick. Bunda simultaneously muttered, "Offense taken."

The two looked at each other, but the gnome had more to say. "We don't need you to fight the bandits, but if you could find the Murley lad, we can be on our way."

"Why can't you find him?" asked Tadok. "You know these mountains better than we three."

"True," said the gnome, "But we fear he went toward the mines, and these hills are rife with wolves. Without Jen, Onlan, or Ren, we are, well..." He looked at his feet in shame, as did the others. "...afraid," he finished quietly.

The village folk stared at them with varying degrees of hope. The three companions conducted a silent conversation with their eyes instead of their voices.

Nick assessed the situation in his head. They hadn't been together long, and while none of them really considered the other two friends, Nick had learned to trust his companions over the last two weeks that they had been traveling together. During that time, they had staved off a number of threats. The first had been when Nick had stood by Bunda's side in a bar brawl in Berin's Inn. He actually hadn't intended to, but he was standing beside him, rather drunk, when a band of local ruffians, blood high of spirits, had tried to make good on their boast to make the Barbarian drink from a trough, and they mistook him for Bunda's companion. Two days later, after leaving town, they had stumbled on a wounded Tadok who had been attacked by an orc war party. Bunda had healed Tadok's wounds with Seirn's power. When they were attacked the next day by the same band of orc marauders, Tadok had appeared with Dorkah and turned the tide in their favor. A week after, while sharing their campfire with a couple of mercenaries on their way to the mountains, Nick had awakened in time to stop them from slaughtering his companions in their sleep. The final threat was the pack of wolves who had gotten too close to them the night before.

But through it all, none had talked in length about their past or of their reasons for traveling west.

Bunda was on some sacred pilgrimage or journey. He was on his way to a temple of Seirn in Sandisan. Tadok was even more guarded. He had admitted to hailing from a small village near Freelan in the north and had said he had business in Sebin. As for Nick, well, he had his own reason for crossing the Suldan Mountains. While Nick didn't expect Tadok to volunteer to help, he was more concerned about Bunda. Bunda was a noble barbarian. He saw the world through the tinted glasses of his god, and in places where the image was too ugly to reflect his ideal world, he strove to fix it.

A gust of cool air and the dull ring of the bell alerted him that another had entered the inn. The murmurs fell silent as a woman in her late thirties revealed herself, dark hair uncombed and dress wrinkled. She must have been a beauty in her earlier years, but her blue eyes were red and puffy from crying. Her hand clenched a silver necklace tightly and she gazed with dull eyes at the common room's crowd.

"Aldeira…" gasped Odetta, who immediately glided over to her. "Come, dear, ye just sit down here by the fire and let me fetch ye some tea, love."

The sheriff's widow, thought Nick.

As Aldeira allowed herself to be ushered to a seat, her eyes locked on Nick and didn't unlock until she was seated. When she spoke, her voice was cracked and hoarse from sobbing, and Nick noticed the bruise on her forehead that Hayek's men had left her when they destroyed her life.

"You," she began flatly, "you buried them. My boys and my husband, I mean." Their lack of response was confirmation. A shuddering sigh escaped her lips. "Thank you," she whispered breathlessly.

Her world had been taken from her in the span of an evening. The horror of seeing her husband killed viciously and then her own boys murdered while she could do nothing was nearly unfathomable. Nearly. Nick shot a glance at the rest of the townsfolk. Sorrow-peppered fury was apparent in their eyes. But more than that was guilt. It hung over the room like an invisible mist. They'd watched their friend and neighbor and his boys murdered, and none of them had had the courage to stop it.

That shame awakened something in Nick. And Garian's voice rang in his mind: *Not because we have to, Nick, but because we can.*

He regretted his next words the moment they left his lips. "We'll find the boy." His eyes locked with the widow's again.

Both Tadok and Bunda snapped their gaze on him. Bunda nodded slowly, but Tadok's eyes held shock and seething anger.

"You speak for us now, Heartlander?"

Instead of answering him, Nick turned to the rest of the townsfolk. Even if he could roll back his words, the gratitude in their eyes bolstered him.

"Good folk, allow me to hold council with my companions." He rose and walked to the door. He purposely left his sword leaning against the wall to make sure it was clear this wasn't a ruse to run. The other two followed silently.

Outside, the winds were strong and carried with them the chilling bite of the mountains in winter. The three huddled underneath the woodshed adjacent to the inn.

"Are you Trin-touched, Sandisan?"

Tadok often called Nick or Bunda by the name of their homes. It must have been some sort of jest or slur in the north since he only used it when exasperated, mocking, or angry.

Nick raised his hand to fend off any further verbal attacks from the half-elf. "No, I'm not. But hear my thoughts and tell me if you find fault or folly in my logic." He had had a few moments to think of his plan and pitch on his way out.

"We have learned that a large band of brigands awaits us on the road ahead. Our supplies and our coin are running low. We spend tomorrow roaming the area looking for the lad. We demand payment in food and corins for this task. If we find the boy, thank Seirn." He shot a glance at Bunda, who nodded approvingly. "If not, we still get payment. We are delayed by only a day in our journey but have enough supplies to circle around this brigand, Dell Hayek, on our way to Sebin."

Tadok was still angry, but he also appeared to be thinking. Good, thought Nick. If he was thinking, he was considering.

"I'm no fool or chivalrous knight, Tadok. I simply see the truth that the road ahead has become even more dangerous than it was before we cut those poor sods down. If you don't like this plan, we can always head back towards Berin's Inn and take the Triumph Road."

The return and detour would add another ten days at the least to their journey. And passing through the mountains this late in autumn held the rising risk of the passes being snowed in the longer they delayed.

Tadok finally accepted the logic in his argument as his shoulders eased back. "No. That would take too long."

Nick didn't know if the half-elf, too, feared the snow, or if there was another reason for his urgency in reaching Sebin, but it didn't matter. He'd won the argument.

"But to be clear—one day. The moment that cock crows on tomorrow's morrow, this village and their sad tale will be at our backs. Are we in agreement?"

Nick nodded. Tadok turned to Bunda.

"And you, Shard?" There was that slur again.

"Aye. And I'm not from Shard, Northerner. There are other Tundrial Islands in the sea." He grunted in disgust.

Nick couldn't help the smile that crept up on his lips but wiped it off instantaneously when Tadok shot him a sharp look.

"Now, let's get back in. My balls are freezing off."

"Mainlanders..." muttered the Seal Shore barbarian, shaking his head.

Tadok only grunted and turned back to the inn.

When he was out of earshot, Bunda put a hand on Nick's shoulder. "That was a good thing you did, Nick," he said, admiration in his eyes.

Nick wasn't sure why, but the tall barbarian's approval sank deep, and he chose the truth when he replied, "It's all she has left. And that boy, the youngest brother, is alone and frightened."

He walked back to the inn, recalling another frightened boy who'd lost his brothers.

2 WITNESSES

"So, where do we start?"

The three were having a breakfast of oat porridge with dried apples and the same nettle tea Odetta had offered them the night before. Nick was thankful as the porridge was a refreshing change from the hard bread and jerky that had made up most of his breakfasts since leaving Berin's Inn.

They had fleshed out their plan and laid out their conditions to the village folk the night before. They agreed on free food and board during their stay and ten gold corins for their services. They'd started at twenty, but Marven was apparently a seasoned haggler. In addition, they would supply them with food for the detour they would need to take to avoid Dell Hayek and his band. There was no sense in starting their search until morning as it was a starless night, and while Tadok's elven blood provided him with improved vision in the dark, Bunda and Nick would be blind as bats.

"I think we need to ask the locals. They can tell us of any known places the boy frequented," Tadok suggested.

"The dwarf said the mine was a good hour's trek to the mountains. We'd best be sure we have time to check it out before nightfall," reminded Bunda.

"Agreed," said Nick. "But perhaps we should split up to cover more ground."

It was a good suggestion. After all, the boy could be anywhere.

"I will start with the Church of the Four at the top of the hill. Priests in villages such as these are often told secrets children wouldn't tell their own mothers. Perhaps the boy or one of his friends had given this Father Sheilagh such a secret," explained Bunda.

Nick nodded. "I'll question the townsfolk. I'll start with the widow."

"I'll join you, Bunda," said Tadok, scooping up the last of his porridge with his wooden spoon. "From the hill I'll be able to scout the lands around us."

Nick nodded, recalling the half-elf's additional talents.

The plan was set.

Nick turned to the bartender and waved his empty bowl. "Any more of this, man?"

The bartender wasn't Marven, but the young red-headed man with the close-cropped beard who'd been silent the night before. A damp cloth in his right hand and a ceramic mug in his left, he absently wiped down the dishes, which had been scoured clean. He nodded, motioning to the large iron pot resting above the fireplace, and beckoned Nick to help himself. Something was vaguely familiar about him, so Nick walked over to the bar after filling his bowl.

"Good morning, sir. My name's Nick Cartright. I never caught your name last night."

The man smiled pleasantly, lowered the mug he was cleaning, and stretched his left hand to Nick in greeting.

"Name's Mica Mun. I help Marven and Odetta at the inn. Fine thing you lads are doing. Seirn and Trin bless you," he added after the introduction.

"Master Mun, you seem familiar. Where do you hail from?"

Mica Mun returned to wiping the mug as he answered, "Originally? Taincross. But I've been this side of the mountains for half my life. I did take Trin's path for a while until the Darveys took me in two years ago."

Taking *Trin's Path* was a way of saying he was a vagabond for some time, with no true purpose or intent. It was a Halfling term, as the little folk were avid wanderers.

"I do believe we've met before..." Nick squinted, trying to connect face to memory.

"Berin's Inn," concluded Mica with a smile. "You used to frequent that inn with the pissy ale...What was it called?"

Nick smiled. "You mean the Giant's Rock?"

"That's the one! But we never used to call it the Giant's Rock, did we?"

Nick laughed out loud and shrugged. "I always liked Gornwin's brew."

"I'm telling you, he pissed in it himself. Come back tonight and I'll show you a real man's drink," he boasted mirthfully.

"Oh, we will. And hopefully we will have reason to celebrate." Mun nodded enthusiastically. "Good luck to you in your search!"

Nick walked back to his companions, who were finishing their tea and putting on their cloaks. He buckled his rapier and slung his own cloak over his shoulders, setting his bow and arrow quiver over it.

The three left, ready to begin their search.

***

The village was small yet functional. The previous night, Marven and Mendel had given them the layout and an introductory description of all its inhabitants.

In the center of the village was the inn, owned by Marven and Odetta Darvey. Mica Mun, the drifter, had been taken on as a bar-hand and lived in a small hut behind the inn. The old couple was clearly childless, but Nick didn't know whether this was due to miscarriages or their children having never reached puberty. Both possibilities were common in these parts. Whatever the reason, they seemed to have taken in Mica Mun as a foster son, and he seemed to appreciate it.

Moving clockwise from the inn, the next house was that of Mendel Argun, his wife, Theia, and their five children—three boys and two young girls. Mendel owned a trade cart and was Suldan Bluff's main contact with the outer world. This made him Suldan

Bluff's Bǣrestman. Which meant that once a month between spring and autumn, he and his two eldest sons would take the road to Sebin to trade whatever produce the village could offer, returning two weeks later with whatever the village could not, along with any news of the larger world. This was common in the more rural villages of Trosia, where folks would pool their resources and send one of their own to sell them at the nearest town or city.

After Mendel's house was the smithy, staffed by Hanlan, the man with the anvil tattoo, and his teenaged son, Trace. His wife had died from a coughing sickness a few years ago.

After that was the small rundown hovel of Yorgen Kooly, the drunk. Yorgen farmed barley and tended an apple grove. His wife had run off a few years back and the man had declined ever since. He still tended his crops but was falling behind in recent years. Nick suspected that he mostly lived off the kindness and generosity of his neighbors. The community of Suldan's Bluff did their best to help each other out in a way that reminded him how the dredges of Shadder Street in Sandisan had taken care of their own. Ironic that those who had nothing to lose were always those with most to give.

The next house, on the other side of the path into the village, was that of Swegan, the dwarf. Swegan was an old dwarf who had seen the fall of *Doar Keirn*, the dwarven homeland of old, which had been destroyed by the Great Orc Hoard over two hundred years earlier. He had been somewhat of a champion in his time, but he'd vowed never to raise his ax and fight for humans since, a vow taken by many members of his race after being abandoned by the Empire in their hour of need. These days he tended a herd of sheep.

Tilly, the seamstress, was next. She lived in a small, two-room cabin with her teenage daughter, Mara. She tended a vegetable garden and spun the yarn from Swegan's sheep. The village gossiped of Tilly and Hanlan, the blacksmith, and their not-so-secret love affair, which seemed to hold great fascination for their neighbors.

The next house was a strange-looking workshop owned by the gnome, Diggericut. The gnome was a self-styled inventor and a history buff, according to Marven. No one knew why he chose this remote settlement, leaving the big cities behind, but he was always kind and neighborly, and the villagers had come to be rather fond of him over the years.

Behind the gnome's workshop was a thatched roof cottage belonging to Ren O' the River, a half-elf who had lived in Suldan's Bluff since Marven's grandfather had settled it. He was a tracker and hunter. Two and half decades earlier, Ren and Jenathy Murley, the late sheriff, had gone off to fight for the Empire during the War of the Broken Crown. When they returned, they had brought with them the Half-Orc named Onlan. Apparently, the trio had been part of the same troop and had created a brothers-in-arms-like bond. Onlan had lived with Ren, and their home was nicknamed the House of Halves. The house stood empty since both of them were missing—their whereabouts, unknown.

The last house, adjacent to the inn, was that of the Murleys. It was here that Nick intended to make his first stop.

The house's windows were all covered in dark cloth, except for one window which held a single fat candle burning in it. A sign of mourning.

Behind the house was a carefully planted herb garden with a wide variety of flowers and herbs. Nick knew none of their names. His street-life upbringing did little in the form of education in things such as these. Odetta Darvey had said that Aldeira was an herbalist and a healer. When Bunda asked why Father Sheilagh, a priest of The Four, didn't take care of the community's aches and illnesses, Odetta, Marven, and Mendel had looked at each other, and finally Marven had shrugged and said that Aldeira was simply better at it. A basket of freshly baked bread, some berry jam, and some hard cheese wrapped in cloth rested on the doorstep, along with a blanket and gown that had been carefully folded. This must have been the work of Odetta, taking care of her grieving neighbor.

Nick took a deep breath, practiced his most sensitive, compassionate expression, and knocked on the door. A full minute later, the door opened a crack.

Aldeira was wearing a thick wool robe over her gown, which looked like it had been worn for the last three nights. Dark circles framed her eyes, making her look a decade older than she probably was. Nick estimated she was in the latter half of her thirties. By the age of her boys and the fact that her husband had fought in the wars, they must have had a marriage which had spanned two decades. They'd probably expected another decade or two together, with a full brood of grandchildren at their side from their three sons.

She said nothing but ushered him in.

The interior of the small, neat house was filled with furniture. A long oak table near the kitchen was either where the family would gather for supper or where she would mix her salves and potions, or both. A sheepskin rug dominated the area by a fireplace, whose fire had been reduced to embers.

Nick motioned to the wood pile. "May I?"

Aldeira nodded and settled in a rocking chair. If the cold bothered her, she said nothing.

As Nick prodded the wood chips into the center of the fire, he said, "I'm sorry for your loss. May the Divine Father embrace their souls and may Trin guide them on their final journey." He thought that was how the saying went, anyway. The widow said nothing, so Nick tried again. "It is a terrible tragedy…"

"How are you going to find my son, Master Cartright?" she interrupted, clearly not interested in his condolences.

Nick nodded, moving on.

"My friends and I have divided our efforts. I will speak with you and the rest of the townsfolk, and they have ventured up to the church to speak to Father Sheily."

"Sheilagh," she corrected. "Why him?"

Nick shrugged. "In times of need, folk often seek sanctuary in temples, shrines, and churches."

"Christopher would never have gone near the church," she said, dismissing the notion.

"Aye? The boy's a bit of a gamin, then? To tell the king's truth, I was one myself at his age." He hoped she would open up to him if she could identify with him. Nick truly did want to find the boy, regardless of what he had told Tadok.

"Chris? No. He was an angel. How he worshipped his father and brothers! He followed them around everywhere. Jen even made him a tin sheriff's badge like his brothers. His brothers, on the other hand, were a handful, taking after their father, but Christopher...he was of me." A smile broke her frown for a moment, and Nick found himself lost in her piercing green eyes. Underneath the years, the sleepless nights, and the endless sorrow, she was a striking woman. And that beauty shone through in that moment as she recalled her deceased husband and sons, but the smile quickly became a bitter sob.

"I'm sorry, I didn't mean..." he began, feeling suddenly like he'd invaded this woman's circle of sorrow.

She waved him off. "No, it's all right. The memories will come. As long as I can see my beloved husband's eyes and my sons' sweet smiles in my mind, let my pain come as it may."

A glimpse of purple puffy faces contorted in terror flashed through Nick's mind, but he said nothing.

"'Tis when the memories fade that my true sorrow will come," she finished. He nodded solemnly. When the silence had lasted long enough, she continued. "Father Sheilagh doesn't hold ceremonies...or hasn't in years. He's an odd one, that fellow. No one goes up to the church much these days and the good Father comes down every couple of days for supplies."

"I see," said Nick. "How far had the boy ever ventured? Does he have a known hiding place—if not the church?"

Aldeira chewed her cheek in thought before responding. "He has joined his father in his roaming around these lands. They have been to the old guard tower, the mines, and the totem tree. All the way up to Broken Axle Bend and the high passes to Sebin. Never more than two days from home. Not with Christopher."

"What's this 'totem tree'? We haven't heard of it yet."

"An old tree near the mines. It has an ancient language carved all over its trunk. Some old form of Karr, I think. Diggeri would know more."

Nick grunted and made a mental note.

"Is there anything else you can tell me that could help?" he asked.

Aldeira's eyes darted back and forth as she tried to remember anything useful. She then shook her head, a frown on her face. "He's a thin boy of eight, with hair the color of mine but curly like his father's. He has a fear of wolves and the dark but likes to climb and is a good swimmer. He loves playing in the leaf piles in autumn and is quick to laugh." Her voice broke, and she couldn't go on. Fresh tears streamed down her face.

"We'll find him, I promise." No sooner had he said the words and a voice in his mind raged, *You fool! And what if you don't find him?*

Nick ignored the scolding from inner Nick and stood up.

"We will finish our questions to your friends and neighbors by noon and head for the mines. In the meantime, I suggest you rest and pray to the gods."

Aldeira eyed him with a mix of skepticism and hope. While she may not trust him and his companions, she would grasp at any thread that would lead to her son, no matter how thin.

He left her in her rocking chair, eager to get to work on his promise.

***

The rest of the questioning didn't lead to much.

Hanlan, the smith, and Trace, his son, had seen the boy run off to the green when his father and brothers were dragged to the tree, but they had not seen him since.

Mendel had searched the sheepfold and the various chicken pens and had found nothing. Like Hanlan, he had seen the boy hide behind the well in the green but had assumed he had run home from there. He, too, supposed the best bet would have been the mine. He had checked the well itself—even lowering a lantern he borrowed from the inn into its depths, fearing the boy may have fallen in and drowned—but there was no sign of a body. Only dark rippling water.

Yorgen claimed he had gone as far as the old guard tower but had seen no signs of the boy. Besides, the adults of Suldan's Bluff had a habit of telling the children that the place was haunted to prevent them from venturing there on their own, and Christopher was a frightened little girl-of-a-boy in his eyes. He had probably run off to the hills and either fell down one of the many ditches and cracked his head or had been eaten by wolves, and they were all wasting their time waiting for him. *Cheery*, thought Nick. He understood why the other villagers detested the sour man.

Diggericut, the gnome, hadn't seen anything. He had been at his shed and hadn't witnessed the lynching. When Nick asked him how he had not noticed the commotion, the gnome pointed to a large leather hood with tinted glass lenses. He explained that he used the hood for his experiments to block out flashes, scents, and sounds.

Nick had asked him about the totem tree and the ditches.

"The totem tree is fascinating!" said the gnome, his eyes lighting up. "The writing there is ancient and is not in any form used by the Karr that lived here before King Nem's conquest. It has some elven characteristics but is clearly not elvish. Actually, is comes from another very ancient people known as..." The gnome droned on about long dead civilizations, and Nick found himself losing his concentration. The events of ages past had little to do with what occurred only a couple days ago, so he interrupted the lecture, changing the subject to the ditches.

As for the ditches, the gnome explained that the whole area had suffered tectonic activity. Following that statement, he had to explain what 'tectonic activity' was. Still, he didn't believe the boy would have succumbed to such a fate. The ditches were known to anyone growing up here, and besides—they were shallow, and the boy could have climbed out easily. Nick had the sense that the gnome loved explaining his accumulated knowledge and would have spent the day doing so if allowed.

He was just walking out of the seamstress's house—she had seen nothing as she and her daughter were hiding in the house during the commotion—when he saw a young teenage girl sitting on the low wooden fence surrounding the house. The girl had a hunting bow slung over her shoulder and a quiver of arrows in hand. She watched him intently.

"Hello," Nick said simply, waving at the girl. Her eyes were ringed with red as if she'd been crying, and her cheeks were flushed.

"Are you going to kill Dell Hayek?" she asked bluntly.

Direct, isn't she? thought Nick.

"No, that's not our intent. We're looking for little Christopher Murley. Once we find him, we'll be off as fast as we can. As should you be."

"Are you craven?"

Nick wasn't sure if it was meant to be an insult or another direct question.

"Against thirty armed, bloodthirsty brigands? Aye. A craven I am, and once again, so should you be." He began walking to the last station of his questioning when the girl called after him.

"John wasn't craven!"

John? It took a moment for Nick to remember who John was. The Murley elder boy. Could he have been the target of this girl's teenage infatuation?

"But John's dead. We buried him." It was Nick's turn to be blunt. The words must have stung, as the girl's freckles flushed even redder. *Good,* thought Nick. By the look of the bow and her set jaw, she was in danger of doing something youthful and stupid.

"You must be Mara, Tilly's lass."

Mara hopped off the fence and set upon Nick with purpose. Her words tumbled from her mouth quickly, as if she'd been rehearsing her pitch all morning.

"The people here may not all be fighters, but we're tough as tree bark. And with you three in the lead, we can fight back. Maybe ambush the bandits when they're drunk, and—"

"None of that," Nick cut her off sharply, scowling. Apparently, his words hadn't quite stung enough. "This is no tail or bard's song. Do you know what men like Hayek do to girls like you?" He let his eyes travel up and down her body for emphasis. She was much too young for Nick. Barely a woman, but he was under no illusion that Hayek's men would care.

Uncertainty tinged with fear crept into her eyes, and Nick drove the point in.

"Do you know what they would do to your mother? And to all of Suldan's Bluff? If you think our three blades would make a difference, then you're a fool."

The girl's jaw was still set, but she blinked back tears, and Nick couldn't help softening his tone.

"If you loved John, don't let his bravery be for naught. He died to defend your honor. Don't soil it on foolish notions of revenge." He had heard that line in a mummer's play years ago. And he remembered it because of the woman who'd delivered those lines back then.

He willed himself to force the memory from his mind and, at the same time, maintained unbroken eye contact with Mara. He had thought those lines ridiculously romantic at the time, but they seemed to fit, and he executed them perfectly.

He sighed and added, "Hayek will find his end someday. Maybe at the hands of his own men, or at the end of a noose or from a hungry ogre, but not from us and not now. And when he does, he will answer to the Divine Father for the suffering he's caused."

The girl stared into his eyes for a few moments. Nick was unsure if his words had the effect he had hoped. She then turned sharply and darted into the house. Nick imagined he could hear sobs.

Nick sighed shaking his head. He cleared his thoughts and focused on the last house. The bartender-drifter's house.

He had spotted him earlier when he was speaking with the dwarf, chopping wood near the inn, and still heard the sound of ax splitting logs. Good. It afforded him some time.

He walked around the back of the house, and when he was sure he was out of sight, he dipped his hand into a hidden pocket sewn into his sleeve and palmed two long needles with odd protrusions and grooves. The lockpicks had been a gift from his older brother, and over the years Nick had perfected their use.

It took him less than two minutes to hear the satisfying sound of the latch in the door's lock tumble into place. He looked around. All was silent, so he quietly opened the door and entered Mica Mun's home.

Inside, the main room was dark with only a few beams of light poking through the makeshift curtains above the two windows: one by the small kitchen and the other near the door.

The house had a single room that acted as a living room and a kitchen, with a small unlit fireplace and an adjacent bedroom. An iron pot hung in the cold hearth. A single cushioned chair sat across from it, and a simple wooden chest stood by the far wall.

Without a second thought, Nick quickly lifted the chest's lid and began rummaging through Mun's belongings. A goose feather quilt, a few cloaks, and changes of clothes were neatly folded within.

His next stop was the pantry. People hid things in pantries all the time. After rummaging through some dried jerky, half a wheel of cheese, and some sour sheep milk—Mica Mun must eat most of his meals in the inn—he found a pouch of coins hidden in a jar of flower. He wasn't interested in the coins for their monetary value, but coins also held information. Twenty gold corins with the serene likeness of Emperor Justice the Fourth of Nemir with a crown on his head. It was a sizable sum for a drifter, and it was clear that they had been minted in the Sandisan, the capital of Nemir. But coins traveled, and the origin wasn't hard proof of anything. He needed to find the token.

He padded over to the bedroom. A simple bed of straw covered in sheepskin was neatly made. A small table with a candle sat in the darkness near the bed with an open book resting upon its top.

'The Rise and Fall of Karrendel.' The book was popular and held legends—probably mostly fictitious stories concocted by the writer—of the sunken city which had inspired the imagination of so many bards and minstrels. He had heard parts of it recited in quite a few taverns and inns.

He lowered himself to the hardwood floor to look under the bed. He reached in and withdrew a scabbarded sword. A quick look at the pommel identified the crafter's mark and smithy, providing evidence of it being from Sandisan. Still, evidence wasn't proof.

He returned the sword and looked around the room. A thought bloomed in mind, and he felt around the edges of the book's leather cover until he found a small bulge. He ran his finger across the binding's stitches finding a couple that were missing. He poked his finger in and slowly withdrew a coin-sized tin hexagon with a crude hand branded into it.

He smiled. It was what he was looking for, yet it was odd. The weight seemed off.

Then he heard the tell-tale sound of a crossbow winch being set and froze.

"Slowly," a voice said calmly. "Hands and fingers stretched."

He turned towards the voice, his hands as far away from his sword as he could physically muster.

Mica Mun stood in the doorway. The crossbow rested in the crook of his left arm, the middle finger of his right hand on the trigger, and a wicked-looking bolt was aimed at Nick's chest.

"What was my tell, Nick Cartright?" asked the man. "Or should I call you Robin Hugh?"

3 THIEVES

Robin panted heavily as he stumbled through the corridors of Undertown—the old section of Sandisan, built in the days of King Nem and since rebuilt again and again. The Undertown was a maze of warrens and ruins. In some places, it had been claimed by the Ailtel Sea, and in others it was dry. A perfect home for the Shadder Hands.

His one hand supported his younger brother, Thomas, who was bleeding from the deep cut in his thigh. His other hand gripped his rapier tightly, which he waved ahead of him almost like a torch. His elder brother stopped in his tracks and turned his head slightly to his two younger brothers behind him, still keeping a watchful eye on the darkness ahead.

"Would you stop waving that thing around like a cock in a henhouse? If Gale's men don't kill us, *you* will." Despite the situation, Garian's voice was light, and Robin knew it was for the benefit of his two younger brothers.

"I need to…rest," begged Thomas, his face pale enough to shine through the beams of moonlight filtering through the grates above. Robin brushed his own matted sandy hair away from his forehead with the arm of his sword hand.

"Gather your strength, Tommy; we can't rest here," he said.

But Garian nodded, overruling him. "We can steal a few moments. Take a look at those bandages, Robby." Garian, six years Robin's elder and nine years Tommy's, was the unquestioned leader of the Hugh brothers. Even if Robin questioned his judgment, Tommy wouldn't. He propped his brother up between two rotting crates and looked at his bandaged leg.

The rag was wet with Tommy's blood, seeping down his pant leg. Robin tightened it and Tommy groaned loudly.

"Hush now, brother," whispered Robin harshly, "lest you bring them all down on us."

Tommy bit his lip but was silent. "How did this happen?" asked the fourteen-year-old lad. "Where did Gale get the men? Was it Silvermanes?"

Garian shook his head. "Sally has an arrangement with them. These are our own brothers and sisters."

"I don't know about that. We've been fighting and running from Hands we've never met before. I think some of the other chapterhouses came to his call. Troll-fucking bastards!" swore Robin.

"Cowards is what they are. Cowards and ingrates. If it weren't for Sallidan, they would still be pathetic cutpurses and thugs. He united them. Gave them a purpose. A family. I'd say they're bloody kin slayers," said Garian.

"I don't think they see themselves as very well-loved cousins, the way Sally's been bleeding their purses and coffers," replied Robin.

Robin knew that his elder brother and he had different opinions about Sallidan "Sally" Merkin, Shadowmaster of the Shadder Hands. In the aftermath of the War of the Broken Crown, Sandisan had received waves of refugees fleeing from the conflict. The ones who stayed in Sandisan found themselves settling near the docks in the poorer sections of the metropolis, specifically in a place called Shadder Street. There, the combination of poverty, desperation, and the political weakening of the country in general bred a small gang of protection racketeers and cutthroats into the largest and most influential crime syndicate the world had seen.

Sallidan had been attentive, and he had been ambitious. He'd grown the thieves' guild beyond the borders of Sandisan, organizing the various crime families, hooligans, and scum of the towns and cities and roads of Nemir into a cooperative, if not coordinated, organization that included about five different chapterhouses and hundreds of operatives from the lowly gutters of Sebin to the courts of Nirn Bay. Guild fences could pass on goods stolen from Netheer under the unwatchful bribed eyes of guards at Taincross all the way to Sandisan or Culidge with no interference. Under Sally, the guild grew from a dominant yet local crime guild in Sandisan to a continent-wide thriving underworld organization, which could destabilize local governments if it chose to do so. Sally had seen the pie, and instead of fighting for a larger slice, he chose to make a bigger pie. Or so Garian believed, and he himself had risen through the ranks to become one of Sally's lieutenants selected often by Sally for missions which required wit and charm, which were the young man's gifts.

Everyone loved Garian. He could be caught with the sack of gold in his hands and still convince both the city guard and the robbed victim that it was all a good-natured prank. Garian's rise through the ranks afforded the brothers a level of respect that wouldn't otherwise have been given to three orphan boys from Shadder Street.

The coup had happened unexpectedly. One moment, the brothers were playing dice, discussing Mother Beya's new girls and jibing Tommy good-naturedly about it, and suddenly Rika crashed into the room through the door with a dagger in her back and two masked assailants pursuing her. Garian and Robin had quickly dispatched the two, but not before they had wounded Tommy.

As they made their way to the large, empty warehouse known as "Sally's Court," they found dead friends strewn along the gullies and alleys of Undertown. Most of them with dagger wounds in their backs or with throats slit, assassinated quickly by those they had thought were friends. Many had looks of shock and surprise in their dead eyes.

Robin's reverie was cut short by shouts coming from a bend in the passage ahead, quickly followed by four figures who burst into the tunnel. It was evident that one of them was fighting off the other three and was losing.

"It's Reigar!" shouted Garian as he leaped to help Sally's older brother and his friend.

"Stay here!" Robin said with a grunt, dashing to join the fray.

Reigar was waving a blood-stained sword, trying to parry thrusts from his three opponents. The two brothers raced towards the melee, their boots splashing in sewer puddles loudly. The large attacker on the left tried to twist towards Garian but wasn't fast enough to stop the tip of the young man's sword as it sliced through his cheek and nose cleanly, spattering blood on the wall even as the man swirled away to protect his face. The second one was better prepared and blocked the young man's thrust with his short sword while kicking him squarely in the chest. The dazed Garian tried to recover, but the man was faster, swatting his sword aside and advancing. He raised his sword to strike but froze in place as Robin's rapier erupted from his throat. His legs buckled, and he crumpled to the wet floor.

The third assailant was larger and was on the brothers with an ax and short sword. He swung them together and drove the two of them apart, which only acted in their favor. With practiced precision, Robin and Garian circled their opponent, flanking him from both sides. Robin lunged forward, and his opponent grinned and sidestepped the clumsy attack. Only to discover the feint too late as Garian's sword plunged into his ribs. Even with blood spurting from the wound, the battle-crazed man twisted, making Garian lose his grip on the blood-slick handle of his weapon. He raised both ax and sword high in the air, bloody spittle flinging from his lips, but before he could bring them down, Robin slammed into him, knocking him to the ground. Robin turned his stumble into a roll and came up a few steps away from the dying attacker. Before the man could rise to his feet, Reigar finally ended the fight by plunging a dagger into the man's eye.

For a moment, all was silent in the corridor except for the panting of three people. Thomas hobbled over to them.

"Is anyone hurt?" asked Garian, resuming the mantle of leadership. "Good. We need to get to Sally."

Reigar shook his head, trying to catch his breath. "Sally's dead. He was the first to go. Gale has his head on a stake. He's already named himself the new Shadowmaster, and his men are settling accounts with anyone who followed Sally. We need to make it to the docks."

If the news of Sallidan's demise shocked any of them, no one showed it. They were partially expecting it, anyway.

"Gale. That fucking eel!" swore Garian, but he was already moving forward.

"Who dunnit? Was it Duke Luthern's men?" asked Tommy, still holding on to that theory.

"No. The Silvermanes tried to warn us. But Sally wouldn't believe his own Hands would strike at him. He trusted Gale."

The four of them made their way down an old sewer tunnel. They could see the moonlight streaming through the large grill ahead. Beyond it, Robin could hear and smell the sea. If he recalled correctly, an old skiff would be resting on the rocks. If they started rowing now, they could make it to a fishing village by dawn, and from there they could head north or west. The Shadder Hands were weak in Freelan and in Seaview.

They carefully moved the grate aside and transitioned from the putrid-smelling tunnel to fresh air. Robin took a moment to stretch his back. The tunnel exited at the foot of the cliff underneath the Bard's Tower. He could see flickering torchlights above where the king's men paced the walls, looking out towards the Ailtel. Robin knew that if they remained quiet, they wouldn't be noticed.

"There's the boat!" exclaimed Reigar a little too loudly. He began running to it. There was a sudden *twang*, and Reigar twisted sharply in mid-run, a bolt buried deep in his chest. The old man fell to the sand and pebbles, blood fountaining out at the foot of the shaft. The crossbow bolt must have pierced his heart as he was still.

The three brothers swung towards the source of the bolt. Above the rocks, dark figures came into the moonlight.

In the center stood Gale the Boon. His black hair was gathered neatly behind his head, and his dark beard hid a faint smile.

"Thus dies the last member of noble 'House Merkin'," he announced with satisfaction.

To his side stood a beautiful woman in a low-cut leather blouse and a matching leather knee-high skirt. Robin recognized her as Delona Ravin, Sally's consort and one of his lieutenants. The way Gale had his arm around her, and by the cold smile on her lips, it was obvious that Sally's romantic notions had been sorely misplaced.

The man who fired the crossbow was dark-skinned and wore darkened chainmail that glinted occasionally in the light of the torches. Robin had no idea who he was, but his strange yellow eyes radiated in a deadly fashion. Another ten figures with swords stood at his side. Some of them Robin recognized as friends and fellow Hands. People he had run heists and played dice with. The betrayal stung deep.

"Ah, Hugh," said Gale, noticing Garian for the first time. "Seems like you have a choice, son. Are you a man who recognizes an opportunity? Or are you looking to follow your master to meet the Divine Father?"

Sally had raised the Hughs from nothing. He had found them on the street begging and pickpocketing, and he saw in Garian what the boy could be and offered him a place at his side. When Garian made it clear that he was a package deal with his brothers, Sallidan simply laughed and told him he must have some real ogre balls, but he would take the two younger boys in as well. He had given them a home and a job and always made sure they were treated fairly by the older and more violent Hands. The lowlifes of Shadder Street knew that to lift a finger to a Hugh was to cross the Shadowmaster.

Garian owed him everything. On the other hand, the only thing which trumps loyalty is family, and he had Robin and Tommy to think of.

But Tommy must have known this, and maybe it shouldn't have been a surprise when his voice rang out in the night: "Suck goblin cock, shit feeder!"

Gale burst out laughing, and his cronies followed their master's lead. Robin looked up. The guards must have noticed the exchange by now. Why weren't whistles blowing? To his dismay, he could see them calmly watching the exchange. Realization sank in. *They were a part of this*, thought the young thief.

"I like his eyes," purred Delona Ravin.

Gale looked at her and then back at the boys. "Then you shall have them," he said cruelly. With a motion of his hand, his henchmen began advancing, swords and daggers at the ready.

Rapier in hand, Robin stepped forward to his brother's side.

"No!" said Garian harshly, shooting his hand out to block his brother. Robin looked at Gale in confusion. Did he have a better plan?

"What's the angle here, brother?" he asked.

"You need to take Tommy and go," he said in a husky voice. "I'll buy you enough time to push the skiff out. There's only one boat here, so they can't follow."

"The fuck you will—" Robin began to object, but Garian cut him off.

"I'm not asking, Robby." Garian's eyes softened, but his voice was steel. "We don't have to all die tonight. And Tommy's our little brother—someone has to protect him. He's afraid."

Robin looked back at Tommy. His eyes were wide and his face pale. His earlier bravado was gone as the enemy advanced, and Robin saw the truth in Garian's words.

Robin looked back and forth between his two brothers, making the hardest choice of his life. Finally, he clenched his teeth and clasped Garian's arm. "You make it out of here tonight! Find a way. *You always do.*"

"I always do," echoed Garian in confirmation, lending strength to

Robin's resolve.

Robin dashed towards the shore, grabbing the confused Thomas by the arm and dragging him towards the skiff.

"What about Garian?" the boy asked, bewildered.

"He's coming," he lied. We're making a break for it."

Gale's men were closing the distance to Garian. As Robin and Thomas pushed the boat into the water, Garian charged the first attacker, taking him off guard and stabbing him with a quick jab to the chest. Even before he dropped to the ground, Garian's sword was already slashing at the second assailant, opening a deep gash in his stomach. He parried a clumsy stab by the third attacker and kicked his feet out from under him, plunging his sword into the fallen man's back.

In the torchlight, Garian fought like a demon. Hacking, slashing, and stabbing. He was everywhere at once, and Robin began entertaining the notion that he actually may win. But his hope turned into crushing dread as one of the attackers slashed the back of his brother's leg, forcing him to one knee. Still, Garian managed to swipe his sword in an upwards arc, catching the man on his chin and sending him somersaulting backward, pelting blood into the sand.

Garian rose unsteadily to his feet but suddenly froze. A crossbow bolt jutted out of his chest. He sank back down to his knees, dropping his sword.

"Garian!" He didn't know if the scream erupted from his mouth or from Tommy's. The skiff was already sixty feet out into the water. Blood rushed up into his ears and his mouth instantaneously turned dry. He grabbed Tommy's head and crushed it to his chest, flattening down in the boat. He could hear the cheers from Gale's men as they closed around his older brother. As if through a dream, he could vaguely see swords and daggers rising and falling. He shut his eyes tightly, willing the images to go away.

He took down four of them! If I had stayed, we could have had a chance, he raged silently. Fuck you, Garian! Fuck you for making me leave you to die!

They floated in silence for what seemed like hours. The undertow dragged them out into the Ailtel, until great Sandisan was just lights in the distance, and the only sound was that of the sea and of Tommy sobbing softly. Then, Robin rose and grasped both ores in his hands and started to row with ashen determination as the sun began to rise on a new and alien world.

He never looked back.

4 PRIESTS

Bunda and Tadok stopped to catch their breath at the top of the stone stairs leading up the hill.

Nestled midway to the top of the hill stood a lonely stone building. The Church was probably as old as Suldan's Bluff. Miners were superstitious folk. Tadok guessed he would be, too, if he spent his days crawling under thousands of tons of rock.

So that would make the church about half a century old. It looked like it had fallen into disrepair recently. Windows were boarded up, the small vegetable garden was untended, and even the sign in carefully carved elegant scrawl was only hanging from one chain and swaying lopsidedly in the wind. Still, the thin stream of smoke snaking lazily up into the heavens was evidence that despite its poor upkeep, it was home to someone.

The lopsided sign simply read, 'Church of the Four Sons', with the Four's divine rune carved underneath.

"Not a very welcoming place of worship…" he commented.

Beside him, Bunda looked at the rundown building disapprovingly. "While I've never felt kinship to the faiths of the Mainland, no cleric of Seirn would allow his lord's house to fall into such a state."

Tadok shrugged. "Maybe he's one of those clerics who spends his time in commune with his god, far removed from earthly needs."

"Priests," the tall barbarian said with a grunt.

"What?" Tadok blinked.

"Priests," he repeated. "Seirn, Geiless, Trin, Obe and Tiel-kah have clerics. The Divine Father, his Four Sons, and the rest of the pantheon known as the Circle have priests or fathers," he lectured distractedly while surveying the building and its surrounding grounds.

"Huh," replied Tadok, "I didn't know that."

"It doesn't matter. This is no way to caretake a holy place," continued the Tundrial cleric of Seirn.

Being honest with himself, temples and churches were not a favored location for Tadok. He had grown up in a village not much larger than Suldan's Bluff, which didn't even have its own hall of worship. The closest thing the village of Sage's Rock had was the spirit shrine in the woods, which the elders claimed was a holy place.

An orphan by the age of six, it was there he had laid his mother to rest—a small boy, six years of age, kissing his mother's cool forehead while the village wise woman put cloves in her mouth and covered her in a white shroud. At the time, he thought about what he would do after, when the pity of his neighbors abated, and they would once again recall that he was a half-elf outcast. They would probably send him to fend for himself. It would take Sellwyn another week to arrive at Sage's Rock and save him from poverty and homelessness. But at the time, standing there in the holiest place he had known, he knew no god was listening to him, and he hated them for it.

Sellwyn hadn't liked places of worship either. Tadok always thought that it had been due to her true nature and origin. So, they both felt like outsiders and avoided the temples and churches of the towns and cities they'd passed through in their journeys. Sellwyn had enough hedge medicine knowledge that she didn't need the assistance of wise women or temples, and there were always potion brewers along the way—enough to allow them to avoid the sacred houses and holy men who made them both feel uncomfortable.

But with Bunda, it felt different to the young half-elf. Maybe it was that the cleric had saved his life when he was injured, or maybe it was that he had come to view the Tundrial as a comrade in arms and not as the stereotype of a human cleric which had been embedded in his mind. Besides, Sellwyn was gone, and it was time to shake off childish superstitions.

Yet, standing at the top of the steps and looking at the church itself, he was once again beside his mother's frail body as snow fell around him, silently cursing the gods for turning a deaf ear to a child's prayers. And oh, how he had prayed in the weeks before his mother finally succumbed to her withering illness.

"Why don't you find this Father Sheilagh while I climb up to that lookout and scope the lands around us?" he suggested.

If Bunda detected the real reason he didn't want to set foot in the church, he didn't let on to it. He was so focused on his disgust at his counterpart of the Church of the Four that he barely noticed Tadok anyway.

"As you wish. But be weary, my friend. Something is not right with this place."

Tadok nodded, removing his gloves and hooking them onto his belt. It was a subtle motion. One which would have been lost on most onlookers. But Bunda had fought alongside Tadok and assuredly knew that this was akin to a warrior loosening the sword in its scabbard or an archer knocking an arrow.

In a fight, Tadok's first go-to weapon wasn't his sickle or crossbow; it was his magic. A gift from an elven grandfather, who he had never known, magic ran in Tadok's blood.

Tadok wasn't truly half-elven. If anything, he was *quarter*-elven. His father had been a human and his mother the daughter of an elven diplomat and a local wise-woman. His grandmother had died when he was only four, but even so, she didn't speak much of his grandfather. He had known very little of the man before meeting Sellwyn, who had introduced herself as a friend of his grandfather. It was she who had taught him how to channel the magic in his veins into spells which could protect him and harm others. She'd explained that it was different from how it was for wizards and mages who needed to study worded incantations which would allow them to draw power from the world around them. No, *his* power came from his very soul. In a fight, he would start with his powers and then draw his steel. If all went badly, there was always Dorkah.

Bunda closed the distance to the large double wooden doors and rapped loudly on the door with the iron knocker while Tadok proceeded up the small path, which continued to the top of the hill.

It took him a little under ten minutes to complete the climb. At the top of the hill, the wind was howling, blowing his brown hair in his eyes. Brushing it away, he took in his surroundings.

Before him at the foot of the hill rested Suldan's Bluff sleepily. It was too far away to make out faces, but he assumed the small figure in the smithy was Hanlan. There was a man near the inn chopping wood and a couple people in conversation near the edge of town.

He closed his eyes and turned his attention within. He dived deep, under the physical layers of fatigue, the minor discomfort of the breakfast porridge making its way through his bowels. Under the emotional level of his insecurity with his companions, his frustration that he was losing time and even his loneliness. Under all that was his center. There, he found the *Flow*.

When he opened his eyes, the village was no longer toy-sized. It was still small, but now he could recognize the blacksmith clearly. The woodchopper was gone, but the rest of the village was much clearer.

He turned his head eastward and could see the ruins of a stone fort. *The old watchtower,* he thought. It must have seen better years. It wasn't a tower at all. More like a courtyard surrounded by a circular stone curtain wall. Tadok wondered at the calamity which had brought down the tower itself. Marven's story hadn't mentioned it at all. When he returned to the village, he made a mental note to ask the innkeeper. Then shook his head to cancel out the notion. It wasn't important. He and his companions had been clear about leaving town tomorrow at first light, and he had every intention of sticking to that plan. His inherent curiosity would need to go unsatisfied, he concluded.

He looked west. The hills were lower than the one he stood on and were covered by sparse trees and foliage. They were all barren, as would be expected this close to the heart of winter.

Tadok followed a path from the village with his gaze until it disappeared into the mountains, which were the famous Suldan Mountains. Legend had it that they were the border markings that ancient gods had set in the age of creation. The large mountain ridge split the continent of Trosia into east and west and stretched all the way from the Everwood in the north to Nirn Bay in the Southern Ocean with few gaps that were passable. One such gap was the pass through which the Triumph Road ran. From the ruined guard tower, Tadok imagined one could see for miles east and west along the road--giving the garrison ample warning if a horde of barbarians or orcs chose to invade.

Tadok's gaze continued to scan the panorama before him. His magically augmented eyes shifted to the church and narrowed. Behind the church was a small cemetery with a couple dozen graves. A shirtless man was toiling with a shovel at one of the graves. What was peculiar was that at least a dozen of those graves had been unearthed, with small mounds of dirt surrounding each.

Bunda was nowhere in sight. Probably chagrining the priest for letting his church come to its current state. He decided to take initiative and descended the path he had taken. At its base, he circled around the church and came upon the cemetery.

The man's sweaty back was turned to him. He was a thin scarecrow of a man with lank gray hair crowning a bald scalp and hanging to his shoulders. He was unshaven, and his breeches were stained with mud and crusted with dirt. A small silver medallion with the divine rune of the Four– which was four beads made of silver, iron, bronze, and copper was turned around and hanging on his back so as not to interfere with his work. His hands grasped a large iron shovel, and he was busy heaping piles of earth and dirt next to the gravestone, which read: 'Here lies Hector–loving father and husband'. A rusty-looking pickax rested against the tombstone.

So, this *was* the priest, and by the looks of it, he was as neglected as his house of worship was.

He was muttering under his breath and hadn't noticed Tadok. Tadok thought it prudent not to sneak up on the man with the large shovel and cleared his throat loudly. "Good morning, sir."

The man jumped and gave out a small yelp. He spun around quickly–the shovel swung in a large arc, confirming that making himself noticed from a distance had been a wise course of action.

His eyes were wide and had dark circles under them, and his teeth were crooked and yellowing, framed by wide, chapped lips.

Tadok raised his hands to show he was unarmed. "No need to be startled. I came from the inn. You must be Father Sheilagh."

The man, who must be Father Sheilagh, eyed him suspiciously for a few moments, then his demeanor shifted. "Ah, yes, friend, welcome to the house of the Four. You must be one of the travelers Mendel mentioned to me this morning."

"Aye," said Tadok with a nod. "We're searching for young Christopher and thought he may have come this way."

Sheilagh's eyes darted around Tadok. He licked his lips. "Have you come alone?"

Something in the way he asked the question set alarms blaring in Tadok's head, and his heart began beating a little faster.

"Yes. My companions are searching elsewhere." He wasn't sure why he chose not to mention Bunda, but a small voice in his head warned that it may be best to keep his assets a secret a little while longer. "Has the boy come this way?" he asked.

"The boy? Oh, little Christopher. No, I haven't seen him. The townsfolk aren't a very god-fearing pack. Don't really come up here anymore. Even during Yernsend or Demon Day. Practically heathens, that lot." His voice managed to somehow be both reedy and hoarse at the same time.

Tadok realized he was gazing at a man who hadn't slept, bathed, or eaten much for a significant amount of time. But it was his eyes that were the bigger source of concern. The bloodshot, shifty gaze and the way his lips seemed to quiver and mutter–this was a man near the border of sanity. The question was from which side of it.

"What," Tadok began carefully, his fingers twitching to form a protective spell, "pray tell, are you doing?" he asked, motioning to the unearthed graves without daring to take his eyes off the man.

Sheilagh seemed to notice the graves for the first time. A mix of emotions washed over his face. Tadok had traveled once with a band of mummers and thespians. He had seen one preparing for a show once, switching his expression between anger, grief, and laughter in a heartbeat. The priest's face was doing the same now, shifting from terror to rage, and then to a crazed grin.

"I told you," he began softly, "These folks are heathens. For years, they've buried their dead in a way unbecoming of good children of the Circle. I'm liberating their spirits with proper rite. Lest they wander the earth as ghoulies or specters…" He spoke as if Tadok was a stubborn child who refused to learn, and anger was creeping into his voice.

"Father, please step away from the grave. Come inside the church and let's have some tea."

"No!" He shook his head in exasperation. "You don't understand! None of you do! I'll show you."

Like a spitting viper, his body lashed out, heaving the iron shovel like a spear, blade first, directly at Tadok.

Tadok was unprepared. He managed to twist away, but the heavy iron tool struck him in the thigh with enough force to numb his whole leg. Tadok, still reeling from pain, backed away towards the gate cursing. His hands rose instinctively, and his fingers danced a well-practiced dance. The ground under Sheilagh's feet suddenly became slick, as if oil had been spilled on marble, and the thin man scrambled to hold his footing, his hands clamping on old Hector's tombstone for support.

Tadok used the time to draw his crossbow, setting a bolt into it fluidly. He raised it, taking aim at his foe.

How his leg ached.

To his surprise and dismay, Sheilagh had closed the distance between them, now holding the pickax in both hands. Tadok loosed the bolt just as Sheilagh swung the pickax with enough ferocity to send the crossbow sailing left, narrowly missing Tadok's hands in the process. The bolt launched to the side, clattering on a tombstone.

Hell, he's strong! He didn't know if it was whatever insanity rested on the man or something else which fueled his strength, but no man that thin should have been that strong.

Tadok suppressed the panic growing in his belly and concentrated. It was second nature to him. In the center of his forehead, a red glow formed, as if an ember was embedded behind his skin. The glow made his forehead nearly translucent, dark veins bloomed around the central focal point between his eyebrows, giving him a burning look. Then he called to her with his mind.

The strange visage gave Sheilagh pause, and he partially lowered his weapon as Tadok stumbled backwards, trying to put enough distance between himself and the rusty pickax.

When nothing further happened, Sheilagh laughed maniacally and advanced on the half-elf. He then froze in his tracks as a low growl rumbled behind him.

5 BULLIES

The boy ran panting through the woods. His pursuers were not far behind. He could hear them laughing and hollering insults and threats about what they would do to him when they caught him. Make him eat tree bark, cut off his ears—he'd heard it all before.

At only eight years of Age, Tadok knew the woods well. Being friendless, an orphan, and an outcast at Sage's Rock gave him a lot of time alone. He would venture far into the Everwood, reaching farther than the other children deemed safe.

He knew that if he made it to the rocky slopes ahead, the older boys chasing him would give up and return to the village empty-handed, mumbling that he was a woodland demon or that the elves helped him, since he was one of their kin and all.

Truth be told, Tadok had never even seen an elf. His mother had been a half-elf, and his father had been very human himself, but he'd never met him, having died while his mother was bearing him in her womb. Sellwyn had explained that despite common opinion, hybrid blood was stronger than pure blood, which was the reason he appeared half-elven. He wondered how a cross between an elf and a dwarf would look. The thought made him snort and burst out a short giggle, which transformed into a cry of pain as his foot snagged on a protruding root and he crashed unceremoniously into the undergrowth.

A sharp pain pierced his ankle, where it settled and throbbed. *Well, there goes outrunning them,* he scolded himself mentally. Tadok crawled on his hands to a small hollow under a fallen tree. There, he hugged his knees, trying to make himself smaller.

The older boys passed by him and stopped. He could hear them arguing amongst themselves.

"Where'd ee' go?" That one was the leader. The one the other boys called Clem.

"I swear ee' ran this way!" They were all panting and huffing.

"If we didn't 'ave to wait for your fat arse, Klancy," scolded Clem.

There were four of them. Must have been twelve or thirteen years old, although maybe Klancy was older. Then Tadok heard footsteps shuffling nearer to his small hideaway. He clamped his hand on his mouth, hoping against hope that they wouldn't notice his feet sticking out of the foliage.

He suddenly felt a sharp pain in his forehead, like his brain was on fire. Despite doing his best to avoid the bullies, he let out a small groan. Now, they were sure to hear him. Suddenly, there was a dull pop in his ears, and the pain in his forehead abated as if it hadn't existed in the first place. From his vantage point between the tree's thick vines and network of roots, he could see the boys looking up the path. They had frozen in place, their faces drained of color. One of them, Klancy, by his size, had a growing wet patch forming around his crotch.

A large dog stood ahead of them. Or, at least, it looked like a dog if the dog had been drawn by a child. It was soot-black and smooth with small black eyes and a wide-open, toothy maw. It had no ears and no tail. Still, it growled menacingly at the band of bullies.

Clem's lip quivered, and he raised a shaky hand to point at the strange creature. "F-fiend!" he stammered breathlessly.

It was all the boys needed, and a collective scream erupted from their throats. The boys turned and ran, shrieking through the woods.

It was over within the span of thirty seconds. He could hear their screams receding.

The woods grew quiet. Then he heard soft paws lumbering closer. And then the fiendish dog was standing before him.

Tadok pulled his legs up in fear. Upon closer look, he could see that the creature also didn't have any nostrils and was entirely hairless. It's skin, which he initially thought of as black, was actually dark gray. It slowly extended its smooth snout toward the boy's face. Tadok was quickly overcome by a sense of peace. He knew in that instant that this creature was no fiend or demon and was not going to do him any harm. He slowly extended his hand and petted the dark head. The creature's eyes closed calmly like a cat being scratched behind its ears.

"Thank you," he said quietly.

The creature pulled back and opened its eyes. Its maw gaped in what looked like a grin, and an alien sound escaped it. Almost sounding like a word.

"*Dor-kah...*" said the creature. Its voice sounded somehow hollow yet rich.

"Is that your name? *Dorkah?*" asked Tadok. He tapped his chest: "I'm Tadok."

To Tadok's bewilderment, the beast replied, trying to mimic his name, "*Ta-dok...*".

Tadok blinked twice, mouth open. Dorkah did the same.

Suddenly, the adrenaline fuelling his blood gave way, and everything flooded back at once. The pain in his ankle, his fear—it all rushed in, overwhelming him, and he broke out in tears. Dorkah stepped forward and nudged her head at his ear. Tadok threw his arms around her—he knew, somehow, that Dorkah was a 'she' and he sobbed, holding her tight.

He wasn't alone anymore. *You'll always be with me*, the boy thought. It didn't surprise him at all that in his mind, she answered.

***

It was already dark when he made it back to Sage's Rock, Dorkah in tow. The hike had been challenging with his sprained ankle. Yet Dorkah had been at his side the whole way. At first, Tadok was still bewildered by the creature, but as the walk continued, he started chatting endlessly with her. Telling her about his mother and father, and about Sellwyn. "She'll love you. Sellwyn likes strange creatures. She's not like the others at home, who are sure that anything not a human is evil." He scowled.

"*E-vil,*" replied Dorkah in agreement. That was something she did, mimic the last words of his sentence. But there was yet a stranger aspect to her speech.

Once, at Yernsend festival in Freelan, he had been with his mother before she got sick. The city, with its high stone walls and minarets, had been a marvel to the boy. His mother had had to drag him along to avoid being stepped on or lost in the wonder of the place. They had stopped when she bought him a hot honey roll in the market. And while the boy ate the delicious treat and licked his fingers, he watched a performer with skin as dark as coffee sing and play a strange-looking lute. Perched on the strange man, who his mother had explained came from the Wetlunds far to the south, was a colorful bird with a large beak. At the end of his sentences, the bird would mimic his words to the laughter and applause of the crowd watching them.

Dorkah was different than this bird. While she did mimic his words, she also seemed to know how to reuse them at the right time. When his injured ankle betrayed him once and he stumbled, Dorkah had been at his side, crying *"Ta-dok!"* in alarm.

When they came upon the village, Dorkah had asked, *"Vill-age?"*

Just how smart are you? he wondered.

There was much more activity in the village than he expected. He could see torches in the village and heard men shouting to each other.

He wondered what the boys had told their parents and was glad that his small cabin was on the outskirts of Sage's Rock.

He and his new companion quietly crept over to the door.

"Wait here," he said to Dorkah assertively. "Stay out of sight." He pointed to the wood pile, which was high enough to hide the strange doglike creature.

"Sight," answered Dorkah.

Tadok quietly opened the door to the hut where Sellwyn was packing her satchel hastily. She shoved in bandages and salves. Perhaps someone was sick or injured. Sellwyn often helped Creya, the village wise woman, when she needed help or replaced her when she was traveling to Freelan to restock her supplies.

The moment the door closed, Sellwyn spun around, and her greenish golden eyes grew to the size of saucers.

"Where have you *been*!" She gasped, grasping him in both her hands. Her slender fingers dug into his shoulders, and she shook him. "Do you know how worried I was? There is some sort of beast roaming the woods, doing gods know what."

He was about to answer but instead winced in pain when he shifted weight onto his bruised ankle.

Sellwyn's anger gave way to her concern, and she started turning the boy around, prodding and pulling at his tunic.

"Are you injured? Did it attack you?"

Tadok finally was able to push her hands away and said, "No, I'm fine. I mean, I twisted my ankle, and it hurts bad, but I'm alright. But—"

Sellwyn looked down at his swollen ankle.

"It doesn't look broken. I should probably put some ointment on it." She began rummaging through her satchel, retrieving items she had only recently inserted into it.

"Sellwyn, I—"

"It's important to take care of an injury first thing. Little cuts and bruises may seem small but sometimes hold unseen dangers to our bodies. I am pleased you like the woods, but when you're there alone, I expect you to be more sensible, boy. Being clumsy is a sure way to get yourself hurt or even killed," she lectured.

"I wasn't clumsy," said the boy defensively. "I was being chased. It was that—"

Sellwyn looked up sharply. "Chased? Was it this beast? Was it a Winter Wolf? A Gleith? A bear?"

Tadok had had enough of trying to get a word into the conversation. "Would you *listen!*" he shouted exasperated. That seemed to shut her up for a moment.

"I was being chased by Clem and his friends. Clem's cousin is here from Goring, and he told him he wanted to show him how to make an elf eat dirt."

Sellwyn's face darkened. Sellwyn wasn't of Sage's Rock. She had appeared once when his mother had begun to fall ill. She had been a friend of his grandfather, so she said. It seemed his mother knew her or knew *of* her and let her in. She had been passing through and wanted to visit the daughter of her old friend and meet his grandson.

At first, the five-year-old Tadok had been shy around her. But his timidness turned to fascination and fondness when she began reciting stories of the days before the war and of her homeland. She had even allowed Tadok to touch her small back-swept antlers which framed her head. Tadok had never seen a *Shadowtouched* before. They were rare beings. Beyond the antlers and the golden tint in their eyes, they looked more or less like elves. Sellwyn had said that some of her race had reddish skin or antlers that protruded upwards, but she was lucky enough to pass through human lands as an elf if she wore her hat or a hood.

Sellwyn had stayed with them for most of the winter. One

morning, Tadok had woken early to see her packing her horse. A messenger had come in the night and had called her back to her lord, King Celestine Goldenbrow, High King of the *Sahangi* Elves.

She had returned a week after his mother's funeral, staying in their cabin for the last two years, effectively adopting the boy.

While she wasn't his mother—a fact she had stated repeatedly— she seemed to deeply care for the boy. She made sure he had food in his belly every night, had taught him to read and write and count numbers.

Sellwyn was beautiful by both human and elf standards. Even though she must have been his grandfather's age—at least—her hair was rich and fiery red, her eyes greenish-gold and she had a smile which would light up a room. Despite appearing like an elf, the men of the village welcomed her openly—the women not so much. She had sent them all away repeatedly. Sellwyn had made it clear to the young boy that no one could know of her true heritage. When the boy had questioned this, she explained that in the world of men, Shadowtouched were often viewed as demons or fiends. As far as anyone was concerned, she was his aunt from his mother's side, come to take care of him after his mother's passing. Luckily, she was very skilled at masking the inhuman aspects of her appearance.

Over time, the villagers, either spurred on by a jealous wife or a spurned would-be-lover, chose to shun the disguised Shadowtouched, creating gossip and rumors about her and her ward—as men often would when the fairer sex rejected their advances.

When Tadok had asked her what a 'Tor-lip' was, as a couple of boys had claimed their mothers had said she was, she had laughed and told him it was what wives were most of afraid of and their husbands most sought. While Tadok had no idea what she meant, she had ended the conversation by explaining that all was better this way. But what she had never accepted was the bullying Tadok had to endure.

"What did that *sikat* do to you?" she asked, scowling.

"Nothing. They didn't reach me. Just as they were about to get me, Dorkah appeared and scared them off."

"Who is Dorkah?" she asked, narrowing her eyes.

"She's my friend. She's like a dog, but different. Don't be mad," the boy said noting her expression. "She looks a little strange, but she's really smart. She can even say words!"

"Tadok, you're not making any sense. What did you see in the woods?"

"Look, she's outside. I'll call her."

Tadok had intended to open the door and call to her. But as his hand reached for the door, his mind called out to Dorkah. His forehead glowed like it had before and felt hot, and suddenly, with no warning, there was Dorkah, resting on her haunches by the fireplace, her strange eyes looking at the both of them and her tongue wagging like a dog's.

Sellwyn leapt backwards, cursing. As she did her hand suddenly blazed into flame, which she aimed at Dorkah, who instantly sprang into a protective stance.

"No, wait!" shouted the boy. His mother had told him that Sellwyn was more than she seemed. That Shadowtouched were often magical and held the gift of the arcane in their souls. Living with her, Tadok had seen her use her magic from time to time. To light the hearth, or to mend clothes and broken crockery. Once he had climbed a tree to show off to her. A squirrel had startled him, and he would have fallen ten feet to the hard ground below. Sellwyn had been there, and to the boy's shock and then delight, she had instinctively pointed at him. His descent nearly stopped in mid-air, and he floated to the ground like a snowflake.

It was clear to him by now that what he had known and seen was only the tip of Sellwyn's power. Like a *Brangroot*, whose short stock and leaves were only a small fraction of the plant; it had a root that could burrow up to three feet under the ground. He was suddenly afraid for his new friend. However, Dorkah's mouth was snarling, exposing two rows of long needle-sharp teeth. Before his eyes, the muscles in her hindlegs flexed, preparing to leap at his adopted mother. He acted.

Tadok jumped between the two, holding his hands outright, his eyes shut as he expected to feel either the searing pain of Sellwyn's flames or Dorkah's jaws crushing his body as her teeth pierced his skin.

To his surprise, neither happened.

He opened one eye, and then the other.

Dorkah was back on her haunches. Her growl turned into a yawn. "Ta-dok," she said simply—the equivalent of a shrug.

Sellwyn looked at them with wide eyes. Her hand was still red as a burning ember, but it was no longer aimed at the creature.

"You," she began and had to swallow to wet her dry mouth, "you…summoned her?"

"No, honestly!" he said, then corrected, "I mean, I don't know." He looked down at his ankles. "I think she comes when I need her."

Sellwyn's hand finally darkened, as if it hadn't been burning like a torch a moment ago.

"I bet she does…" she said, mystified.

Dorkah chose that moment to pad over to the boy and nudge her head against his neck.

Sellwyn made a subtle motion and her eyes flashed for a moment. She seemed to be scanning the creature, looking at Tadok from time to time. She gingerly raised her palm to his forehead, like she did when he was ill, then immediately drew it back.

"She doesn't mean me any harm, and I know she won't hurt you either, Sellwyn," he said, trying to assure her, using the same tone she would use on him when he was crying, and she wanted to calm him down.

Dorkah raised her head, her black eyes turning to the Shadowtouched. "*Sell-wen,*" she said in her hollow voice.

Sellwyn blinked in surprise. Her features finally calmed, and a faint smile emerged on her face. She nodded slowly, as if understanding. Her shoulders slumped, and she sighed audibly.

"Well, then. Welcome…Dorkah," she said, looking at the boy and his new friend.

Tadok's eyes shot up to the woman, and a grateful grin lit up his features.

"Does this mean she can stay with us?" he asked hopefully.

Sellwyn slowly nodded. "Yes," she said. "She can stay with us. But unfortunately, love, *we* can't stay here anymore."

She knelt beside the boy, resting one hand on him. And after a moment, the other went on Dorkah's smooth head.

"Pack your things. We're going on a journey."

6 ZOMBIES

Sheilagh spun around to face Dorkah, whose large maw was bared, revealing her pointy teeth. Her jet-black pearl-like eyes had narrowed to slits, and a low rumbling emitted from her throat.

With no further warning, she pounced—razor sharp claws extended from her front paws.

Sheilagh tried to twist out of her way but wasn't quite fast enough. Dorkah slammed into him with force, her claw tearing three gashes in his side and knocking the priest back a couple steps.

He cried in pain and stumbled out of the creature's way. As he did, he swung the pickax with all his might. The spike punctured Dorkah's midsection, just above her hindleg, and Dorkah howled in pain.

Tadok felt the pain himself. He had that bond with Dorkah. The pain for him wasn't as if he had received the blow himself, but as if a second set of nerves—dulled by being once removed, was setting off warning bells in his brain. Dorkah must have felt the numbing pain in his thigh the same way.

Dorkah lunged at Sheilagh, and her jaws clamped over the long wooden handle of the pickax. For a moment, the two wrestled over the weapon. In any other situation it may have looked comical, as if a man was trying to wrestle a branch out of his hound's jaw to play fetch with him.

Sheilagh's uncanny strength seemed to come into play, as Dorkah was unable to rip the long tool from his grasp despite the cords in her neck heaving under her smooth black-gray skin. She changed tactics.

Her powerful jaw suddenly clenched down on the wooden shaft, crushing it in an eruption of splinters.

The crazed priest dropped the two parts of his weapon and

56

skipped back. Dorkah was panting; dark blood oozed from the wound in her side. Sheilagh seemed to ignore his own injury despite his blood streaming down to his breeches from the three gashes under his ribs.

Sheilagh suddenly withdrew a short stick-like object from his pocket. It was strange-looking. The handle part was dark ironwood, but the top half ended in a nob and was entirely white. It was too small to act as a club, and it took Tadok a moment to realize what he was holding and the danger he and his Dorkah were now in.

While Tadok was no wizard, Sellwyn had taught him enough to use his own hereditary magic, as well as lessons about the way magic worked. So he knew a spell wand when he saw one.

It was impossible from a cursory glance to know what magic the item held. What spells had been infused into the small rod. But if he drew it now, Tadok expected it to be nasty.

Dorkah, get down! he mentally commanded her, and the creature complied, flattening on her belly.

But no beam or lightning bolt escaped the tip of Sheilagh's wand. There was a sound, like a bell ringing and a tiny puff of green smoke, but nothing else.

Tadok began to think the thing had misfired and stood back up, as did Dorkah.

"That didn't work out too well for you," he said, a triumphant smile on his face.

Suddenly, an overwhelming stink of rotting flesh assaulted his nostrils.

"You were saying?" It was Sheilagh's turn to smile.

Around him, sounds of clawing and hollow moans escaped the open graves in the cemetery. The hairs on the back of the half-elf's neck rose, and his body shivered when the first rotting hand emerged from the grave.

The hand was that of Hector, loving father and husband that he was. As he climbed out and straightened up like a macabre marionette, Tadok reflected on how he didn't look so 'loving' right now.

Hector had probably been interred no less than a year ago. It was enough for nature to take its toll. Gray rotting flesh hung in tatters from his partially exposed bones, and as Tadok watched, he was graced with the grotesque image of something with multiple legs crawling out of his empty eye socket and back into a gaping hole in the cadaver's withered cheek.

All around him, the deceased residents of Suldan's Bluff were awakening from their eternal slumber. There was more than a dozen of them—each in different stages of decay that ranged from dry skeletons to horrifying corpses in their fully intact burial shrouds.

At that point, Tadok regretted that the people of Nemir didn't cremate their dead, as was customary in the Seal Shore Isles.

As Hector stumbled into range, Tadok limped over to Dorkah and drew his sickle. He slashed out at the undead thing with a wide backhand, cleaving the creature's jaw clean off its skull. If the lack of a working jaw bothered the late Hector, he didn't show it. He continued forward in a shambling advance, arms raised, bones protruding sharply from the tips of his gray finger.

Dorkah leaped on the dead man's back, powerful jaws crushing his skull to a gray pulp. That seemed to stop the zombie, but the rest were closing in.

Dorkah slashed another zombie with both claws, severing its spine and cutting it effectively in half.

Tadok slashed at a skeletal fellow with a gray bristling beard, but his sickle stuck, lodged between the thing's exposed ribs. The bearded zombie swung a bony hand, catching Tadok on the side of his head. It was like being slapped with a dry branch and his vision blurred for a moment. Blood seeped down from his pointy ear. He shoved the thing with all his might, and it fell over into one of the exposed graves.

As more closed in, Tadok wondered in numbing terror if once they ripped him to shreds—would he too rise and join the priest's ghastly retinue?

But just when it seemed he was about to find out, bright sunlight blinded him. The undead hissed or groaned—in the case of those who could make air escape their rotting throats—and instinctively tried to turn from the source of the light. Behind him, Bunda's voice chanted or prayed, or whatever clerics of Seirn did when they called upon their lord's might.

In an instance, the dead mob surrounding him fell to the ground, smoke curling off their bones and flesh.

Tadok braved a quick glance behind him.

Bunda was standing tall, seal cloak billowing out behind him and long braid blowing in the wind—almost like a tail. His face was serene, yet also commanding. He held Seirn's glowing medallion–half a solar disk–in front of him, pointed directly at the undead. For lack of a better term, Tadok found him majestic.

Tadok had heard about the champions of Seirn being able to banish the undead back to their afterlives–but had never seen it before.

For the first time in a long time, Tadok found himself rethinking his alienation of faith.

7 GODS

When no one answered the door, Bunda opened the large door himself. It groaned on its hinges but swung open rather easily.

Bunda walked in and surveyed his surroundings.

Inside, the church had a tall, vaulted ceiling. Stained glass windows in better times would have allowed the light to filter into rainbows as it washed over the wooden pews. Now, the windows were dull and grimy, even boarded up in some places. The rows of pews were misaligned and cracked. A thin layer of dust caked their wooden seats, indicating that the parish they had been designed for hadn't sat on them for quite some time.

Tapestries hung from the walls, their edges frayed and moldy. The tapestries depicted the four sons of the Divine Father.

The dark-bearded muscular fellow holding a scythe was Legeth the Reaper, Lord of Autumn, Death, and Rebirth. The pale woman with golden hair and piercing blue eyes was Agreina, Mother of Winter—or the Ice Witch, as she was often referred to—Lady of Night and Mystery. A helmeted warrior in green armor brandishing an ax was Carrodus the Champion, Bringer of Autumn, Master of Harvests and Protector Maidens' Virtue. The last Son was Tinnias, the Flame-Haired. His domains were summer, crafting, healing, and toil.

Candles were set in alcoves along the inner walls and on the two pillars in the middle, but only a few were lit. At the end of the hall rested a small dais with a podium and a large stone altar with divine symbols carved into its base.

Despite the rundown state of the place, Bunda couldn't help wondering who had funded it. This was no mere village shrine or chapel, consisting of a single room with an altar and podium. The church was more reminiscent of the temples erected by wealthy nobles who wished to leave their mark and legacy on the land during their lifetime. Or to obtain divine favor in the heavens after it.

Places of worship were of special interest to Bunda. Ever since he had climbed the stone steps of Darakeila—the holy mountain in Shard on which rested the temples of the Tundrial, he had been mystified by the homes of the gods on mortal soil. For one, the architecture in some places was stunning. Arches and ornate columns, the high domed ceilings or the alters. But more than anything—the art. The detailed and the abstract, the statues of saints and heroes, and the paintings of heavenly battles. For Bunda, it was what being a Journeyman was all about.

The other reason was that he felt a sense of peace when stepping into temples and churches. As if he was closer to the beings who had created the world and had designs for all men. It was a tug he felt going directly to his soul, confirming that everything had a reason, and even if Bunda didn't understand it, his master, Seirn the Dawn Father, also called Heaven's Torch and the Righter of Wrongs, *did* understand, and that was good enough.

Seirn had become more popular in the mainland since the War of the Broken Crown two and a half decades earlier, and he had stopped in every one of his temples on his journey from the moment he stepped off the ship in Culidge. But when a town or village lacked a temple of Seirn, he had never hesitated to pray in a house of another deity, such as the churches of the Four Sons. The smaller the villages got, the more dominant the 'Circle' churches became. These houses of worship would often represent a few deities, such as the Four Sons, and one daughter. Bunda assumed that it was as good a choice of faith as any for an agrarian community.

But Bunda wasn't here for the decorum.

"Hello?" he called in his best booming voice. When no one answered, he repeated and added, "Show yourself, kind custodian of the Faith, for I am Bunda of the Jams, Journeyman of Seirn." A proper announcement was customary.

No one answered.

Bunda slowly walked down the center of the aisle towards the dais. A small door behind it must have led to the priests' private chambers. Perhaps he was sleeping.

Think, boy. In his head, Bunda heard the voice of Garlan Ice Sail, his father. *You have other senses.*

Bunda closed his eyes and listened. The howl of the wind was confined to the outside of the church. Yet a few broken windows near the vaulted ceiling allowed enough of it in to give a low whistling shriek above.

He sniffed and could detect the smell of the old oak wooden benches, mold, and the faint scent of cloves and incense from the thuribles resting near the podium. Underneath it was an almost undetectable scent of decay. Of rotting organic matter.

Bunda made his way to the dais, trying to locate the source. As he came upon the dais, a flurry of wings sent him jumping back as a couple of pigeons launched into the air from behind the altar, frantically trying to get out of the way of this rude human intruder. Bunda followed the two birds with his eyes as they took refuge in the rafters above, leaving a trail of gray and white feathers, slowly floating gracefully to the floor.

He cursed himself for being too jittery, but he suddenly froze. *The feathers.*

Bunda traced their trail to the floor. While they floated down, swaying from side to side, at a point near the foot of the podium, they suddenly sailed to the right as if pushed by an unseen hand. *Or a breeze of air,* he thought.

He neared the podium's base, the point where it rested on the floor, and sure enough, a breeze of air blew out from a small space between wood and stone. It was upon this flow of air that he could smell that stench of rot he had picked up a moment ago.

Looking around him one last time to make sure he was alone, he braced both hands on the side of the wooden stand and pushed.

The podium wasn't heavy, and it easily shifted to the side, revealing a narrow wooden trap door.

He smiled in satisfaction. The wooden planks lacked the coat of dust that covered other items in the church's main hall. He bent over and hooked his fingers underneath the wooden door and pulled it open. The portal opened to reveal a set of wooden steps leading into the darkness below. Now that the door was open, the reek he had barely smelled before assaulted him, and he covered his nose with the back of his hand.

What would he find down there? A forgotten larder? A body?

Bunda held his medallion and uttered a prayer in the Divine—a language reserved for requests between mortals and gods.

His eyes flashed a deeper blue for a brief moment, and he began scanning the darkness. While it was still dark, he could now see the shifting prism of energy flowering in various colors. The *Auras*.

It was faint, but it was there. A reddish-dark tendril that kept flickering and shifting on the edge of his field of view.

Whatever was down there reeked of a more sinister stench—one which couldn't be picked up by even the keenest noses.

"There is something evil here..." he muttered to no one in particular.

He drew his saber. He whispered another divine incantation and ran his hand along the blade. As he did, his palm left a trail of fire along the edge, turning the curved weapon into a flaming sword in the name of his master.

In addition to making the weapon significantly more powerful, this would take care of the darkness.

Armed with his flaming sword and his faith, he steadily stepped into the darkness.

8 DRUIDS

"*Latktan Kulit'an!*" roared the crowd, raising ceramic mugs of ale, mead, and wine, which sloshed over the drunken hands of their owners.

The blessing was in old *Alan-Nemtang*, the ceremonial language of Tundrial, which was a mixture of their old Karr language and the language of King Nem's people when they first arrived at their shores. "Reign Wisely." It meant and was often offered to new clan leaders, kings, druids, or even fathers of when they sired sons. On that specific spring morning, it was aimed at Greffik "Iron Tooth" Majess, newly elected Druid of Tarthen Island.

Tarthen was actually two adjacent islands connected by a series of five bridges. The port below was smaller than the one in Shard, the capital of the Seal Shore Islands, but as it was more southern, it was often a favored stop for ships traveling north from the Wetlunds after circumventing the Snake Marshes. Also, the clans of Tarthen were known to be more hospitable than other Tundrial.

Tarthen wasn't just one clan. It was comprised of various clans, such as Graykine, Stilserd, Draketoth and the Jams, which were more of a collection of smaller clans and families who voted together during Moots. Tarthen also held four temples, giving homage to Geiless, Tiel-Kah, Trin and Seirn, and welcoming travelers who wished to pray before journeys, or thank the gods after their completion.

Now that the chief druid of Tarthen had been announced, it was time to bless the acolytes and initiates of the four official faiths—a custom which represented the blessings the *Nemfolk* had received from the local tribes and their druids when they began settling the islands five centuries ago. The people who'd lived in these lands before Nem's migration were feral and uncouth, following the law and rule of twelve high druids. When Nem's people arrived, they had initially been attacked by the local folk who inhabited the islands–the *Karr-alan*. But Nem's people brought with them steel and magic and the Karr-alan were quickly defeated.

The Karr-alan initially named these foreigners *Tundrial*, which was Karr for 'Thunder-Folk' – as they had come out of the western storms. Recognizing the invaders as the new alphas, the Druid Council came on their bellies to Nem's captains, pledging their spear and heart to them. In return, Nem decreed that the druids would continue to practice their beliefs and customs on the Islands, but Nem's people must be allowed to settle them peacefully. Over time, the invaders and their indigenous Karr-alan fused, as people do, and the Tundrial rose to be one nation.

In general, the Tundrial respected religion. Any religion. Their attitude was basically that life was hard enough as it was–why take the risk of angering someone's deity? Even when they pillaged and looted, temples, shrines and churches were never defiled.

The ritual of Subjugation, as it was known, was a remnant of the surrender of the Karr-alan of the Seal Shore islands to Nem's people all those years ago.

Standing in the front row a little to the left was a figure who was a little taller than the rest. At the age of eighteen, Bunda took his first step as a priest of Seirn. The new Druid of Tarthen, one of the thirteen druids on the druid council, was kneeling before him and his twelve peers in mock tribute as the Druids had done over five hundred years ago.

"We accept you as you accept us. We are one and the same, man and nature. We are *Tundrial,*" the thirteen young acolytes recited together. When they finished, the druid rose to his feet and the crowd cheered and hammered their mugs on the long wooden tables which had been set in the clearing.

Bunda and his fellow followers of Seirn exited right to allow another thirteen students of Tiel-Kah in their white cloaks to take the stage.

Bunda advanced through a crowd of congratulators and back-slappers to a table at the back where his brothers sat, waiting. Somber looks on all their faces.

"Where have you been, Brother? Father will skin your miserable hide for missing the ceremony," said Ulan, the eldest of the lot.

"What do you mean, where was I? Do you not have eyes? Did you not see me receive old Iron Tooth's blessing?" he asked in surprise and a little anger. His brothers never seemed to take interest in any of his activities or his life.

He swept his long braid away from his shoulder so they could clearly see the golden half-sun symbol that hung from a narrow silver chain.

The holy symbol was way too expensive for Bunda. It was a family heirloom handed down to him by his uncle who had also been a cleric of Seirn.

"I'm a cleric of the Dawn Father now. And you lot best show some respect lest I curse you with a pox and your dicks fall off.

Ulan's face stayed stern. Golen, the youngest of his three older brothers, stared at Bunda with wide eyes. "Seirnites can do that?"

His horrified look was so comical that none of them could hold the ruse any longer, and all four doubled over laughing.

Migril, his large gut still shaking with laughter, was the first to recover. He pointed a meaty finger to Golen, "You need a dick in the first place to have it fall off, boy!" The rest of them roared with invigorated laughter, and even Bunda, who was considered the most serious of the four brothers, couldn't help himself.

Each in turn embraced him, slapped him on the back, and congratulated him. His brothers were proud of him, and Bunda felt himself overcome with emotion. Still, his joy was flecked with an undercurrent of sorrow that he couldn't show his new medallion to his mother. He wondered where she was. If she was even alive. Did she still love him? Five years were a long time. Perhaps her life as a slave was something she strove to forget–her son along with it. He didn't want to believe that.

The ceremony had ended two and half hours ago, making way for the feast. And as the feast progressed, the songs became bolder, as did the women. The men began drinking each other under the table. Occasionally, one or two would try and corner a slave girl pouring drinks or bringing food. The nimble ones managed to avoid the drunken advances, but some of the others simply took it with defeated eyes and did what they must to survive. It was the Tundrial way.

His thoughts were cut short by an imposing figure who cast a shadow in the setting sun.

The man who walked over was tall—towering at six-foot-five from sole to crown. He had broad shoulders and a barrel chest. His braid was entirely the color of iron, but his beard held the man's original Auburn hair color. He crossed his arms to his chest, covering a tattoo of a longship.

"A word with you, boy," his father said with a growl.

The revelry stopped. The brothers looked at each other. It was unclear if their father was angry or not, but he *was* serious. This was not a time to test his patience.

Bunda wouldn't be intimidated. Not anymore. He drained his mug calmly and rose to his feet.

"What do you want, Garlan Ice Sail?" He could have called him father, but he chose to call him by the name everyone else called him. It was an obvious show of disrespect or at the least alienation, but Bunda didn't care. Whether coming from the ale or from his new standing with the faith, Bunda felt power in his gut. He was done being afraid of this man.

To his surprise, Garlan's eyes softened. "A word with you—*please*," corrected his father.

In all of his eighteen years of life, Bunda had never been on the receiving end of a polite request from his father. It had a more significant effect than the actual word itself and deflated his bravado. He took a swig from his brother's mug and walked off after his father into the woods.

They continued their walk in silence for another five minutes until they were out of earshot of anyone at the party, when Garlan finally stopped. He didn't look Bunda in the eyes. His hands were tying and untying his leather sword strap—and he looked anxious. Bunda was curious.

Without looking Bunda in the eyes, he said, "You and me, boy, we've never really seen eye to eye on many things."

That understatement was the equivalent of calling Nem the Conqueror a simple ship captain, thought Bunda.

"But there is something I need you to know." He sat down on a fallen tree trunk and motioned Bunda to join him.

"They say it's bad luck to lie to a cleric, and even if you weren't one, some secrets rot in your heart until their stench is overwhelming for the soul. The truth is"—the old man swallowed hard before proceeding— "I've always loved your mother, and I will until I die."

This was *not* what Bunda was expecting. Garlan had taken Tarillian on a raid. The raid was conducted on a small village in the Shield Mountains. But it hadn't unfolded like most. The irony of it was that the Tundrial war band had encountered an orcish raiding party in the outskirts of the village. The orcs had had the same intent as the Seal Shore Barbarians, and before the raid, the warriors had to contend with the orcs. The fighting was fierce, and his father's party had lost at least half its men. To add to their disappointment, the spoils from the village had been meagre. Fortunately for Garlan, he had found Tarillian and decided to take her home, back to Tarthen as his slave.

Contrary to popular belief, Tundrial treated their slaves better than other masters around Trosia, provided they didn't break the law, repeatedly disobey their master, or try to escape. Their servitude was limited to a number of years depending on their situation when enslaved. It was considered bad form to harm or rape a slave, although the exact definition of rape probably differed from the way it was perceived in the mainland. Forced concubinage was acceptable for slaves, and what happened during a raid, when the blood was hot, was usually excused. But killing a slave would still be considered murder. It wasn't uncommon for slaves to be offered places in the clan after their servitude was done. Garlan eventually fell in love with the blonde girl and made her his third wife, the first two dying in childbirth and drowning on a voyage. Tarillian was never treated poorly, and definitely far better than her days as a slave

Bunda had been raised believing she had loved his father back, although he never understood why. While his mother was gentle and kind and delicate, his father was rough and temperamental. He often came home drunk, and his mother and he would argue and often fight. Although, to the best of his knowledge, Garlan never raised a hand to his wife—something that was acceptable in the Isles. No one would have batted an eyelash if Tarillian had a bruise or two the morning after talking back to her husband and master.

Then, five years ago—with no warning—his mother had simply vanished off the island. Garlan had been so enraged that he named her a *Biellkah*, a traitor. For slaves, this meant the slave had betrayed their master's trust and was now deemed less than human. If he was found by any Tundrial, he was empowered to exact violent justice on the traitor-slave. How hurt must have Garlan felt to accuse his wife this way, thought Bunda.

"My mother...?" asked a bewildered Bunda. "Then...why would you mark her so?"

Garlan shrugged, then sighed. "Men do foolish things when they are angry. Or hurt." He added the last as if it was hard to admit how much she had broken his heart. He looked at his boots. "I didn't know she was unhappy. We argued, but it is said that a man and his wife will only cease to argue when they are buried beside each other. So, I thought nothing of it. When she left me, I assumed the worst. That she had given her heart and bed to another. Rage filled my heart and turned me into a fool."

Bunda sat motionless for a full minute. "Why tell me this *now?*"

Garlan looked up directly into the eyes of his youngest son. When he spoke, his voice was steady and clear. "Because I respect you, boy. You've grown to be a fine lad, and I suspect that is from your mother more than from me." He scrubbed his hand through his gray hair.

"Your uncle and namesake was the smarter and better of us. I was the brute and the muscle. If he had been by at my side and not at the bottom of the sea, I wager he would have made me see reason. And today I watched you rise in front of old Iron Tooth and was so proud. I was proud for your uncle and for my forefathers and for your mother. It ached my old heart that she couldn't see it herself."

How ironic, thought Bunda, that they had shared the same thought at the same moment exactly.

"I want things to be different between us, boy. If I am ever blessed enough to lay eyes on my sweet Tarilly again, I want to be able to tell her I did right by her boy." He finished his sentence and looked at Bunda, holding his son's eyes for a long time. "Perhaps then, she will forgive me." He said the last in almost a whisper, and Bunda needed to strain to hear him.

"Father I—" Bunda's reply was interrupted by a scream, which ended abruptly with a slap and a short yelp. He leapt to his feet.

His father trailing behind him, Bunda rushed through the woods to the source of the sound. There in the moonlight, by a small fire in the clearing, Bunda saw Tarthen's new High Druid, stark naked, standing near a young slave girl. His woad body tattoos shone off his large gut and back, while she was stripped to the waist, pale breasts shuddering in the moonlight, tears streaming down her cheeks, but she dared not say a word. Iron Tooth's intentions were made obvious by the brazen erection pointing towards the trembling woman. No, not woman–she was more of a girl. She couldn't have been older than fifteen or sixteen.

Bunda was unarmed, but he raised a thick branch from the ground. His father, who had caught up with him, grabbed his arm. *"What are you doing?* Is your mind Trin-touched?" he whispered harshly. "That is the High Druid of Tarthen! And she is a slave girl."

Cold rage iced Bunda's heart. "So was my mother!"

He shrugged off his father's grasp and dashed into the clearing, swinging his makeshift weapon. His blow caught the High Druid by surprise on the back, sending him rolling in the mud and leaves. Bunda placed himself between him and the girl as the naked man rose to his feet with murder in his eyes.

"That was a mistake you stupid sniveling whelp!" He growled.

Suddenly, the branch in his hands began twisting and turning until it became a snake. Bunda flung it towards the fire with a shout. The druid was on him, pummeling him with his hands, which were now bear claws. Bunda tried to protect himself but was being slashed by the animalistic claws jutting from the man's paws.

All the while the druid screamed threats and profanities: "I'll gut you like a fish! I will rip off your ears and stuff them up your arsehole! I'll turn your skull into a chamber pot, you shit!"

Bunda took a step back and clasped his medallion, *"Selis, Si' ami!"* he intoned in the divine.

Suddenly a glowing ball of bright light split the darkness, washing the whole clearing in pale rays. Bunda shoved the globe straight at Iron Tooth's face.

"Aaargh!" he yelled, averting his head and covering his eyes with a bear claw. While the globe had no physical manifestation–only light—it was enough to blind the druid and allow Bunda to roll away from his attacker.

Iron Tooth shook his head and blinked away the flashes in his vision. His rage was even greater than before. His lips began to move, and his eyes began glowing; terror gripped at the young cleric's heart.

Suddenly, vines sprang up from the earth and wrapped around his ankles, yanking him off his feet. Before he could rise, more vines wrapped around his wrists and chest. He was pinned to the earth; the air slowly being crushed from his lungs. The druid stood darkly above him. Eyes and woad tattoos glowing in the night. He raised a large rock which was intended for caving in Bunda's skull and then froze.

Garlan's arm had wrapped around Iron Tooth's neck and was holding a slim steel knife to man's throat. "Throw it aside, Greff."

Greffik Iron Tooth did nothing of the sort. "Are you *mad*, Ice Sail? I am the High Druid of Tarthen. How *dare* you interfere?" Spittle was flying out of his mouth in rage, but he made no move against the knife.

"And she is a child-slave girl. And he is an anointed son of the Dawn Father. And I am *still* a Thunder Warrior. But most importantly, he is my son. I'll saw your throat ear to ear before I let you harm him." To make his point, he pressed the knife ever so slightly against his throat, enough to lightly break the skin.

Either the threat worked or his arms were simply getting tired of holding a rock above his head because Iron Tooth tossed the large stone to one side. Bunda sighed in relief. Not that there was much air in his lungs by that point, anyways.

"Now release him," ordered Garlan.

The vines withdrew and Bunda stumbled to his feet, gulping in air and leaning shakily on a tree. "This is far from over. Once I tell the council—"

"You will need to explain to them what your own hands were doing, Iron Tooth. This," he said, motioning to the girl, "is not our way. It's not even the way of a *real* man."

Garlan turned to the girl. "Go," he ordered curtly, and she bundled her tunic around her chest and ran, stumbling through the woods, still sobbing.

Garlan turned back to Iron Tooth, and the two older men stood in silence. Garlan held Iron Tooth's fuming gaze without flinching.

It was Iron Tooth who first broke the eye lock. "If it won't be tonight, it will be tomorrow. Or the next day. Or the one after that. But one day that boy will die by my hands, for the island itself does my bidding."

Garlan sighed and looked at his feet. He looked sadly at Bunda, and Bunda was suddenly aware of the how old his father was. The weight of losing a brother, countless comrades in arms, cremating one wife and the empty dress of another, and finally being left by a third…the man had known pain and hardship, and had hidden it behind a wall. *It was easier to understand why the universe punished you if you were resigned to being a shit,* thought Bunda.

71

When his father looked back at the druid, his voice was clear. "From my gut, I couldn't give a gnome's ballocks where you shove your dick. But others may. And I ken that ye can't be leaving a boy who gave your rump a good slappin'." Iron Tooth began to protest the account of the fight, but Garlan simply raised his voice and continued: "So, I have a proposal for you, Greffik 'Iron Tooth.' My son will take the road and wear the cloak of the Journeyman, leaving Tarthen behind and keeping the setting sun at his back."

Bunda swung around towards his father. "Wait, what?"

"Your shame will no longer be on this Island, and I will take a god-witnessed oath to keep it a secret."

Iron Tooth weighed his options. While he could take on Bunda alone, Garlan was a well-known and strong warrior. He had once bested an ogre in single combat and had swam for two days all the way from Tarthen to Liarth, a nearby island.

Garlan, as if to ease his decision, drew his sword, switching his dagger to his other hand. "Which will it be, druid?"

Iron Tooth's eyes narrowed, but then he took a step back, and Bunda's heart thudded in his chest. "So be it. The boy has by sundown tomorrow to have left these shores behind, or the land itself will be the weapon of my wrath."

Garlan nodded, and the two backed away from the campfire, heading back to the feast.

They didn't speak until they were closer to the party. The bards were already drunk enough to unjustly torture the songs they were attempting to play, and most of the guests had gone home.

"Thank you, Father," said Bunda finally.

Garlan paused. He turned his weary blue eyes to the stars above. "You were right, boy. When you said that I didn't understand. I love her, but I've never really seen the world through her eyes." He turned to his son, "But *you* do. And I'll be cursed 'fore I let Iron-Tooth-Little-Cock cut you down.

"So, you will travel the road. Stop at temples and do Seirn's bidding." Garlan surprised Bunda by suddenly crushing him in an embrace. With his lips close to Bunda's ear, he whispered harshly, "And find your mother if you can. Tell her," he swallowed before continuing, "tell her she took my heart with her."

9 BROKEN MEN

At the bottom of the stairs, the smell was overwhelming. He was standing in some sort of large cellar or basement. Rows of barrels lined the walls, and a door at the end of the room was slightly ajar. The stench of carrion coming from it was overwhelming.

Bunda carefully walked up to the door. He took a deep breath, muttering a prayer to Seirn, and flung the door open, shoving his burning sword into the darkness.

Before him was a scene from nightmares.

The room was roughly twelve by twelve feet in size, with a low ceiling. The walls and parts of the floor were covered in runes and psychotic scrawling in a language Bunda didn't recognize. Across from the door rested a large wooden table. The table was strewn with rotting entrails, hunks of flesh and bits of bones. The wood was stained with blood—some old and some fresh—dripping and pooling on the floor beneath it. Two thick candles resting on the corner of the table flickered and burned, giving off the only light in the room aside from his sword.

Bunda's wide eyes grew even larger as he saw an iron cage in the corner of the room. In it was a man.

The man was large and muscular. His clothes were in tatters, and Bunda could clearly see fresh wounds and what appeared to be ritualistic carvings in the prisoner's flesh.

The torture must have taken its toll, as despite the man's size, he shied away from the light, sinking into the corner of his dirty cage and shielding his eyes from the burning blade in Bunda's hand.

Bunda was speechless. He had expected to find something horrible in the hidden room. Dead animals, maybe even a human body. But the scene before him was horrifying beyond his expectations.

He raised his hand and cast a light orb spell. The orb shone like a miniature sun, casting out all shadows. Bunda flung the orb at the ceiling, where the ethereal light source stuck.

He gingerly walked towards the man, sheathing his sword and dousing its flame. "Be calm, man. I mean you no harm," he said to the broken man. "I'm a cleric of Seirn, the Dawn Father," he added, hoping it would soothe him and inspire some level of trust.

The man slowly raised his head, blinking at the bright light in the room. It was obvious that it had been some time since he'd seen a light source stronger than the candles on the table.

His face exposed, Bunda could tell by the prominent jaw, short pointy ears, and grayish skin that this man had orcish blood. A memory clicked in his mind.

"Onlan?" he asked, hoping this was the half-orc deputy Mendel and Marven had mentioned in their story the night before. After all, how many half-orcs would one find in such a small village?

At the sound of his name, Onlan seemed to relax, and he looked at Bunda in disbelief. Then he lunged at the bars. It was clear that while the retired soldier was strong, he hadn't eaten in weeks and caged as he was, could not stand or stretch. His muscles had fallen victim to atrophy. There was no malice in his sudden movement, only desperation and hope that maybe this was the end of his torment.

"Stand back," Bunda commanded. Bunda drew his sword. Exposed to the air, the blade immediately burst into flame again.

Good, thought the Tundrial Cleric. *The spell had held.*

He thrust his burning saber into the lock, chanting in the Divine. The lock grew red hot, and Bunda kicked it with the sole of his boot. The weakened metal cracked and fell off. Bunda swung the iron door open, the rusty iron hinges creaking loudly.

Bunda outstretched his hand to the half-orc. Onlan timidly took the cleric's hand and slowly climbed out of the cage.

"Careful," warned Bunda as he assisted the broken half-orc. "The latch is still hot as embers."

Out of the cage, Onlan's cramping muscles prevented him from stretching to his full height. As he rose, his knees buckled and Bunda was forced to catch him before he crumpled to the ground.

"Who did this to you?"

Onlan opened his mouth to answer, but only a weak, animalistic sound escaped his cracked lips. He motioned to his mouth, and to Bunda's horror, he saw that the man's tongue had been cut out of it. And apparently recently, based on the dark stain on the front of his torn shirt.

Bunda hissed in anger and surprise. "Let's get out of here," he said.

Supporting Onlan, he exited the gruesome torture chamber and made his way back to the church. Once he was back in breathable air and sunlight, he inspected the half-orc's wounds.

While Onlan was obviously no stranger to a blade, based on the various old battle scars on his body, his more recent wounds were clearly an act of sadism.

Whoever had done this to him had done it slowly and with great precision. Strange symbols and characters were carved into the man's back, chest, and legs. His whole body. Even his face hadn't been left untouched, with long vertical gashes slashed into his cheeks. Furthermore, the wounds hadn't been allowed to heal—some being deliberately reopened time and time again.

Bunda called once again upon Seirn's holy might and began sealing the still-seeping wounds, but he couldn't heal everything.

For one, Bunda was spent. He had called upon his god's power several times today, and it was wearing him down. There was only so much of the divine that mortals could wield without resting. Also, some of the damage was too extensive for healing magic, and only rest would help.

Bunda tore down one of the less rotted tapestries from the wall and covered the broken man with it. He then removed his water skin and offered it to the half-orc, who eagerly gulped down too much too quickly and erupted in a fit of coughing and sputtering.

"Slowly, friend," he cautioned. He had seen sailors who had washed up on the shores of Tarthen, having gone with no food or water for days or weeks, and how their throats would constrict due to lack of nourishment.

"Small sips," he instructed. Once the man's thirst was slackened, Bunda tried again. "Who did this? Was it the priest?"

Onlan's eyes widened, but before he could answer, Bunda heard a shout from outside the church. He jumped to his feet, drawing his curved saber, and looked to the source of the sound. He realized it was coming from behind the church.

"Stay here," he ordered Onlan, who, considering his weakened state, had no choice but to comply.

Bunda walked out the door and started to circumvent the building. As he advanced, another sound came from the source of the commotion—this one a low hollow growl. *Dorkah*, he realized and picked up his pace.

As he cleared the building, another horrifying sight greeted him.

Tadok and Dorkah were side by side, fighting what could only be described as a host of the dead.

Ice crept into Bunda's heart as he observed the macabre site. Rotting corpses of men and women—even children—were closing in on his friends. A shirtless man with a maniacal look was laughing and spurring the undead attackers on.

An eyeless skeletal woman in a blue wedding dress slowly turned her hollow sockets toward the barbarian, the dusty joints in her neck creaking. It was too much for him, and he froze in stark terror.

Why are you dawdling, boy? This is what you were ascended for! his father's voice snapped him out of his stupor.

Although he had never seen the living dead before, it was known that in ages past, evil necromancers and unholy clerics of the Fallen—the enemies of Seirn and his heavenly companions—had wielded dark magic to create whole armies of the dead. The champions of Seirn had been tasked with destroying those abominable hosts. Until today, Bunda had imagined it all ceremonial. Legend and tales of ancient history in far-off lands.

But this was now. And the living dead were here.

A sudden sense of calm drowned out all smell and sound. All fear melted away, and there was only him and his god.

The sun was out and shining on his face. In its warmth, he felt his god's touch. He embraced the holy warmth around him and, grasping his medallion, channeled all of it at the creatures before him.

The light washed out of his outstretched hand, engulfing everyone in his field of view. While Tadok, Dorkah, and the shirtless man were unaffected, the undead seemed to hiss and groan and collapsed where they stood, their grayed flesh and yellowing bones smoldering and sputtering.

When it was done, nothing moved. Not even a twitch. The dead were back where they belonged.

Tadok looked back at Bunda and nodded gratefully.

Bunda smiled, then sagged against the wall of the church. It was too much. In the span of half an hour, he had had more holy magic coursing through his body than he normally had in an average week.

"No!" yelled the shirtless man. "No, no, no, NO!" he repeated, as if denying the loss of his puppets enough times would undo it.

He pointed the object in his hand—a wooden black and white wand with a knob at the end—at the corpses around him, but before he could do anything else, two-hundred and seventy pounds of Dorkah barrelled into him, knocking the man to the ground. Dorkah pinned his arms under her and growled through rows of pointy teeth.

"I wouldn't move an inch, Father," said Tadok as he advanced towards the man. He briefly bent down to dislodge his sickle from the ribcage of the corpse who had entrapped it. When he rose, he winced in pain and massaged his thigh.

"Are you injured?" asked Bunda in concern, though he wasn't sure he could do anything more for him today. He would need rest and meditation first.

Tadok waved him off. "I'll be fine."

Bunda motioned to Dorkah, her dark blood still seeping out from the wound in her side.

"Dorkah will heal by herself once she returns to her realm," said the half-elf.

Tadok leaned by Father Sheilagh and pressed the sharp edge of his sickle against Sheilagh's throat. "One word that doesn't sound Nemirian, and you'll be joining your friends," he threatened, referring to the host of corpses.

Bunda retrieved the wand from his hand. On closer inspection, he could see that it wasn't just wood painted in black and white. The lower half of it was black ironwood, the kind that came from the Dark Marshes to the south. The other half of the wand was actually bone. Along it, strange writing covered it in letters he had never seen before. Actually, that was incorrect—he saw them twenty minutes ago in the man's torture chambers.

The thing looked ominous. And while the spell had already died out half an hour ago, he knew that if he had used his divine vision, the thing would have radiated evil like a noxious steam.

"Who are you? Why did you attack me? Where is the boy?" Tadok started hurling questions at the man.

"You don't understand!" wailed the priest in anguish, "*She* was very clear! I must complete the ritual."

"Who is '*she*'?"

"My mistress. And she will reward me greatly when she has her glorious victory." Sheilagh's voice was crazed, and he had a feverish look in his eyes.

Bunda started asking his own questions.

"This ritual. Is that what the runes were for in the cellar? And all the dead animals?"

The priest nodded, tears streaming down his eyes, yet Bunda couldn't tell if they were the manifestation of sorrow, fear, or joy. Tadok shot a glance at Bunda but was mindful enough not to ask him anything in front of their prisoner. His curiosity would wait.

"Why did you torture the half-orc, Onlan?" demanded Bunda, using what Nick had called his ship-commanding voice.

"I wasn't torturing him! Can't you see? I was letting him loose. Setting him free so he would be ready to serve her," said the priest, as if anything in that sentence made any sense.

"A couple of contradictions there, man. Want to try that again?" said Tadok, grabbing a fistful of the man's thin gray hair. His icy voice and the grim set of his lips were enough to send the priest over the edge.

He suddenly screamed, and Bunda thought that maybe Tadok had used his blade on him, but Tadok seemed as surprised as he was. Tadok didn't release the man's hair, but he drew his blade back half an inch from his throat and scanned the man on the ground before him. Dorkah had taken a step away, leaving only her paw on his two legs. Tadok spat in disgust as he saw the wetness growing around the man's crotch.

Bunda surveyed the bodies. They lay where they had fallen, and not knowing the town, there was no way to know who each was, and which grave they had climbed out of. Still, it was Seirn's divine doctrine that the dead were respected. And these poor souls had been tortured enough by the man who should have been the warden of their final resting place. But first they had a prisoner to interrogate and a broken half-orc to return home.

"Let's take him into the church," he said, "and continue this inside."

Tadok nodded and raised his captive to his feet. He encircled the man's neck with the crescent of the sickle. The inner edge was as sharp as the outer, and if it had once been used to cut through bushels of wheat, it could easily slice the man's throat if he made a sudden move.

"What was that about Onlan? Wasn't he the missing half-orc?"

"Missing no longer," replied Bunda as they walked around to the church's entrance.

"Is he dead?"

"No, but I found him close to it."

Tadok looked back at Dorkah and nodded to her, echoing some telepathic dialogue the two had shared. In an instant, the creature popped out of existence. As if she hadn't been there a moment ago.

Dorkah was a true mystery. Neither she nor her master were evil—Bunda had checked using his spiritual vision when they first met. In fact, it was almost as if the two shared their aura between them. Still, Dorkah's existence and Tadok's magic were a source of concern for the cleric. The thing was, that to the best of Bunda's knowledge, magic was divided into four fundamental groups.

The first was divine magic. Magic provided by the gods to their mortal followers which reached back to the age of creation and the *Cei'lasteel*, the divine covenant between gods and mortals. It was bestowed on the devout and the champions of their gods. Then there were the druids, whose magic originated from the spirits of nature, like that of Stone Tooth and his ilk. It was wild as nature was, and it took much training and discipline to control. The third was the Arcane. Magic wielded by the mages, who studied them for years and, in time, learned to bind the energy around them to their will using carefully worded incantations. The last—and most unpredictable—was that of the *Coritiath*, which was an elven word meaning *magic-touched*. They were often called sorcerers and were shunned in many places. The Coritiath cast spells that drew magic from within their souls. Many grew mad and dangerous. Bunda thought about all that power coursing through one's veins without the guidance of a deity and shuddered.

To Bunda's best understanding, Tadok was such a spell caster. And while he wasn't evil, and Bunda had begun to consider him a friend, it was clear to him that Tadok was still guarded about his past and his strange companion. While Bunda didn't pry, it certainly worried him.

As they entered the Church, Onlan was sitting on one of the

benches, his eyes blank and staring at the wall. He was huddled under the tapestry exactly as Bunda had left him.

The man jumped as the door opened, and the trio came in.

Now that Sheilagh had nowhere to run, Tadok shoved him forward. "It's best you start talking," he said to the man. "Who is this mistress you keep blabbering about?"

The priest backed away from the two, his eyes wide as saucers. He opened his mouth to respond, but his answer was squeezed back into his throat as two callused hands enclosed around the man's neck.

Onlan had leaped so suddenly from his seat that none of them could even react. His tongueless mouth gaped in a silent snarl, and his sunken eyes blazed in rage. It took him only a second to cross the distance between him and Sheilagh, clasp the priest's bony neck, and squeeze.

"Wait!" yelled Tadok as Bunda sprung towards them.

Sheilagh sank to his knees, eyes and lips bulging. His broken nails clawed and scraped at the large half-orc, reopening some of the wounds which Bunda had healed earlier. But Onlan didn't seem to care or even notice. Saliva flecked his lips. He didn't seem to even see Bunda and Tadok in the room.

Bunda reached him and locked his hands on Onlan's wrists, trying to pry them off the priest's windpipe. It was like prying an iron grate off its hinges.

Sheilagh's feet kicked up a frenzy, but his frantic clawing began to weaken and finally his hands fell to his sides. To finish it off, Onlan jerked the man's chicken-neck, which gave way in a sickening snap that echoed off the room's high-vaulted ceiling. Only then did Onlan finally let him go, and he slumped to the floor, his head twisting impossibly to the side, his eyes bulging from their sockets.

Bunda was reminded of the boys he had buried less than a day ago at the hangman's tree. Their eyes had puffed out the same way. But while they had been innocent victims, and their murderers needed to be brought to justice, he couldn't fault the half-orc who, by all evidence, had been horribly tortured for weeks by the dead man at his feet.

The church was silent. Then, Tadok summed it up.

"Shit."

10 SPIES

"What gave me away?" asked Mica Mun, crossbow still trained at Robin's chest.

Robin had no illusions as to his ability to dodge the bolt. While it may not hit his chest, it most likely would lodge in his shoulder or ribs, and his eventual destination would still be the same—just with a longer and more painful journey.

"Well, it was two things," he said with his hands spread wide. *Good, if we're talking, I'm not dying,* he thought.

"For one, you shook my hand with your left. So, I bargain you have a mark on your right."

"Maybe I'm simply left-handed," suggested the bar-hand.

"No. I saw you wipe down the bar with your right."

"Observant," he said simply. "What was the other thing?"

"I've never heard of a tavern called 'The Giant's Rock' or the 'Giant's Cock in Berin's Inn'," he answered smugly.

"Ah, I should have known." Mica smiled. "A child's mistake. But then again, you Hugh boys were always clever. I thought Garian was the smart one of you three. How is the old boy doing?"

Robin's smile faded. If Mica had known about his brother's fate and was feigning innocence, he hid it well.

The truth was that since leaving Sandisan that night, he had done everything to avoid the Hands. Once he crossed the mountains, he had not set foot on Kingdom soil again. The Shadder Hands' influence in the lawless lands of Suldan-Karr wasn't as strong as in the heartlands of Nemir. It was true that thieves and bands of outlaws thrived in lands where the law was weak, but *thieves' guilds* did not. They needed structure to climb and politics to exploit. Sally's fingers were in the pocket of half the nobles and the magistrates in Nemir, selling information, offering delicate favors, and occasionally assassinating rivals. A wealthy merchant needed to know about deals being made behind his back, the head of a church needed to pay off his mistress, or a noble needed a particular item stolen from another—they all turned to the Shadder Hands. And if they didn't, Sally would still know about it and know how to make use of that knowledge. However, in the chaos which befell the lands of Suldan-Karr after the War of the Broken Crown, where marauding orcs and hordes of Tundrial barbarians would sweep in and do as they wished with the local population, it was difficult to maintain consistent sources of power. Besides, the lands had been ravaged so badly in the last two and half decades that there wasn't much left to steal. Sure, there were bandits and local outlaw brotherhoods, but gaining their loyalty or even cooperation was a difficult and risky task.

Mica's eyes narrowed. "He didn't make it out, did he?" he asked. He raised his chin, reading Robin like a way sign. "He picked the wrong side," he summarized.

Robin said nothing.

"Well, that's a shame. Truth be told, I never liked your brother. He smiled too much. But I did respect him. An honest thief if there ever was one."

"And which side did you pick, Mica Mun?" Robin chose to change the subject. "Allegiances broke that night. Are you here at Gale's command?"

Mica chuckled. "You think Gale would have reason to send a man to hide in the middle of nowhere? For what end?"

Robin raised an eyebrow. "Perhaps he needed a remote safe house to peddle loot between the coast and Sebin. Or perhaps for the same reason he sent Dell Hayek here."

Mica cocked his head, as if considering the notion, then shrugged. "No, I have no connection with Gale or with Hayek, his rabid dog. Before the coup, I even tried to warn Sally, but he wouldn't believe me. Believe me or don't, I've left that life behind."

Robin flashed the small coin in his hand. "Yet you still keep your marker," he argued.

"Yes. I felt it may have use one day," Mica answered. Robin gave him a skeptical look. Mica sighed. "The night of Gale's coup, I left Sandisan. People I didn't like were ascending the power ladder, and it was a time of scores being settled. I didn't want to spend my nights with my back to the wall. These people"—he motioned to the village outside the window, a movement which made Robin a little nervous considering the crossbow he was gripping— "actually took me in. A little suspicious at first, but they have grown to accept me, and I them. It's a good life," he summarised. "At least it *was* until two nights ago."

A thought crossed Robin's mind. "So, you *don't* know why Hayek is here?"

Mica shook his head. "I don't. At first, I thought they were simply avoiding the Triumph Road and were just a roving band of cutthroats. But if they were, why did they ride off? Why not murder the town and take whatever was here?"

"Based on the innkeeper's tale, they wanted a steady tribute," replied Robin.

"What tribute could Suldan's Bluff possibly offer? Besides, winter will be upon us shortly, and the roads will be impassable. The town's meager food supplies would quickly run out if they had to feed his men and having a band of hungry murderers at your back tends to be rather risky for the person leading them."

Robin folded his arms. "In that case, why do *you* think Dell Hayek is here?" The answer to his question was less important to him than the answer to the question of what Mica would do if he folded his arms. It still didn't give him the tactical advantage needed to make a move, but it showed him that he was either getting some leeway from his captor or was successfully distracting him.

"I'd never heard of Hayek during my days as Silk for Sally, which means he's either new or was in Gale's camp during the coup."

So, you were *a Silk*, thought Robin.

A Silk—in the Undercity lingo—meant a person was Sally's eyes and ears. It was their task to know of any underhanded deal, power struggle, or ambitious upstart within Sandisan. As it was also their task to keep Sally in the know about any member who wanted to double cross the guild, they were often shunned by other guild members, which was why they kept their tasks and positions secret from their peers. The fact that Mica was openly telling Robin about this was evidence that he may be telling the truth about leaving that life behind.

"To be honest, at first I thought *you* were in cohort with Hayek. Coming into town less than two days after Dell's lynching of the sheriff and his boys. I knew you the moment I saw you in the inn but was rather certain you didn't know me," said Mica.

"Me?" asked Robin in surprise. "Why would we go to the trouble of cutting them down and burying them if we were Hayek's men?" he argued.

"Exactly. It makes no sense. So, the real question is—why *are* you here, Robin Hugh?"

Robin answered without hesitation: "With the way things have been going in the lands west of the Suldan, we thought it wiser to follow the road less traveled. We thought that this close to the winter passes closing, we would be more or less alone on the roads." That part was actually true, and the best lies were those of omission.

Mica gave him a sardonic look and said, "Let's say I believe you're stupid enough to discount wolves and bears and any other hungry predator who doesn't give a *Gobbo's* balls about the roads. My question is: why are you returning to Nemir after five years?"

Robin wasn't expecting that and didn't have a rehearsed answer. At least, nothing came to mind which would fool the former Silk.

"Well...I...Suldan-Karr has become so dangerous," he stammered.

"Bollocks," said Mica. "You said so yourself you haven't been back to the Kingdome of Nemir since that night. You can obviously take care of yourself, and there is nowhere better to disappear than between here and Culidge. You've changed your name, so the half-elf and the barbarian probably don't know your secret, and you're choosing backroads to avoid any Hands you see."

Robin took a deep breath and decided to tell the truth. He was gambling that the man had reformed somewhat or was at least in worse standing with the Hands than he was.

"It's my brother. My other brother, Tommy. We parted a couple years ago, and it appears he's in trouble. I need to get back to Sandisan to help him if I'm not too late." He looked him straight in the eye.

"So why stay and find the boy? Why entangle yourself in the affairs of these folk?" he asked. Mica was clearly no fool.

"I swore I wouldn't turn my back on another brother. And in my mind, I see that boy alone and afraid. Master Mun, I may be a thief and liar, but if a back-stabbing Silk can redeem himself, then so can I."

Silence followed. The two former Shadder Hands eyed each other over the wicked arrowhead peaking dangerously from the front end of the crossbow. Mica cocked his head, training his eyes on Robin, as if he was listening to an unseen voice in his head.

Finally, he nodded once and lowered the crossbow, but he was careful not to remove the bolt. Robin's own sigh took him by surprise. He hadn't realized how nervous he actually was.

"Well, what happens next?" he asked.

The red-bearded man shrugged. "I'll keep my secrets, and you keep yours."

"Agreed." Then, as an afterthought, he asked, "And you know nothing of the boy?"

"I was sure you offered that to get a free meal. I must say, I'm impressed by your devotion. However, I fear you may never find the boy in time, if at all."

"Why is that?" asked Robin, laying the token on the table.

"You have quite a lot of land to search. And the sun has reached midday."

Robin's mouth twisted in thought. Then he looked up at the bar-hand. "My friends are searching the Church of the Four Sons. If we had to choose one more place, where would Trin most favor us?"

"If you chose one place, it definitely wouldn't be the church," he answered.

Robin raised his eyebrows. "Why is that?"

"That man, Father Sheilagh, is madder than a halfling mummer. The whole village stays away from that place."

"Really? Are my companions at risk?" he asked, wondering if perhaps they shouldn't have split up.

Mica waved the notion away. "I doubt it. Your friends seem capable enough, and the man may be stark raving mad, but I don't believe he could do them any real harm."

"So, if not the church, where would the child go?" he pressed.

Mica thought for a moment. "Perhaps the mines, if he was scared enough."

"Then that is where we shall go," he stated.

Mica was looking out the small window towards the village green. "Looks like our parlay has come to an end, *Nick Cartright*. It appears your friends have returned. And, oh my," he suddenly added that last part, a look of surprise on his face, "it seems that they have found a missing member of our community. Not the one you were looking for, mind you, but mayhap Trin *is* on your side..."

11 WOLVES

"So, the bodies are currently rotting in the sun?" asked Robin Hugh, trying to fill out the final details of the amazing account his companions had given.

The three were walking across the low hills towards the mountains. The sun was already far enough in its daily journey to cast the shadows from the mountains over them. The sky was clear above them, but distant dark clouds amassed like a gathering army in the west. Bunda, who knew much more about weather than the two of them, had stated that that storm would be upon them within a day, and Robin didn't cherish the thought of being outside in it. Maybe they would be lucky enough to find a remote cave to weather it.

"We couldn't very well re-bury a man in another's grave, could we?" answered Bunda. It was clear he didn't like the idea of leaving the bodies without completing the burial rites, but they had had more pressing matters, and this was a task the people of Suldan Karr could complete. Besides, they had needed to get the half-orc, Onlan, back to the village.

When they arrived, they stirred up quite a commotion. Onlan had been gone for weeks, and the village was grateful to see him back alive. They stared in horror at the wounds he had endured. Aldeira was the one to take him in. Despite her own anguish, Onlan was a close friend of her late husband, and taking care of him must have been a welcome distraction from her grief.

Tadok took Robin aside and told him of the ordeal they had faced, while Bunda, with Onlan by his side, accounted it to Mendel, Marven Darvey, and the dwarf, Swegan, who seemed to be acting as village leaders during this crisis.

At first, they had been suspicious and disbelieved it. But Onlan, despite being unable to talk, nodded, confirming that they had a mad necromancer living in their midst all this time. Robin wondered how he would have reacted and couldn't come to a conclusion. In a village like Suldan's Bluff, few things changed. The talk of the year could have been a bad harvest or news from far-off other places that Mendel or a rare traveler would bring in. Kidnap and torture, the dead rising–the first was something that happened in other places, and the second was something that never happened at all. In less than a week, they had lost their sheriff and his sons to a horrible murder and discovered that their spiritual shepherd was a murderous lunatic with power over the undead. Robin thought it was wise to continue searching for Christopher and let the village folk deal with this recent blow in their own way, lest someone decide they had something to do with it.

He had filled them in on his own morning, leaving out his conversation with Mica Mun. It wasn't half as interesting as theirs, though.

"And there was no sign of the boy in the basement? Could he have been murdered by Sheilagh?" It was a gruesome thought, but Robin could only fathom what crazed priests did in their spare time and why.

"He seemed to know nothing of the boy. Just kept going on and on about his mistress," answered Tadok. "I think he was preparing the half-orc for some sort of ritual sacrifice."

"And no, there were no signs of him in that gods-cursed chamber. Only dead animals," added Bunda.

Robin thought silently for a few minutes as they walked the old path. A thought came to him, and he resumed the conversation. "Bunda, what sort of dark god would want a retired half-orc soldier as a sacrifice?"

He knew little of the divine. There was the Circle, of course, which included the Divine Father and the Four Sons. Those were common in the heartlands. Then there was Seirn, the Dawn Father, Obe the Shield, and Trin the Knave or Wanderer. There was a sea god or goddess whose name he couldn't remember. There was Sheleen, goddess of Beauty, and he thought that someone had told him there was an elven and a dwarven god, but he didn't know their names. Were there also evil gods? Whose followers would sacrifice half-orcs and boys?

Bunda slowly nodded. "In the age of creation, it is said that the gods chose sides. Those who believed in the rise of mortals and those who sought to destroy or dominate them. These dark gods were collectively known as the Fallen. Over three centuries ago, my lord, Seirn, sent his followers on a holy crusade to root out the followers and temples of some of these gods and cleanse them from Trosia. It doesn't mean, though, that their worship is not still practiced in the darkness. But as to the goddess that the priest followed," he shook his head, "The man had surely forsaken the Four and desecrated his church and symbol. I've never seen such writing before."

Then Tadok surprised them both. "I have."

When the two looked at him confused, he added, "I've seen those symbols before. And they aren't symbols; they're letters and words in a language known to few alive today."

"So, what are they? Some form of elven?" asked Robin curiously.

"No, of course not," said Tadok, waving off the notion as obviously absurd. Robin regretted asking the question and exposing his lack of education.

"It is *Shadowtang*. The language of Hell, or the Abyss. The lower realms." He looked at Bunda. "Where your god banished the Fallen."

Bunda stopped in his tracks. He looked at Tadok, and Robin felt the tension rise. "Tadok, how do you know this language?"

Tadok stared him in the eyes. There was no anger or shame in his eyes, only a calm, calculating look. "I once had a teacher who showed me how to master my powers. She knew this language and taught it to me."

Robin may not have been properly schooled and could only read basic Nemirian, but he could proficiently read people. That was a language one needed to know early to survive on Shadder Street. Learning to know whether a person was going to turn you in or if a bully had the guts to back up his threat were important skills—ones which could often not be learned more than once. It was clear to him that while Tadok wasn't necessarily lying, he was leaving a large portion of the story out.

"Tadok, that language is evil. The hand that wrote it was evil. Even knowing that language could be dangerous without proper guidance—" began Bunda.

"Guidance? Like that of Seirn? An ax can be used to cut a tree or a man. The ax is never evil, Shard. Even when its wielder is."

"The language of Hell is no ax—it's a poison," replied Bunda heatedly. The slur to his god was probably a worse insult than being called Shard again, despite being told numerously that the Tundrial was from Tarthen.

Robin needed to diffuse the situation. "Okay, so what, pray tell, was written on the walls?" he asked Tadok, hoping to distract the two and change the subject.

Tadok snapped his glare in his direction. After a moment, he shrugged, deflating. "I don't know," he said. "It was in a dialect strange to me. All I understood was a mention of 'the Temple' and another two words which could mean 'dark altar,' or something like that."

Robin blinked. "Well, that's ominous."

Tadok nodded, resuming his pace towards the mines. "On the advantage, though, he wasn't a priest of this mysterious deity."

Bunda scowled. "He wasn't a chosen of the Four Sons, that's for sure. I don't care if I had the medallion. After his deeds, none of the circle would have given him their embrace."

"That's exactly my point. He didn't cast any spells."

Robin ran a couple steps to catch up to the half-elf and walk beside him. "Wait, didn't he raise the dead? I would consider that a pretty fucking unnatural power..." he said sarcastically.

"He did," nodded Tadok, "but not with a spell. He used that wand." Robin's blank stare was evidence that he wasn't following, so Tadok rubbed his eyes in weariness and explained. "Anyone could have cast the spell to infuse that wand. For all we know, that wand could be five hundred years old. If he had the divine touch like our friend here, he would have called on his mistress for her power and not just used a tool. You don't need to be a priest or cleric to use a wand. Hell, *you* could use that wand, too, if you learned how to activate it," he said motioning to the Heartlander.

Robin cocked his head, considering such a power at his beck and call, but then saw Bunda staring at him suspiciously. "I would never do that, mind you!" he said quickly.

"My point is," continued the half-elf, "that he could have found that thing and gone mad trying to decipher the letters on it. He may not really have any mistress—he may be utterly and psychotically mad and forsaken by The Four."

They walked on in silence for the next ten minutes, each in a council of his own thoughts.

The sloping hills were low and easily navigated. Most of the trek was open fields of grassland dotted with dogwood, birch, and ash trees, making the trip to the mountains take a little over an hour. An old trail led to the mines. Deep grooves in the path marked the passing of countless carts filled with the precious silver extracted from the mines, but they were old and faded.

The path led to a large open expanse at the base of the mountain. The dark opening of the old mine stood out like a cavity in the tooth of a titanic giant. An old, partially collapsed wooden building must have been the depot, as one would expect in an active mine.

Off to the right of the mine was an unusually tall redwood tree that seemed to stick up vertically out of the earth. The first odd thing about it was its perfect ninety-degree angle, a clear contrast to the twisted trunks of the ash and birch trees. Nature isn't usually that precise, thought Robin.

The second odd thing was the figure planted on top of one of the branches, hugging the trunk. His perch was halfway up the tree, about twelve feet from the ground. It was impossible to identify the person from this distance, but the cause of his unusual choice of resting places was obvious.

At the base of the tree lay a pack of mountain wolves.

There were a total of nine of them, and by their relaxd manner, they had been there for some time. They were waiting patiently for their prey to lose his grip on the tree and plummet to the ground, or perhaps for him to get desperate and try to escape. The chances of the first seemed inevitable, and the chances of the second seemed very unlikely.

"That doesn't look like the boy," said Tadok. His natural eyesight was better than his two fully human companions.

"Do you think those are our wolves?" asked Robin, thinking of the pack that had tracked them two nights ago. The pack that he had scared off by shooting one of them. Did wolves seek revenge?

"Maybe," answered Bunda.

"I guess it doesn't matter," said Tadok, slinging his crossbow off his back and knocking a bolt onto the track.

"There are quite a few of them, and they're probably hungry," said Robin. "Do you have any magic that can help us?" he asked, turning to Bunda.

"Not much. I've rested a little on the way, but to fully rejuvenate and use my lord's powers, I need sleep and meditation. Still," he said, drawing his curved saber. He whispered something and drew his palm across the flat of the blade, sheathing it in fire again.

"Well, that's not nothing," said Robin. He turned to Tadok and said, "I think you need to call upon your demonic dog."

"Don't let her hear you saying that," said Tadok, closing his eyes for a moment. His forehead glowed like an ember, and suddenly Dorkah was there, popping into existence silently. Her side had fully healed, with no traces of the wound Tadok had reported she received during the fight with the false priest.

"Why? does she speak?" asked Robin, chuckling. Dorkah turned to him and said, "*Speak*" in an inhuman voice, and Robin's chuckle died in his throat. Tadok smiled smugly.

"How do we attack?" asked Bunda.

Robin assessed the land between them and the wolves. "If I can go unnoticed across this plain, I can climb one of those trees there. From there, I believe I can pick off one or two of them before they choose my tree over theirs. Unless they can climb, I can continue shooting them off one by one until they tire. In the meantime, Bunda can help the man down and see if he can run. By then, hopefully, there won't be enough to challenge the three of you," he said, laying out his plan. He checked his arrows.

Fifteen. That should be enough, he thought. Robin had become quite the archer in his years as a sellsword. And if the wolves chose to surround his tree like they were surrounding the poor fellow out there, he could make every shot count. The trick was getting there unnoticed.

His two companions looked at each other uneasily, but finally Bunda, then Tadok, nodded.

His fear turning to excitement, he grinned at them giddily.

"Seirn be with you," said Bunda.

"Try not to end up like that fellow," added Tadok.

"*Fellow*," agreed Dorkah.

Robin stared at her, still unsure how he felt about Dorkah talking. Actually, he didn't know what he thought about Dorkah generally

He wasn't a total stranger to magic. Growing up in Sandisan, Robin had seen his share of priests and mages. The latter were sometimes street performers, some were hired magical muscle, and at least on one occasion, one wielder of magic had been a mark his brother had spotted. Oh, how he had been furious with Garian about that botched-up robbery. They had thought he was just an overconfident foreign nobleman. But when the man suddenly took flight and began raining down bolts of fire at them, it was all they could do to get out of the way and back to the protection of the Undercity.

"Imagine he turned Tommy into a frog or a newt!" he had shouted once they had caught their breath.

Garian hadn't been able to stop laughing. "T'would have been an improvement, Brother!"

The memory brought a smile to his face, and he forgot about Tadok's talking beast as he crept along through the tall grass, doing his best to stay low.

Dogs had uncanny hearing, and he bet wolves did as well. The bigger concern would have been their sense of smell. So, Robin walked a wide circle around them, making sure he was downwind of them. Luckily for him, the winds were strong. The problem was that that advantage would turn against him in the next part of his plan. Shooting an arrow into the wind would be challenging, so he chose a closer tree than the one he had originally selected. The one wasn't as large as his original choice, but if he perched on the two upper branches, he believed he would be secure and out of range of those canine jaws.

After what felt like twenty excruciatingly long minutes, he managed to reach the tree undetected. Slinging his bow over his back, he leaped up to the lowest branch and begun to climb.

One of the wolves looked up at him but chose to do nothing.

When he managed to reach the top branches, he realized it would be a challenge to keep his balance on both branches at the same time. So, he selected the sturdier of the two and wrapped his legs around it firmly. He gingerly released the other branch to test his weight against the strength of the branch beneath him. It swayed but held.

Good, he thought. He looked at the ridge where Bunda, Tadok, and Dorkah had been. Bunda had already begun moving into position to sprint to the tall tree once the wolves charged at his.

He carefully drew his bow and held it parallel to the ground. It was a form of archery which lacked the accuracy of the normal straight hold, but it was the only way to wield it while seated on the branch.

A few more members of the pack had turned to watch the spectacle. They must have found the human-squirrel an odd site.

He notched an arrow, pulled the bowstring back, and let loose at the first wolf who had spotted him. The arrow clattered on a rock next to him, and the wolf snarled while the rest of the pack sprung to their feet.

"Shit," he cursed, knocking another arrow. He was down to fourteen arrows, and the wolves were still planted in place. Soon, they would hear or smell Bunda, and his battle plan would collapse.

He drew back the second arrow to his chin. He couldn't miss this one. He let the arrow fly. The sound of a twang from the bowstring was overpowered by that of a dry crack, and the branch snapped. He dropped twelve feet to the ground below.

The wolves charged.

12 LESSONS

Tadok, Bunda, and Dorkah waited silently on the hill overlooking the meadow before them.

Tadok absentmindedly removed his gloves and hung them from his belt. He winced as he put pressure on his leg again.

Bunda noticed and turned to him. "I think you should let me look at that."

"It's fine. Just bruised."

"You know, 'tis often the little scrapes and bruises which hide more serious damage."

Tadok smiled, not taking his eyes off Nick advancing silently in the field below.

"It's not a laughing matter, Tadok," said Bunda, misunderstanding his reaction. "I've seen men come back from battle with a small cut on their hand or leg, refusing to have us treat the wound, only to have it fester until the limb had to be removed."

"No, it's not that. You simply remind me of someone I knew."

"He sounds like a wise man. A healer?"

"*She*, and no, she wasn't. Although some would say she *did* have a healing touch."

Bunda nodded. "Well then, *she* was a wise woman. And a healer's touch is the gods' blessing."

Tadok smiled wryly. "Not sure you would say that considering it was she who taught me that ancient language you were sermoning about before."

He didn't know why he said it. It had no value beyond provocation. Bunda may have been naïve and misguided, as so many devout were, but he was the closest thing he had to a friend for a long time. Beyond Dorkah, anyway. Mocking Bunda's faith was probably not wise. What would Sellwyn have said?

On the one hand, she had no patience for the pious, considering them stuck-up and superior idiots. But she had always chided him on allowing his temper to get the better of him. There was smart, and there was wise. The smart man would know how to get out of the trouble that the wise man knew to avoid. At the moment, he was being neither.

"When I said that—" began Bunda hotly, but Tadok cut him off, pointing at Nick.

"He's made it to the tree. You best make your way around. A wolf runs faster than a man."

Bunda seemed annoyed about being cut off in the middle of the argument, but, looking at the meadow, chose to postpone it to another time. Flaming saber in hand, he began trotting down the hill, keeping low.

Tadok looked at Dorkah, who was staring at him.

"What?" he asked the creature.

"*Bun-dah*," she said simply.

Tadok rolled his eyes. "Not you, too."

Dorkah cocked her head to the side—the equivalent of a shrug—and started pawing at an anthill, sending the little insects into a frenzy.

The truth was that Tadok was never good at making friends. His relationships were divided into those who abandoned him, such as his mother and his surrogate mother, and those that never would, such as Dorkah. There was no middle ground. These new companions were temporary. They would accompany each other to Sebin, maybe Sandisan at best, and they would go their separate ways, and he and Dorkah would be alone again. Truth be told, that was really all he needed. But he had to admit that there was a certain comfort in having someone to talk to who said more than one word in return.

"Damn!" he suddenly cursed. In the field ahead, Nick suddenly dropped to the grass below his tree. While he couldn't hear it, he could imagine the branch cracking and Nick thudding to the ground.

He shifted his gaze to the pack. They were no longer lying about the tree lazily and were on their feet. Before his eyes, they rushed towards the fallen Heartlander in haste. They would close the distance within less than a minute.

He glanced at Bunda. The barbarian must have seen it, too, as he changed his trajectory. He was no longer hunched over but charging at his top speed towards the ensuing melee.

Tadok needed no further cue and sprung down the beaten path, Dorkah at his heel. She needed no order or vocal command. The bond between him was enough for her to sense his needs and wishes.

She quickly overtook him, sprinting like a cheetah, leaving a trail of dust in her wake.

Tadok regretted not empowering her with a defensive spell. Dorkah may have mostly healed her wound from the fight with the priest, but so many adversaries at once may overwhelm her.

His mind raced faster than his feet, trying to think of any spell he could muster that would turn the odds in his favor. Could he draw his crossbow in time? Even if he could load the bolt without slowing down, which was no mean feat in and of itself, it would be impossible to hit anything at his breakneck pace. Besides, he'd be just as likely to hit Nick as anything else, and if he slowed down to take aim, he wouldn't make it in time.

There was only one thing he could try, but it was a long shot.

As he watched, Nick regained his footing, swiftly drawing his thin rapier. The lead wolf leaped at him, jaws wide. Nick sidestepped, stabbing it through the throat. But the weight of the leaping animal tore the blade out of his hand, and when he turned to the next one, he was unarmed.

The next wolf lunged at Nick's leg, fangs latching onto flesh, and the young human fell to the ground.

The grass was mercifully tall enough to conceal what followed as the rest of the pack closed in.

***

"No! This is a waste of time," said the ten-year-old half-elf to his Shadowtouched adopted mother.

"Only because *you're* wasting time."

It was springtime, and the scent of lilacs filled the air thickly, as did the buzz of insects. But beyond the buzzing insects and the chirping birds, the clearing was empty, aside from the two of them and Dorkah.

The spot was secluded enough from the halfling camp that no one would hear their exchange or the sensory signature of what they were doing. Actually, by the distant sounds of festivities, no member of the traveling caravan would hear them regardless of how loud they were.

The caravan was no different from a half-dozen others they had joined over the last two years. They had been with this particular one for two months, and Tadok already knew their time with the traveling little folk was coming to an end. He could feel Sellwyn's restlessness.

Since leaving Sage's Rock, they had traveled continuously. Sellwyn had made sure they never stayed in one place too long. At times, they would stay in a village or a town for a few weeks and Sellwyn would sell her services as a healer, concocting salves and medicine for the sick and wounded or performing minor feats of magic at inns or taverns. When she did the latter, their stay would often be shorter.

Tadok had asked her why that was once, and she had explained that magic attracts attention, even the simple tricks like she did to entertain locals. At times, men would try their luck with the pretty women, which would also hasten their departure. Sometimes, those men would be a little too aggressive, especially if drunk, and Sellwyn would need to employ her magic more forcefully. When that happened, they would spend the next week or more heading as far away as possible, often leaving the bewildered would-be lover croaking like a toad or having developed a rather severe case of loose bowels.

The good thing about halflings was that they moved around a lot, were usually kind to strangers—if those strangers employed the same kindness back—and didn't seem to be sexually attracted to anything much taller than them. So, traveling with the halfling caravans made sense. On the downside, they basically traded in gossip. And what better gossip than the Shadowtouched Sorceress and her half-elf boy who had been with them since the last town?

Tadok also truly enjoyed the campfire stories, the music, and the tumbling performances they practiced every evening after a day's travel. Sellwyn didn't even have to perform or treat the sick. She would if asked to, but it never seemed to be a prerequisite to join the caravan.

The caravans would travel from town to city, peddling their wares, including anything from spices to fortune telling and magical potions, which sometimes actually worked. When they reached a city, it often saddened the boy as he knew that either before entering or upon leaving civilization, they would take their leave of the little folk.

The first time it had happened, he had been furious with her as he had made a few friends. But by now, he had gotten used to it and realized there was no use in getting too close to anyone if he wanted to avoid the emptiness of losing them. So, he mostly kept to himself, studying the books and scrolls Sellwyn would provide him with and practicing his magic when they could find secluded spots like this one.

Their private constitutionals had a second advantage to them: Dorkah.

The one iron rule imposed by the sorceress was that only in the direst of threats could he summon the creature in the presence of others. It often meant he had to endure days without her by his side—something the boy disliked tremendously.

So, even when he found his adopted mother's training grueling, he knew that it would allow him time with his only true friend, and he would look forward to it.

Currently, his friend was trying to befriend a frog, which kept leaping away as she came near it. The frog must have been terrified as what looked like a cross between a black dog and a lizard sauntered up to it, sniffing with no nostrils and lolling its tongue. Tadok was confident that Dorkah would never eat it, as he had never seen her consume anything at all. It didn't mean she wouldn't unintentionally step on the thing and squash it.

"Focus, child." Sellwyn's voice snapped him back to the task at hand.

He sighed and composed himself. He drew a breath and willed his mind to look inward. His sensory layers melted away. No, that was inaccurate. They were still there but were transparent. The best comparison his child's mind come up with was the tricks he could play on his mind while looking at a reflection in a pond. He could will his mind to see the fish and the rocks below, or he could shift his mental perspective and see his rippling reflection.

He could still hear the sounds of the clearing. Could see Dorkah and Sellwyn. He felt his body telling him he had eaten too many of Minda's oat cookies and also that he had a slight headache. He could feel his skin go clammy.

And there it was.

Underneath it all was what Sellwyn had called the *Flow*. A mass of underlying energy without form or function—but with purpose.

Sellwyn spoke to him at his external sensory level. "Can you see the Flow, Tadok?"

"Aye," he answered, keeping his communication to a minimum lest he lose his grasp on it.

"Good. Now draw it to you."

He did as he was bid, willing the swirling mass to bend and shape to his design. It reacted, and a sense of exhilaration filled his young heart.

Sellwyn must have understood his expression and encouraged him. "Now, use the words and the gestures," she instructed calmly.

Carefully, Tadok repeated the phrase he had recited again and again for the last few weeks. As an aspiring sorcerer, he didn't require the arcane commands to perform magic as mages did, but it helped him train. In any case, it was very short—maybe four syllables. But it had to be precise. Any deviation in tone or pitch at his level of control and the spell would fizzle into nothing. Simultaneously, he raised his hand, touching his thumb to the center of his middle finger. A sudden popping sound came from his outstretched hand, and two miniature fireworks crackled into the air in front of him, bursting in a flash of light and color. He had never gotten this far in the spell. This was certainly a surprise. Although he couldn't feel any heat, the flash made him jerk his hand back, unlocking his fingers. The small balls of light and color winked out of existence immediately, and Tadok fell to his knees in defeat.

"I told you, I can't do it! Why do you keep making me?" he shouted at the Shadowtouched woman.

"Curb your temper, Sage's Rock," she replied calmly, although there was a hint of annoyance at his accusation. "You were almost there."

"But *why* was I almost there? This spell is useless unless you want me to be on stage with you in the taverns. Doing tricks for Sorins."

"It's not useless at all. It's for your protection," she replied, beginning to raise her own voice. "It's an alarm that you can use to alert me if ever you're in trouble."

Tadok wouldn't back down. "If I need a spell for my protection, why don't you teach me the one that shoots flames from your fingers or that energy shell you used against the bees at Sheleen's Home."

"Because, oh great sorcerer," she began mockingly, "if you lost control of the color and light spell, nothing happens. If you do so with the flame hands, you set yourself on fire."

"So? I've got Dorkah to protect me," he argued, pointing at the creature.

That seemed to stop Sellwyn before she could retort, and she turned towards the beast thoughtfully.

After a pause, she said, "Yes, Dorkah is your loyal companion and protector. She is what the elves of Andunleen call an *Eith'lin*, which means *apparition* or *eidolon*."

She looked at Tadok, who obviously had no idea what any of it meant, so she elaborated.

"Very few individuals can directly control the flow. But there are those of us out there who can. You and I are such. But even rarer still are those who have the raw power to bind and shape it into a complex creation such as an independent creature. Dorkah is a raw construct of your essence made alive by your will."

Tadok was thoughtful. "You mean...*I* created her?" he asked, looking at his creation. Sellwyn paused. She seemed about to say something but hesitated. Then she smiled and nodded.

"How did I create her? She's alive. I think."

"I don't know. It would take a truly powerful soul and normally a lifetime of training to create an Eith'lin. The kind of lifetime reserved only for elves. I've never heard of it in a young boy before."

His expression then twisted into exasperation. "Which is why casting a color-light spell shouldn't be evoking such whining from you. Now, back on your feet. Start again."

Tadok sighed and went back to the task of trying to shoot mini fireworks from his hands.

***

Once the path reached the bottom of the hill, Bunda shuffled to his left and into the undergrowth. He remained as hunched as he could to avoid detection while trotting through the tall blades of grass, careful to keep the flames dancing along his blade away from them lest he start a brush fire.

He was sure to keep both the wolves and Nick in his sight. The Heartlander was in position, locking his thighs around one of the top branches of the tree. He pulled back his bowstring and let loose an arrow. It missed.

The wolves rose to their feet and began snarling and barking at their attacker.

Bunda picked up his pace. The distance between the stranded man's tall redwood tree and the tree Nick had chosen wasn't too far. And Bunda realized he would have precious minutes to help the man down and get him to safety while Nick was keeping them distracted.

There were no wolves on the Seal Shore Islands, but Bunda had heard stories long before he had encountered them here in the Suldan Mountains. He had heard enough about them to know that they were intelligent hunters. They normally didn't attack men unless provoked or very hungry. In this case, they were both. And this was a large pack.

Any moment, they were likely to see him or pick up his scent. While he didn't expect them to attack him right way, they would never let him close to the man on the tree. Their prey.

He heard a loud cracking sound, and he turned his head to the tree Nick had inhabited. To his dismay, Nick and the branch he had been sitting on were gone. A moment later, the blond man stumbled quickly to his feet at the base of the tree, bracing his left hand on the trunk. Sure enough, in a chorus of snarls, the wolves were charging at him.

"Seirn!" he swore. He changed course and started sprinting directly at him. But he was too far away.

Nick managed to dispatch his first assailant but lost his sword in the process. The next one was luckier and managed to lock his canine jaws on his leg.

Nick fell to the ground in a howl of pain, trying to dislodge the powerful jaws from his shin. Before he could, two other wolves reached him, salivating jaws snapping.

The first one went straight for his throat. Nick instinctively blocked with his left hand and screamed as the large wolf's fangs sank into his forearm, while the third wolf caught hold of his boot in his maw, yanking it off his foot.

They're tearing him apart! thought Bunda in alarm.

Still twenty feet away from the jumble of man and wolves before him, Bunda did the only thing he could and hurled the flaming saber with all his might, praying to his master that he hit the wolves and not the man.

Whether fortune or skill, the blade struck the hindquarters of the wolf, which had clenched down on Nick's hand. The beast yelped in pain and, seeing the flames, darted away in a frenzy, which only set him more ablaze.

Bunda had no time to lament the loss of his weapon. Without slowing down, he reached the first wolf, who had Nick by the leg, and kicked its midsection with all his might, sending it tumbling into the air. The wolf landed a few feet away and scrambled to its feet, teeth barred at the new threat.

Nick wasted no time. Rolling over to his first attacker, he yanked his sword out of its dead throat, spraying an arc of blood into the air, and stabbed the third wolf who had taken his boot. The boot thief leaped back in pain.

Bunda helped him to his feet and leaned him against the tree. His left hand and leg were bleeding profusely, and his face was pale. Bunda would have to see to that eventually. But he had more pressing problems.

The rest of the pack had made their way to them and now surrounded them, still seven strong.

They had a new respect for their prey and, thankfully, refrained from charging them head-on. But Bunda and Nick were now surrounded, effectively flanked, cut off from any escape route—not that they could have run. The wolves snapped, barked, and snarled at them. They smelled blood, and they smelled fear. It was only a matter of time before the first attacked, and then the rest would follow.

"Come on, bastards!" he shouted at them, goading them to attack. He realized it was more for his own nerves than anything else. If he was going to stand before Seirn in the next few minutes, he wanted the last moments of his life to be in brave defiance, not cowering on the ground.

But the anticipated meeting with his maker would have to wait. There was a sudden burst of sound and light, and as he turned his head, a cacophony of color and flashes filled the sky to the south. The wolves paused, growling at the strange fires in the sky. And then, a dark shadow, a little larger than the wolves, crashed through the field, kicking up dust and blades of grass as it charged into the nearest wolves.

Dorkah leaped forwards, razor-sharp talons poised like daggers. The wolf she had attacked went down in a spray of blood.

The combination of the lights and this new threat was too much for the rest of the pack, and it broke rank.

Maybe she had killed the Alpha, thought Bunda. He'd heard that was a thing with wolves. They scattered in every direction, yipping and barking as they tried to put as much distance between themselves and their prey-turned-predator.

Dorkah darted after them, growling as she pursued. She overtook one of them, leaping on its back, two long rows of needle-sharp teeth locking on the poor creature's spine.

The wolf howled in pain, trying to twist towards its attacker. Dorka jerked back her head, and the wolf collapsed to the ground with a final whimper. She raised her head, her face wet with blood, looking for her next victim when she suddenly froze, looking back the way she had come, hearing a silent command from her master.

Tadok stumbled into view, panting in exertion from the sprint or from the spell. Or both.

"That...was quite a show," said Bunda, looking at the half-elf in wonder.

Tadok nodded, still breathing heavily, hands on his knees, as Nick collapsed.

Bunda rushed over to the fallen man. His leg looked to be the bigger problem of the two.

He held his open left palm over the wound, praying that Seirn would grant him one last miracle. Blood flooded out uncontrollably now. Nick's face was white and pasty. Bunda tore his leggings open. It was ugly. Worse than he had initially thought. The wolf had not only sunk his fangs into his calf but had torn a large chunk of flesh out. He couldn't bandage this. Not in time.

He closed his eyes and concentrated, his hand clasping his medallion tightly. It was so hard to focus.

He turned his face up to the last rays of sun peeking over the mountain. *Dawn Father, give me strength*, he prayed.

Nothing.

And suddenly, he felt his left palm grow warm and then hot. He risked a glance and sighed gratefully as the flesh around the wound seemed to knit itself together. *Thank you, my lord.*

It took another ten seconds for the wound to fully close. And when he wiped off the blood, a scar had already formed.

Well, that's strange, he thought. Seirn's healing magic had never left a scar before. When it was successful, it would leave clean and unbroken skin where the wound had been. He must have truly been dipping into the bottom of the barrel of his holy reserves. It didn't matter, though. Nick was breathing less raggedly, and he seemed to even smile weakly.

"I think that plan went pear-shaped," he said.

"Aye. You were supposed to stay in the tree," said Tadok as he sat down heavily next to him.

Bunda walked over to the smoldering corpse of the wolf he had thrown his sword into. It hadn't made it too far and, luckily, hadn't started any fires. Just a black smoking husk in the center of the beaten dirt path. The divine power could heal. The divine power could harm.

He yanked his saber from the charred wolf. It had lost its flame by now.

Tadok regained his feet and helped Nick to his. The wounded man was cradling his arm, and Bunda remembered he had also been bitten there as well.

But Tadok was already tearing a strip from Nick's tattered pants to bind the wound. It would do for now.

He turned his attention to the redwood tree

The man who had been stranded on it was now carefully climbing down. At the final branch, he dropped to the ground and nearly lost his feet. As the three neared him, Dorkah at their heels, he drew a long dagger from his belt and looked at them suspiciously.

"Friend or foe?" he asked, his voice croaking the way voices did when their throats hadn't had water for too long.

"Friendlier than the wolves," replied Nick with his most winning smile.

The man had probably been up on the redwood tree for days. He was sunburned, his lips were chapped, and his hair and clothes were disheveled and stained with sweat. Underneath all that, he was tall— easily a head above Bunda— and had the unmistakable markings of a half-elf, including slightly slanted blue eyes and pointed ears framing his dark, matted hair.

"You must be Ren o' the River," said Bunda, offering him his water skin.

The man put away his knife and eagerly took the skin offered, pressing it to his cracked lips and taking in a deep swig. Like with the half-orc, it ended in a sputtering cough, and Bunda said, "Easy, man. There's enough of it to last. We have food, too."

"Thank you, sir," he said once his cough subsided. "You know my name; may I know yours?"

"Aye. My name is Bunda. This is Nick Cartright, and that is Tadok."

"And what is that?" he asked, motioning to Dorkah, who was sniffing at various rocks the wolves had rested on previously like a hound, probably trying to read 'canine'.

"*That* is Dorkah," replied Tadok, "And you needn't worry about her."

Ren nodded slowly, clearly not reassured.

"Well, I must thank you and the gods who sent you," he continued. "That pack had me stranded up there for three days. I was contemplating my escape when you came. Wondering how far I could run."

"In your weakened state? I would be surprised if you made it to the wagon path," stated Bunda simply.

"Agreed, Master Bunda. So, thanks again."

"You've been up on that tree for three days, you say?" asked Tadok. When Ren nodded, he continued. "Did you happen to see a boy of ten pass through these parts? Maybe snuck past the wolves and into the mine?"

Ren narrowed his eyes and slowly shook his head. "Haven't seen any boys pass by. Besides, the wolves would be shitting him out by now if he had."

Bunda was relieved. He had feared that that would have been the answer and end of young Christopher Murley.

"What were you even doing out here?" probed Nick, and Bunda noted Tadok was staring at the redwood tree.

It was a peculiar sight. For one, it was the only redwood tree around, easily towering over the surrounding birch and ash trees. The odder thing was that the entire length of its trunk was carved with elaborate runes. The language was indecipherable, but as Bunda had expected, it matched the strange scrolling he had seen on the walls of Father Sheilagh's torture chamber. He took an uneasy sidelong look at Tadok, who had walked up to the tree and laid his hand on its trunk, tracing his finger over the twisting grooves.

"I was looking for a friend. A large half-orc named Onlan who's been my brother since the War of the Broken Crown. He went missing from my village a couple weeks ago and Jen Murley, our sheriff, and I have been searching for him. I thought he may be in the mines. When I came out, the pack was waiting. I'd left my bow over there as I thought I may need to do some lifting. Much good it would have done me..." he trailed off, seeing that three of them were eyeing each other.

"What is it? Have you seen my friend?"

Tadok turned from the strange tree and stated simply, "Well, we have good news and bad news."

13 SCHOLARS

It was dark when they finally made it back to the village. The trek had been slower than their journey to the mines due to Robin and Ren's conditions. When the village was in sight, Tadok sent Dorkah to hunt and feed. At least, that was what he told Ren. Robin had already learned that she didn't actually need to eat anything, and Tadok was most likely sending her back to whatever magical layer she hailed as home.

Breaking the news of the events in Suldan's Bluff that Ren O' the River had missed was difficult. At first, he didn't believe it. It was a lot. In the span of one conversation, the half-elf hunter had learned that the village had been subject to the attack of raiders. His good friend, the sheriff, and two of his sons had been murdered. His other best friend had been tortured by a member of his own community. And within a few days, the bandits would return.

As they had walked in silence, Robin had noted the tears which streamed down the man's cheeks.

The other problem they were facing was that night was upon them, and they had been unsuccessful in finding Christopher Murley. This, more than anything, weighed on his heart.

When they entered the village, a small crowd greeted them. Robin could see Marven and his wife Odetta; Melvin, the dwarf; Swegan, the blacksmith; Hanlan and his son; and the gnome, Diggericut. He noted that Swegan had a two-handed war-ax slung across his back, and Hanlan had a sword hanging from a baldric at his side.

When they saw Ren, they rushed to his side, alternating between embracing him and bombarding him with questions.

"Let's get him inside," said Odetta, cutting the questions short. "'Tis freezing out here, and the poor man needs a good bowl of stew in his belly."

Followed by the rest, she ushered Ren inside the inn. Marven stayed behind for another moment, locking eyes with Robin. He was silently asking about the boy. Robin looked at the ground and shook his head.

"We found nothing."

Marven sighed in disappointment. Then his eyes brightened up. "Wouldn't say that," he said cheerfully. "In the span of less than a day, ye've found two lost sheep. If ye keep at it, gods allowing, you'll find the lad tomorrow."

Robin hesitated momentarily. Then nodded.

With that assurance, the innkeeper smiled, satisfied.

He turned his gaze towards the hangman's tree. "Now let me find that fool, Yorgen. He was supposed to be keeping watch and must be off in some drunk stupor." He started towards the tree and called back over his shoulder, "Head to the Lodge. Odetta has made her famous mutton and apple stew."

As soon as he was out of sight, Robin turned to his companions. Tadok was furious. When the innkeeper was out of earshot, he said, "We were agreed. We leave at first light."

The half-elf's voice was steel and his eyes intent.

"Be reasonable; we still have at least two days."

"That's not the point!" he spat. "If we leave tomorrow, we have a better chance of avoiding Hayek. For all we know, he could return early. Even if he doesn't, he has horses. If these people are still here, he could easily run them down and torture it out of them that we were the ones who cut down the sheriff and they could overtake us. If he's as bloodthirsty as evidence would suggest, he may choose to take our heads as an example to others. He seems keen on examples," he said, motioning to the distant hangman tree. "The closer we are to the safety of Sebin, the better off—"

"Sebin isn't safe either," Robin blurted out.

Bunda, silent so far, raised an eyebrow. "How so, Nick?"

Robin hadn't intended to release that information to his friends. This was the wrong time to breed suspicion and admitting to being a retired member of the same organization Hayek was from wouldn't be helpful.

"Do you remember when Mendel called Hayek's crew the Shadow Hands?"

"It was Marven Darvey, not Mendel," corrected Bunda helpfully.

"What?"

"It was Darvey, the innkeeper, who called them Shadow Hands," he repeated.

Robin shook his head to clear the interruption. "That's not the point. Darvey misheard. Dell Hayek and his men are *Shadder Hands.*"

If he expected any realization to dawn on his companions, he was disappointed, so he explained: "The Shadder Hands are Gale the Boon's men. They are the strongest band of cutthroats, thieves, smugglers, and pushers in Nemir. He has ties from Sheleen's home to Netheer. And Sebin is one of his most important strongholds. I reckon that Hayek's band hail from Sebin and take orders from the Shadow Mistress of Sebin herself."

He couldn't be sure, but rumor had it that Sebin was gifted to Delona Ravin from Gale for betraying Sally.

I like his eyes.

He shuddered internally, remembering that horrible night.

"If Hayek knows it was us, Sebin's walls may hold no safety for us anyway. If you think death in an ally is preferable to one of the roads, you're a fool." Robin was doing what he did best—he thought on his feet and pressed on, the words forming almost faster than he was thinking them. "The only way we survive this is if we get the townsfolk to be gone before Hayek returns. And they won't do that if we don't bring them the child or the child's body!"

The two looked at him suspiciously.

"How do you know this?" asked the half-elf.

This was the part he was hoping to avoid. *The best lies are mostly truth*, said Garian's cheerful ghost in his head.

"I've...run afoul of them before. They killed my brother and hounded me over the Suldan mountains." That wasn't a lie.

"What exactly did you do, Sandisan?"

"I...witnessed a murder. Not one I enjoy reliving." *That* wasn't a lie, either.

Bunda's voice was calm and filled with empathy when he spoke. Gods knew how Robin's story was playing out in his head. "The gods watch over your brother's soul, Nick. Why are you returning to a place that holds such peril for you?"

"Because I have another brother. In Sandisan. And he needs me." *Mostly truth.*

Tadok's anger hadn't faded from his eyes. "So, we've been

traveling with you while you've had this Gale the Goon's mark on your back all this time, all the time knowing full well that we, too, are now in his hunt just by being associated with you?"

"I don't recall bashing on you for knowing how to speak demon, half-elf," he replied hotly. "We all have a story, and you choose when to tell yours. It wasn't your concern until a moment ago."

Tadok's lips were a thin line of cold fury. Before it could get out of hand, Bunda took a step towards them in case he had to break up a fight. "Friends," he began, but Tadok ignored him.

"What's to stop us from turning you in to Hayek and Gale? Be rid of his ire *and* make some coin at the same time."

Bunda swung his eyes in shock to Tadok, momentarily speechless at the suggestion.

Time to gamble.

"Because you're not the type, Tadok of Sage's Rock."

"You know nothing about me."

"I know you charged into a pack of hungry wolves today to save my hide. Besides, considering that you don't let Dorkah come out and play in villages, towns, and cities, you may want me to watch your back in Sebin."

Tadok's lips were still pressed together, but his eyes showed he was considering Robin's words.

"I also believe you have your own demons to take care of, and I don't mean Dorkah."

He'd struck something as Tadok averted his eyes for a fleeting moment. "That's none of your—"

"Business?" finished Robin, now on the offensive. "I agree. It isn't. So, let's make a deal, half-elf. We guard each other's backs but guard our own secrets, as long as one doesn't endanger the other."

Silence and an intense gaze followed. Finally, it was Tadok who broke.

"*One* more day, Sandisan." He lifted his index finger for emphasis. "One. And if you find further excuses to delay, I'll take my chances on the road alone."

Robin could have mentioned that that idea hadn't worked out for him so well last time, but a caravan master had once told him that when the buyer pulls out his coin purse, you shut your gob. And Tadok was buying.

The half-elf stormed off towards the inn.

"You never asked me, Nick."

Bunda's voice startled him. He had nearly forgotten about the man. He turned to the tall barbarian. "I assumed Seirn's way would have demanded you help the innocent..."

Bunda waved the argument away. If his silver tongue had worked with Tadok, the magic must have evaporated with the Tundrial. "Seirn's teachings can be interpreted. If I were to put thought into this, I would council for the good villagers to flee while they could. Their odds of standing up to the cutthroats or finding their lost boy are small."

Before Robin could think of an argument, he went on, "But that is a decision they may still make tomorrow. I will pray to my master that we find the child tomorrow, but there is another matter at hand."

"Oh?"

"This place is odd. I can feel a...taint." His mouth twisted as if it was a bad aftertaste. "There is something ancient here. I wish to study it more. I believe the runes on the tree and those in the priest's cellar have something to do with it. And I will need the half-elf's help to decipher those dark runes."

Robin slowly nodded. Whatever made him stay and give Robin another day would be helpful.

As Bunda turned and walked to the inn, Robin remembered something. "Totem tree," he called out. Bunda turned, eyeing him in confusion. "The gnome. He called it a 'totem tree'. He said he'd studied it when he first arrived."

Bunda looked at him for a moment and then scratched his beard thoughtfully. Then he shrugged and entered the inn.

***

The inn was fuller than it had been the night before. In fact, everyone in town besides Marven, Yorgen, the seamstress, Tilly and her daughter, Mara, and Aldeira were present. Apparently, she had been caring for Onlan, the half-orc. Robin assumed she would also be happy to see her late husband's other friend return. She needed all the support she could get right now.

The villagers seemed to rejoice at the return of their two lost members, but underneath the relief, the conversations had an anxious undertone, and it seemed that many kept looking out the windows into the silent darkness, as if expecting Dell and his raiders to galop onto the green at any moment.

Ren was seated on the bar with a small crowd around him, asking him questions. He nodded at their questions and replied curtly between spoonfuls of soup. It wasn't apparent if it was the ordeal or the news of the loss of his friend which was responsible for his sombre mood. Both would have been just reasons, thought Robin.

Tadok was seated at the same table they had inhabited the evening before, and Bunda and Robin joined him. The trio ate in silence. Tadok was still brooding, and Robin didn't want to test his luck with the half-elf.

Within a few moments, Mica came over with a tray and bowls of mutton stew, keeping an innocent look as he poured their drinks and laid their food on the table. Nothing in his eyes or demeanour hinted at the conversation he and Robin had shared that morning at arrow point. Robin noted that Mica's right hand was bandaged, covering the Shadow Mark. Bunda noticed it, too.

"What happened to your hand?" he asked.

Mica looked at it as if noticing it for the first time. "Oh, this? The men and I went up to the church to re-bury the remains of the former citizens of Suldan-Karr you encountered. My lodged a large splinter in my hand while I was digging." He lied as easily as he took breath. A true Silk.

"It wasn't an easy sight, mind you," he continued, shooting a glance at Mendel. "I think Mendel's father was buried with Marven's aunt's arm."

Robin smiled, but Bunda's face darkened. Robin laid a hand on his friend's arm. "Easy, friend, it was a jest, wasn't it, Master Mun?" he said, giving Mica a 'not-a-time-to-jest' look.

"A man's eternal rest is not a subject of mockery," said Bunda in a deep and serious voice.

"Of course, master Journeyman. We took great care, I assure you," he replied hastily.

"Did you enter the undercroft in the church?" asked Tadok, ignoring the exchange.

"I didn't, but Swegan and Diggeri did," he said, never taking his eyes off the scowling Bunda.

He quickly retreated back to the safety of his bar, lest the Tundrial cleric force him to exhume Suldan's bluff's cadavers just to check that everyone was buried with the right set of bits and pieces.

After a few minutes of slurping and chewing, Robin chose to break the silence by asking, "Was it the same language, Tadok? I mean, the words in the church and the wand and those on the totem tree Ren was hiding in?"

Tadok thought carefully before answering, his eyes trained on his drink. He was clearly still mad at him but finally made the decision to be social.

"Yes and no. It appears that they are of the same letters, but they make no words. Or make no sense. I'm thinking maybe it's the same language but from a different era."

"Why would that matter?" asked Robin. He barely read one language, so he was impressed and humbled that Tadok spoke and read at least three.

"Language changes over time."

"Is that so?" asked Robin with raised eyebrows. "Why?"

"Imagine you met your grandfather," began Tadok. The task was rather difficult for Robin. Being the bastard son of a Shadder Street harlot, he hadn't known his father, let alone his grandfather. "You would find some of his words and terms a little different from yours, as they change with the fashion of the time."

"Okay," Robin said and nodded to show that he was following and genuinely curious.

"Now imagine you were talking to your ancestor from the age of Great Nem. How many grandfathers would that be?"

Robin was worse with numbers than with reading, and after thinking on it for a few moments, Bunda came to his rescue.

"About ten," answered the Barbarian, and by Tadok's nod, it must have been a better answer than his, which was going to be fifty.

"So, ten grandparents, all with slightly different words and speech, would make the language sound rather different. Some words would be the same but understanding a sentence would be like understanding halfling speech."

That was easier, as he knew halflings. They had the annoying tendency to switch in the blink of an eye between Nemirian, elven, dwarven, and even *Xayel* in some cases. This would make it impossible for someone not fluent in all languages to follow, even if he understood a few words here or there.

"Yet, in the days of Nem, the Nemfolk spoke *Nemtang*. It's still spoken today in the Seal Shore Isles in ceremonies," said Bunda, trying to contribute to the conversation.

"True. And when Nem's people finished conquering the lands and establishing the empire, their language fused with the tongue of the Karr and is what is today known as Nemirian, or common," he explained. "But *this*, is far older than Nemtang or even Karr. Even the Shadowtang I was taught differs from it. I understood very little of it."

He finished his drink and dried his stubbly chin with his sleeve. He then motioned to the gnome who was passing by at that moment.

Diggericut looked over his shoulder to understand who the half-elf was motioning to; a look of surprise washed over his face when he realized he was the person of interest. He walked over to the table carefully, apprehensive about what this stranger could want from him.

Tadok pulled over the fourth empty chair, motioning for him to sit. The three-foot-tall gnome climbed up to the chair, propping himself on his knees so his head and shoulders passed the surface of the table.

"No cause for alarm, little one," began Tadok in an attempt to calm down the nervous gnome, "I am told you have a unique expertise on the history of these parts."

Diggericut considered this for a moment, then nodded. "I do," he began, "Any gnome worth his beard knows history, but if you want to hear the village history, Marven's family has been here for about sixty years. And if it's the war which piques your curiosity, then Onlan and Ren fought in it. And going farther than that, Swegan saw the fall of Doar-Keirn. Granted, he was only a boy, but he has a good memory and—"

Tadok cut into his words by leaning forward. "No. The stories I seek are older, from an age that no living human, dwarf, or even elf could remember. But a *student* of history may."

The gnome's eyes comically grew to the size of saucers.

"We wish to know more about the Totem Tree. The one near the mines."

Diggericut saucer eyes brightened up—apparently entering a field he enjoyed discussing. All uncertainty previously shown had vanished.

"It's fascinating, isn't it!" he said enthusiastically. "It's a rather local tradition. I haven't seen anything like it anywhere else, but there are at least twelve documented in the mountains, and I suspect there were more once, although time and woodcutting may have diminished them. When I first arrived, I had sent a carefully worded letter to the gnomish cartographer's college in Sandisan—those gnomes travel farther than anyone. Unfortunately, no one had seen anything like it. I had spent days sketching it, too." He suddenly realized he was ranting and turned up to Tadok. "What do you want to know?" he asked.

Tadok nodded. "First, who made them?"

"Ah! A fascinating mystery. Have you ever heard of a people called the *Cleith*?"

When they all stared blankly, he continued. "The Cleith were a nation which had formed city-states on the west side of the Suldan mountains. They are an important to the development for humanity as they were the first humans to use arcane magic. Before that, we only know about the elves using magic. Over the centuries, enough trade and intermarriage with the nation of *Kinnal* on the east side of the mountains formed the Karr."

"And it was these *Cleith* who made the trees?" asked Robin, trying to prove that he, too, had a scholarly instinct.

"No," laughed the gnome, "that would be ridiculous! The trees are around two thousand years old and the Cleith didn't exist before the age of Man-Ascending, one thousand years before Nem."

"Two thousand!" asked Tadok in shock. "How would the runes survive?"

"Magic," answered the gnome, clearly not appreciating the interruptions, "but I'll get to that."

"The Cleith, who used the dwarven alphabet, had an extensive library which was found in the ruins of the city of *Karmorgar*, which is today Westerwick."

Too many names, thought Robin in dismay.

"It was in this library where they found documents of an even older human society, called the *Terrodites*." He paused to let it sink in. By the confused expressions, not much had. He went on.

"These Terrodites lived in these parts *two thousand* years ago! And it was these ancient humans who made the totem trees," summarized the gnome.

"Were they known to worship demons or wicked gods?" asked Bunda thoughtfully.

"Hmm." The gnome massaged his jaw in thought. "From the little which is known, their trees were their spiritual focus. The same way you would bend your knee to a statue of the Seirn. But I had assumed that it meant their gods were of the spirit world or of nature–like druids."

"Then why would they be scrawled with the language of shadows?" asked Tadok.

"The language of shadows? You mean...of the Abyss?" asked Diggericut putting a shocked hand to his mouth, as if he regretted uttering the word.

"And of Hell, and of other lower realms," answered Tadok, not intending to be deterred by the name of a place. "The Totem Tree, the undercroft, and this," he said, drawing the wand they had taken off of Father Sheilagh that morning. He handed it to the gnome, who took it carefully, drawing a set of round spectacles, which he placed on his nose to examine it.

"Where did you find this?" he asked in wonder.

"We took it off the late Father Sheilagh, just after he used it to raise a pack of undead to attack us."

The gnome was silent as he examined it. If the fact that the thin rod had been used for such a nefarious purpose disturbed him in any way, he didn't show it. The only emotion on his face was that of pure academic interest.

"This is a mage's wand," he stated.

"Well, obviously," answered Robin, still trying to show he was a contributing participant in the conversation.

"And look!" He pointed at the small letters and runes covering it. "It has the same writing as that of the tree!" he exclaimed excitedly.

"It's Shadowtang, and our friend here can read it," added Bunda.

Tadok shot him an annoyed look but didn't say anything.

Diggericut looked up sharply at Tadok.

"This means you can decipher the writing on the tree?" he asked hopefully. Gnomes loved puzzles and mysteries.

Tadok shook his head.

"The writing on the tree is different. There appear to be no words, as if their author knew the letters but not how to assemble them."

The gnome looked disappointed. "A shame. It remains a conundrum."

"Well, not really, if you think about it."

They all turned to Bunda, who had spoken between mouthfuls of stew. When he realized they were silently staring at him, he looked up.

"Isn't it obvious?" he asked. Apparently, it wasn't, so he explained.

"The tree. It grows," he stated simply.

Diggericut was the first to catch on.

"So, over time…"

"…The letters would be pushed farther apart as the bark expanded," completed Tadok.

"Aye." Bunda nodded. "In the Seal Shore Isles, trees are venerated by druids. If what you say is true about the tree being two thousand years old, it was much smaller a thousand years ago. I'm no druid, but a redwood tree like that one would grow about an inch per year when it was younger, and slow down as it grew older. It probably grew at least two hundred feet over the last thousand years, too."

"I'm impressed, Tarthen," said Tadok, finally calling him by his correct origin. "That explains why the letters are clear, but the words have dissolved."

The gnome suddenly leaped to his feet excitedly, standing on his chair. Some of the other patrons of the inn turned to look at him, but he didn't seem to care.

"Then I can calculate it!"

"Calculate it?" asked Tadok.

"Yes! If we know approximately how the tree has grown, and I've full sketches of it, which I made almost a decade ago, I can compare them to the location of the letters today and know how much they've drifted apart. Then I can transcribe the original text," he said, out of breath. "This is so exciting!"

"So exciting," repeated Robin, but his sarcasm was lost on the other three.

The conversation droned on into the evening until, finally, Robin stood up yawning. He immediately winced, remembering his wounds.

"T'has been quite a day. Zombies and wolves and all. I'm off to bed."

With that, he climbed the narrow staircase to his room.

The room was one of two the Miner's Lodge had to offer guests. It had four beds, arranged at the four corners, and a single shuttered window. The room was situated above the hearth, and the chimney chute actually went through the inner wall, heating the room comfortably. A small peer in the shoot acted as a hearth and allowed one to dry wet clothes along with an iron crane for a tea kettle. A clever architectural design sucked the air upwards to avoid filling the room with smoke. A large sheepskin rug dominated the floor, and there were shelves and two chests for anyone who wished to place their belongings in the room. Despite this, the three of them had never unpacked, and their travel gear rested at the foot of each of their beds.

After relieving himself of all the ale he'd imbibed in the chamber pot, he gingerly stripped off his clothes and examined himself in the spotted standing mirror which stood next to the door. He shivered and opened the iron grate in the chimney shoot wider to heat the room.

The scar on his calf was an angry red misshapen mark, and he had dark bruises on his shoulder and ribs from where he had hit the ground. He winced as he carefully removed the bandage from his hand. Nothing was severed or broken, but the puncture wounds were already puffing around the edges. He washed his hand carefully in the bowl of clean water on the single table in the room. He hoped that tomorrow Bunda's healing magic could speed along its recovery, as it itched like hell.

He lay down in his bed, carefully removing folded parchment from one of the secret pockets in his cloak. He read it again as he had every night for the last month.

What did you get yourself into, Tommy? he thought.

Finishing the letter, he blew out the small candle next to the bed, hoping to reach a deep enough sleep before Bunda or Tadok stumbled into the room and woke him up.

But sleep was slow to come.

The last thought that drifted through his mind before he drifted off was, *What have I gotten myself into, Garian.*

14 MUMMERS AND THESPIANS

"...So if thee love me, don't let my sacrifice be for naught. Life is too precious for foolish notions of revenge, my sweet King Celestine. With these words of wisdom, I leave thee to the bosom of the Father," said Dilal weakly. And then she died.

There was a moment of revered silence and then a round of booming applause. A moment later, Dilal took to her feet, removing the red handkerchief, which was supposed to represent the blood from her mortal wound. She clasped hands with Norton, who had been the elven King Celestine Goldenbrow a moment ago, and they both bowed deeply for the audience, who responded by clapping even harder and stamping their feet on the makeshift wooden benches. The rest of the troupe joined in and bowed several times more.

She was good. Robin had to give her that.

They had been with the Lionheart Theatre for three months now. And despite having seen 'The Price of Freedom' at least ten times now, he still found himself drawn into the story towards the end. Robin assumed part of it was because the tale was a good one. Probably one of Garitone's best. The other part was the amazing emotional performance Dilal executed as she transformed into the beautiful General Argalei of Freelan.

Leaning on a post at the entrance, he watched her as he always did at the end of the show. The flushed cheeks, the bright green eyes, the genuine joy at seeing the success of the play. Tommy had called her a flower with the heart of a lioness, and Robin had to agree.

She caught his gaze from the stage, and Robin averted his eyes in embarrassment. But when he lifted them again, hoping she hadn't seen his admiration, she was still staring at him. Before he could look away again, her humble smile split into a grin that made his heart flutter, and he had no choice but to grin back. He applauded. Still smiling, she winked at him, and Robin's smile slowly faded.

It had been a successful evening for the Lion Theater, and Corwin Lenther, the old dwarf who headed the troupe, was generous with the ale and mead.

The townsfolk of Taffin's Grove, a three-day ride out of Sea View, had already returned to the protection of their wooden walls and palisades, and the theater's caravan guards were more at ease.

Robin, Tommy, and Dilal were sitting on a log across from the wide, slow moving Trotten River, enjoying the cool summer's night air. The river was alive with the reflection of a million fireflies as they danced in small clouds of stars above the water. At a distance, the sounds of Norton's flute and Kodiander's lute filled the air in the center of the caravan circle. One of the halfling mummers, Jolin—or was it Dalin? Robin could never tell—was juggling five colorful balls above his head and laughter echoed from the performers who were now the audience.

"...My dear, I am spent, and his cock was all bent..." Tommy sang as Dilal giggled.

"That's not how it goes! The words are 'and with that, far he *went*'," she corrected him between bouts of laughter.

"My version makes much more sense. If he's spent, how would he go far?" answered Tommy, taking a swig out of the jug of mead and passing it over to Dilal.

Robin grinned, whittling a small block of wood. He had plans to try and make Dilal's likeness in it. He wasn't an expert woodcarver, and his last attempt had looked more like a melted troll, but he had taken a lesson from Kodiander and wanted to try again.

It had been three years since they'd left Sandisan. The brothers didn't talk much about the night of Garian's death; it seemed to be a painful topic for both of them. Besides, survival had been more of a priority than anything else.

They had headed west, crossing the Suldan Mountains through Sebin into the chaotic lands of Suldan-Karr—a place where one could disappear. Despite a more difficult beginning, the brothers transitioned from stealing what they needed to survive to selling their services for hire. They avoided heist jobs or trafficking as Robin feared they would draw the attention of local crime lords, which in turn would reach Gale.

It was apparent that Gale was closing scores with anyone who had backed Sally. At first, Robin assumed Gale wouldn't put effort into finding them. Garian was the one with clout among the Shadder Hands. But he had made contact with an ex-hand he knew in Sebin a few weeks after the coup—a man named Gromel who had been a fence before a two-year stretch in prison had set him on the straight and narrow path. He had been a friend of Garian from the start, and Robin was hopeful he would take Tommy and him in. A few days after he had met him in Sebin, Gromel and his whole family had been butchered in their home by Gale's men. Robin and Tommy had been lucky enough to be out of the small house at the time. They had fled Sebin and left Nemir behind, changing their names. Robin would introduce himself as Nick, and Tommy changed his name to John. Even after crossing into Suldan-Karr, they had been careful to never stay in the same place more than a few weeks, changing inns frequently. Work for two armed youths was abundant in the lawless lands beyond the Suldan, and Nick and John Cartright made do.

But their time with the Lions had been different. The troupe of traveling performers went from town to town, bringing joy and laughter where there was none, as Corwin Lenther liked to put it.

They were two of eight sellswords the caravan employed. They spent their days guarding the caravan as it passed through the old roads and their evening policing the crowds which turned up. From time to a couple of local drunks would get too rowdy, and Robin and Tommy would firmly set them on their way back to town. There had even been a case where Dilal and her little sister Shinara had been attacked by a trio of goblins when they had made camp. Robin and Tommy had dispatched the little monsters easily and earned the troupe's gratitude and trust.

But it wasn't the Lion Theatre's favor which Robin found himself coveting.

Robin had had his share of women in Sandisan. The Hands had investments in many different businesses in the Shadder Street and in the docks and quite a few brothels. Mother Beya's was the Hugh brothers' favorite, and they were often treated like family there. This was probably since they were.

While Robin had been only three when his mother had died, she had originally been one of Beya's girls. When she'd gotten pregnant with Tommy, Beya had allowed her to take care of the books and earn her wages with her head and not her body. Garian said that that was how she knew Sally, as she was the one to hand over the Hands' share every week.

While Garian was every girl's favorite customer, with his roguish good looks and his natural charm, Robin and Tommy had their fair share of willing ladies to choose from too. Beya never even charged them the house tax as long as they were polite and respectful of her girls.

Beyond the various girls he'd tumble every so often, there had been one disastrous relationship with another cat-burglar, a girl named Sonya, which had ended rather poorly, and one memorable weekend with a noble's daughter when her parents were away.

But through all of it, he had never felt the way he did when he was around Dilal. She took a liking to him and his brother instantly and shared more and more time with them. Dilal had been with the Lion Theatre for ten years now. She and her little sister had been rescued from a fate on the streets of Culidge when Corwin had found them. He had a soft spot for children, which Robin admired. It reminded him of Garian and of Mother Beya. He had taken in the two girls as costume seamstresses at first. Dilal had shown her stage talents early on and quickly rose to stardom in the troupe. At seventeen, she could turn the heads of any warm-blooded mortal with her lithe form and infectious laughter. Robin often found himself lying awake in his cot, still smelling her flower-scented perfume in his mind before sleep would take him.

He was smiling much more than ever since Garian's death, as was Tommy. Thus, his little brother didn't mind when he continued to sign on for another run and then another as they continued to follow the Lions around Suldan-Karr.

A lone figure walked over to them. It was Angst, the grizzled old bear of a guard who had been with the troupe for years and acted as Corwin's unofficial captain of the guard.

"Nick? Is that you, lad?" he asked, squinting his eyes in the darkness.

Robin rose to his feet. "Over here, Angst," he called. The man walked over to them, frowning at the jug of mead.

"Sorry to disturb the fun, but I need one of you two boys. Guss, that half-elf-half-dogshit from Westerwick is sodding drunk and drooling behind the mummer's tent."

"That's the third time, Angst. I told you he couldn't stay away from it."

The old man grunted tiredly. "Aye, you were right. Doesn't change the truth, though, that I need a man on night's watch."

Before he or Tommy could protest, he raised his hand to placate them.

"I know the both of you did a full day's work today but Kier is taking on the dead-man's watch and everyone else is in town. My word—you'll get Guss's pay for the day, and I'll replace you in two hours when the others return. I only need one of you—whoever is closest to sober."

Tommy and Robin looked at each other. He guessed that either one of them could pull off two hours of guard duty, but Tommy was smiling the way he never had since they had lost Garian, and Robin couldn't bring himself to cut that short. Besides, it would give him time to finish his little art project.

He turned to Angst in mock resignation. "Fine. But you better get rid of that idiot before he causes any more trouble, Angst."

Angst nodded enthusiastically. "He won't be coming with us when we leave tomorrow."

Robin waited until the old brawler was on his way and turned to Dilal and Tommy, who had been watching the whole exchange silently. When the three locked gazes, they all burst out into an uncontrollable fit of laughter.

Robin, still chuckling, gathered his belongings and headed to the guard station at the entrance to the camp.

"There better be something in that jug when I get back, John. You owe me, brother."

He walked off into the night to the sounds of Dilal and his brother attempting to sing the '*Weary Sailor*' again.

By the time he reached his post, he was humming the song himself.

"*...and his cock was all bent...*" he sang to himself and chuckled. Tommy did that a lot. Warp songs with funny or rowdy lyrics.

As he whittled the block of wood, he tried to recall Kodiander's lesson.

"Break it up into shapes and lines," he muttered under his breath.

As he worked, he envisioned Dilal's face. The thin brows, her long brown hair, the color of mahogany, her cheeks and small delicate nose. His mind continued to wander, and he imagined her wearing a blue dress with flowers in her hair. He would be there with a fresh new tunic. He could buy a nice one in Seaview. He didn't know which faith Dilal designated to, but he was sure he could find a priest of The Four, or maybe a cleric of Sheleen in one of the villages. He certainly didn't care. If he could be with her, it was time to stop running. He allowed his fantasy to build in his mind, imagining summer nights like this one with his love and his brother. The image was sweeter than the mead.

"Calm down, lad, you don't want to frighten her..." he said to himself. But she had given him so many signs over the last few days that he would need to be blind not to see it. The lame excuses to ride with Tommy and him. The flirting, the lowcut blouses she seemed to be wearing more and more around them. And she'd winked at him at the play.

This isn't a moment to be bashful, you fool, echoed Garian's voice in his head. *The girl obviously has taste for Hugh,* he said as he always would when Robin was considering which girl to pick at Mother Beya's. Robin smiled, thinking of Garian. How he wished he could talk to his older brother at that very moment. His surrogate father. His best friend.

He looked up at the block of wood and smiled. It really *was* a likeness of her. He made a mental note to remember to thank Kodiander for the expert advice.

By the time Angst plodded over, he was eager to get back to her.

As he walked back to the log by the river, his heart began thudding in his chest. He would show her the small wooden likeness of her and profess his feelings.

He made it back to the log within a few minutes, using all his will to refrain from running.

As he neared the two who were still sitting there, he suddenly stopped cold in his tracks. At first, he wasn't sure what he was seeing. In the darkness, their two heads seemed to fuse into one, as did their hands. And then as he heard Dilal moan softly, his heart sank into his boots, and he looked away.

Aye, she did have a hunger for a Hugh—just not for *Robin*

Hugh. His mind replayed all of his encounters with her with this new spin, and the sweet memories became bitter. All the time shared, all the flirting. It had all been when both he and Tommy were together with her. But she had winked at *him*, he thought miserably. This had to be a bad dream.

He stood there, his feet planted into the ground, not sure if he should disturb them or leave.

"Nick!" It was Dilal who had seen him.

He turned and began to walk away, but Tommy caught up to him.

"I was going to tell you, brother."

"How long, Tommy?" he rounded on him, forgetting himself and using his brother's real name.

Tommy lowered his voice and looked around frantically to see if anyone had heard.

"Hush, someone will hear," he whispered harshly.

"Answer me," said Robin, no apology in his voice.

Tommy took a deep breath without unlocking his brother's eyes. "Since Torik's Inn."

Robin silently calculated in his head. "So over two months. And you said *nothing*?"

"No, because I knew you'd anger this way."

Could his brother have known Robin's feelings? And he had advanced in his courtship anyway? The thought iced his heart in cold rage.

"Robin, we've been running and hiding for three years. Every time we begin to be at peace, you take us to the wind again."

Mild relief. So, at least Tommy didn't know how he felt. He didn't know that Robin was ready to stop running, too. At least he was until five minutes ago. Robin took the part Tommy had written for him, just as the actors took the parts Corwin Lenther cast for them.

"That's because I still possess all my wits. You seem to have lost yours at the sight of a twat with pretty bust," he said, regretting the words as soon as they were voiced.

Tommy's face flushed in anger.

"Don't call her that," he said warningly.

Robin held his eyes for another few moments and then turned, continuing back to his tent.

"Just be ready for travel by the cock's crow," he called over his shoulder. "We're leaving tomorrow."

"No." Tommy's voice was flat and hard.

Robin turned back, staring at his brother in the moonlight.

"I'm done running. I love her."

"You have no idea what that means, lad."

"You mean that *you* don't know what it means, Brother," retorted Tommy. "Ever since Garian, you see no joy in anything. Over the past few weeks, I've seen you smile. I've seen you happy. I thought you finally were."

I was, thought Robin bitterly.

"Don't be a fool, Tommy. Do you know what Gale will do to this entire Troup if he finds us here?"

"Which is why we're leaving." It was Dilal's voice, which rang out as she joined them.

Robin turned to Tommy. "You told her?" he asked in shock.

Tommy's jaw was set, and he pulled himself up to his full height—half a head above Robin. The crying boy, with his head buried in Robin's chest in the small skiff floating in the Ailtel that night, had grown up.

"I keep no secrets from the mother of my child," he answered in defiance.

Robin was at a loss for words as the new information sank in. This night was not holding back any punches.

"Tommy, you fool," he finally said, shaking his head.

"That's all you have to say to me?" Tears of rage welled up in his little brother's eyes.

Robin turned to address Dilal. "He may be a love-struck idiot, but if you value your life or that of the child you claim to carry—you'll stay well away from us and forget our names. We have dangerous men after our heads."

If the threat or the insult to her integrity phased Dilal, she didn't let it show. She simply smiled hopefully and said, "Tommy isn't the only love-struck person here, Robin. So am I. And I've been scared my whole life. For the first time, I'm not. And I know there are many places in Trosia where we can disappear and live happily. Tommy, me, you. Even Shinara.

"Robin, you may have lost family, but there is a new one to be gained. You're so intent on looking over your shoulder that you're blind to what is ahead."

He had to admit—she had a way with words. He gazed into her green eyes, lamenting what could have been. He would have preferred to be caught and tortured by Gale over living a life in the shadow of her and Tommy's happiness. The happiness she should have shared with him.

And at that moment, Dilal understood and averted her eyes in embarrassment and sadness.

Or was it pity?

Of all the blows received that night–her pity was the worst. Robin's jaw hardened, and he turned on them both.

"I'm leaving tomorrow Brother. With you, or without you."

That was the last time he saw either of them

15 NEWCOMERS

Tadok woke from a dream in which he had been standing on a cliff over the sea. Was it the Ailtel Sea? He couldn't be sure. Sellwyn was there looking out across the waters.

She was crying, her shoulders shuddering under her silent sobs. He raised a hand to her shoulder, but she shrugged away.

"What has been done cannot be undone, love," she whispered into the wind.

He wanted to ask her what she meant. To tell her that Dorkah and he would come for her. But no words escaped his dream self's mouth. His vision swam as sunlight washed over his face, blinding him, and he blinked awake.

He was in his bed at the Miner's Lodge; the curtains had been pushed open, and sunlight filtered through the dirty window.

Shirtless and on his knees, Bunda was deep in meditation, sitting in the center of the room surrounded by motes of sunlight. His lips moved silently in prayer as his arms carefully rose to the light, his fingers spread to filter the light into beams on his face and chest.

Bunda's back was covered in tattoos. Intricate artwork in motifs of sea and sun.

A groan from the other bed alerted him that Nick had also awakened.

"Every damn morning…" the Heartlander muttered sleepily.

Finishing his morning prayers, the Tundrial rose to his feet and washed his face in the water basin.

"For a man with a hole in his hand awaiting Seirn's healing—I'd not complain so much, Nick Cartright," smiled Bunda, water dripping from his beard to his muscular chest.

Tadok rose and walked over to the window, opening it a crack and staring out. When he was sure no one was outside, he proceeded to relieve himself of yesterday's drink.

"You know, there's a perfectly good chamber pot in the corner," said Nick, yawning.

Tadok didn't answer him. The thought of pissing in the same jug Bunda and Nick had been using seemed revolting to him.

Bunda was inspecting Nick's wound, mumbling a prayer to Seirn and letting his hand hover above it. After a moment, the holy magic completed its mission and Nick flexed his smooth hand.

"As if I've been graced with a new hand," he said in awe. He then looked at his calf and at the red-white scar.

"Why didn't my leg heal the same way? Without the scar?" he asked with a puzzled look.

Bunda frowned. "It puzzles me, too. But it is to be expected as I called upon the Divine time and time again yesterday. There is a limit to how much power mortals can wield."

He turned to Tadok. "How about you, Tadok Starkin?" he asked, motioning to Tadok's own leg.

Tadok tested out the limb. There was a nasty-looking large bruise from where the shovel had hit his thigh, which was already shifting from dark blue to greenish yellow. He gingerly prodded it and winced. Then smiled at the cleric.

"All good. Save your magic, Bunda."

The trio got dressed and collected their belongings for the day.

***

On the way down to the common room, Tadok reflected on the day ahead of them. They didn't really have any new leads. He supposed they could either go south of the village, assuming the boy had run out to the fields and gotten lost in the night, circumventing the village from the south. It was unlikely, as Christopher had spent his entire short life here, but perhaps in a moment of panic he got turned around.

The other option was to check out the old watch tower. A few people in town had discouraged that notion, as local children were traditionally made afraid of the ruins through ghost stories. But again—the boy may have lost his wit in his flight. Wherever he was, it was clear that he was unable or unwilling to return, as he evidently hadn't done so yet.

That didn't bode well.

Despite all of these questions on his mind, Tadok couldn't stop thinking of the ancient runes on the tree and in the priest's cellar-turned-torture-chamber. He had never seen the Shadow language before beyond the runes and letters Sellwyn had taught him as a boy. In some strange way, he felt a connection to the sorceress when he observed the familiar runes. Late at night, before sleep had taken him, he'd poured over the runes in the moonlight. He hadn't needed any candle or lantern to see them—a gift from his elven grandfather. He had deduced that they held no more magic in them by applying a magic-sense spell, but the runes themselves still held a certain fascination for him.

He pondered this as he entered the common room, intent on sitting at the table they had designated as their own table for the past two days.

To his surprise, the table wasn't vacant. It was occupied by a bald man with a tattoo of a snake behind his ear and his companion, a thin young man with a goatee.

Tadok surveyed the rest of the room. Another table was seated with newcomers.

The one closest to the bar seated three burly men in dirty brown cloaks. One had a long scar over his lip, another had gray hair and an eye patch, while the last scratched a bushy beard with a three-fingered hand.

Near the door, a half-orc the size of Onlan leaned against the doorframe. All of the men were clearly armed.

He took one look at Bunda, and the hair on the back of his neck rose. Bunda's eyes flashed blue, and it was clear to Tadok that he's employed what Nick had called his 'evil-sense'. His lips pursed, and he took in his surroundings, ready for a fight.

Beyond the men, Mica was standing by the bar, pouring ale from a newly opened keg, and both the Darveys were standing in the opening to the kitchen, fearfully avoiding their glances.

Tadok assessed the situation as the three of them crowded the entrance from the stairwell. The patrons hadn't noticed them. He, could only assume they were Hayek's men—unless this village was extremely unlucky to attract another band of raiders. They hadn't made a move, so he expected them to wait for them to fully enter the room—allowing them to overpower and flank them utilizing their greater numbers. They were outnumbered two-to-one.

He could summon Dorkah, but that may not pass over well with the villagers. He was sure he could draw his weapon in time, and maybe even use some spell as a distraction, but that would only buy him a few moments.

To his surprise, Nick walked over to the bar whistling, seemingly oblivious to the situation.

"Good morning, Master Mun," he said cheerfully. "How wonderful to see more guests in the Lodge. Is that a fresh keg?" He grabbed two of the filled mugs, nodding gratefully to Marven and Odetta Darvey.

Before anyone in the room could react, he swung around to the table seating the bandits so fast that in a blink of an eye, the two mugs shattered against the faces of Three-fingers and Scar-lip, stunning everyone. Shielding his face from the splatter, Gray-hair didn't have time to even see Nick's dagger as it jetted out of his hand and sank into his throat all the way to the hilt. He fell back, gurgling blood.

The common room exploded into chaos.

Snake-tattoo leaped to his feet just as Bunda barrelled into him - shoulder first.

Nick, hands free now, grasped the table his three surprised opponents had been seated in and upended it, knocking Three-fingers to the floor.

Goatee slashed at the Tundrial with a short sword, which Bunda managed to block with his drawn saber, mere inches away from his throat.

The half-orc roared and charged at them, raising a wicked-looking wooden cudgel with four spikes on the head. Tadok pointed at the floor under him, drawing upon his Flow instinctively. The floor was suddenly as slippery as if the brigand's boots were slathered in grease. The large half-orc slid uncontrollably over the wooden floorboards and tripped over one of the chairs, crashing at Tadok's feet.

Tadok deftly unhooked his sickle and flipped it into a reverse hold. Leaping over the half-orc, he slashed at Snake-tattoo's back, leaving a red gash visible through his shirt. The man yelled in pain and twisted around, punching Tadok squarely in the face.

Tadok's vision swam, and he felt nausea in the pit of his stomach. It was a good, solid fist in the face, and he had a second to wonder if his nose was broken. He reeled back on unsteady legs. His attacker, snarling through clenched teeth, drew a long knife.

"I'm gonna tear yer ears off, son!" He growled.

Time to stop pulling his magical punches, thought Tadok. He whispered a few short syllables, and his left palm suddenly crackled electrically. As Snake-Tattoo charged him Tadok slashed low with his sickle, which Snake Tattoo easily slapped aside. That was exactly what Tadok hoped he would do.

He shot his left hand forward, grasping the man's face. Sparks, smoke and a sizzle erupted simultaneously from Snake-Tattoo's face, and he frantically tried to pull away. Tadok pressed forward, knowing his only chance was to keep hold of the man's burning face. The knife blindly slashed his right forearm, causing him to drop his sickle and grunt in pain. A few seconds later, the man dropped like a sack of potatoes to the floor—still twitching, but clearly dead. A charred, hand-shaped imprint was embedded on his smoldering face.

Tadok surveyed the rest of the room.

Scar-lip, face still dripping with ale, slammed one of a pair of hand-axs he was armed with into the bar where Nick's hand had been a moment ago. Nick, out of mugs and daggers, somersaulted backward over the bar, crashing and shattering ceramic and glass.

Scar-lip tried to free his ax from the wooden bar but gasped as Mica Mun suddenly slashed a broken mug across his throat. Blood erupted from the wound almost immediately, spraying the bartender, the bar and the bottles behind as the man went down.

On the other side of the room, Goatee and Bunda were going at it blade for blade. Goatee had speed, and Bunda had reach. The problem was that with Goatee's superior pace, he could get two attacks in for every one of Bunda's strikes, and Bunda was losing ground, keeping on the defensive.

Tadok bent down to fetch his sickle to aid his friend, when a large hand grasped him by the throat from behind. The half-orc.

The large brute lifted Tadok clean off his feet with both hands and slammed him into the stone wall of the inn.

Tadok had already used up his electricity charge and, with his airway cut off, was prevented from using more magic. He slapped futilely at the man's arms and face, but the grip only tightened. He wondered if he would pass out from being choked or his neck would snap and which of the two would be the better death.

Time to summon Dorkah. He concentrated as his forehead began to glow. Suddenly, his vision bloomed into white stars as the half-orc slammed him again against the wall, cutting off the summoning.

The half-orc suddenly bellowed in pain, dropping the half-elf to the floor, and turning around. As Tadok's vision cleared, he could clearly see the hilt of a kitchen knife protruding from the half-orc's back as he advanced on the now unarmed Marven Darvey.

Tadok wasted no time and leaped at the half-orc's ankles, hugging them with all his strength. Unfortunately, he wasn't strong enough to trip the larger foe, who looked down at him, snarling.

Near the bar, Nick had finally unsheathed his rapier and was dueling with Three-fingers, who had a similar rapier.

Nick's blade was a flash of silver through the air, stabbing at the other man, who managed to bat away Nick's every slash and jab.

Three-fingers slashed upwards and Nick bent backwards, narrowly avoiding being eviscerated. He brought his sword up to block the man's return downward slash and spun into his guard. Now it appeared as if Three-fingers was embracing Nick in some strange dance, the crook of his elbow wrapping around his throat, as his sword slid down to the basket hilt of Nick's own blade. Suddenly, Nick switched tactics. He dropped the sword from his right hand, simultaneously grabbing the man's hilt with the same hand and dexterously catching his falling sword with his left. He flipped the blade and plunged it under his armpit, catching the surprised man off guard. The man staggered backwards, his left hand clutching his side as blood seeped from between his fingers.

Nick allowed him no respite. He advanced on him, his sword back in his right hand. He batted Three-finger's rapier out of the way and plunged his own into the man's heart. Three-fingers gasped and slumped to the floor.

At the same time, the half-orc leaned down and clutched a fistful of Tadok's brown hair, yanking the half-elf to his feet. Tadok yelped in pain, tears forming in his eyes. He kicked with all his strength, catching the half-orc in the groin, who in turn dropped Tadok back to the floor with a groan, both hands dropping to his injured manhood.

On hands and knees, Tadok began to crawl away but was kicked viciously in the ribs, flipping him over and onto his back as he wheezed for breath.

Across the room, Bunda dropped to one knee as Goatee got lucky with a slash to his thigh. He managed to block another strike from the man but dropped his saber. Goatee grinned triumphantly, raising his sword, but Bunda suddenly spoke a word in the Divine and pointed at his face; a ball of bright yellow light instantly formed right on top of his nose, blinding the man and causing him to try and shield his face. It was no use as the epicenter of the light globe was the man's own nose. With his enemy distracted, Bunda regained his sword, stabbing upwards right into the man's diaphragm. He dropped to the floor, the ball of light illuminating the mask of shock and confusion frozen on the dead man's face.

The half-orc roared at Tadok, flecks of spittle flying out of his mouth. He raised his foot above Tadok's head, intent on ending this half-elf nuisance once and for all, when Nick bull-rushed into him with left elbow, catching him directly under the taller half-orc's armpit and pushing him to the side. As he did so, Nick managed to stab the larger man three times in the ribs, striking like an angry viper.

The half-orc, panting now, was still standing, blood streaming from the wounds in his back and his side. Bringing his arm down and catching Nick in a headlock, he spun around, catapulting the young man into the newly risen Bunda, causing them both to collapse in a heap of limbs and grunts.

Staggering but still standing, he turned back to Tadok. The half-orc took a step towards him, but suddenly froze, hovering over the confused and breathless half-elf. The brute then collapsed to his knees and slumped forward right on top of Tadok. A hand-ax was lodged in the back of his skull.

Odetta stood there shaking from the adrenaline, which had loaned her the strength to kill the brute.

The inn was now silent, aside from a few tinkles of glass falling on the stone floor and the heavy breathing of all of the survivors. The whole fight had lasted less than five minutes.

The common room was in shambles. Glass and ale were strewn all over the floor and tables and chairs had been overturned.

Bunda slowly rose to his feet again.

"Is anyone injured?" he asked, ignoring the cut on his own thigh.

Now that adrenalin had drained out of his body, Tadok relived every hit and cut with a vengeance. Still panting, he weakly raised his arm, and Bunda was at his side.

"You may be a bit concussed," he said, examining his head. "And your nose," he began, gingerly examining the half-elf's face with his fingers. Suddenly, he gripped his nose with his right hand and the back of his head with his left and twisted it with a sickening crunch. Tadok cried out at the unexpected pain, and fresh blood gushed out of both nostrils, but now he could breathe again.

"The tenderness of Seal Shore care…" he said hoarsely, wiping his nose and mouth with his sleeve.

Bunda hid a wicked smile as he passed his hand over the wound in his forearm, healing it with magic.

"Thank you," said Tadok as Bunda helped him up to a chair.

Nick was checking each of their assailant's bodies.

"They were Hayek's men!" cried Marven in fear and anger.

"gods, I should hope so," answered Nick sarcastically, without raising his eyes from his work. "Otherwise, this was a terrible way to greet new guests."

"Where is the rest of his band?" asked Bunda, peering out a window.

"It was only them. No one else rode into town," said Odetta.

"So, these were some scouts? Left behind to watch the village?" asked Nick.

Mica Mun shook his head. "No. They came in shortly before you arrived in the room, looking for you three."

"I told them ye'd'd already left, but they didn't believe me," said Marven in a pleading voice. "They threatened my Oddi," he cried, voice cracking.

"It's quite alright, master Darvey," said Nick, calming the old man down.

"And thank you for aiding us. Seirn knows, you probably saved our lives, and that took much courage," added Bunda.

The implications of this sank in. Marven, Odetta, and Mica had raised arms against Dell Hayek's men, and even personally killed two of them. Their lives were forfeit when the bandit leader returned. Odetta burst into tears and retreated to the kitchen. Marven looked at Tadok with a mix of apology and fear and followed his wife to calm her down.

Tadok turned to Nick and Bunda.

"Will we have a problem with them?" His eyes followed the innkeeper and he spoke in hushed tones and trying to avoid the bartender's ears. Mica seemed to be preoccupied with sweeping the shattered crockery behind the bar.

"You mean, will they turn their hide and sell us to Hayek when he returns so they can save themselves?" asked Nick. "It won't help them, and I think Marven knows that." He raised one of the untouched mugs of ale, sniffed it, and drank deeply, wiping foam from his chin.

"Besides," shrugged Bunda, "They wouldn't have taken arms against them had that been their intent. They could have simply let them finish us off."

Nick looked at the entrance to the kitchen with a worried frown creasing his forehead.

"We have bigger problems," he said. "These cunts were looking for us."

Tadok nodded in understanding.

"Then this tells us two truths," he said. "First, Hayek's men are camped nearby. Second. while probably not the Darveys, there is a *Silk* among the village folk."

Nick choked on his drink, and for a moment, the sound of sweeping of the glass and ceramics halted—then resumed as fast as it had stopped, making Tadok wonder if he had heard it at all.

"Why do you say that?" asked Nick, still coughing and sputtering ale.

"What is a 'Silk'?" asked Bunda at the same time.

It was clear the barbarian wasn't familiar with the term. Tadok sighed and explained.

"A 'Silk' means a spy or traitor in the Heartlands. We have been here for two nights, and Dell's men come hunting for us. They were trying to ambush us, which means that they knew we possess the means to protect ourselves. The only way they would know this is if someone in the village was selling his honor for something."

Nick seemed to consider this. He finally nodded.

"I think you're right, Tadok. But which one?"

There was a moment of silence as each tried to consider the people they'd met over the past two days and who could have turned on them.

"I could use the Divine-sight," suggested Bunda, "Malice can't hide from Seirn's eye."

Nick grimaced. "The problem with that is that you assume this was done with malice. The traitor could simply be a man or woman afraid for the safety of their family and the village. They could reckon that turning us in would be the lesser of evils. And I'm not sure lesser evils would count against your spell."

Tadok nodded. These people were afraid, not wicked. It could be Mendel fearing for his family, or Tilly thinking of her daughter. Or maybe even Aldeira, hoping against hope that Hayek's men would give her information about her son.

That gave him an idea.

"What if Christopher is alive and in the hands of Hayek's men."

The other two looked at Tadok, considering the notion thoughtfully.

"The way I see it," he continued, "The boy is either reluctant to return as he's still afraid, unable to return because he's dead, or unable to return because he's captured. The first seems unlikely."

Nick stood up.

"Well then, we have three questions to answer. First, if I were a band of fifty cutthroats, where would I hide."

"We're not going to look for the band of fifty cutthroats," Tadok stated flatly.

"Of course not. But knowing where a broken floorboard is saves a foot from splinters."

Nick continued his list.

"Second, who's been talking to Dell and his men? If we answer question number two before we answer question number one, we may be able to learn the answer to question number one."

"Lest not forget we still have to find the boy," added Bunda.

"Not forgetting," replied Nick quickly. "But I don't want to stumble on the bandit encampment if it can be avoided. I'm thinking perhaps whoever sold us to Hayek may know more than he or she's told us about the boy."

"What was your third question?" asked Tadok.

Nick looked around the common room.

"Where can we hide six bodies?"

***

"So once again, Marven and Odetta Darvey own the inn," said Tadok, trying out the list for the third time.

"Aye," answered Nick.

"Mendel and Theia and their boys do the cart runs to Sebin and Berin's Inn. He's the Baerstmann."

Nick nodded with a grunt, steering his horse around a fallen branch.

"Tilly is the tailor and Mara is the daughter."

"She also owns two cows, so she's also a 'milker'," added Bunda, trying to contribute to the conversation.

"Not helping," stated Tadok flatly. "And the correct term for that is 'dairywoman' or 'milkmaid'."

"That's a very confusing name for such an occupation. Mine is better..." mumbled the large barbarian stubbornly.

Tadok had no idea why this was so hard. He could speak four languages and read three of them. This should have been easy—but it wasn't. The names and the faces simply didn't align. He decided that he had passed through so many towns and villages in his journeys that learning names seemed to be a waste of time. Nick was the exact opposite. They had been there for a little over a day, and he knew every single one of them, including their occupation and relationship with their neighbors. Even Bunda seemed to be doing better than him. The most galling part of it was that he truly didn't want to learn these people's names and know them any more than he had too.

The problem was that for their plan to work, they all needed to know who each man and woman were as best they could.

"Alright, so Aldeira is Jen the sheriff's widow. Mica is the bar hand,"

Nick nodded, encouraging him to continue the test.

"Diggericut is the gnome, and Swegan is the dwarf. Yorgen is the old drunk, and Hanlan is the half-orc and Onlan is the smith," he completed triumphantly.

"Almost," answered Nick. "Onlan is the half-orc, and Hanlan is the smith. And you forgot Ren O' the River—the half-elf tracker."

"Oh, I remember the half-elf, Sandisan. We nearly fed you to the wolves rescuing him yesterday."

"Good," said Bunda. "Because we're here."

It had taken them two hours to dispose of the bodies. They had agreed to store them in the cellar of the church temporarily. Thankfully, the six brigands had left them six horses.

By the time they had returned to the village, they could clearly see that the citizens of Suldan's Bluff were preparing to leave. Windows were being boarded up and cartwheels mended. An atmosphere of tense anticipation was in the air. The only house which didn't seem to be preparing to leave was the sheriff's house. The windows were still covered in black cloth, and the fat candle was still burning.

"I'm thinking that poor Aldeira's neighbors may not have the nerve to stand behind their boasts anymore," said Bunda sombrely.

"Do you think they'll really leave her?" asked Nick.

Bunda shrugged, motioning to the bustling village folk as they packed up their livelihoods.

Nick nodded grimly. "Where I come from, they say that the largest balls shrivel when the cock gets kicked."

Tadok grimaced and turned to his companions.

"Have you considered that expecting them to stay by her side is a bigger evil? One born of both cowardice *and* folly?"

The two were surprised at the intensity of his words.

"These people prepare to risk their homes and travel these roads, which are lousy with predators—both beast and man. They do all this because the notion of Hayek's cruelty is worse, and expecting them to stay for one child is like asking the whole ship to drown to save one man."

He knew he'd somehow tangled up the metaphor by Bunda's raised eyebrow and Nick's look of confusion, but he didn't care. His point had been made.

He had been such a boy. How he had resented the 'Clems' of the village with their large families and loving parents. Even before he'd lost his mother, she had been ill. At the age of six, their roles had been reversed, with him caring for her as she slowly wasted away before his eyes. His village had been indifferent to their suffering. If it hadn't been for Sellwyn, he would have starved come winter or resorted to begging and thieving in Freelan. When Sellwyn had left him, he was alone again. That is, besides Dorkah.

The truth is that when all was merry in the world, people were generous and friendly. They shared, they protected, and they supported. Strip that away, and they would all turn into wolves.

No. That wasn't accurate. Wolves lived as a pack even when times were tough. Tadok tried to think of an animal in nature that turned on its herd, pack, or pride to protect itself, and couldn't. It seemed to be a human trait.

This lesson was one he had been taught and learned again and again. *You come into the world alone, and you leave it alone.* Rely on others—and be weak and vulnerable. The people of Suldan Bluff were no different.

By the time they reached the inn, it was already midmorning. They paused, standing in front of the large door.

"Five Corins says this turns out badly, Sandisan. That they chase us away from here or attack us. This is a terrible plan," said Tadok gloomily.

"I'll take your wager, half-elf. And this is a very *good* plan."

"I'm a terrible actor," replied Tadok skeptically.

Nick smiled wistfully. "I know. We've played cards."

Tadok shot him an angry stare. He still suspected the Heartlander had cheated in that game.

Nick widened his smile to show he was jesting.

"Look, all you have to do is act is as yourself. Glowering and sullen."

Tadok was beginning to regret agreeing to this, suspecting this plan had been laid out for his maximum humiliation.

"Exactly!" exclaimed Nick, pointing at Tadok's angry glare. And with that, he got off the horse salvaged from the bandits and entered the inn. Tadok and Bunda did the same.

Inside, the entire village was occupying the common room, which had been cleaned and set up again. Still, the signs of the fight were clearly visible. The bar had a large ugly notch in its center where an ax had lodged into it, and no amount of scrubbing had fully removed the dark stains of blood on some of the walls and the floor.

Everyone was here. Even Aldeira and Onlan were sitting next to Ren in the back. Onlan still clearly showed the scars of his ordeal, both in body and mind. While he seemed to be listening to the bustle and chatter, his eyes would often drift and gaze at nothing, then he'd squeeze them tight and shake his head to clear it when Ren or Aldeira would put a hand on his shoulder.

When the village folk noticed the three companions had entered the room, the murmurs and chatter waned, and the room was quiet. All eyes on them. Bunda moved over to the back of the room, sitting on the stairwell leading up to the second floor.

Marven nodded to them and walked over to the fireplace, which seemed to be the center stage in the room. He cleared his throat.

"Yer all here now," he said, addressing his neighbors. "So, about two hours ago, Hayek's men came back to the Lodge."

His sentence was followed with frantic whispers as the villagers began panicking.

Tadok surveyed the crowd to see if anyone seemed unsurprised by this information. Nothing conclusive.

"All right, all right...settle down ye lot," said Marven attempting to subdue the rising anxiety.

Nick stepped in.

"Allow me, Master Darvey," he came to stand by the innkeeper, who gladly yielded the floor to him.

"Marven Darvey is correct. We came down this morning only to be ambushed by six of Hayek's men."

"Gutless bastards!" swore Swegan the dwarf.

"As Trin's luck would have it, that was a big mistake on their part," Nick said grimly.

He made contact with each set of eyes in the room as if trying to make the point clear to every one of them. Tadok knew that underneath the facade, it was more about reading their reactions than conveying Nick's own. He finished his sweep by glancing at Tadok. Tadok gave him a barely visible shake of his chin.

Nick continued.

"There were six of the bastards. Heavily armed. They came at us with knife and sword. They didn't expect two things." He paused, as if for dramatic effect. Once again, he scanned his audience, finishing with Tadok. Tadok darted his eyes to Bunda, who made a subtle negative motion with his finger. *Stall.*

"They had no knowledge that we are armed with magic and that three members of Suldan's Bluff had the hearts of lions." He motioned to the Darvey's and to Mica Mun.

Odetta covered her face in her hands, and Marven looked embarrassed. Mica Mun continued staring at Nick intently.

The crowd's attention was now on the Lodge's owners and the bartender.

"Didn't think you had it in you, old man," said Hanlan, smiling slightly, punching him lightly with his beefy hand.

Mendel's wife—Tadok couldn't recall her name now—hugged Odetta for support, while he in turn gathered all five of his children closer to him.

"You're Magi?" squeaked Diggericut, looking at Nick with a look of wonder.

"Not I, but my friend Tadok is a master of the arcane and Bunda here is a chosen of the Dawn Father."

The crowd looked at Bunda with reverie and wonder and at Tadok with suspicion and fear. All except for Yorgen, his bleary, bloodshot eyes eying the door.

"Together with Mun and the Darveys, we put those dogs down. None survived," he said, once again pausing and scanning.

"Did you kill the leader?"

The voice was Mara's. Tilly's teenage daughter. Her eyes were hard as steel. Her mother shushed her in embarrassment.

"No. The coward wasn't here."

"Where are the rest of them?" asked the dwarf, Swegan.

"Where are the bodies?" asked Yorgen at the same time.

"Did you scare them off?" asked one of Mendel's sons.

Nick raised his hand to halt the barrage of questions. He glanced at Tadok and then at Bunda. Both nodded curtly. Now was the time to play their gambit.

"Those aren't the right questions. The true question is, who in Suldan's Bluff has betrayed us to Hayek?"

There was a moment of silent shock, and then the room erupted in commotion as the news sank in. Every citizen looked frantically around the room, trying to identify who the wolf among them was.

"One of us?" asked Mendel in shock.

"That's madness!" shouted Hanlan.

"Who would do such a thing?" asked Tilly.

"Fortunately," continued Nick, raising his voice over the din of the crowd. "We have a way to find out."

Like a herald, he extended his arm towards Tadok with a flourish.

"As a master of the unseen, Tadok can summon creatures of the Eld. This ancient magic will bring forth a Dorkah-Demon, which can sniff out deceit and treachery."

Tadok couldn't help the scowl that twisted his lips. No matter, it simply made him seem more menacing.

"None can hide from the Dorkah-Demon. It will sniff out the traitor, eat his flesh, and consume his soul. So, if any wish to confess now, you can save yourselves a painful death."

The audience looked at him and at Tadok in a mixture of fear and skepticism.

Bunda walked over to Mendel's wife and her children.

"Take the little ones outside now," he said in a soothing yet firm voice.

She looked up at him in surprise but immediately started ushering her children out the door.

"I want to see the Dorken-demon!" wailed a five-year-old as she yanked him out the door.

"Bullocks!" spat Yorgen, crinkling his veiny nose.

Nick locked eyes with the sour man intently for a moment. He then turned back to the rest of the room. Looks of skepticism turned to outright fear.

"Master Cartright, there must be another way," said Marven in a shaky voice.

"Unless the craven turncoat wishes to confess his sin—I see none. You needn't fear if you are innocent."

He turned to Tadok and nodded.

The entire room gasped as Tadok's forehead began to glow, and suddenly, the space before Yorgen which was empty a moment ago, was suddenly filled with the dark form of Dorkah.

Dorkah appeared with wide black eyes and an open maw, tongue lolling lazily. Panic filled the room, accompanied by screams and curses.

Tadok had often wondered what Dorkah's home was like. Was it a cave? Or an island? Or some unfathomable strange dimension where others of her kind roamed. But the Eith'lin's home, like her origin, was shrouded in mystery, even to him—her bonded soul. What he did know was that when she answered his summons, she was always happy to see him, filled with curiosity and excitement.

It took him a heartbeat to update her mentally on the situation and the plan. Be vicious, he silently commanded her.

Her disposition shifted instantaneously. She rocked back on her haunches, her toothy maw transforming into a menacing snarl, which was directed at Yorgen.

The man shrieked in terror and backed away. Dorkah edged towards him, step by step.

Gods we'd better be right! he thought.

"Stop this madness!" shouted the dwarf, drawing his battle ax.

Onlan was on his feet, drawing his own weapon, and Hanlan

stood protectively in front of his Tilly and Mara. Even Mica Mun drew a loaded crossbow from beneath the bar, aiming it at Dorkah.

This was going horribly wrong. Any moment now one of them would attack the Eith'lin or one of them, and this would become a bloodbath.

***

Bunda, like Tadok, had been against the plan from the start. Had he not fought beside the half-elf's beast in the past, he wouldn't have trusted it or the sorcerer. But Dorkah had proven time and time again that she was fiercely loyal to Tadok and would obey his every command. But even if Dorkah could be controlled, could they control the people of Suldan's Bluff? People in these remote hamlets and thorps tended to be superstitious. Add to that the fact that they had been through hell on earth over the last few days, including discovering that they had a hell-worshipping cultist necromancer masquerading as their community priest for the past few years. This was a very dangerous game Nick was playing.

But the Heartlander had convinced them both that they didn't have time to conduct a full investigation, and every moment that the spy in their midst roamed free, more information about them and the people of Suldan's Bluff was given to Hayek. At first, they had thought to try and bluff the traitor into revealing himself by claiming that one of the brigands had already exposed him before he died. But Nick pointed out that it was probable that whoever it was, his fear of Hayek's fury should he double cross him was far greater than any earthly threat they could make. Thus, it was time to use an unearthly threat.

During Nick's theatrical speech, they had all tried to read the crowd in hopes that the spy would mark himself by his reactions. They had agreed that only if all three of them suspected the same man or woman would they go forward with this plan.

The moment Yorgen started edging for the door was when he suspected. His question about the bodies boosted his confidence in those suspicions. Looking at both his companions, he gathered that they had come to the same conclusion.

But now, he could see how this plan was going sideways as the villagers drew weapons. Could they diffuse the situation without bloodshed? He wasn't so sure anymore.

Luckily, thank Seirn, he didn't need to find out.

Yorgen shrieked and backed up to the wall. Before anyone could say anything else, he turned to Tadok, pleading.

"I beg you! Get it off me! I didn't know! I didn't mean nuthin' by it!" he wailed.

Dorkah halted but didn't alter her threatening stance. Her black eyes still locked on the terrified man.

"Is there something you wish to tell us, Master Yorgen?" asked Nick calmly.

"I...I did it to save the village!" stammered the old man. "He said they wouldn't hurt us if I told them who cut down Jen Murley."

He dropped to his knees, tears streaming down his eyes.

"The Dorkah-Demon can smell lies, Yorgen," said Nick solemnly.

On cue, Dorkah growled and leaped at Yorgen, jaws opened wide. She halted inches away from his face, dripping saliva from her pointy teeth. Yorgen screamed in unbridled horror. The rest of the crowd stood frozen in shock at the exchange.

"Aye! I took their coin! But 'tis true that they promised to spare the village. I swear on all gods! 'Tis the truth, I beg you! Please believe me..." he trailed off, sobbing.

"And what of the priest? Did you know about him?" asked Bunda.

"No! I knew nothing of him, and neither did Hayek's men."

Nick and Tadok exchanged glances and then looked back at Bunda to get the barbarian's approval.

Yorgen was hugging his knees, sobbing. He was beyond lying. Bunda turned to the other two and nodded his own consent.

And just like that, Dorkah vanished.

The inn was awash in stunned silence. Then, before anyone else could react, Aldeira marched over to Yorgen and slapped him so hard across the face he toppled onto his side, shuddering and sobbing.

Ren was at her side, trying to pull her off the man, but there was no need. She retreated back to her seat, her furious eyes never leaving Yorgen. She said nothing.

At this inadvertent sign from Aldeira, the villagers came back to life.

"You fucking coward!" bellowed the dwarf.

"Craven fool!" muttered Hanlan.

Odetta was shaking her head in disgust. "How many times? How many *times*, Yorgen, did Jen save yer sorry arse? He even went all the way to Berin's Inn to trade coin for yer freedom after ye got yerself locked up a year ago! We all pitched the collection pouch for that!"

Diggericut vomited in the corner.

"You were one of us. How could you?"

"*You* should be swinging from the tree, you sack of sheepdung!" shouted Mendel, pointing at the door in the direction of the hangman tree. The villagers answered with scattered nods and grunts of affirmation.

Bunda stepped in, positioning himself between Yorgen and the crowd.

"You have a right to desire justice. But in the eyes of the gods, he's wronged us more than you. And revenge is not Seirn's way."

"Besides," added Nick. "He's got information to tell us first."

***

Half an hour later, the inn was cleared. The only remaining villagers were Maven and Odetta, Aldeira, and Ren–who was acting Sheriff.

They had bound Yorgen to a chair, but by the looks of him, he wasn't about to run. The encounter with Dorkah had scared the sourness right out of him, and all that was left was a shell of an old, broken man.

Bunda wondered what had made him so. He had heard it mentioned that his wife had left him years ago, but his bitterness had probably driven her off in the first place.

Marven had said that Yorgen's father had been an angry drunk himself. He had hated Yorgen as a child, being in his mind an inferior son to his eldest, who had died as a child. Growing up, he had known only rejection and beatings.

Bunda couldn't help feeling sorry for the man. Had he not had his brothers and his faith, would Garlan Ice Sale, his father, have molded him into someone like Yorgen?

He fiddled absentmindedly at his medallion as Nick conducted his interrogation.

So far, they had gleaned that the bandits had found Yorgen while he was checking on his apple grove, and the man had begged them to spare him if he gave them information. Bunda was sure that this was a lie, and apparently Nick and Tadok weren't believing it either. But whether his story was true, or he had actively sought out the brigands, the information was useful.

"So, this man, Eilah," said Nick, "He's Hayek's second in command?"

Yorgen shook his head, eyes on the floor. "No. His second in command is Sledder, Butcher of Themston. But Eilah is the man who I spoke to."

"The one with the snake tattoo," repeated Nick. "How much did he pay you?"

Yorgen mumbled something.

"I didn't quite catch that," said Nick, leaning closer to the old man.

"Twenty Corins," said Yorgen more loudly.

"Twenty Corins?" asked Ren incredulously. "You would sell us out for twenty Corins?"

"I wasn't selling *you* out, half-elf!" shouted Yorgen. "I was selling them out. Eilah said the village would be spared."

"And you believed him, Yorgen Thalesten?" said Adeira, piercing him with a withering gaze.

"These strangers had the gods-blessed decency to do what none of you had the courage to do. And even after, they could have left without entangling themselves with our business, but they stayed here to help find my boy, and you would sell them out for twenty sodding Corins? *Where's my boy!*" she shrieked.

"I don't know, Aldee. He wasn't there. I swear!"

'He wasn't there'. So Yorgen was at the raider's camp, thought Bunda.

"Don't you dare call me Aldee, traitor!" Aldeira looked like she would slap him again, but Nick continued his questions before she could.

"Where are they hiding?"

Yorgen paused, glowering at Nick defiantly. Nick leaned back in his chair and looked over to Tadok innocently.

On cue, the half-elf sorcerer closed his eyes, and his forehead began to glow faintly.

"The tower! The old tower!" yelled the old man hastily. He had no desire to see the Dorkah-Demon again.

Nick raised his hand to halt Tadok and looked intently at Yorgen. "How many of them?"

"I only saw ten. But they had a wizard with them and a huge half-orc. A giant of a man. The one they called 'The Butcher of Themston'."

"Good, Master Yorgen. You may be of use yet," said Nick, calming the man down. "What were they doing there?"

"I don't know."

Nick looked at Tadok again, who rose to his feet.

"I swear!" insisted Yorgen. "But..."

"Go on."

"The wizard was in a fit. He was shouting at one of them that, 'If Hayek knows any old dead languages, he should get his bloody arse over there and open the damn thing himself'."

"What was the wizard trying to open?" asked Tadok.

"I don't know. They kicked me out with the coins and told me to stay away from the inn in the morning. They said that Hayek would grant me favor when he returns."

Tadok drew his wicked sickle and advanced on Yorgen threateningly.

"It's all I know! I swear!"

"You've been doing that a lot, recently..." commented Bunda. His pity for the old drunk was being replaced by revulsion. Dell Hayek had no intention of sparing any of them. It was clear. When he found whatever it was he and his band were looking for, they would turn their attention to Suldan's Bluff. They would kill the men, make sport of the women, and kill the children. There was nothing for them of value here, and leaving witnesses was ill-advised, even in the lawless lands of Suldan-Karr. Yorgen was a foolish idiot for thinking otherwise. They'd take their twenty gold corins back from his dead corpse and laugh while doing so. Bunda knew raiders. He was raised by raiders. While the Tundrial had their own code of honor, which may have seemed odd to Mainlanders, they were hard people with little sentiment for disrupting and ending the lives of the villagers and townsfolk who had the misfortune of being their victims. Unlike Hayek's cutthroats, the Tundrial would usually take the women and children as slaves once the battle was done, and the defenders of the village had the fight viciously stripped away from them. It was the Tundrial way of life. A life which secretly brought shame to the young cleric.

Nick put a hand on Tadok's arm gently.

"I think that's all we'll get from this sorry sack of shit."

Turning to Ren, he asked, "What will you do with him?"

Ren, who had been quiet for the duration of the interrogation, chewed his lip, considering his options.

"Not sure. Truth be told, we don't have a jail or anything like that in the village. We've never had the need to cage men."

"I know of a cage," said Tadok quietly.

***

As Ren and Hanlan, the smith, lead the prisoner up the hill to the church, a crowd had already gathered outside. They watched in sullen silence as their life-long neighbor was dragged off to the cell which had only yesterday been a madman's torture chamber.

How their lives had turned upside-down. In the span of less than a week, three murders, one missing boy, one tortured member of their community, and two others who had proven to be not what they seemed. A traitor and a madman. Oh, and brigands and zombies to boot.

Bunda couldn't help admiring their resilience.

"So what do we know?" asked Nick, sitting on the barrel next to him as Tadok joined them. They were out of earshot of the others and thus took the opportunity to talk.

"We know you've sent us down a hell-path, Sandisan," said Tadok bitterly. "If the plan was to disappear east while the villagers head on their merry way west without Hayek knowing about us—that plan's a very leaky boat right now."

He wasn't wrong. There was no telling what Yorgen had passed on to the raiders. They hadn't made their destination a secret in the village, and according to Nick, it was clear Hayek had connections in Sebin. Furthermore, the old guard tower gave ample vantage across the road in both directions. It would be an easy feat for Hayek's men to ride down both themselves and the villagers when they saw them escaping town.

"Look at the bright side, half-elf," said Nick, not being baited into a fight. "We know there aren't more than four or six of them right now since we killed six. That means they won't try and attack before

Hayek returns."

"You haven't been listening, then," snapped Tadok. "They have a mage and some half-orc giant with them. What will you do when fire and brimstone rain down from the sky on you?"

Bunda looked across at the old broken tower in the distance. He could only imagine the bandits surveying the village, searching for their dead friends. Did they see the horses carrying the bodies up the hill? Were they planning an attack that night? It was barely an hour's ride down to the village. If they had, they would have probably charged in. Unless...

"They can't leave the tower."

Both Tadok and Nick looked at him.

"Why is that?" asked Tadok.

"Because if they could, they would have by now. They are under orders to hold the tower and search for something. Actually, the wizard is under those orders. And Hayek doesn't seem to be a man whose orders are lightly disobeyed."

Each one of them was considering his words, so he continued.

"They know that six men couldn't kill us. Their companions haven't returned, so they know something's amiss. Which means their best option is to bring more men. But they must not have enough to punish the village and to hold their post and carry out their task. So, their only choice is to wait until Hayek and the rest of his men return. So it isn't fifty bandits. There must be fewer than ten in the fort."

Nick suddenly took on a sly smile.

"Are you sharing my thoughts?" he asked the barbarian.

Bunda considered it. He hated the idea that Hayek and his men would go unpunished. And if he were correct, and there were only half a dozen of them, perhaps with careful planning they could strike at them from the darkness. On the other hand, there were still more unknowns than knowns in this. Before he could decide, Tadok shook his head heatedly.

"Absolutely not!" he said harshly. "Yorgen is a drunk. We don't know truly how many men there are and when Hayek is returning. Besides, if you are concerned about his rage and retribution about us burying the sheriff or even killing his men while defending ourselves— imagine the ends of the earth he will chase us to if we raise a sword against his stronghold. And all this without truly knowing how powerful that mage is."

His eyes were blazing. He was furious. While Nick had managed to sweet talk him into agreeing with his plans for the past two nights, it was clear the half-elf sorcerer had reached his edge. And while Nick was a capable swordsman, and Bunda had Seirn's blessing—it would be suicide to attack the tower without Tadok and Dorkah.

"We leave *tonight*," he said in an uncompromising tone. "Under the cover of darkness when the tower can't see us. The villagers should do the same so they may get as much ground between them and these Shadder Hands before Hayek returns. If you are correct, barbarian, then maybe, *if* Trin loves them, that is, they can reach Berin's Inn before he butchers them."

The three stared at each other in tense silence for a full minute. Finally, Bunda nodded, conceding that this was the best of all options. Not because he feared the three of them couldn't take on the bandits in the tower or even the danger of attempting it alone with Nick. But looking at the villagers, he realized they were all in mortal danger if they didn't leave that night.

That left the matter of the boy.

"We still haven't found the child," he said with a sigh.

"And sadly, I suppose we never will," answered Tadok. He was still angry, but he softened his voice an inch.

"We did everything we could. We endangered our lives, not once, not twice—but thrice trying to find that boy. This is where the search ends. If not for our own sakes, then for theirs," he said, pointing at the villagers scattered about the green.

Nick sighed in resignation. For once, this was an argument he couldn't win.

"I best go talk to the widow and let her know we've failed."

"No, not you. Him." He pointed at Bunda.

Nick began to argue, but Tadok raised a finger to stop him before any words left his mouth.

"Every time you talk to one of the villagers, you somehow get us into further trouble."

"You're exaggerating," began Nick.

"Am I? You have a kind heart, Sandisan. Trust me, it is a weakness, and one day it may get you killed. And I want to be nowhere near you when it does."

Nick's eyes flashed in anger, and he was about to retort, but

Bunda stepped in.

"I don't think a kind heart is a weakness, but he's right. It's best I speak to her."

When Nick seemed unconvinced, he looked at the sky. "Look, 'tis still five or six hours until sundown. Why don't you continue the search? Even if you don't find a living boy, a dead one may still offer her some solace."

He turned to Tadok. "You should speak to Marven and Ren. Explain to them that they need to leave tonight if they are to have any chance of escape."

In agreement, the three men split up.

As Bunda walked over to the widow's house, he thought of the first time he'd been sent by the temple of the Dawn Father to console a griever. Death was treated differently in the isles. Tundrial who died in battle were celebrated as heroes. Boys were taught not to cry for their fathers and wives, and mothers would often do their weeping alone or with only their closest circles. People were expected to return to their lives within three days of mourning. But what happens when they don't?

In that case, when the pain was too great for an individual to withstand, the responsibility for support fell to the faith. The Seal Shore Isles had a number of those. First, of course, there were the spirits of land and sea. Those were represented by the druids—a faith so old its origins were linked to the first humans to ever settle the isles—thousands of years before Nem's arrival. Then there was Geiless, Mistress of storms and oceans, also known as the Sea Bitch. Being seafarers, the Tundrial gave the larger slice of the faith pie to her. Then there was Teil-Kah, Lord of Crops and all things which grew. He was the patron of the harvests and of children, so his popularity was obvious. Trin the Wanderer was next—since who wouldn't want a god of luck on your side? And finally, Seirn, the Dawn Father.

Seirn was a relatively new faith in the isles, only going back one hundred years or more. Seirn was a blatant contradiction to the ways of the Tundrial. He was god of Justice and Defender of the Innocent. Something that didn't always fit in with the way of life of the Seal Shore barbarians, who were infamous for laying waste to the western coast. However, Seirn's teaching didn't forbid battle. Even battle for gain. The Seven Doctrines of the sun god, which were the backbone of the faith, forbade harm to children—which the Tundrial would avoid in any case—and promoted valor. In addition, the clerics of Seirn were the best healers, which the Tundrial valued greatly. Bunda attested the rising popularity of the deity to the coming of a plague which had washed over the islands fifty years earlier. According to the accounts, Seirn's healing was said to have saved thousands. His faith had gained a place of honor in the Seal Shore Isles ever since.

Two years ago, a longship had been dashed against the rocks in a storm, sinking to the bottom of the Silver Ocean. Most of the crew managed to swim to the safety of Tarthen's rocky shores, but one man–the captain didn't make it. There was nothing unusual about that in and of itself. The sea claimed many Tundrial every year. But what *was* unusual on that day was that the captain was a follower of Seirn.

Bunda had known him in passing, seeing him in the temple, giving tithes and prayer to the sun god before setting out to sea. So naturally, he had attended the funeral with the High Herald of Light, the head of the temple.

After two weeks, the man's ten-year-old son came to the temple, claiming that his mother would not eat or drink or sleep. She was wasting away. The boy was the eldest of a family of six children, and without their father and their mother, the family would be doomed.

The High Herald of Light was on a holy pilgrimage to Darakeila in Shard, and the Master of Rays was ill, so the task fell on the shoulders of Bunda of the Jams, who was the eldest of the initiates.

Bunda had been terrified. He rehearsed his words the whole way to the mourner's home, but when he entered the house, he'd forgotten all of them. The small house was in disarray. It was obvious that the mother had been useless over the last two weeks. The captain must have been too poor to own slaves, as none were in sight. The dishes were dirty, the pantry was empty, and the crying toddler of barely two years of age was clearly sitting in her own soiled clothes.

Instead of saying a word, Bunda had collected the crockery. Gathered firewood for the hearth. He then drew water from the well for drinking and rinsed dishes and children in the nearby stream. He spent the rest of the day fishing, gathering fruits and nuts and cooking for the family. By their ravenous hunger, it was clear that this was the first meal they had had since the well-wishers had left. At night, when all the children were fast asleep, he found the widow sitting on the porch, gazing at the waves crashing on the beach below.

He was about to wish her well and be on his way but instead decided to sit by her side in silence. Only for a moment. The moment became ten minutes, which stretched into thirty and then an hour. He never said a word, and never moved from her side. Just watching the waves as they washed over the sandy shore in the moonlight.

Finally, after that hour, she spoke, and Bunda listened. She began to talk about how she and her husband had met. About how she had been terrified to tell her father he had gotten her pregnant before they were wed. She talked of how nothing ever scared her husband, and he would make jests which would always make her laugh, even during the most serious of times. She spoke of how he had attempted to make a treehouse for their son, but it had crashed on top of him. Bunda said nothing of his practiced lines. He just asked questions, smiled when she was reminiscing, and laughed when she told a funny story. When dawn broke, so did the widow, and she sobbed into his shoulder for a full hour. When the sun's rays broke over the horizon, he pointed at the growing golden disk. He had told her that her husband was with Seirn now. He instructed her to close her eyes and asked her if she could feel her husband's touch on her cheek in Seirn's warming rays. The widow smiled and nodded. She was at peace.

The next week, she and her six children arrived at the temple to give prayer to Seirn. And they did again and again every week until Bunda's last days on Tarthen. The woman had found employment as a kitchen maid in Korey Red-Coral's hall, and her eldest son had been initiated into Seirn's temple last year. She'd never spoken again to Bunda, but every time he saw her, the gratefulness in her eyes was apparent.

After that, the High Herald had seen that Bunda had a gentle touch with mourners, and he had been sent again and again to comfort those in need. Despite the grimness of his new duty, Bunda never resented it. Giving guidance to those whose lives had been crushed was one of the most noble callings the young cleric could imagine.

And now, he stood outside Aldeira's house. He took a deep breath. Muttered a prayer to his lord and knocked on the door.

16 DENIZENS OF THE DEEP

It had taken Robin two hours to search the groves south of the village, and by the time he returned, he was thirsty, sweaty, and muddy.

He had crawled into a cave, which was scarcely more than a crack in a rock, hoping to find the boy, but it was in vain. Not wanting to give up, he continued into every gully, climbed over every rock outcropping, and even waded into a muddy pond, ambivalently hoping to step on a body.

He couldn't put his finger on why this obsession with finding the boy had taken him. The Robin who had run with the Shadder Hands wouldn't have made such a fuss–especially considering the perils they had faced and the ones yet ahead if they didn't get themselves the hell out of Suldan's Bluff.

When he closed his eyes, he imagined the boy lost and afraid. Was he huddled on a tree branch? Was he stuck in a ravine? Was he even alive? The boy must have been in such terror seeing his beloved father and brothers murdered before his eyes.

He had seen his brother murdered before his eyes. The Hugh brothers were also three. He'd abandoned his elder to die and his younger to whatever fate awaited him.

The boy is not *Tommy,* he scolded himself in his head, shaking it.

As he arrived at the green, he could see that Tadok's warning had been heeded. The villagers were completing the task of packing up their entire lives into whatever they could carry on their backs and were getting ready to head to the east under the cover of darkness.

By now, all men and many of the women were armed. Daggers, wood-cutting axs and bows, in addition to some of the weapons which had been carried by their would-be assassins that morning.

Good, he thought. Even without the brigands at their backs, the road ahead held many dangers.

Bunda, who was helping the villagers draw buckets of water from the well, saw Robin coming over and nodded to him. He offered him a ladle of water which Robin, took thankfully.

"No success, Nick?"

Robin simply shook his head. "But he has to be out there somewhere," he insisted in frustration.

Bunda looked at him with pity but said nothing.

"Don't look at me like that, Journeyman." He scowled. It was enough he had the Half-elf's judgment to contend with; he didn't need the barbarian's as well. "I know he's most likely dead. But at the least, I need to find the body."

He motioned to Aldeira's house, which was the only house in the village not showing the signs of preparation for departure.

Bunda shook his head sadly. "She won't leave, Nick. She wants to be here in case he returns," he shrugged.

"Well, I guess I can't fault her," said Robin. "What mother would intentionally leave her child?"

A surprising look of pain crossed the Tundrial's face. As if he had been slapped. Robin wondered what ghosts he was hiding. Had the barbarian left a child in the Isles? Weren't Journeymen celibate?

He was wondering whether to press the subject as he lifted another ladle of water to his lips, but something caught his eyes before he drank. A glint of metal dancing in the water. He poured the content of the ladle into his hand, catching the small tin circle. The flat circle wasn't much larger than a coin. Or a badge.

He looked up at Bunda sharply, then tossed the ladle aside and peered into the darkness of the well.

"What is it?" asked the barbarian, looking over Robin's shoulder into the well.

"This badge. What does it remind you of?"

"That's a badge?"

"Not a real one," said Robin, trying to peer into the darkness. All he could see was the reflection of the water. The well was deep. "More like what a father would give to his boy so he could play at being a deputy."

Bunda's own eyes widened as he understood.

"Stand aside," he commanded.

As Robin obeyed, he clasped his medallion and pointed into the darkness below.

A miniature sun-ball appeared above the water, illuminating the cavernous deep.

The pit below the well was much larger than the man-made pier above. From their vantage point, they could see the walls of the cavern.

"Can you command it to move around?"

"No. It will only shine where I point it to when I cast it."

Robin cursed under his breath. That gave him an idea. He leaned into the well and cupped his mouth with both hands.

"Hello!" he yelled with as much volume as he could muster. When no answer came, he tried again. "Cristopher!"

People were gathering around them.

"What did you find?" asked Ren. Bunda handed him the tin disk. He held it up to the sun, inspecting it.

Moments later, most of the village was there, shouting into the darkness of the well. However, it was no use. Even when Aldeira called to her son, only silence answered back.

The three companions stood at the back of the crowd grimly. The odds of finding the boy alive lowered as the odds of finding a body rose.

Robin caught Swegan by the shoulder. "How deep would you say that cavern is?"

Dwarves knew caves just as well as elves knew forests, and Tundrial knew the sea.

Swegan stroked his salt-and-pepper beard in thought. "The pit's about twenty feet. And the water's about six or eight feet deep in the center."

"Really?" asked Tadok. "I'd expect that by the end of summer you'd have drained most of it."

"This well ain't a water pit. There be an underground stream that feeds it."

He smiled at Tadok's look of surprise. "The Suldan is old. The very spine of Trosia. You humans seem to think that there is nothing of value under your feet. For every stream and pond you see above ground, there is twice that below."

"I'm not fully human," shrugged the half-elf.

"Hah! Elves are even worse," he laughed and went back to peering into the well.

They watched the people of Suldan's Bluff in silence for another moment.

Then Tadok spoke, "You know what must be done…"

Bunda nodded. "I'll do it," he said, stripping off his seal-fur cloak.

"No, it's better I do it." Robin sighed. "I'm the better climber."

"Oh yes, we've seen," answered Tadok with the hint of a smile.

Robin grinned. "Well, at least if a branch breaks, I'll have water to meet me below this time."

***

Half an hour later, with a rope tied to his mid-section, Robin started scaling down the well, with the village witnessing it in anticipation. The afternoon shadows from the mountains replaced the warming rays of the sun and Robin wasn't too eager to meet the cool waters below—especially after drying from his wade in the pond. He nodded to Bunda, who clasped the rope with both hands, followed by Ren, Onlan, and Hanlan for support, and began his descent.

He wore a cap provided by Tilly, on which Bunda had cast another light spell so it would illuminate the darkness in the direction he turned his head. He took a moment to fasten it on his head and looked down. The water reflected on his unnatural light as his hands and feet tested out the protrusions in the uneven brick wall. While Bunda and the townsmen may have been carrying his weight, Robin couldn't bring himself to let go of the wall completely. It simply went against his own survival instincts, so the descent was slow going.

About halfway down the well, the brick masonry gave way to a large underground grotto. The handholds disappeared with the walls as they widened around him.

"Lower me down!" he called up to Bunda, who complied as he began slowly sinking down to the water. Whether due to the exertion, the tension, or the humidity, he was sweating buckets under his cap.

Careful not to move too much, he surveyed his surroundings in the darkness. The cave was about twenty feet in diameter at its widest, and the floor was entirely submerged in water. Now underground he could hear nothing but the constant tempo of dripping water from the stalactites which lined the uneven ceiling.

He stared intently into the water as his boots broke the surface and shivered as water seeped in through the lining. Suddenly, he dropped six feet with no warning, plunging him into the cold, dark water.

Panic gripped his heart as he clawed at the rope, sputtering and gasping for breath in the cold darkness.

"Sorry Nick!" Bunda called from above. "Are you alright?"

The rope was now tight again, and Robin tested the waters, relieved to find hard—yet muddy—rock beneath his feet.

"I'm unhurt!" he called back up. He avoided the urge to look up at Bunda, for he knew that in doing so he would render himself blind to the darkness for a moment as his eyes adjusted to the murk. Years of sneaking around at night had taught him that light could illuminate, but it could also blind you. If used correctly, a clever thief could use the same light to make himself invisible to the people who were trying to use it to see him.

Now that he was on solid ground, he waded through the dark waters, doing his best to penetrate their dark surface with his magical light.

A three-day-old body, unless weighted, would be floating by now as gasses bloated the decomposing corpse. Robin was somewhat relieved not to find the floating corpse of the child. As he shined the light from his cap around the cave, he noticed something that didn't reflect it the same way as the water and stone walls did. He waded over to the wall to fish it out of the water.

It was an overcoat. A *child-sized* overcoat, he thought as he held up the soaking-wet garment. He then noticed a fissure in the wall, which must have been the source of the water which Swegan had mentioned. It was barely a crack, but a small child, having removed his waistcoat, could have squeezed through.

He shone the light into the dark crack. The narrow tunnel beyond disappeared into the water. The only way to explore it was to dive after squeezing into the crevice—which he couldn't do.

"Fuck!" he cursed, slamming his wet palm against the smooth unyielding stone. He stood there in frustration, water up to his armpits lapping at his chest. There was nothing he could do.

Suddenly, something brushed his boot under the water, and he jerked back instinctively.

He wasn't alone in here.

Drawing his rapier, he began backing up to the center of the grotto, rotating from side to side, trying to detect further movement.

There! Something broke the water surface to his left. It was large and only six feet away from him. He slashed at the water and at the invisible creature, his breath coming in shallow gasps, as fear threatened to engulf him.

"Bunda!" he yelled without looking up. "Pull me out!"

The rope, which had been slack to allow him to explore, began uncoiling in the water as Bunda and the others started slowly pulling it back.

There it was again. This time ahead of him. A scaly, slick torso lazily cut through the waters again. Whatever it was, it was no fish.

"That thing's the size of Dorkah," he muttered. Scanning the water franticly, he yelled, "Hurry, Bunda!"

He felt the tug of the rope as he was lifted off the floor of the subterranean pool slowly. Far too slowly.

The water rippled again–this time behind him. Robin jerked around, trying to face the creature. It only served to initiate an undesired slow spin as he hung from the rope.

"Stop your dancing about!" yelled Bunda from up above. It was clear from his tone that dragging him up was more of an effort than lowering him down.

His boots finally emerged from the surface, showering well water in their wake.

He was nearly three feet in the air, gently spinning above the water, when the creature erupted from the dark pool in a spray of water.

In the light, with his magical cap, he saw it, and it wasn't the size of Dorkah.

A serpentine torso, a foot wide and over eight feet long, its neck ending at the triangular head shot out of the water. Its white, milky eyes topped a narrow maw lined with rows of nail-like teeth, which were gaped impossibly wide and aimed directly at Robin's face.

Robin yelped in terror and slashed his rapier at the thing, slicing a gash in its smooth snout, knocking it aside. It dived angrily back into the water.

"Bunda! Hurry the fuck up! There's bloody deep eel down here!" he screamed. In response, he began rising in faster jerks.

He had never seen a deep eel before beyond a painting on the side of a ship in the docks at the harbor in Sandisan. Half legend, the salty sailors of the Ailtel talked about them with fear and reverence. The tales told of hellish creatures that were ten feet long and could leap over small boats, dragging unfortunate sailors to the depths of the inland sea. Robin had always assumed that these were tall-tale exaggerations. Until now.

The water erupted behind him, and Robin tried to twist around, but it was too late. Powerful jaws clamped over his left leather boot, yanking him three feet down to the dark water.

Pain lanced through his foot as the eel's teeth sank through his leather sole into his flesh, and he shrieked in horror and pain, stabbing down at the creature.

Was an eel's bite venomous? His panicked brain tried to recall the stories he had heard as he thrust his sword down at it frantically.

The pressure from the rope around his midsection from his companions trying to lift him to safety with the additional weight of this monstrous water serpent was so tight he feared his spine would break. That is if the creature didn't kill him first.

Hanging there in the darkness between the black waters and salvation, with the monster latched on to his foot thrashing about in the water, fear gripped him like never before. His mind racing, trying to remain calm enough to escape his dire situation, Robin had an idea.

He stabbed down again, but this time aimed for his boot buckle. His slim blade fit snuggly under the buckle, and he ripped it forward with all his strength. The leather strap gave way, and his boot, along with the eel, dropped back into the water with a large splash, and he was wrenched upwards. Unfortunately, his sword slipped from his slick hand and somersaulted into the dark pool.

Bootless and dripping blood and water from the hole in his stocking, he watched as the creature thrashed and thrashed in frustration below, trying to sink its fangs into its prey again. But he was too high up for it now.

As he was lifted into the light, he never stopped watching the waters as they calmed, the nightmarish predator below finally realizing it had lost its meal.

Strong arms gripped him, yanking him over the lip of the well and into the evening's air. Robin collapsed on the grass, panting.

He looked over at Bunda, who had collapsed beside him. His hands were raw and bleeding, and his face was red with the effort of dragging Robin and his undesired passenger up.

"This village—" began Robin, who paused, coughing. "This village never stops giving," he muttered mirthlessly.

***

"Stop fidgeting, Nick, you're not a little girl," said Bunda sternly, smearing a salve provided by Aldeira to his injured foot.

"I don't understand why you're rubbing that foul slime on me. Can't you simply magic the wound shut?" replied Nick, sniffing at the ointment.

Bunda paused. "My lord's healing has closed the wound. Mostly. But it doesn't seem to fully heal the flesh. Perhaps Deep Eels *do* have venom in their fangs. The ointment needs to be rubbed into the wound for it to work."

"Think of the advantage, Sandisan." Tadok smiled. "It could have gone after your balls."

"Well, I wouldn't be rubbing *that*, then," stated the Tundrial cleric flatly.

After a moment's pause, the three simultaneously burst into laughter. The joke wasn't very witty, but the tension, fear and frustration all let go at once, and Tadok was grateful for the shared mirth.

Perhaps it was because he was feeling guilty about allowing Nick to spelunk the well alone. He practically shamed him into doing it. Or maybe it was that they were finally leaving that made him a little giddy.

The laughter faded into a few sporadic chuckles, and Tadok could see the disappointment in Nick's eyes.

"Nick," he said, with all the tenderness he could muster, "we did what we could. And at least we've brought a measure of comfort to the widow. She now knows of the fate of her boy and can mourn him. Far away from here."

"We didn't find the body," said Nick stubbornly, but he did so without looking him in the half-elf's eyes. He was defeatedly accepting that there was no way a boy of ten would survive in the den of such a predator. No, Christopher Murley had hidden in the well and dropped into it. He'd then found his end in the jaws of the Deep Eel. Tadok hoped it had been swift. Whether it was or wasn't, the boy's strife was over, and his spirit could now be laid to rest. It was a tragic end, but an end, nonetheless.

A knock on the door disrupted the conversation. Bunda stood and loosened his saber while Nick reached for his rapier, only to remember he'd lost it in the well. Cursing, he drew his dagger, then nodded to Tadok.

The half-elf put an ear to the door, and when he heard nothing, he opened it a crack. He peered into the hall, almost missing the child-sized gnome standing there. He gently swung the door open.

"Yes, Master Diggericut?"

The gnome was wringing his hands with a mixture of tension and excitement. "I did it!" he announced, bypassing Tadok and entering the room.

It was clear by their blank expressions that they had no idea what the gnome was talking about.

"The runes, I fixed them. Well, *fixed* isn't the most accurate term, but I factored the age of the tree and its standard growth and where the runes would have been back when the tree was young, using the first letters as anchors." He stood there beaming like a street magician who'd completed his trick and was expecting applause. When none came, he exclaimed, "They formed words, Master Tadok. *Words!*"

"What did those words say?" asked Nick, curious.

"Well, I don't know *that!* It's *Shadowtang*. But you can read it," he pointed at Tadok, "right?"

Tadok had to admit he was curious. He'd believed the task of realigning the wording on the totem tree would be impossible or at least take a lifetime of work and it would remain a mystery. He'd heard gnomes were masters of engineering and other academic pursuits, but the sheer geometry of the task was daunting. And Diggericut had deciphered the puzzle in a day.

"Let's see it, then," he commanded.

Diggericut produced a folded sheet of hemp paper from the recesses of his apron. The creased page was littered with tiny schematics and calculations, scrolled in the gnome's miniature handwriting. He flipped it over, and among the mathematical equations, a single verse was evident.

Tadok scanned the page, his fingers following the letters and words. He then flipped it ninety degrees, running his finger on the words again.

"Shadowtang is written from top to bottom?" asked Bunda, curiously.

"Sometimes. It's a two-dimensional language," replied the half-elf.

"Whoever spoke it or wrote it had a different mind, unlike that of humans or elves or dwarves."

Tadok was about to begin reading it when a thought nagged at the back of his mind.

"Master Diggericut," he began. "These ancient Karr who lived here. The ones who scrawled these letters and used totem trees..."

"The Terrodites," supplied the gnome.

"Yes, these Terrodites. Why would they write in *Shadowtang?* Wouldn't they use elven or dwarven characters, like other Karr nations?"

The gnome eyebrows knitted together, and he scratched under his cap. "I've been considering this myself. The answer is yes. They should have written Karr's words in elven, probably. In fact, the other totem trees discovered all had words in Karr. No mention ever of *Shadowtang* in any of the accounts."

"Why would they defile their holy shrine with such a foul language?" asked Bunda.

"That's still a mystery, but perhaps the content which was written will shed light on the matter," suggested the Diggericut hopefully.

Tadok shrugged and flattened out the page near the candle on the desk and forced his mind to bring forth all he had learned of the ancient language from Sellwyn.

"'*Know...men of the...earth*' or land, perhaps," he read hesitantly. "I don't know *that* word. But here it says, '*Malaketh is lord of sky...of land, of sea and of...mountain. He will take*' or maybe it says *claim* something. It's unclear."

Truth be told, it was a marvel he could read any of it. If they were correct and the author of this ancient text had carved it so many centuries ago, logic dictated that it was removed from whatever the Shadowtouched spoke and wrote in present day. On the other hand, as opposed to Nemtang, the language spoken by the humans of Trosia in the past, *Shadowtang*, or "Shadow Tongue," was spoken by a race that lived for hundreds of years. Sellwyn looked in her thirties by human standards, and she had once confided in him that she was over two hundred fifty years old. Perhaps their tongue hadn't shifted the way that of the shorter-lived humans did. He read on silently, then paused.

"The next bit seems unrelated. And unclear."

"Well, go on, half-elf," said Bunda in anticipation.

Tadok took a breath and cleared his throat. *"Blood, flesh, bone, ash...death'.* That's all of it."

There was a moment of silence as the three men and one gnome digested what they had heard.

"Is it a ritual?" asked Bunda at the same time as Nick asked, "What's a Malaketh?"

"I have no answer to either question," he shrugged.

"Very curious," said Diggericut. "Perhaps the wise men of the Enlightened Academy in Sebin can decipher the meaning," he suggested hopefully.

"We'll be sure to consult with them when we complete our journey to Sebin," said Tadok. He reached for his coin purse. "How much do I owe you for your service, Master Diggericut?"

The gnome seemed confused, then waved Tadok away. "No coin needed. I love Suldan's Bluff, but opportunities for such scholarly challenges are rare and far between. This exercise was pure joy!" he said clasping his hands in glee.

"If this place is so boring for you, how does a scholar such as you find himself here?" asked Bunda.

"My focus. I'm a *geologist*," he stated.

"And what is that, pray tell?" asked the Tundrial.

"I study rocks."

"Doesn't that make you a dwarf?" snorted Nick.

"No," the gnome laughed, "although many of the best text and information about rocks comes from dwarven accounts, my study is more academic in nature."

"What could be so academic about rocks?" asked Bunda. Being island dwellers, the Tundrial had never been miners and had either traded or raided for their metals and precious stones. Tadok assumed Bunda's knowledge of the components of his own saber were as lacking as Tadok's own knowledge of seafaring.

"Rocks are fascinating!" The gnomes grinned. "And it isn't only about rocks, but also the study of mountains, and caves and the movement of the earth."

"The earth moves?" blinked Nick.

"Well, yes—what did you think earthquakes were?", said the gnome.

"Earthquakes are Obe's rage," said the cleric, referencing the god of war.

"I've heard that earthquakes happen when the dwarves dig deep and tickle their god," shrugged Nick.

The gnome laughed at the last. "Whatever the cause, the Suldan mountains are plentiful when it comes to the quakes. More so in the past. I suspect a very large quake, the kind which breaks mountains, happened in this very spot about two thousand years ago. I've been spending the last few years trying to prove my findings and send them to Sebin."

Tadok glanced out the window. It was already dark. Outside on the green, he could see Mendel and his family packing as many supplies as they could on their cart, and Hanlan had boarded up his shop and was staring at it forlornly.

"Speaking of Sebin, it's time for us to be on our way, and for you, Master Gnome. I am grateful for your help and wish you success in your study of...rocks," he said.

The gnome nodded and bid his farewell.

"Gnome?" called Nick after him. "Would you know where I can find an unused boot?"

***

Packed and ready to go, the three made their way out of the inn. They had to make a quick stop at Tilly's, which Diggericut had recommended as a footwear solution for Nick.

The green was a bustle of activity, as the people of Suldan Bluff readied themselves to abandon the village. Mendel and Odetta Darvey were staring at their Inn, both silently weeping.

Ren was hugging Aldeira's shoulders as she finally agreed to leave her home and her tragedy behind. Tadok couldn't imagine the maddening grief that must have engulfed her. By the absent stare in her eyes, she had a long journey ahead of her.

Onlan the half-orc stood to the side, a longsword on his back. He was carefully guarding Yorgen, who they had mercifully decided to take with them to Berin's Inn instead of leaving him to the mercy of Dell Hayek, which he probably deserved, thought Tadok.

Diggericut was chatting with Swegan, the dwarf, who was talking about the ancient-looking battle ax the dwarf held in both hands.

Mendel and his family had packed their cart, which held most of the supplies for the journey for the entire village. The little ones sat on top of it while their mother hushed their excitement.

They made their way to Tilly's cottage, but just as they were about to knock on the door, it swung open, and the seamstress burst out of it.

"She's gone!" she wailed and collapsed in Bunda's arms. "Mara's gone!" she sobbed.

"Gone where?" asked Swegan rushing over.

"What happened?" asked Bunda.

"I spent the afternoon delivering cloaks to everyone for the journey. Warm wool for the cold nights. When I returned, she was nowhere to be found. She also took her da's hunting bow and ax. She went to the tower!" she cried in anguish.

"Calm down, Tilly. How do ye know that be her destination?" asked Marven, trying to calm the weeping woman.

Tilly pointed with a shaking hand to the open door to her cottage with a shaking hand. Tadok frowned as he read the words carved into the wood.

Justice.

"Damnit!" cursed Nick. "That silly girl."

"How long since you saw her?" asked Tadok. Perhaps they could catch her before she made it to the tower.

"The hearth's cold. At least three hours," said Tilly, breaking down in sobs again.

Yorgen chuckled evilly, and Onlan smacked him on the back of the head to shut him up.

The whole village was looking at them hopefully. Again.

Tadok was about to shake his head in refusal when Nick grasped his arm.

"Private council," he said softly and drew Bunda and the half-elf out of earshot of the rest.

"We don't have a choice," he stated grimly.

"You're not the one to decide when I have choices, Sandisan," replied Tadok angrily.

"The things they will do to her! Have you no heart in that cold half-elven chest of yours?"

"Aye, I have a heart. I also have a head between my pointy ears, and I seem to use it more than you!"

"This village has suffered enough!" he growled, raising his voice.

"But not by our fault!" answered Tadok, raising his own voice.

"It *is* my fault!" Nick shouted.

Bunda put a large hand on each man's shoulders. "Hush the two of you!"

He turned to Nick. "How is this *your* fault?"

Nick sighed, looking at his feet.

"Yesterday, she came to me asking if we were going to kill Hayek. Apparently, she had fancied the sheriff's eldest son. I spoke rather harshly to her, hoping to avoid the very event that has happened. I never believed she would actually be foolish enough to do it," he finished shaking his head.

"It makes no difference. She made her own choices," said Tadok stubbornly. This village seemed fixated on destroying itself.

"I'm in agreement with the Heartlander this time," said Bunda quietly.

Tadok turned on him, about to retort, but Bunda cut him off. "Tadok, there is a difference between a dead boy and a living girl."

Tadok scowled. "She's already reached the tower by now, which means she's already dead. So, the comparison remains the same."

"Bunda is right. They will take their time with her, and as horrible as this sounds, it gives us time to rescue her."

The thought made Tadok shudder. The marauders had definitely reasoned by now that the three of them had dispatched their companions that morning. Their frustration at not being able to leave their posts and exact their revenge on them would be taken out on the sixteen-year-old girl brutally. Still, getting the three of them killed wouldn't save the girl.

"And you think three men can take on the remaining bastards in the tower, and their mage, *and* their giant of a commander?"

"Four men." The voice was that of Ren, who had silently joined their party. "Besides, I know these lands better than you three. I can get us to the tower undetected."

Onlan silently stepped forward to join them, but Ren put a hand on his large chest gently. "No, my friend," he said. "Not this time. You're the last defense the village has. You need to get everyone to the safety of Berin's Inn."

Had the half-orc had a tongue, he may have answered. But the silent exchange between the two friends surpassed words. Finally, Onlan stepped back, nodding.

Tadok threw his hands up in exasperation. He threw his pack to the ground and slung his crossbow over his shoulder, counting the bolts in his quiver.

"What are you standing about for, then?" he growled at them. "Let's get this over with. And Sandisan," he looked at him, not sure if he wanted to curse him or slap him. "Get some fucking boots!"

17 SENTRIES

Under the shadow of a half-moon, the four of them hiked up the winding path to the tower. The night sky was shrouded in dark clouds, which made the way even more treacherous. They dared not light a lamp or a torch for fear of becoming a beacon for whatever watch the bandits had set in the tower. From time to time, Ren would stop and look at a footprint or a broken branch or an overturned stone.

Bunda cursed under his breath after stumbling for the fifth or sixth time. He couldn't help the jealousy creeping into his heart at that moment for Ren and Tadok's sight. It was known that elves, like dwarves, could see in the dark, and that the trait was passed down to their offspring—even the half-bloods. He wondered why the gods had blessed the two races with long life and improved senses. Or perhaps the question is why they had cursed humans. An average dwarf lived three or four times the lifespan of a human, and elves closer to five times. His training had taught him to trust in the divine, but it would be nice to be able to see more than the outline of Nick's back as they made their way in the darkness.

He cursed again as his boot slid on a slick rock, and Ren stopped ahead of him. He couldn't actually see the half-elf, but he heard him, and ahead Nick halted in his tracks. After a moment, the ghostly figure of the hunter approached them, motioning them to come near.

"These tracks show where she left the path, probably in hopes of avoiding the eyes on the tower—which was smart," he said, pointing at nothing that looked any different to the barbarian's eyes. Then his voice became grim. "And these tracks show that she was being followed by a man."

"So, they did see her," surmised Nick.

"Perhaps that is better," suggested Bunda. "If she attacked them from the shadows, they may have killed her on sight. If she was detected before she could strike, there are better odds she's been captured and still alive."

On the other hand, a single assailant could have overpowered the girl, raped her, and slit her throat, not wanting to share his prize with his fellows. The thought was too grim to voice out loud, but he knew they all had shared it.

They pushed on leaving the path behind, following both sets of prints, as a bitter cold rain began lightly falling to the ground. The drizzle made the foliage and earth beneath their feet slick and hazardous, and Bunda kept his eyes focused on the ground, counting on the two half-elves to warn them of any danger ahead.

The tower now loomed before them. A black foreboding obelisk darker still than the night behind it. It was too dark to make out its features, beyond the shape of the curtain wall surrounding it and jagged peak of the tower where the upper floors had caved in.

Ren had stopped again and pointed at it silently. Now that he focused his eyes, he could discern a dim flickering light which glowed softly over the top of the wall, confirming that this was the bandit's camp and base.

"I can't hear anyone. Perhaps Trin favors us and they're deep in slumber," suggested Tadok. "If we can surprise the mage and the half-giant, we could have a chance."

"He's no half-giant, just a man. A half-man, half-orc, to be precise," said a voice behind them and Bunda spun around drawing his saber in a fluid motion and peering into the blackness behind, eyes wide.

"Put away your swords. I have a crossbow bolt trained at one of you, and you know not who, so it could be any of you."

After a moment, a shadow stepped out of the trees they'd passed a moment ago, with a loaded crossbow in hand. Before Bunda or any of the others could act, he lowered it to his hip and raised his other hand to show he wasn't intending to make good on his threat.

"I wondered where you were, Mica Mun," Said Ren.

"And had I had my way, you would have kept wondering Ren O' the River."

Mica Mun stepped into the little light they had from the moon.

Bunda could barely see his features.

"I have my own business to attend to in Sebin and was intent on taking my leave," continued the mysterious bartender. "Unfortunately, I saw Tilly's girl making her way up to the tower with the dangerous combination of stubbornness and foolishness. Both afflictions of youth."

"And?" asked Ren taking a step forward. "Why didn't you stop her?"

Micas had the decency of looking ashamed. "She was too far ahead, and the guards spotted her. Foolish girl tried to fight but was easily taken."

"Is she alive?" asked Tadok, and Bunda wasn't sure which answer he wanted to hear. The consensus in their party was clear. Dead children, they could leave, and living children must be retrieved.

"She was, as far as I saw," he said, and Bunda heard Nick let out his breath in relief. "The bandits jeered and laughed at her attempts to fight, saying something about the fun Dell would have with her. Which means with any luck, that her honor is still intact, as Hayek hasn't returned from his errand. If you hurry, you may still have a chance to rescue her."

"'You'?" asked Ren suspiciously. "And where are you going, Mun?"

"I told you; I have other affairs."

"I never took you for a coward!" snarled the hunter harshly, taking a step towards the man. As he did, steel flashed in the night as a long knife appeared in Ren's hand. But before he could reach the bartender, he stopped in his tracks as the crossbow was suddenly aimed at his chest.

"Lower your voice, you fool!" he whispered harshly. "Unless you want to announce yourself to Hayek's men."

Bunda had his sword raised again before he could think about what he was doing. He didn't think Mun was a coward. He'd acted on his own initiative in the bar that morning, taking out one of the bandits with only a broken bottle. He couldn't see his face, yet he was pretty sure that fear wasn't the emotion that he wore at that moment.

"You can't shoot all of us, you bastard!" growled Ren, but he stayed where he was.

"I don't want to shoot *any* of you," replied the bartender calmly. "So don't force my hand."

When Ren finally relaxd, he lowered the crossbow again. "I've been standing here for an hour debating what to do. I have no wish to see harm come the girl, yet I can't risk my own mission."

"And what mission is that?" asked Tadok. "How do we know you aren't in league with Hayek? Waiting to betray us once we move on the tower?"

"Because I would have killed you already if I were."

"Or perhaps you stumbled upon us, knowing full that while you may be able to take one of us out, you'd be dead before you could draw another bolt. So the wiser path would be to act the friend and fool us while alerting the tower."

Mica Mun was silent as he stared at them. His face was a dark shadow in the night, with two pinpoints of light where his eyes reflected the moon.

"Or perhaps Yorgen isn't the only greedy bastard in Suldan's Bluff. When you learned about Yorgen, you realized there were Corins to be made by selling your honor and friendship, and you crept up here like a thief in the night. Then Trin smiled upon you by delivering the four of us into your hands, offering you the perfect gift for Hayek." By the time Tadok was finished with his theory, his whisper was so harsh it was barely a whisper at all. Bunda was grateful for the falling rain, which must have masked the noise of their exchange.

But Tadok's accusation made sense. And Mica wasn't refuting it. He edged slowly to his right, hoping that Mica was as blind as he was in the darkness. Striking with his saber would draw too much attention. But he did have a spell which could cause him to lose his concentration for a moment. Enough for them to reach him before he could let the bolt fly.

"So now you're a Silvermane?" asked the bartender, referencing to the King's Secret Police.

"No. But *you* are."

Bunda's spell stuck in his throat as he turned to look at Nick, the source of the allegation. They all did.

In the moonlight, Nick seemed to hesitate, as if he hadn't meant to say what he did. He sighed, closing his eyes in resignation.

"That's why your mark didn't feel right. It was a counterfeit. You could never get the proper combination of clay into it the way they do in the Undercity. And that's why you said you'd tried to warn Sally," he said, ignoring their stares. "Reigar had told my brothers and I that the Silvermanes tried to warn Sally about Gale. That was you, wasn't it."

"You better start making sense, Sandisan," said Tadok, his own crossbow was out.

When Mica answered, his chuckle was tinged with cruel mirth. "A fine ally you've backed yourself into, lad. Push forward and share secrets, retreat and lose trust."

"What's he on about, Nick?" asked Bunda in confusion.

Nick turned his face up to the moon. As he did, Bunda could see the frustration on the man's wet face. He hadn't meant to speak, but now he could no longer take his words back.

"His name isn't Nick," Began Mun. "It's—"

"Robin," said Nick, "Robin Hugh," he said quietly, squeezing his eyes shut.

"Talk," commanded Tadok, his crossbow now trained on his Heartlander companion.

"Before I do, know that I haven't lied to you."

Tadok snorted. "I think you lied to us the moment you introduced yourself."

"Well, yes, I did that. But from that point I've told you only the truth," he said, then looked away. "Yet not all of it."

He took a deep breath. "I told you my brother was murdered by Gale the Boon and that I'm seeking my younger brother Tommy as I fear he's in their clutches yet again. What I didn't share was that at the time of my brother's murder, I was one of them. A Shadder Hand. As were my brothers."

As he spoke, Bunda clutched his medallion and uttered a few whispers in the Divine. He blinked his eyes, so the others wouldn't see them flash as the Divine Sight augmented his normal eyesight. When he opened them again, the night was as dark as it had been. But now he saw the auras floating around each of the other four men, like ghostly palls.

Ren O' the River's aura was strong. An aura of peace and tranquility. Tadok had the angry, conflicted aura he'd had when they'd met nearly a month ago. There was rage and pain there, but no malice or ill will. Next, he scanned Mica Mun. The aura around his was cold and calculating, yet underlaying it all were the telltale colors of duty and loyalty. Not to them, but perhaps to the crown. Finally, he focused his magical site on Nick, or Robin or whatever his name was. His Aura was a maelstrom of pain and fear. Of regret. Yet under it all was an overwhelming aura of the need for redemption. As if only *that* would abate the pain he felt.

"Five years ago, there was a civil war within the ranks of the Hands. Gale's faction won and purged any who were loyal to the old guild master. My brother included."

"And we should trust you now?" asked Tadok. "Perhaps your goal is to return to the graces of this Gale, in hopes that he will return your brother."

"No. I swear it by any god you put faith in, Tadok."

"That's good enough for me," shrugged the Tundrial, sheathing the blade and turning back to the tower. He couldn't see Tadok, but he could imagine the incredulous stare aimed at his back.

"You're not serious, Tarthen!"

"How many times has he fought by your side, half-elf? How much blood has he shed in the last two days alone?"

Tadok was at a loss for words.

"Whatever his past. Whatever his true goals—they pose no threat to us." He glanced at Nick, the man he'd fished off the dirty floor of a tavern in Berin's Inn when they met. "You have my trust, Nick. I mean Robin."

Even in the darkness he could see Robin's look of gratefulness, and the emotion was mirrored in his aura.

By Tadok's exasperated sigh, he knew that it was settled.

"Where's Mun?" asked Ren suddenly, in alarm.

In the interchange, the bartender, who was actually a secret king's spy, had disappeared into the darkness.

"You needn't worry about him. He has his own mission to carry out," said Robin, searching the night.

"Then let's get this over with. We've been standing here clucking like a bunch of chickens for far too long," said Ren. He began walking to the tower again, his bow in hand.

The three pressed on into the rain and shadows. Ahead of them, loomed the old guard tower ominously.

***

Making sure he was out of the others' line of site, the man on top of the wall yawned as he lowered his breeches and began urinating into the bushes below. When he finally emptied his bladder, he shook himself as men do to get it all out. Then he shuddered and gasped as Robin's dagger silently drew a dark line across his throat. Robin's other hand cusped his mouth to stifle any noise. When the man stopped struggling, Robin quietly lowered his body over the wall into the puddle of both blood and urine he'd just made below.

He crouched motionless for a moment, testing the night for any commotion which would indicate that the man's companions had heard. When none came, he nodded at the rest of them who silently scaled the wall, gathering behind a cracked stone wall which was still partially intact. They were out of the attacker's field of view, and Robin carefully peeked around the corner.

Five of them. Two were having a conversation near the main building, and three surrounded the main campfire, which was located in the center of the courtyard, sputtering and popping in the light drizzle of rain which fell consistently throughout the night.

He took in the upcoming battlefield. The tower had seen better days. In its prime, the tower would have stood three or four stories high, with a curtain wall surrounding a courtyard which was forty paces across, housing stables, a smithy and an outhouse.

The tower had collapsed in on itself, leaving only the lower floor intact, and the stables had been reduced to a pile of stone and wood. The smithy still stood, but its roof had partially caved in. As for the outhouse, well, as the guard he dispatched had demonstrated, the entirety of the ruins was now the outhouse.

The main tower was built over the northern curtain wall, and to its left sat a strange contraption which had seen better days.

A Nemirian scorpion, mused Robin. Robin had seen plenty of them on the walls of Sandisan and in other cities in Nemir. A single scorpion could launch a spear through a horse or pierce a shield, a plate armor chest piece, the human encased in it and finally come out the back plate. But looking at its broken bow and odd angle, Robin surmised that it would be immaterial in this fight.

"Okay, seems like we can execute the *second* plan," he said, referencing the attack options they'd discussed on their way. "But I don't see the half-orc or anyone who looks like the mage."

They nodded in unison and crept to their positions.

Unstrapping his bow, he looked sideways at his companions. Ren had knocked an arrow, and Tadok carefully winched back the bolt in his crossbow. Bunda leaned his saber on the low wall and grasped his medallion.

Taking a deep breath, Robin nodded, and four things happened all at once.

The silence was cut by two bow twangs and one sharp clack from the crossbow. Ren's arrow hit one of the two men near the door in the chest and Robin's planted itself in the second man's stomach. Tadok's bolt was less successful, thudding into the rotting door behind them.

The central fire suddenly surged into a fiery blaze twice its size, and the three bandits sitting around it yelled, stumbling back and shielding their blinded eyes.

Before they could regain their senses, Dorkah pounced out of thin air, landing on one of them and clamping down her jaws on his face.

One of the other two screamed as his companion, regaining his sight, lunged at the Eith'lin, rapier stabbing. His lunging stab glanced her skull, leaving a slim cut on her scalp, narrowly avoiding her eye.

Robin wasted no time. Dropping his bow, he leaped off the wall and landed nine feet below. As he did, he rolled forward deftly, regaining his feet at the same time as he drew his dagger. It reminded him of his days hopping from rooftop to rooftop in Sandisan with his brothers and he didn't even notice the grin which split his face from ear to ear.

Behind him, Ren had also dropped from the wall, followed more slowly by Bunda. Tadok was already setting another bolt.

The man who had screamed had recovered his senses and attacked Dorkah with a short sword. Dorkah rocked back on her haunches, avoiding the clumsy slash and leaped at the man slashing him with razor-sharp talons, forcing him to retreat.

Robin had reached the man with the rapier. The man noticed him and slashed at him with the slim sword. Robin ducked under the blade, feeling it split the air above his neck by an inch, and lunged upwards with the dagger, burying it in the man's ribs. The man staggered and tried to bring his sword to bare, twisting away from

Robin. Robin shot his left hand out, catching the bandit's wrist and preventing him from pulling it back for another strike. They wrestled like that for another five seconds, and then the man's knees buckled, and he crumpled to the ground.

Across the campfire, Dorkah and the other guard were slashing at each other with sword and claw. The bandit was backing away from her, his teeth clenched. Dorkah suddenly charged again, and the man yelped and dodged away, but not before the Eith'lin drew three red slashes across his left arm. The man screamed in pain again and slashed at Dorkah's back. But his strike was blocked by Bunda's saber with a loud ring of steel.

Bunda stepped forward, and raising his left fist, he punched the man squarely in the face. The man staggered back, shaking his head, and Bunda used the opportunity to plunge his curved blade into his heart, dropping him instantaneously.

Leaping over the body of the man Dorkah had killed, Ren reached the man who had been the recipient of Robin's arrow. He had his back turned and was clutching the shaft protruding from his gut and fumbling with the door handle, hoping to retreat into the safety of the building. Ren leaped at him, locking his left arm around his throat as he plunged his knife repeatedly into his chest, spattering blood across the door with every stab. He released the man who slumped against the door…which suddenly flew open with enough force to launch the dead man three feet away and knock Ren to the ground.

Out of the door frame emerged a huge behemoth of a man, crouching to avoid hitting his head.

He was obviously of orcish blood with incisors slightly protruding from his lower jutting jaw and a sloped bald forehead. His skin had a grayish tint, and he was easily over eight feet tall. He wore only breeches, and scars crisscrossed his hairy chest. He wielded a long-shafted ax in ham-sized fists.

Ren scrambled to get out of his way, but as he rose, the large half-orc kicked him squarely in the ribs, sending him sailing forward six feet away. Ren groaned in pain, weakly rising to one knee.

Instead of advancing on them, the half-orc surveyed the courtyard as two additional bandits armed with short swords came out of the door and took positions on either side of him.

"So what's this then?" he asked in a booming voice. "Come to get your little chit back?"

Taking the rapier from the dead bandit, Robin came to stand protectively over Ren as Bunda took up his other side. Tadok, who'd come down from the wall, joined them.

"Aye. So how about we avoid the bloodshed, and you hand her over to us," he said, feeling none of the bravado he was trying to convey.

"Stall," whispered Bunda next to him, out of earshot of the half-orc and his cronies.

Robin grinned at the large man. "You must be the wizard we keep hearing about."

"Wizard, he says!" roared the half-orc in laughter. "Not close, little man, but don't you worry. I can magic you into a pile of guts with this," he said raising his ax.

Robin smiled slyly. "You know, we had the pleasure of slitting the throat of another half-orc mean fuck like you this morning. Any relation?"

The half-orc's visage shifted visibly, and his eyes darkened beneath his protruding brow.

"That was my brother, you little maggot," he growled. "And don't you fret, I'm a much meaner fuck than him!"

And with that, he charged at Robin, ax raised high above his head, ready to cleave the Heartlander in two.

Robin tried to get out of the way, but the half-orc's reach was too long. He heard Bunda shout something in the Divine and felt more than heard the rush of air behind him, and a shadow was cast over him in the flickering light of the campfire. Bunda's saber swung above his head, locking with the large ax in a jaw-clenching clang.

Dodging out of the way, he glanced at the cleric. He was still the same, but he had grown nearly twice in size, standing a full head taller than the half-orc. He stepped forward with a long stride and slammed his shoulder into the half-orc's pig-nose. Blood spurted out his nostrils as the cartridge gave way, and the half-orc took a step back defensively.

Robin didn't even pause as he leaped at the brigand on the left, stabbing at him with his newly salvaged rapier. The bandit managed to swat the sword out of the way and lunged at him, opening a bloody gash in his shoulder.

On the other side of the courtyard, Ren and Tadok were

engaging the other guard. Ren was still clutching his likely broken rib, teeth clenched. The man's attention was on the hunter, keeping him at bay with his longer weapon. He slashed the back of his hand, forcing Ren to drop his knife and shout out in pain. Tadok took the opportunity to slice low with his sickle from the man's flank, catching the bandit below the shin. It wasn't enough to penetrate man's leather leggings, but it did allow Robin to trip him directly on to Ren. Both men went down cursing.

Meanwhile, the half-orc had gotten over Bunda's magical growth spurt and was hacking mercilessly at the Tundrial Cleric. Bunda was losing ground, backing up towards the campfire.

Bunda's lucky break came when the half-orc swung too wide, and he stepped forward stabbing him in the shoulder. The Half-orc bellowed in pain and slammed the shaft of his ax into the side of Bunda's head. Bunda staggered back, kicking the fire's embers in a shower of sparks. He swayed drunkenly as the half-orc, blood dripping from his broken nose, charged at him, roaring.

Just then Dorkah pounced out of the shadows, landing on the brute's back, all four sets of talons sinking into his flesh and latching the Eith'lin onto him like a cat.

Robin couldn't observe Bunda's fight anymore as his own opponent charged him with his short sword. He dodged the thrust, only to receive the man's knee in his stomach, knocking the air out of his lungs. Doubled over and coughing, he twisted as the man tried to stab him again with his blade. He feebly managed to raise his sword, and the bandit's stab glanced off it, narrowly missing his ear, but opening a mean gash in his other shoulder. He staggered backward and drew his dagger with his left hand. The bandit grinned at him and stepped forward, fainting right, then left.

He's toying with me, he thought. Well, he knew how that game was played. He stepped back weakly, his sword hand swaying. He blinked back the sweat from his eyes as blood ran unbridled from his two shoulder wounds. His enemy grinned and went in for the kill. At that moment, when his opponent swung his sword to hack his head from his neck, he quickly brought his rapier up, blocking the swing and plunged his dagger into the man's eye. The bandit shuddered once and then slid off the blade to the ground.

He assessed the rest of the scene around him. Bunda was swaying like a drunkard as blood dripped down a long gash in his scalp, matting his hair and blinding his right eye. Luckily, the giant half-orc was preoccupied with Dorkah. He swung from side to side, trying to reach the smaller Eith'lin, but she was too well centered between his shoulder blades. He backed up towards the curtain wall and slammed Dorkah between his muscular back and the crumbling stone wall. To Robin's surprise, Dorkah held on, only digging her claws deeper into his back.

To his right, Tadok managed to unfurl Ren from the bandit, and before the latter could rise to his feet, he pulled his hair back and slit his throat as the man tried in vain to twist out of his grasp.

The half-orc changed tactics. He suddenly grasped his ax in both hands and flipped the ax head upwards. Robin immediately knew what was about to happen but was too late to stop it. He heard Tadok scream 'No!' as the half-orc swung the ax over his head at his own back, burying it deeply into Dorkah's back, a few inches left of her spine.

The Eith'lin howled in pain but stubbornly wouldn't let go. The Half-Orc tried to rip the ax out of her, but it must have been lodged in her ribs. By now he was losing strength and blood for the half a dozen cuts in his back, and he dropped to one knee, panting.

Robin sprinted towards the wounded half-orc, but Tadok got there first, slashing his sickle across his exposed stomach. The curved blade tore a long gash in the half-orc's fat belly under his navel, and blood spurted out, followed by the giant's intestines, which began to unfurl out of their rightful place. He gave up his ax and covered his ravaged stomach with one hand, slamming his other into Tadok's chest, causing the half-elf to double over in pain and drop to the ground.

Robin made the rest of the way to half-orc. He sidestepped the man's second punch which was unfocused and weaker than the one which had felled Tadok, and plunged his thin blade into the exposed section between his neck and right shoulder. Robin kept thrusting it down into him until it was half-way to the hilt, piercing tissue, muscle, lungs and finally exiting through his left ribcage. Blood sprayed from the half-orc's mouth as he exhaled his last breath, and he fell face forward to the ground in a widening pool of his own blood and viscera.

Robin panted and checked on Dorkah. She ignored him and limped over to Tadok, who painfully adjusted himself to a sitting position. Axe still lodged in her back like a strange mast in a ship, she nudged her smooth snout into Tadok's neck.

"*Tadok...*" she gasped.

"You did good, girl," he said, running his hand across the smooth black hide. He looked up at the ax and winced. "Yes. It's time to rest."

"*Rest...*" rasped the Eith'lin gratefully.

He didn't make a move or utter any spells, but Dorkah suddenly vanished. The bloody ax dropped to the ground where the Eith'lin had been a moment earlier.

"Will she be alright?" asked Robin, helping the half-elf to his feet.

Tadok nodded. "She heals in her own realm. But it does mean we won't have her services for the rest of the night." He looked at the open door of the tower, frowning.

"I hope we won't need them," said Robin and began walking over to Bunda, cleaning his newfound sword on the cloak of one of the dead bandits on the way.

"We still haven't met the wizard," he said uncertainly.

Bunda had shrunk back to his original size as Ren sat him down, his back to a wall.

"How is he?" asked Robin.

"Concussed," answered the hunter simply.

"And you?" asked Robin, motioning to his ribs.

"A few broken ribs. No worse than your shoulder."

Robin had forgotten about the shoulder wounds, but now that the adrenalin of the fight was waning, the searing pain had returned. He crouched down next to Bunda, who had his eyes closed.

"Hey Bunda!" he called loudly, "I need my cleric friend." Bunda's eyelids snapped open, and he tried to focus on Robin, but his eyes kept rolling back.

Ren reached into a small pouch he carried with him. "I have something for him," he said, extracting a small vial. "A small gift from Aldeira."

"I'll open his mouth," suggested Robin.

"His mouth? You want to kill the man?" asked Ren. "This is *Soin* Sauce."

He opened the small vial and gingerly placed it under the barbarian's nose, allowing him to smell it. The effects were miraculous, and Bunda snorted and opened his eyes wide, fully conscious.

"Amazing! It actually works," marveled Robin. He'd heard of the dwarven concoction which could wake anything which wasn't dead but had thought it was an exaggeration told by bartenders and drunks.

"I think an ox kicked me in the head," he muttered, wincing as he touched his scalp.

He raised his hand to his head and whispered a few words as the wound healed miraculously, leaving only the drying blood on his hair and face.

He rose to attend to the others just as the rain suddenly began pouring heavily.

"We'd best continue this inside," warned Robin.

The four of them hobbled into the darkness of the tower.

18 BROTHERS

During the golden age of the empire, Suldan-Karr had been a relatively peaceful province. It was dominated by vast planes and fields, surrounded by the Suldan Mountains to the east, the Shield Mountains to the north, and the Silver Ocean to the west. Farmers from villages and homesteads paid tax in the form of coin or food-rent to the center of power which was seated at Culidge. There, the Ducal family of Markine ruled dynastically for generations. Sure, they had to fend off raids from the Orcs in the north, but they were few and sporadic. The Tundrial, even the Seal Shore Barbarians, had been relatively pacified turning raid into trade, mostly.

But the war had taken its toll, transforming Suldan-Karr into a chaotic no man's land. It began when the Tundrial overthrew their overlords, returning to their raiding ways. They had then turned their wrath born of centuries of subjugation on the mainland and on the inhabitants of the mainland.

At that time, Emperor Murishad Arkine had died, and before the crown prince could take his place, he was assassinated on the way to his coronation. Thus, the Empire cracked in what was later known as the War of the Broken Crown.

The Empire sundered, with the duchies of Larka, The Wetlunds, Netheer and then Arga declaring independence and ejected the Nemirian government from their lands. Lord Timothy Talon, who had claimed the crown of Nemir through an old dynastic (and somewhat dubious) link to the House of Arkine waged war against the empire's former vassal states and provinces. He had no men to spare for the lands to the west as the Tundrial invaded. They had pillaged, looted and destroyed any town or city which tried to raise sword or bow to them, as they made their way along the Road of Triumph, finally being defeated at Sebin. After that, they retreated to their island homes with the riches they had plundered and the slaves they had taken.

The War of the Broken Crown had left Suldan-Karr a ravaged land in which every city or town was on its own, fighting to keep alive from winter to winter, and struggling to pay homage or ransoms to the Seal Shore Barbarians. The shrunken land of Nemir, now ruled by Talon who'd changed his name and title to Emperor Justice the Fourth despite being the the only man to call himself 'emperor', having lost four-fifths of the empire, simply did not view the broken Suldan-Karr as lands worth fighting for. Not with his more dangerous neighbors to the east, plotting.

And in the bastard lands of Suldan-Karr, there was no place better to disappear in than Berin's Inn.

Originally a halfway inn sitting entrepreneurially on the Triumph Road it straddled a fork between Culidge to the west, and Sea View to the south. Over the years, it had grown into a bustling border town for merchants and travelers crossing the Suldan mountains. The last point of civilization before journeying into the mountains, and the first a traveler would find when he emerged from them.

It was here that Robin found solace in anonymity after leaving Dilal and his brother. Work as a sellsword was always to be found, and faces changed so often that no one took a second glance at strangers.

It wasn't that he could call it home, so much as he could remain numb to his past, spending his days working for the merchants and traders and his nights drinking and whoring.

No one had recognized him except once, when he'd run into Kodiander from the Lion's Theatre. It had been in a crowded street, and he had watched as the small man was about to be knifed in an ally by a band of teenage ruffians. He'd come to his defense, scaring off the boys. If Kodiander hadn't been in mortal danger, he would have avoided him, but he couldn't let a man who'd been kind to him die in a dirty ally.

Kodiander had insisted on paying him for saving his life, but Robin refused. He knew that if he gave the performer any hint that his sword was for hire, he would have insisted to hire him as a bodyguard, and that would have brought too many painful questions and memories of Tommy and Dilal.

He'd settled for allowing Kodiander to buy him a meal and a few drinks, and they talked for a while. Robin advised him that should he make his way through Berin's Inn again, he should spend his nights at an Inn named the Dark Candle. The inn was guarded, belonging to the mayor's family, and the lice population was relatively low. Worth the extra few sorins.

He hadn't seen him again. Perhaps his experience in Berin's Inn brought him to avoid the town all together.

One day, he'd returned from a job north of the town. It was a band of orcs that was harassing a few villages near the mountains, and he'd joined a group of fellow mercenaries hired to drive them out. The orc band had been thirty warriors strong, but the mercenary platoon had surprised the orcs at dawn, scattering them to the winds.

He was sitting in a private corner of the Black Candle, counting his pay, out of eyesight, when June Ashly, the bartender walked over to him.

"Nick, a rider came in last night with a letter for you."

The words didn't seem to make sense to Robin. Who knew him beyond the sellswords and mercenary bosses in the town? Was it another job? Bosses and recruiters didn't send letters to find hired muscle.

"The rider said he came from Sandisan and was apparently paid handsomely to deliver it here as it was his only cargo."

Sandisan. This was beginning to look suspicious.

"He only parted ways with it when I described your person to him."

Robin realized June would continue talking until he paid her to keep silent. Well, that's what he got for counting his coins in the common room of an inn, even one such as the Candle which he patroned often. He should have known better. Instead of continuing to berate himself, he handed the her a stack of five Sorin's to keep silent. When the woman left, he looked at the letter.

It was folded neatly and tied together with string. There was a wax seal which was unbroken in its center.

He raised it to his nose and sniffed it. Paper, horses and…it was faint, but undeniable. The scent of lilacs. He'd known only one woman to wear such perfume, and it was etched into his dreams of her.

He dropped the letter onto the table as if it had turned into a hot ember. He looked around the room to see if anyone had noticed him do so. When he was satisfied that he had his privacy, he gently broke the wax seal and unfolded the letter.

Dear Nick,

I hope this letter finds you. I thought Trin's luck would favor me if I used your selected name. I met Kodiander a few months ago and he told me that you could be found in Berin's Inn at the Black Candle Inn. He said you're still the noble soul he knew, but he didn't explain why.

I know we didn't part on the best of terms, and I imagine you wish to be left in peace. I hope you're as happy as Tommy is. Your brother truly loves you. And he misses you, although he isn't likely to admit it easily. You Hugh brothers are of the same stubborn mold.

I want you to know that we're living in Sandisan and aside from our Son, Garian, we also have a daughter—Egwen. Both Tommy and I tell them stories of their uncle and how the two of you saved me from the goblins. I pray to the Four that they will meet you someday.

However, I write to you under less happy circumstances. A week ago, Tommy disappeared. I searched every corner of the city, but no one has seen him. Then a juggler friend of mine told me that he had seen Tommy with men of ill repute at the docks several times over the past few weeks. He'd seen him with Shadder Hands.

Unbelievable, thought Robin. *How stupid could you be, Tommy! First, you return to Sandisan, and then you actually return to Gale's court?* He read on.

Tommy had never said a word to me. He was always so careful to use our chosen names and avoid any contact with the Hands, so I'm shocked and confused, Nick. And scared.

I don't know what he's gotten himself into, and you're the only person I can think of turning to.

I beg you to come to our aid. If not for your brother, then for me. And if not for me, then for your nephew and niece.

You can find us above the bakery at Lark's Corner. The one that sells the black bread.

I beg of you to come quickly.

Yours truly,
Dilal Hugh

Dilal Hugh. Perhaps she had thought that signing off the letter with that name would awaken familial love, yet it only awakened the pain he'd numbed over the past two years.

And what could he do? It must have taken at least a month to reach him with this letter, and it would take him another month to reach them if he left today. He may rush to the capital of Nemir only to find Tommy in the loving arms of Dilal with his two kids on his knees. The image was bitter and filled him with anger. Then another image, the alternative image, filled him with dread. If Tommy hadn't returned by now, what chances were there that he even still drew breath?

He shook his head to clear the thought out of it. No, he was too far away and still, apparently, too bitter to take action. *You cooked this stew up yourself, Tommy,* he thought. *You eat it alone.*

***

When sleep refused to come that night, Robin decided he needed reinforcements to combat the inconvenient insomnia.

He wasn't in the mood for the Candle's more upscale clientele. He needed to drown his sorrows in a booze dive.

The one he had in mind was at the south side of town, near the wall. The ale was strong, and the women were cheap. Maybe he would play dice, or maybe he would get in a brawl. Both seemed appealing to him as he walked down the dark muddy streets. Few out and about gave him a second look. Just another bravado with a sword.

As he entered the *Stuck Pig*, the place was already bustling with the bottom-of-the-barrel of Berin's Inn's society. The ceiling was obscured with a mist of smoke accumulated from dozens of tobacco pipes and from the firepit in the center of the large room.

A dark skinned Xayel from the Dark Marshes was playing a flute while his wife or sister danced to the drunken jeers of the patrons. Serving woman were doing their rounds with platters filled with frothing mugs of ale or steaming piles of meat, trying to avoid the groping hands of the more drunk and boisterous patrons. Joy girls were sitting on laps and fondling various patrons, although 'girls' was a generous term as many of them seemed past their prime.

Robin made his way to the crowded bar. The only available place he could squeeze in was between a soot-faced minor for whom the bar was already a pillow and a muscular-looking Tundrial barbarian with a long braid and shaved sideburns. Seal Shore barbarians were not uncommon in Suldan-Karr. It had been over twenty years since they had ransacked Berin's Inn, focusing more on the western coast of Suldan-Karr these days, yet people still eyed them with suspicion and kept their distance from them. But after spending time along the Silver Coast, Robin knew that a single Tundrial was nothing to worry about unless provoked. They could even be friendly. It was when they were in a band or a war party that fear was warranted.

So, Robin tapped a silver Sorin on the polished oak bar and ordered a mug of mead. He was in the mood to get 'I-have-no-idea-how-I-got-to-my-room-and-who-is-that-next-to-me' drunk, and ale simply wasn't up for that task.

He downed the drink in two gulps, the cloying sweetness of it masking the strong alcohol, and immediately ordered another. His Sorin should be good for at least two more.

By his third drink the flute player had been replaced with a pair of dwarves with a viola and a strange contraption which they'd introduced as an *Organetto*, which seemed to be all pipes and billows.

The music played wasn't too bad, or perhaps he was far along enough in his quest for inebriation that his standards had lowered.

As a comforting haze of drunkenness began to wash over him, he noticed a group of five burley-looking teamsters looking in his direction with stern faces.

Confidence boosted by the mead, he raised his mug to them and smiled charmingly. Or at least he thought he looked charming at the time.

The group looked at each other and glowered at Robin. Two of them pushed back their chairs and marched over.

As they neared, he downed his fourth mug and dismounted his barstool.

He looked at them and then confidently called over the noisy room, "You lads should truly watch yourselves; this establishment is too purple for you. People pay for drinks here in sorins, not bits."

The lead teamster, a large man with a red face and bushy beard, scowled. "Your kind shouldn't be drinkin' eer with civilized men," he said with a thick Culidge accent.

"That was basically what *I* said. You can't use the same insult *I* used on *me* back at *you*," he slurred. Wait. That didn't sound right.

Someone was saying something beside him, but it was difficult enough to focus on one conversation.

"I think you've drunk enough with men, and it's time you tried the horse's trough," threatened the man.

"Thank you for the invitation, but you lads aren't my type of company. Besides, I may catch whatever afflicts you," he retorted drunkenly.

The man bared his teeth and advanced.

Despite his drunkenness, instinct kicked in and Robin thrust his foot forwards, kicking the man below the knee. As he stumbled forward, Robin slammed his forehead into the man's nose.

The three teamsters who'd remained at the table kicked back their chairs, jumping to their feet. The second man who'd advanced halted in surprise, and Robin took the opportunity to jab his elbow into his ribs. He succeeded in causing the man to double over but lost his own balance and fell to the dirty floorboards. The two men's companions were on him instantaneously, kicking him furiously from three directions. He curled up into a ball to protect his face and head as their boots continued to hammer down on him.

He was vaguely aware of a large figure grabbing the two of them by their collars and slamming their heads together.

Everything went black.

***

When he regained his senses, he was looking at the stars and could hear waves lapping at the boat he seemed to be lying in.

"Wasn't your finest moment, brother," said Garian, steadily rowing the two ores of the skiff.

"They started it," he muttered, wincing at the pain in his head and ribs. Something was strange, but he couldn't put his finger on it. Why was Garian even here? Where were they?"

"You used to be smart, Robby," said Garian, rowing in strong, steady strokes. "You never used to pick a fight without me and Tommy."

"Yeah, well, maybe you shouldn't have died," he answered. Yes, that was right. Garian died.

"What are you doing here, Gar?" It seemed like a simple question, thought Robin.

"I came to talk sense into you. Don't you think you've been drinking and whoring long enough?"

"Nothing better to do," answered Robin, trying desperately to focus. The rocking of the boat was making him nauseous. "My older brother died, and my younger brother ran off with the woman I loved. Sounds as good an excuse as any to drown my sorrows."

Garian stopped rowing and folded his hands over his knees. "You didn't kill me, Robin," he said sadly.

"I left you to die. I may as well have."

"Perhaps. And perhaps you chose to save Tommy."

"The three of us could have taken them," he insisted stubbornly.

"For argument's sake, let's say you're right. Why would you choose to abandon your brother yet a second time?"

"I'm not abandoning Tommy. He made his own choices. He abandoned *me*."

"Did he?" asked Garian.

Robin couldn't find an answer. The rocking of the boat was taking its toll on his stomach, and he was considering were to vomit.

"Brother…" began Garian.

"What?" he asked.

"Brother…" repeated the ghost.

"What!" he shouted.

"Brother, are you alright?"

Garian's face swam out of focus and another face replaced it. Pale blue eyes stared at him instead of Garian's green ones, and in place of his brother's brown curls, the head before him was piqued by a black low mohawk which was gathered in a long braid.

"Can you hear me?" asked the Tundrial who'd been drinking next to him.

They were outside, and he was propped in a sitting position with his back to the wall of the inn. The music and voices were distant and all the pain of the fight came rushing back. Robin groaned and vomited four or five mugs of mead.

"There you go. Let it out…" soothed the barbarian.

He offered him a water skin, and Robin drank thankfully after wiping his mouth. He spat out the water, trying to get rid of the aftertaste of the mead.

"That was a kind thing you did. Few in these lands would have defended one of my people. Seirn bless you."

"Defended…" he began, putting the pieces together. Now the teamster's insults made a more sense.

"Let's get you to your inn," said the tall Tundrial as he lifted Robin to his feet.

"My name's Bunda, by the way. Bunda of the Jams."

19 SPELLCASTERS

The rain pattered on distantly as the four of them made their way into the tower. A hallway with a door on each side ended in a spiraling stairwell. The stairs leading up were terminated in the rubble of the collapsed upper levels, but the stairs leading down seemed intact.

They carefully checked the two rooms to the side of the hallway and found no living person inside. One room had rows of sleeping mats and makeshift cookfires. The other had an assortment of rotting wooden crates, a barrel filled with scorpion bolts and all manner of other supplies which had been left when the tower was abandoned.

"There seems to be nothing of interest here," said Robin as he and Tadok returned to the hallway. Bunda had completed healing Ren's ribs and his own wounded scalp.

"How's the shoulder?" asked Bunda.

Robin flexed his arm then nodded.

"You?" he asked, turning to Tadok.

"I'm fine," replied the half-elf.

Tadok suddenly heard a noise from the stairwell and held up his hand. He silently motioned in the direction.

"There are more men down there. Maybe the girl, too."

They all nodded, and Robin advanced, taking up the lead.

"Hold a moment," said Tadok. He was tempted to call upon Dorkah, but he knew the Eith'lin needed time to heal. They were on their own this time. Still, Tadok was a sorcerer and had a few other tricks up his sleeve.

He reached down into his center and grasped the Flow. He whispered a few words in the Arcane, laying his hand on Robin's back. A soft blue glow engulfed the Heartlander and then disappeared as soon as it came. It took about ten seconds.

"What did you do to me?" asked Robin, a mix of apprehension and bemusement in his voice.

"We're about to face a mage. I don't know his powers, but this will protect you somewhat from his attacks."

"Why not cast it upon yourself?"

"If this turns into a wizard's duel, I don't believe I have the training to be victorious," he answered.

The truth was he'd never faced a mage before. Unlike sorcerers, whose training focused on controlling the inherent magic within them, mages studied for decades to manipulate the magical energy around them and shape it to their will. Their lessons also included how to attack other magic users and counter their spells, which he'd had no proper schooling in. In addition, few of Tadok's spells were direct attack spells. Sellwyn had been adamant about training him in spells which augmented him or Dorkah and not the fire or lightning spells she could muster. After she had left, Tadok had tried to learn by himself, but it was difficult. He had mastered the electric palm spell he'd used that morning, but it required that he get close enough to touch the mage, and he wasn't sure he'd get the chance. His best bet was to distract him long enough for Robin to plant a dagger in his back.

"I'm trusting you to kill him, if I cannot."

Robin nodded in understanding, and the four of them advanced. Robin and Bunda lead and Ren and Tadok held the rear.

They quietly crept down the winding stairwell. The torches were few, but annoyingly prevented his eyes from adjusting to the dimness as they had outside.

At the bottom of the stairwell stood a small landing and a large wooden door.

Robin pressed his ear to the door listening. Tadok didn't need to.

He heard men's voices. Too low to make out words, but there were a few of them. Then, under it all, he heard a female voice. Whatever she said, it was defiant and angry. The men laughed at her.

Robin examined the lock and nodded to his companions, signaling the door was unlocked.

"On three," he whispered as they prepared.

When he reached three, he shoved the door open with all his might.

The gust of wind from the sudden eruption of the door blew out the fat candles standing in a pool of wax on the table in the center of the room.

Four sets of eyes looked up at them in surprise as Tadok and Ren picked their targets and discharged their arrows. Unfortunately, they simultaneously picked the same guard and both arrow and bolt thudded into his chest. He rocked backwards and then slumped forwards onto the dice they'd been gambling with.

The other three jumped to their feet as Bunda and Robin charged into the room.

It wasn't a large room, spanning twenty feet across in a perfect square. The opposite wall held three cells with rusty bars, and there was a corridor leading to the right. Four torches sat in old sconces jutting out of the cracked stone walls, offering dim, flickering light even without the candles.

Robin barreled into the man who'd been sitting with his back to the door as he tried to turn to meet his attacker. He stabbed him repeatedly with his rapier as the brigand tried in vain to get his sword out of his scabbard.

The last two brigands managed to get their weapons ready in time. The one Bunda had charged at blocked Bunda's saber, cursing as he was driven back.

The other drew twin daggers and hopped up onto the table, stabbing down at Robin's face. The Heartlander managed to evade at the last moment.

Ren dropped his bow and drew his long knife, charging the man on the table with a wild slash. The man was nimbler than anticipated and vertically jumped up above the hunter's attack. As he landed, he slashed at Ren's face, and Ren cried in pain, retreating with his hand over his face.

No time to deal with that now, thought Tadok as he drew his sickle and joined the fray.

Bunda continued pressing his opponent back towards the cells. Seeing an opening, he stabbed with his saber, but the brigand dodged left. Bunda's sword scraped through the rusty bars, and the bandit took the advantage, slamming his shoulder into the barbarian's arm forcing his to drop his sword.

In the table in the center, the nimble bandit darted his foot out of the way as Robin attempted to trip him with his rapier, and stomped down on it, pinning the slim blade to the table.

Robin cursed as the man on the table slashed outwards with both blades hoping to slit his throat. Robin let go of the rapier and jumped backwards, electing to lose his weapon but save his life. Seeing his advantage, the table hopper leaped off the table, pressing Robin back to the door.

Tadok was frantically debating which one of his disarmed friends needed him most when he felt the air crackle and tasted ozone. His brain registered what was happening just in time for him to drop to the floor as a spider web of lighting sizzled above him connecting to one of the sconces behind where his head had been, blasting it into twisted dark metal. Looking to the source of the lighting attack, he noticed the mage had entered the fray from the hallway.

He was a stout man with two sets of chins under a patchy beard. He wore dirty maroon robes covered with frayed embroidery set to look like magical runes. Cruel beady eyes looked out from a bushy brow. He grinned at Tadok, exposing tobacco-stained teeth.

Tadok rolled to his feet as the mage moved his chubby hands in a series of intricate gestures and shouted a sentence in Arcane. Two crackling balls of red energy formed above his head and shot out—one at him and one at Ren.

He had time to instinctively form his Flow into a magical barrier before him just as the globe crashed into it in a shower of sparks. Ren wasn't so lucky.

Peering out of one eye, he ducked under the globe, which narrowly missed his head. To his surprise, the magical projectile made a U-turn behind him and connected with his left shoulder blade. Ren screamed, and the smell of charred flesh filled the room as he fell to the ground, writhing in pain.

The mage stared at Tadok, and his grin widened. He licked his lips and put his hands together, pointing them at the half-elf, and chanted a magical phrase again.

Tadok recognized that spell and knew that his magical barrier would be useless against it. Bending low, he darted at the table and flipped it over, scattering dice, coins, and a dead man in all directions. He managed to get behind it in the nick of time as a stream of fire hit the center of the table. The rotting wood began to smolder and then burst into flame, forcing Tadok to scramble to find new cover.

Behind him, the dagger-wielding bandit was trying to skewer Robin. Robin had pulled his own dagger and was trying to keep him at bay but was losing ground. The bandit stabbed forward with his right dagger, which Robin managed to catch with his own with a loud ring of steel upon steel. Unfortunately, that left him exposed to his left dagger. The bandit saw his opening and stabbed Robin in the chest. To his surprise, instead of penetrating flesh, there was a flash of blue light emanating from the point of contact, as if an invisible armor had intercepted the blade—which it had, thanks to Tadok's spell.

Robin smiled and shrugged at the look of shock on the bandit's face. He then jabbed his index and middle fingers of his left hand into the man's eyes. The bandit retreated, blinded, and Robin pressed forward, slashing at the man, cutting a long gash across his chest.

Bunda and his own opponent were wrestling now. By now, both had lost their weapons. The man was strong and taller than the barbarian and was using it to his advantage. He'd managed to get Bunda in a headlock and was slowly crushing the life out of him. He was also leaning all his weight onto the cleric, attempting to force him to the ground.

Bunda had one hand on the man's arm, and the other held the cell bars which had cost him his sword, desperately trying to keep his feet on the ground and his airway open. By the look of him, he was dangerously close to losing on both fronts, his eyes bulging and his knees shaking.

"Stop fighting it, barbarian. Your life ends here and now," growled the man, his stinking breath moist on Bunda's ear.

Suddenly, changing tactics, Bunda let go of his captor's arm and grabbed both bars with both hands. He mustered the last of his strength and pulled the bars as hard as he could, launching the man's head into them in force. The hold on his neck eased immediately, and Bunda gasped for breath. The bandit was dazed and had fallen to his knees. Not letting him recover, Bunda grabbed the man by the hair and slammed his head into the bars repeatedly until he dropped to the ground limply, his face a mass of blood and broken teeth.

Near the entrance to the corridor, the mage was preparing his next attacks.

"Hold still, you little shit!" he commanded. Tadok raced through his mind, going over his spells, trying to think of anything that could counter the mage's attack. Suddenly, the man who had been fighting Robin backed into him, his left arm covering his eyes. Robin, who'd been about to stab him, twisted to narrowly avoid skewering Tadok.

"Don't interfere, half-elf!" Robin shouted at him as the man took the opportunity to reel away.

He was about to retort when his words dawned on him. *That was it! He's a mage.* Tadok didn't need to cast any spells—just to interfere with *his.*

Taking a step away from Robin's melee, he turned to the Mage and flung his sickle at him with all his strength. The blade somersaulted through the smoke of the burning table but was too high and clanged against the ceiling of the corridor behind the mage. Still, it had done exactly what he'd hoped it would, and the mage was forced to duck and halt his casting. Tadok knew that the hand motions needed to be precise, as did the verbal incantation. Any error, a single syllable misspoken or a twist of the wrist at the wrong moment and the spell would fizzle into nothing.

Tadok leaped over the burning table and crashed into the fat mage. Punching him in the gut. As he doubled over, he raised his knee right into his nose, crushing it. The mage tried to retreat back into the hall, and Tadok pursued, picking up his sickle as he advanced.

The mage recovered and stared at him in panic above the blood gushing over his mouth. He raised his hands again to send another scorching fire spell, but Tadok sliced upwards, embedding the point of his sickle into the man's double chin, the blade sinking three inches in and piercing his brain. Tadok could even see it through the man's open mouth. The mage's beady eyes rolled up into his head, and his hands, which had been about to turn Tadok into a human bonfire, spasmed involuntarily as he died.

Behind him, Robin had regained his rapier and had made short work of the last guard, stabbing him in the right arm with his sword and then in the left armpit with his dagger, burying it to the hilt. The man spat blood and dropped to the ground.

All was now silent in the room except for the crackling of the small bonfire which had been the table.

"Hey!" a high youthful voice split the silence. "Are they all dead?"

***

"I can't do much for the eye. That's beyond my powers, but at least this will stop the bleeding." Bunda took a step back to examine his handiwork. While he'd heard of miracles performed by saints in which limbs had regrown and blind men could see, the best he could do is heal flesh and fractured bones. The lopsided bandage around the tracker's head covering his eye would have to do. Satisfied, he walked around Ren to look at his exposed back. The flesh where the magical bolt had struck him was pink and raw, and skin was puckered in a circle about the size of an apple. It was an ugly wound.

"Do you feel any pain?" he asked Ren, lightly prodding the wound.

"No. Seirn be praised."

Bunda wasn't convinced. His healing magic had repaired some of the damaged flesh, and blood was obviously circulating in tissue which was charred and necrotic a few minutes ago, but this wasn't the way it was supposed to work. The flesh should have been as smooth as it was before it was struck, with no scarring or any indication that it had happened. To be fair, since his daily meditation in which he rejuvenated himself spiritually, he had cast his light ball twice, used his divine vision, caused a campfire to blaze and enlarged himself–which was his most taxing spell. He'd also used Seirn's healing numerous times. He was, once again, spent. He hoped that was all it was. He had a sinking feeling it was more than that. As if Seirn was passing on his divine power through a veil.

Robin and Tadok had gone down the hall, and he could hear them speaking in low voices. The burning table had been extinguished, and the bodies piled up in one of the cells.

Mara was sitting sullenly on one of the chairs in the corner of the room. She'd been surprisingly cheerful when they'd opened her cell doors, shouting insults at the dead bandits. Her high spirits had been crushed when Robin scolded her with such ferocity that by the time he was finished, her lip was quivering, and tears were streaming down her face.

The truth was it was no laughing matter. Men had died, and they had risked their lives. Ren probably lost his eye permanently. The worst of it was that Bunda was unsure that the people of Suldan's Bluff would be able to escape Hayek now, considering the delay.

Their time window was tight as it was, gaining only two days ahead of Hayek at best. Mara's escapade may be the difference between the safety of Berin's Inn's walls and being massacred on the roads. So he resisted the urge to console the girl and allowed her to stare gloomily at the wall as they prepared to return to Suldan's Bluff.

"Bunda, can you come here please," called Robin from the corridor.

Bunda looked at Ren who nodded confirming he was okay and proceeded into the corridor from which the mage had emerged.

The corridor was only wide enough for one man to walk without his shoulder touching the stone walls. There were two rooms on the right. One had obviously been a storage room, and the other was another cell.

At the end of it, the smooth stone masoned walls gave way to crumbling roughly hewn granite. He could see the flickering of their torch beyond a bend and joined them. The tunnel ended abruptly in a dead end. Tadok and Robin stood in the small alcove examining an obviously man-made wall which was covered in etched runes. On the stone floor were littered sheets of papers, sketches and drawings of the runes, measurement tools and charcoal pencils.

"What do we have here?"

Robin answered without looking. "Appears to be a door, but I see no latch, lock or hinges."

"Its nature is magical," added Tadok.

Bunda pointed to the runes. "And that? Is it *Shadowtang*?"

Tadok shook his head. "The letters are elven, but they form no elven words I've ever heard.

"Perhaps it's the language of that island of theirs in the northern sea," suggested Robin. "You know, it's apparently where elves originally came from before settling in Arga. I can't recall the name—"

"*Andunleen*," said Tadok, still examining the wall, tracing his fingers along its surface. "And first, the *Sahangi*, who you call elves, settled the northern forests centuries before it was called Arga. And second, I speak the language of Andunleen, and this isn't it."

"It's Karr," said a voice behind them.

The three turned as one and found Mara standing behind them.

With all eyes on her, she looked away. "At least, that's what Merklese, that fat wizard said to the big half-orc."

They continued to stare at her in silent skepticism.

"Look, I'm telling you the truth," she said, exasperated. "After they threw me in the cell and gave me an account of what Dell Hayek would do to me when he returned, they treated me as if I was air. They spoke and chattered amongst themselves as if I'd been forgotten. But I listened. And the half-orc, the one they called 'the Butcher' came in demanding to know when 'it' would be open. And Merklese had told him 'soon', as he'd solved the riddle and the door was carved with 'Karr'. He said it was *Terrodite* Karr," she said, unsure how to pronounce the alien name.

Tadok looked back to the wall and stroked the stubble on his chin thoughtfully. He bent down and picked up some of the marked sheets of parchment on the floor.

"I thought the Karr were human, not elves," said Robin in confusion.

"The Karr *were* human, but they had no writing of their own. They used elven or dwarven letters when they wrote. No sure about these Tarrodites, though."

He found what he was looking for on the parchment and presented it to the rest of them.

"It appears the wizard Merklese was kind enough to translate this before dying."

"How considerate," said Robin.

He unfurled the parchment on the marked wall, so he could look at the runes and their translation at the same time. He then frowned.

"What is it?" asked Bunda.

"This is nonsense," said Tadok curtly. "These are just random words. Death…Ash…these two mean night and day, and that's mountain. This says Blood. It just seems like a list of random words in no order which makes sense."

"Perhaps the translation is mistaken?" suggested Robin.

The half-elf shrugged. That answer was as good as any other.

Bunda could see the frustration in Tadok's eyes. He believed that one of the reasons he'd cooperated with Robin's hunt for the boy was his growing curiosity with these relics of the past they were seeing. While he wasn't too enthusiastic about the young sorcerer's obsession with these undoubtedly evil objects, it had helped them in convincing him to let them find the remains of the boy and the girl, so he hadn't pressed it. But now, he could see a similar frustration in Tadok's eyes as he'd seen in Robin's. Both his friends had come to the end of their quest and come up empty-handed. Despite his best attempts to hide it, he'd seen the half-elf's eyes light up when the gnome had managed to decipher the writing on the totem tree…

An idea fell into place in his head, and he smiled lightly because he knew he was right.

"I think I know how to open it," he said.

Tadok and Robin looked at him curiously.

"Pray tell…" said Tadok handing him the parchment.

"I will, but two things first."

He turned to Mara. "Mara, return to Ren now," he commanded using his ship-captain's tone.

She began to protest, but one angry look from Robin and she shut her mouth with an audible click.

"As you command, sir," she said impertinently and walked off down the hall.

Waiting until she was around the bend in the corridor, Bunda grasped his medallion and breathed a word in the Divine. His eyes flashed blue for a moment, and his vision adjusted to see the auras. He could see Robin's aura of desperation, and Tadok's aura of internal conflict, but he focused his attention on the door.

And there it was.

It was faint, yet undeniably there. A reddish black pall emanating off the door, just barely visible. Some evil lay behind the door, or perhaps had created it. If it was the latter, it must have been so evil or so powerful that its odor lingered two millennia after it had been constructed.

"Well?" asked Tadok, recognizing the spell he'd used. "Are we facing an evil door? A sinister wall perhaps?"

Bunda ignored the sarcasm. "Yes. There is evil beyond it, which is why I asked the girl to leave before we open it."

He looked at the parchment again, hesitating.

"Whatever is beyond this door, will probably hold danger. This evil may even be beyond us."

The three stood in silence for a moment.

"I don't believe knowledge in and of itself is evil, Bunda," said Tadok quietly. Bunda, whose sight was still augmented by his divine vision, could see the auras of longing seep into Tadok's normal signature auras like wine mixing with water. The half-elf was eager to find out what was beyond the door.

"I have another reason to present," offered Robin. "Whatever it is, Hayek would go to great lengths to find it. We've cost him his wizard and his men. A day from now, whatever artifact or knowledge inside, may be what we have to bargain for the safety of the people of Suldan's Bluff. And if not with Dell Hayek, then with his benefactors. The Hands are a pragmatic lot. If they want this, they will kill or bargain for it. This may save our lives tomorrow even as it endangers them today."

With that, it was agreed.

Bunda compared the parchment to the door and began.

He found the words he was seeking and began pressing his fingers to their carved indentations in the correct order.

Blood.

Flesh.

Bone.

Ash.

And finally, *Death.*

Just as it had appeared on the inscription of the totem tree.

When he pressed the last symbol, the door suddenly began to glow softly. A moment later, it shifted and slid with the sound of stone grating against gravel.

"I don't understand," said Robin. "The Totem tree was in Shadowtang. Why would the door be written in Karr?"

They pondered it in silence, staring into the murk. Ahead of them, a tunnel disappeared into darkness.

"Let's find out," said the half-elf. And with that, Tadok took a step forward into the darkness.

***

Before entering the tunnel, they had sent Ren and Mara back to the village. There was no sense in taking either of them with them, considering Ren's injuries. Besides, they had agreed that it was high time the villagers were on their way. They only asked that they make sure to leave them supplies and horses salvaged from the bandits who'd attacked that morning.

In the tunnel Robin led, and Bunda took up the rear. Each of them held a torch as Bunda had elected to preserve his dwindling spells.

The tunnel was obviously manmade. Not paved or lined with

brick and mortar, but carved out of the rock, nonetheless. It descended gradually as they progressed.

Bunda ran his hand along the limestone walls.

"Who do you suppose made these tunnels? Dwarves?"

Tadok shook his head. "If dwarves had made them, they would have been shorter and wider. These were obviously made for humans."

"I also think dwarves would have reinforced—" began Robin turning to look at the two of them, before Tadok tsked at him in annoyance, shielding his eyes.

"Must you shine that in my face, Sandisan?"

Robin moved his torch away from the half-elf's eyes, muttering an apology.

"It's bad enough that thing is blinding my sight. Why are you even leading the way? My vision in darkness is better than either of yours."

Robin smiled a crooked smile. "How many times have you broken into places where folk kept things they wanted safe?" asked Robin matter-of-factly. "Because I've done so many times. And in such places, the rich and powerful often leave the nastiest traps they can think of."

They continued in silence for another minute.

"So, you were a cat burglar?" asked Tadok. "I figured you for a pickpocket."

Robin snorted. "I hate pickpocketing. The scores are low, and if your mark catches on, you better be a fast sprinter. No, my specialty was entering manors and vaults. So, picking locks, climbing and finding the traps laid out for me. All the while doing it silently enough to avoid getting caught," he explained and smiled over his shoulder, just as the ground gave way beneath his feet.

One moment Robin was walking a few feet in front of them, boasting about his talents, and the next he'd disappeared in a cloud of dust. A six-foot-wide gap in the tunnel floor now occupied the place where the Heartlander had stepped.

Bunda and Tadok rushed to the newly emerged ledge in the floor. The cleric coughed and waved his torch ahead of him to clear the dust.

"Robin, can you hear us?" he called into the pit.

"I'm fine. I think," came the voice from below.

When the dust cleared, they could see Robin laying awkwardly at the bottom of the large pit which was ten feet below the surface. It had been lined with wooden spikes, but from the look of them they had all snapped brittlely when the Heartlander had landed on the rotting wood.

"Nothing broken or wounded but my pride," he said, and finished with a fit of coughing.

Tadok smiled down at him.

"You're a terrible thief, Sandisan. Lucky you've retired."

20 VICTIMS AND SURVIVORS

The Triumph Road stretched endlessly across the barren hills and empty fields. Despite being half a millennium old, and despite the millions of boots, hooves, and wagon wheels that had trodden on its cobbled brick stones, the road showed little wear and tear. A testament to the marvel of dwarven craftmanship.

It was said that when Nem had begun his march east, he'd laid waste to any town or city who opposed him yet showed mercy to those who saw wisdom and swore fealty.

The dwarves of Doar Keirn probably had little to fear from the invader, despite his mega-army. They were tucked away in their fortress city under the mountains in the place where the Suldan mountain range met the Shield mountains.

It was unclear what made the dwarves ally with Nem the Conqueror yet ally they did. They showed their support for the invader by paving a marvelous road all the way from Culidge to Sebin. A wide road which his cavalry could ride and his men could march upon.

In times of peace, the road had been the bloodline which connected east to west, as caravans would make their way to the coast ladened with goods and ore, only to return with grain, salt, red corral and anything traded up the western coast.

Centuries later it would once again feel the thundering march of an army as the Seal Shore Barbarian horde ravaged their way across Suldan-Karr like a wave which finally broke against the walls of Sebin.

And half a jubilee later, two men walked its smooth paved stones.

Bunda had found Nick to be good company. The mercenary from Sandisan obviously knew these lands and was open to sharing his knowledge and campfire with the Tundrial. He'd expected the animosity from the people of Suldan-Karr, having known the stories of his countrymen's exploits over the last two and a half decades in these lands. He knew that given the chance, the cold shoulders would turn into hot hostility, and having another sword at his side was prudent. Nick wasn't yet a friend, but he could see how he may become one by the end of their journey. While Nick would never be a devout follower of Seirn, he certainly entertained some curiosity about the faith and its structure.

"So, after being an acolyte for seven years, you need to be a Journeyman for another five before you may return home? And be celibate to boot? That explains why I haven't encountered more clerics of Seirn out and about. You're the first I've met," he said, chewing on a blade of tall grass as they trekked their way across the western lands of Trosia.

Bunda chuckled. "Not all of the servants of Seirn become Journeymen. There are other ways to promote the faith of the Dawn Father."

"So why did you choose this path instead of keeping to the warmth of your temple's hearth and the safety of its walls? I don't know much about the gods but traveling around Suldan-Karr alone seems like a good way to meet them. I don't know if you noticed, but your countrymen certainly left their mark on these people."

Bunda mulled over Nick's words. The truth was that Bunda had never craved adventure for its own sake. He loved the Seal Shore Islands, especially Tarthen. The forests, the cliffs, rivers and waterfalls. For him, it was a paradise, even during the cold, bitter winters. Truth be told, he had trouble sleeping when he couldn't hear the sea crash against the shore.

His brothers had been his best friends, and whatever he was lacking in his soul was filled by the temple and the faith. He was aware that many Tundrial his age flocked to the banners of war band leaders intent on raiding other islands or the mainland for glory and riches. Ulan, Megril and Golen had been among them and often traded war stories, which left him feeling an outsider. It wasn't that he was weak or frightened of combat. The sons of Garlan Ice Sale had been trained in combat from the day they could lift a stick in the air without falling down.

Had he not attacked Greffik Iron Tooth, three months ago he would be sweeping the floors or the temple grounds, or attending one of the more senior cleric's lectures.

"I believe that Seirn's light can only be fully understood when one gains perspective. The kind of Perspective gained on the road."

That sounded ok. It wasn't too far from the truth, he thought. He wasn't ready to share with his new almost-friend that he'd been banished from his home.

They continued walking and talking as the sun rose high, drying up the morning mist which blanketed the fields around them.

As they reached a bend in the road, Robin halted in midsentence, his hand moving to the hilt of his blade.

Bunda strained to see what had halted the man.

The road, which passed over a small bridge over a dry ravine, showed the carnage of a battle. A recent battle, seeing as the carrion eaters hadn't picked the flesh off the bones of the dead yet.

They both drew their weapons and walked across the bridge carefully.

Halfway over the ravine was a covered wagon. It was facing west and hadn't had a chance to complete its way across the stone bridge. The horses were nowhere to be seen. The wagon's one side was pincushioned with arrows, and a dark stain, which must have been blood, stained the dun-colored canvas. The old, cobbled road was also stained in various places with dried blood. Grislier than the blood stains, were three humanoid figures who lay in different positions around the wagon, each of them had been left where they had died, and all of them were clearly orcs.

Bunda knew well that the lands north of the Shield Mountains were inhabited by orcs. These lands, known as the Barrens, were a cold wasteland of the orc's own making. It was said that in ages past it had been verdant. But of all the races who walked the lands of Trosia, the orcs appeared to have been put on the earth for one purpose only—to destroy.

Orcs didn't farm or trade. They hunted until an area was depopulated of game, and then migrated to a new location. If another people or tribe was already there, well, that wasn't a problem. The orcs hunted them, too, sparing no man, woman, or child, even if they were from another orc tribe. If the winter was bad enough in these parts, raiding parties would make their way across the Shield Mountains and pillage the villagers and caravans along the Triumph Road.

But even worse than their raiding practices, orcs had an appetite for the flesh of human women–and not in the dietary sense. When they'd satisfied themselves, they would leave the woman alive. It was a peculiar custom, considering that they showed no remorse in killing everything else. But something about killing a female who held their seed, even if unwantedly, was against their doctrine. As a result, northern Suldan-Karr was littered with human-orc half breeds, and the children of those half-breeds.

"This isn't the entire war band," said Nick, nudging a dead orc with his boot. It was missing its head.

"I never knew orcs road in wagons," said Bunda.

"They don't. This wagon belonged to a human."

The wagon had a chest that had been tipped over, spilling its contents of clothing and cutlery. The rest of the wagon was filled with farming supplies and blankets.

"Look at this one," called Nick. "No human did this".

Bunda poked his head out from behind the tarp. Robin had turned a body over and dragged it over next to a second body. Bunda could clearly see that it had been attacked by something with teeth and talons. Animalistic claw marks crisscrossed the thing's face and chest, and its shoulder was mass of ruined flesh and muscle.

"There are two more of them across the bridge," said Robin, gazing at the far bank of the brook.

The last one on the bridge was lying on its stomach, and, when it was flipped over, showed severe burn marks around its neck. "If this is what happened to the orcs, where did the humans go?" asked Nick.

Bunda hopped down from the wagon and pointed to the side of the road under an old oak tree.

"I think they suffered the same fate, but were treated better for it."

Three cairns had been set in the shade of the tree. Two were large enough to cover adults, but the third was smaller, and at its head was a ragged cloth doll, which was stained with blood. A child was buried there.

The two of them stood in solemn silence at the foot of the fresh graves. The person who'd done them the courtesy of administering their final rites had obviously been in a hurry and hadn't had the time or ability to dig a proper grave.

Despite the desire they both had to leave the place, Bunda insisted on burying the orcs. Nick had been shocked by the cleric's insistence, thinking at first that it was a jest, but he soon understood that Bunda wouldn't continue the journey without completing his task and helped.

The thing was that for Bunda, it wasn't about kindness or pity. The orcs were scourge, and he was glad they were dead. They'd obviously been those to attack. In fact, had Bunda been here during the attack it was a certainty he would have been doing his best to send them to their sightless god, *Illmeth*. But Seirn had decreed that any creatures with a soul, including orcs, needed proper burial. Whatever a person did in his or her life, it was for their own deities to decide the fate of their soul once its mortal coils had been shed. Bunda also suspected it was about preventing the dead from rising. If the myths held any truth, one of the great missions of Seirn and his followers was to stamp out any undead ghoulies or ghosts which roamed Trosia. Everyone knew that there was a risk of that happening when the dead weren't taken proper care of.

It didn't mean he had to do it nicely, though. They piled all four bodies at the foot of rock wall of the dry ravine and simply piled the stones they found upon them. They took no satisfaction or pleasure from the work–simply completed it grimly so they could move on.

***

It was sundown when they saw him. The survivor.

The man was slumped over with his back to a pine tree. The bottom half of his tunic was stained dark with blood, and his right arm hung in a way it shouldn't have. They closed the distance to him apprehensively. Nick had drawn his bow and nocked an arrow into it, his head swiveling around, slowly scanning the surroundings. This could easily be the setup of an ambush.

Bunda knelt down next to the man. His skin was ashen, and pointed ears poked through brown hair matted with sweat and blood. The wound which had let out so much of the man's lifeblood was a long slash in between his ribs.

Bunda lifted his sword and placed the flat of the blade gently under the man's nose. It was weak, but he could see that the polished steel under the man's nostrils was fogging up.

"He's alive," he called back. *But not for long*, he thought.

Satisfied that no orcs were hiding in the tree line, Nick returned his arrow to his quiver and joined Bunda.

He looked at the half-elf.

"What luck," he muttered. "Sadly, my friend, I think he's beyond saving."

Bunda ignored him. Grasping his medallion with his left hand, he allowed his right to hover over the nasty wound in the dying man's side. He turned his face up to the setting sun and spoke in the Divine.

"*Appriyas durmey lo'unra Seirn Ugledeiah.*" He intoned deeply.

His medallion began to feel warm, and shortly after that, warmth spread from his heart to his hand, and a soft blue glow illuminated the wound. He heard Nick's surprised gasp as flesh knit itself back together.

After a moment, the man's breathing deepened and steadied. Then, his eyelids fluttered open, and his eyes tried to focus.

"...Old tower..." he rasped.

"What?" asked Nick.

His eyes focused on Nick and narrowed. His hand suddenly shot out to grab his shirt.

"Easy friend," said Bunda, "You're safe. Seirn has healed all your wounds."

The man's head slumped back forwards.

21 THE FORGOTTEN

The long tunnel ended in a small cave. The far end of the cave had a stone wall with a large hole in the center. The hole looked as if the wall had been blown apart, and bricks and large chunks of masonry were strewn around it. They'd been covered by a thick layer of dust and dirt, indicating that they had lain where they had fallen for countless years.

None of them spoke, but Robin shone his torch around the cave, searching for any trap or enemy. When there were none, he nodded to Bunda and Tadok and stepped through the hole.

They found themselves standing in a large room. It would have been larger had the left side of the room (Robin wasn't sure where north was anymore) not collapsed. The floor was littered with bones and weapons. A battle had commenced here long ago.

The room was well-lighted, not from torches, but from stone panels in the ceiling which shone with a pale blue light.

"It's a spell," said Tadok, following Robin's gaze.

"We are in some sort of an entrance hall," said Bunda.

The far end of the room, which was still intact, held a large set of doors reinforced by steel bands. The doors were easily ten-feet tall.

Robin knelt down, examining one of the skeletons. The man who those bones had belonged to had worn a dark robe and had held a curved sword. He'd died from an arrow which still rested in his eye socket.

Other robed skeletons were strewn across the hall with similar weapons. Among them were the remains of their enemies, who seemed less homogeneous in their attire and weapons. Two of them were clearly dwarves, and another was probably an elf, along with a few others who were humans. It was hard to tell as time had taken its toll on this place. Scorch marks, dulled by the centuries, were visible on the walls, the floor, and on the corpses themselves. Not all the dead were killed with sword or arrow.

"I'll wager that those were defenders," said Robin, pointing to the robed figures. "See how they are positioned with their backs to that door? And these were their attackers," he pointed to a human and a dwarf partially buried by rubble. "I wonder who won?"

"No one won," said Bunda gravely, staring at the ancient battle site.

"Why do you say that?"

"Because there was no one left to bury the dead."

Robin noticed Tadok had wandered over to the large double doors.

As Robin neared, he could see Tadok's eyes flash yellow for a moment.

"This door is also guarded by magic," he said, staring at it intently.

The door was covered in the same Shadowtang runes which they had seen in the Father Sheilagh's torture chamber and on the totem tree.

Tadok squinted at the twisted letters.

"It's...a riddle," he said softly.

"Again?" Robin rolled his eyes.

Tadok ran his fingers along the words.

He straightened up. "Alright. I think this is what it says:

"My terror, a sword. Lance of life's end.... is death not darkness? Light ended, death's kiss."

They stood in silence, pondering the riddle.

"The hell does that mean?" asked Robin, his eyebrows knitted in concentration. "Seems rather grim."

"Wait," said Bunda suddenly. "I think that's the point. It's describing 'Despair'."

Tadok looked at the inscription again and shrugged. "I don't know. It's an ancient language. I may not be reading it right."

Bunda nodded. "It seems fitting for this place anyway. Try 'Despair'," he said the last loudly.

Nothing happened.

"Perhaps you should say in in Shadowtang," suggested Robin, a little disappointed that Bunda had thought of the answer before him.

215

"*Sulta!*" said Tadok loudly.

Still nothing.

"Try while pushing the door as you say it."

Robin and Bunda set their hands on both doors as Tadok repeated the word in a commanding voice.

"*Sulta!*"

The door didn't budge, but the letters glowed in an angry red blaze.

There was a rattle behind them, and Robin swung around drawing his rapier. To his rising horror, the bones started to drag and roll around the large room, as if being sucked into a central spot. When they reached the center of the room, they began to pile on top of each other, and a massive shapeless form began to rise.

"Fuck!" he cursed.

They braced for what would come next.

The thing that was born from those bones of the dead would give Robin nightmares for years to come.

"Seirn protect us!" breathed the cleric.

Before them was a centipede-like creature made of bones and bound with magic. It rested on dozens of bony legs connected haphazardly. A long, snaky spine made of the spines of all who had died here ended in a mass of skulls. Two arm-like appendages which were a collection of whatever bones remained extended from beneath its head-of-heads and ended in dozens of sharp ribs which served as talons. An unholy reddish glow bloomed in a hundred empty eye sockets as it turned the cluster of skulls which was its head at them. In unison, each jaw dropped open, and it roared deafeningly from countless lines of broken yellow teeth.

It advanced on them, scuttling on a hundred legs with unnatural speed. They all leaped aside as both of its hand-like limbs crashed into the doors, splintering bone fragments in all directions.

Robin was up on his feet within seconds and lunged at the monster from its flank, stabbing it between two oddly shaped legs. But his thin blade slid between the bones and joints without doing any damage. The creature swung its skull-mass head like a club, hitting him in his shoulder and propelling him through the air. He rolled three times before sliding to a halt.

"My blade is useless against it!" he called to the others, searching the ground for a better weapon.

Meanwhile, Tadok, at the creature's other flank, rose to his feet and weaved his hands in a short series of intricate finger motions ending with his index finger pointed at the ground. The floor beneath the creature's feet suddenly became slick and oily, and fifty sets of bony legs skidded and slid, trying to gain a foothold. Finally, the beast collapsed, crashing into the stone floor.

Bunda leaped on its back, hacking with his saber, but his attack was only marginally more effective than Robin's had been. The beast easily twisted around and clasped it with the ribs which made up its fingers, closing them around the Tundrial like a cage and lifting him off his back. The bones constricted, trying to crush the barbarian.

Robin found a double-edged dwarven battle ax lying on the ground where its owner had lost it many centuries ago. He lifted the heavy weapon and launched at the bone-monster with an overhead slash.

Robin had always preferred light weapons which were fast and discreet, and he handled the ax clumsily. When he hacked down with it at the base of the creature's arm, which held his companion, two things happened. The first was that the joints gave way and the arm disconnected from the body, sending shards and splinters in all directions, and the second was the archaic rotting shaft of the ax broke off with the ax head lodged into the creature's side. Despite losing his weapon, the bones which had been crushing Bunda fell apart as if the invisible force holding them together was there no more and the Tundrial was dropped to the ground unceremoniously. He rose to his feet and stumbled towards Tadok, who had drawn his sickle and was about to attack.

"Wait!" the Tundrial called to him. He held his medallion, muttering a prayer, and to Robin's surprise, the saber in Bunda's hand began to glow.

"Distract it!" he commanded, handing the sword to Tadok.

Robin had his own trouble as he was doing his best to dodge and duck under the barrage of attacks from the creatures remaining hand. He rolled under a particularly mean slash of ten bony fingers, which would have scraped the skin off his back if they had been a foot lower. As he tried to get to his feet, his boots slid on the floor, which had been greased by Tadok's spell, and sailed up into the air, landing him painfully on his back. He groaned in pain, unable to move for a moment.

The beast's head loomed above him, and dozens of teeth started snapping as it raised its head. Robin was unsure if he would die from the bites of all those jagged broken teeth or if he would be bludgeoned to death by all those skulls.

Before he could react, an explosion of multicolored light and sound erupted around the creature's head as Tadok cast his firework spell.

The bone-monster drew its head back instinctively and scuttled as its feet slid on the slick floor, kicking Robin out of the way.

Robin rolled away and managed to regain his feet beside the sorcerer.

"Give me that," he reached for Bunda's saber, which Tadok handed him with no objection.

He used the beast's temporary distraction to attack its legs. This time, the glowing blade managed to sever through three legs effectively, and the creature roared from its many mouths.

It reared around towards him and swung its head like a mace at him. He stepped aside, slashing with Bunda's consecrated sword, sending skulls flying and removing a chunk of the thing's head. If the loss of the missing skulls affected it in any way, it didn't show. And before Robin could reflect on it, the creature's hand raked his legs, opening gashes in both of his shins and knocking him to the floor.

Before it could take its next action, bright sunlight filled the room. Robin turned his eyes to Bunda. The cleric stood tall; his medallion which he wielded in his extended hand, was too bright to look at.

The creature shrieked and hissed as smoke began curling up from its bones. It tried to retreat to safety, but Bunda pressed forward, howling in righteous rage.

"I am the seal of light! I am the servant of the Lord of Morning. Seirn commands and banishes you creature of death!" he thundered at it.

The bone creature could do nothing but raise its one remaining arm to shield its head from the searing light.

"Begone creature of death!" screamed the cleric again.

A strange rasp escaped fifty skulls, and suddenly, the whole creature exploded, sending bone fragments shooting outwards from it.

Robin grunted as something lodged in his forearm, and he heard Tadok shout in pain.

And then the room was silent.

Robin stood up and dislodged a finger bone from his forearm. He was covered in bone dust, and the blood left streaks as it ran down to his elbow.

Tadok was in worse shape. He was lying on the ground with a rib the length of a dagger lodged in his side.

Bunda was at his side instantly, examining the wound.

"Hold still," he commanded the half-elf, as he yanked the bone shard out of his stomach. Tadok moaned in pain.

Bunda muttered a healing spell and laid his hand above the wound. The bleeding slowed down but didn't stop.

Bunda looked concerned and confused.

"Why isn't this working!" he snarled in frustration.

He was about to try again when Tadok held his hand.

"I'll be ok, Bunda," he whispered carefully sitting up.

Bunda dug into his satchel and produced a bandage and the salve he'd been given by Aldeira. He smeared it on the strip of cloth before bandaging the wound with it.

"What in nine hells was that?" asked Robin a minute later when it appeared they were all safe. The dust was still clearing.

"The spirit of a guardian," answered Bunda. "Left here in wait for any who didn't know the proper command to open those doors."

Robin looked at the doors. "But we answered correctly! What other answer could there have been?"

They stared at the doors in silence.

"Perhaps it wasn't what we answered but what we actually did," said Tadok after a few moments. He carefully rose to his feet with Bunda's help.

"It could be that the guardian reacted to the two of you as you tried to push the doors open. Perhaps only he who speaks the word can open it."

Tadok walked over to the double doors again and put both hands on them.

Before any of them could react, he yelled, *"Sulta!"* and shoved with all his strength.

"Wait!" called Bunda, but it was too late. The letters blazed red again, but the doors didn't move.

Suddenly, the bone dust and fragments began shifting again to the center of the room.

"Tadok! It's happening again!" cried Robin. "Quick, back into the tunnel!"

"Gods be damned!" cursed the half-elf, in frustration.

"Wait," said Bunda, running over to the door as Robin ran in the other direction. "You said Shadowtang could be read top-down. What does it say if you read it in that direction!"

Tadok, who was about to make his retreat, halted thinking about it.

The bones were beginning to pile up again in the center. Many of them were shattered and broken, and Robin found himself morbidly fascinated about what new shape the spirit of the guardian would choose this time.

Tadok looked back at the door and began reading the phrase again frantically, his finger tracing the words from the top to the bottom this time.

"My lance is light, terror of death ended, a life's not death, A sword ends darkness's kiss!"

"Hurry the hell up!" yelled Robin as he kicked a skull that was rolling towards the dreaded thing which was forming in the center of the room. The skull rolled away, only to reverse its roll midway and return to its original trajectory.

This is hopeless! he thought. But then it dawned on him.

He turned back to the door.

"It's 'Hope'! The answer, is 'Hope'."

Bunda and Tadok looked at each other.

Behind them, the bones piled into a spider-like thing with a scorpion tail edged with two long broken femurs.

"Maler'ekum!" yelled Tadok and shoved the doors.

This time, the letters blazed blue, and the scorpion thing collapsed into a pile of bones.

The doors swung open.

"Who would have guessed such a password in a place like this. Good answer, Sandisan," said Tadok breathlessly, leaning against the door.

***

Bunda's magical globe of light illuminated the vast ancient

chamber, blooming high above the floor and pushing back the shadows. The air was damp and oppressive.

Four massive stone firepits were placed at the sides of the great hall. When lit, supposed Robin, their light would illuminate the hall all the way to its fifteen-foot-high ceiling. The ceiling itself was held aloft by two rows of four wide circular stone pillars, each ornately carved with glyphs. Bunda's magical light shone off a waterlogged corner of the room. The pool at the far end of the chamber flowed from a large crack in the wall. The crack ran all the way up the ceiling, where it spiderwebbed in every direction.

But the most prominent feature in the room was a dais at its end and the large throne which dominated it. There, seated on the ancient throne like some archaic king giving court, was a skeleton. The master of this place, and the master was no human, elf or dwarf.

The creature which had died on that throne was huge. Easily nine feet tall if it had been standing. Two long horns curved up from the front of its skull and skeletal wings hung from its shoulders like a cloak. Its enormous, clawed hands were balled up in fists on its lap, and its sightless eyes gazed out at them.

"Seirn..." whispered Bunda in awe.

"Is that creature going to stand up and attack us?" asked Robin. "I've had my fill of fighting dead things today." His tone was meant to sound light, but it did nothing to mask his fear.

Bunda's eyes flashed blue for a moment, and then he narrowed them, slowly shaking his head.

"I don't think so. But whatever it was, it is the source of evil that has corrupted this place."

"'tis a demon," said Tadok quietly.

Robin tore his gaze away from the dead thing long enough to notice another robed skeletal figure resting with its back to one of the pillars. It was clutching something to its chest.

He walked up to it and carefully pushed its arms away with his rapier. The skeletal arms fell off their shoulder, exposing a leather-bound book.

Tadok leaned down and retrieved the tome from where it had rested for a millennium, carefully opening its cover.

"Careful, friend. It may be trapped," cautioned the cleric.

Tadok nodded, indicating he *was* being careful.

"This is a journal," said the Half-elf, "and its written in

Shadowtang".

He sat down next to the skeleton as if it wasn't there and opened the large tome on his folded knees, and began to read, translating as he spoke.

"*The journal of Malaketh, Lord of Misery, Lord of Calas'tholem.*"

"We've heard of this Malaketh from the totem tree," said Robin.

"Aye, we have," agreed Tadok. "Now hush."

He read on.

"*It is a Tuesday when I awake in a circle of stone and glass. Banished and naked in this realm of humans. I rage. The usurpers can not kill me, so they cast me out. Damned to walk the lands of mortals. My wrath is endless. I find a temple on the hill. The mortals within think their god can save them. By the last of them, they think their god has abandoned them. My rage is unquenched. There is a village of humans near the temple. I kill them all. Then I kill the next village and the next.*

I bask in the blood of my victims. But still, I rage day and night. Then, one night, as I sleep in a bed of the corpses of those sent to stop me, I hear her voice in my dreams. She shows me my crown and the path to reclaim it. I accept her quest. I awaken with the Way Stone in my palm. I set off to find a crossroad. I will extract great pain and suffering on the usurpers. I will tear their flesh and devour their bodies and souls..."

"This goes on," muttered Tadok.

"Lovely," said Robin as the half-elf leafed to the next page. Then the next. Then a third page.

"Ah, here he continues," he said clearing his throat.

"*It is a Sunday, sixty days since my exile. I find the crossroad in the mountains that the mortals of this land call the Sul'than. A human shaman swears this is the place in this wretched realm as she begs for her life. By dawn, she begs for her death. I flay the skin from her body to make this journal.*"

"Ugh," grunted Bunda in disgust.

"*There is a settlement of humans who worship trees. I want to devour them and taste their pain and suffering, but I cannot. They will build my mistress's temple.*

It is Eithday. One hundred and four days since my exile. The humans try to rebel, so I..."

Tadok's eyes widened in horror. He swallowed and went on.

"*So I eat ten of their children as punishment. The women who wail and weep are devoured as well. So that they may be with their children. I keep the remaining children with me from this day. They do not rebel again.*"

"It is a Tuesday. One hundred and fifty-five days since my exile. The humans have completed my mistress's temple. I command them to erect a tree of worship in my name. I then drown them in fire and blood. Their blood and tears sow the land, seeping into the earth and becoming veins with the temple at its heart. The children I keep. I mark them and sacrifice one a week to her. When the last has been devoured, it will be the zenith, and the barrier will be at its weakest. Then the portal will open, and I will return to Calas'tholem and punish my betrayers."

Tadok turned the next page and raised an eyebrow.

"I rage! In the moment of my triumph, a human girl robs me of my revenge. She escapes mere hours before the zenith. I must find her as she beares my mark. I cannot complete the ritual without her. I scour the lands around my temple in vain. The zenith passes. I shriek and tear the land. I vow to make her suffer eternally for her insolence. I curse her and will exact a great revenge on her body and soul.

"It is Monday, two hundred and sixty days since my exile. The lands around me are devoid of life. Every mortal, every beast, I consume in my unending hunger. Even the trees are poisoned by the blood. My kingdom on this earth is death and desolation.

"It is Friday, seven hundred and sixty-three days since my exile. They send champions to destroy me. They come with magic and with the word of their gods. But I destroy them all. They call my realm Clud'rum which means, Death Land in their language, and they call me "The Terror of the Sul'than Mountains".

"It is Tuesday, nine hundred and ninety days since my exile. A curious thing happens today. Humans once again brave my lands. But they do not come to attack. They come to serve. They are the Followers of Shei-Z'a, which is her name in human realms. They come to me on their bellies like worms. They offer to do my bidding and bring me mortals to sacrifice to her and open the gate with the Way Stone. She has sent them. They come bearing gifts. Ten young priestesses of Seirn. I sacrifice half to her in celebration of the continuation of my quest. The other half entertain me for weeks until they succumb, their bodies giving out long after their minds have been crushed."

Robin looked up at Bunda. The cleric turned toward the demon's skeleton, his jaw set grimly. His lips were pursed, and his eyes were so filled with rage that tears welled at their corners. Robin saw his fists balled and his knuckles white, and gathered that it was taking all of Bunda's will not to charge at the dead thing.

He put a hand on his shoulder. "He's long dead, my friend. Let's allow Tadok to finish the journal so we can learn how he was undone."

Bunda shut his eyes and sighed. When he opened them, he nodded to the half-elf to continue. Robin could see that the demon's account was taking its toll on Tadok as well. He looked like he may vomit.

"Eithday, one thousand and nine hundred and seventy days since my exile. This is my last day on this earth. My acolytes bring me victims for years. I soak the land again with the blood of the innocent, and the zenith approaches. I prepare with the Way Stone. I taste my revenge on the usurpers."

Tadok turned to the last page, and to his surprise, it was stained dark where it had soaked up blood.

"My demise. In my moment of triumph, I am betrayed yet again. As I perform the ritual, holding the Way Stone and touching the blood aquifer with my soul, they attack. She is leading them. The girl. The one who escaped me years before. They cut down my pitiful acolytes and attack me with sword, and ax, and spell. I cannot lose my prize again, and must fight them with half my strength. I rejoice, as my regret is that I'll leave this realm without punishing the girl for every miserable day she stranded me in this putrid land. Even in my weakened state, I destroy them, but then she hurls her dart at me. It strikes me, burrowing into my body and soul like a worm. It hurts more than any man-made dagger should hurt. It reaches my heart. In my pain, I pull back, and the blood in the earth answers my scream of agony. The earth shakes and buries my temple, crushing the girl and the last of her companions. Her dagger saps my strength, and I retreat to my throne room. It is here Malaketh, the…"

Tadok stopped abruptly, leafing back and forth in the book.

"That is all. He must have died in mid-sentence and this fellow took the journal, but was still buried in this tomb," he surmised.

They stood in silence for a full minute. Then, as one they walked up to Malaketh, Lord of Misery, the Terror of the Suldan Mountains.

Upon closer inspection, they could see the shine of metal in the creature's oversized ribcage. Bunda whispered something, and his saber suddenly lit up in flames.

"Wait," said Robin. He leaned in and withdrew the dagger that had killed the demon so long ago.

It was a simple weapon. No jewels on the hilt or runes running along its blade. The only notable thing about it was that no rust covered it, and the edge was keen and sharp as if it had seen a whetstone that morning.

"There's something in his fist," said Tadok, prying open Malaketh's hand.

How many lives had those claws ended, thought Robin. *How many had begged for mercy as his fists closed over their throats.*

Tadok removed the Way Stone from Malaketh's skeletal hand. It was about the size of a quail's egg. Smooth like any other river stone. It had one single swirling icon carved in its center. It didn't glow, or shine or do anything spectacular.

Tadok took a step back and nodded to Bunda.

Bunda stabbed his flaming blade into Malaketh's breastbone, cracking and splitting the ancient skeleton. The flames quickly curled around bone as if the Dawn Father himself was eager for revenge.

"Get the book," Bunda commanded.

Tadok seemed as if he would protest, but after seeing the Tundrial's hard eyes he simply nodded. Robin retrieved the horrific account of Malaketh's sojourn in Trosia and cast it into the bonfire which now sat on the throne of the demon.

They watched in bleak silence as the holy fire consumed the demon and his journal. After seven minutes, Malaketh's spine collapsed under the weight, and his skull fell off, bouncing on the floor and rolling off the dais.

Robin pursued the blazing skull, not wanting to lose control of the fire in the enclosed chamber. When he reached its resting place between the pool of water and one of the massive stone firepits, his breath caught in his throat.

"Seirn!" he exclaimed, burrowing from Bunda.

There, in the corner behind the firepit, was Christopher Murley.

22 KIND STRANGERS

Tadok's eyes shot open, but he couldn't move. The ropes binding him were smothering, crushing down on his arms and chests. Where was Dorkah? The bandits were shaking him and torturing him with...mint?

He let his eyes focus. Above him was a ceiling made of tarp. Sunlight filtered from outside, and he could smell the fresh mountain breeze sweeping in the scent of lilies, so common on the footsteps of the Suldan in autumn.

He was not in the bandit's camp. He wasn't bound in ropes, but in the folds of a thick wool blanket. He wasn't being shaken; he was gently rocking in a wagon as the horses plodded down along the Triumph Road.

The scent of mint came from a ceramic cup being presented by a young girl who couldn't have been older than six. He looked at the girl, unsure of whose eyes were wider at that moment. He pulled aside the wool blanket and saw that his shirt had been removed and fresh clean bandages had been wrapped around his midsection where the Bandits had cut him.

"Where am I?" he asked the girl hoarsely, ignoring her offering. "How long have I been here?" he asked when she didn't answer his first question.

The girl remained wide-eyed and held her tongue, and she instinctively hugged a small ragdoll meant to look like a girl, but one of the buttons was missing from her eye.

"Woh!" a voice called from the front of the wagon, and it came to a halt.

A moment later, the flap at the back of the wagon was cast aside, and a smiling weathered face poked itself in.

"Ah! The Father be praised! Yer awake, half-elf," said its owner.

"Ye've been in and out for nearly two days now, young man."

The man hopped into the wagon. He was in his forties, with a sun-weathered face with wrinkles on the side of his eyes, which folded perfectly as he smiled at Tadok.

"Don't ye mind our Layla, she don't speak so much," he said putting a farmer's coarsened hand on his daughter's head affectionately.

"Is he awake?" came a matronly voice from the front of the wagon. "Did he drink the tea? Tell him to drink the tea, Dalton, it's mint and apples."

Dalton smiled at him again, indicating the steaming mug in Layla's small hands. "As ye've gathered, I'm Dalton, this is Layla," he pointed to the girl, "And the songbirds voice ye be hearin' from there is Sima, my wife. Do you have a name, traveler?"

"Tadok..." he mumbled, still trying to adjust his head to the situation.

The last thing he remembered was stumbling through the brush at night, trying to get enough distance from him and the carnage he'd left in the bandit camp. He must have lost consciousness. Days of being tied, beaten, and drugged had merged together into an endless nightmare. He wasn't sure how long he'd been a prisoner, but he imagined it had been at least three days. He winced as he gingerly touched his bruised forehead, where they had clubbed him repeatedly.

"Easy now, friend. You're safe now," said Dalton, his smiling face serious yet comforting. "We found ye half naked in the tall grass beside the road. Ye donna need to tell me what 'tis about, but ye can when you're ready. Fer now, drink up. Gain yer strength."

Tadok gingerly took the teacup from Layla, trying to look less threatening. He sipped it and then drank deeply, swallowing it in a couple of gulps. It was hot and burned the roof of his mouth, but he didn't care considering how parched he was, and the tea felt great as it flowed down his stomach.

When he'd slacked his thirst, he handed the cup back to Layla and whispered a rough, thank you.

"Two days?"

"Aye," nodded Dalton. "Ye were mumbling something about a torc or a dorkal, whatever that is."

"Did...you see a dark creature out there when you found me?" he asked, dreading the answer. He didn't know if any of the bandits had survived, but if they had, news would spread about the half-elf and his demon dog soon enough.

He'd summoned and lost control. She'd torn the bandits apart. Not that they didn't deserve it.

The blond girl had met him at an Inn on the outskirts of Berin's Inn. She'd told him she held a personal taste for half-elves and spent the evening under his arm, making sure his wine cup was always full. In the morning, he awoke alone with a continental headache. He cursed himself for a fool, but since all his belongings were intact, especially the sealed letter for Lord Shandel of Sebin, he counted his blessings, paid an alarmingly high bar tab, and continued on his way.

Messenger life wasn't too bad. The solitary life afforded him time on the road, away from others. Time to spend with Dorkah and to practice his magic far from the eyes of those who would persecute him for his strange art and stranger companion.

But that morning had been different. As he rounded a bend in the road, he saw her, but she wasn't alone.

There had been four of them. They attacked him before he understood the true nature of his folly. He was too slow and hungover to react in time. He'd been able to burn one of them with his electrical palm spell, but the moment they realized he was a spellcaster they knocked him out. From that point, it was all hazy.

They had taken him back to their camp, and they must have drugged him. They assumed he may be worth a ransom and tried to torture him for information. They must have been disappointed in the contents of his light coin purse. But the letter to lord Shandel, which he'd been paid to deliver, must have fooled them into thinking he had worth to the wealthy.

One of the bandits, a sadistic creature they'd called Toren, had decided to try a more direct tactic of trying to glean information from him and had attempted to carve something in his flesh under his ribs. It had proven a big mistake.

The pain had brought his senses rushing back to him and with their return, came the Eith'lin.

Dorkah had truly lived up to her demonic reputation that night. She'd ripped Toren's throat out and set to work on the rest. Even the girl had died in terror, begging for her life, but Tadok had no control over Dorkah. He was too dazed to command her and could only convey his pain and fear to her. When she was done, the camp looked like a chicken coup after a visit from a rabid wolf. Tadok had sent Dorkah back to her interdimensional lair after she'd freed him, and he stumbled, weak, and confused away from the carnage.

Dalton was looking at him in confusion, shaking his head in concern.

"When I was...sleeping, did my head change color perhaps?" he tried again, realizing how odd the question was now that it had been voiced.

Dalton grinned and nodded. "Tha' nasty bruise on yer head started red but is now blue and will likely pass through another color or two before it clears up."

Tadok sank gratefully back into his beddings.

***

By nightfall Tadok was strong enough to join Dalton and his family near the fire. Dalton's family prepared a potato stew, which they served with foraged nuts and berries and some hardtack bread.

Most of the evening's conversation was dominated by Dalton and Sima arguing good-naturedly over events in their lives and who said what to whom.

Layla listened with rapt attention and even giggled when her father sang an old amusing song about a tortoise who wanted to be other animals. Even Tadok was smiling by the end.

Layla finally fell asleep in her bedrolls by the fire, peacefully hugging Sindra, her doll, and Sima went off to clean the dishes in a nearby stream.

Dalton rose to better cover his daughter, smiling down lovingly.

"How long has she not spoken?" asked Tadok.

Dalton sat back down on his log and sighed. It was the first time a look of sadness crossed his smiling face.

"'Bout two years ago, her brother died when a horse kicked in his head. Layla was there. One moment the two children were laughin' and playin' and the next Cal was gone."

Tadok looked away awkwardly. "May his maker guide his soul," he said quickly.

Dalton shrugged. "'Twas a cruel die roll of Trin. Nothin' to do about it. She still has us."

Tadok nodded. Dalton had stated it accurately. Life was hard in Suldan-Karr, especially for the serfs and peasants. The withdrawal of Nemir had left a void with no central government to police the lands. While it meant villages weren't taxd for food-rent, it also meant they were on their own. A good harvest – gods be praised. A blight or a raid...well, Suldan-Karr was littered with the remains of the unlucky.

In Suldan-Karr there were a hundred reasons why a child wouldn't see adulthood. Growing up in Arga had its own challenges. The winters were cold, meaning those who didn't prepare could starve, and the Everwood was filled with creatures that could end the life of a human or an elf. But unlike those who lived west of the Suldan, the citizens of Arga had nothing to fear from Tundrial, since their islands were far to the west. Orcs had been purged from the Everwood centuries before by the elves and while bandits existed, they weren't bold enough to attack the settlements. Suldan-Karr, on the other hand, had all of these in spades.

"What of ye, Mister Tadok? Where are yer kin from?"

"I was born in the north. In a small village in the Everwood. Near Freelan."

"Ah, that explains why ye talk strangely, beggin' no offence, sir."

"Aye, it's all right," said Tadok with a hint of a smile. "But my father died before I drew my first breath, and my mother passed from a sickness on my sixth winter."

"So ye've been alone since? Ye poor thing!" said Sima as she rejoined them, taking a spot on the ground close to Dalton, who put his arm around her. Tadok assumed her pity was brought on by his youthful elven looks. He was nearing his twenty-fifth birthday, but probably looked in his teens by human standards.

"No, I was quite alright. A woman, a healer who'd known my grandfather, took me in and raised me."

"So what brought you all the way here from your Everwood?" asked Dalton.

"We traveled a lot. My foster mother would sell her services from town to town, helping those in need."

"She sounds like a living *Gotsan*," said Sima.

Tadok chuckled, "I don't know about that, but she assuredly helped many people."

'*Gotsan*', was old Karr for 'saint', or 'godsend'. In his mind, he saw an image of Sellwyn performing for drunken crowds, and he smiled.

He was not a religious man by any account, but he was confident no saint had ever hopped on tables and performed their miracles for sorins and bits.

When he bedded down, he did so in a heavy wool cloak and bedroll generously loaned by Dalton. They had expected him to spend another night inside the wagon, but he protested, saying he had taken up their wagon space long enough and he was feeling well enough to sleep on the ground by the fire.

"Well, if you're bent on braving the cold, why don't you have these," offered Sima, handing him a pair of leather, fur padded gloves. The gloves were warm and soft, but when Sima wasn't looking, he removed them. His magic relied on the nimbleness of his fingers. If he needed to call upon his flow, he didn't want a slow or erroneous gesture to result in a misspell or harmful result.

As he gazed up at the stars, he wondered where Sellwyn was. It had been nearly seven years since they had parted, and he didn't think of her as much as he used to. True, he was definitely an adult by human standards when she had left, and he could survive on his own—as he had. He was no healer and would be too embarrassed to cast magic in front of a tavern full of strangers, but he discovered that there was money to be made by those who were brave enough to travel the roads of Trosia with messages from one noble or trade-baron to another. And he could certainly take care of himself, as long as he could summon Dorkah. The downside of it was that he dared not summon her when people were around, lest he be accused of demonic activity. But Tadok never minded the solitude. It was Sellwyn who was good with people – not him. In fact, Dalton and his family were the first people he'd met in a long time with which he didn't feel the itch to leave as soon as he could.

Sellwyn may have taught him magic, history, numbers and languages, but the vagabond lifestyle she'd raised him into did little to teach him how to befriend anyone. Perhaps she'd known all he would need is Dorkah when she'd left, that night.

He'd simply woken up one morning in the inn outside Cherry Brook with a purse of fifty corins and a no explanations. Where she had gone and why, were mysteries which he couldn't answer. As he gazed sleepily at the stars, he wondered once more why she had abandoned him.

***

The next day, he sat in the back of the wagon with Layla. To his surprise, Dalton's family actually owned not one, but two books and Layla had opened one on her lap and was reading. Books were a true rarity with the lower classes of Suldan-Karr; thus, it was surprising that wheat and barley traders from a village outside of Westerwick like Dalton and Sima would own two of them. The truth was that not many people from the rural places in Trosia were as lucky as he to be schooled by a learned woman such as Sellwyn. Had she not come into his life, he would have likely stayed illiterate like most of the children of Sage's Rock. Who cares about reading or writing when the harvest needs to be reaped. He knew that in the larger cities, many of the churches offered basic schooling – but that wasn't available to the majority of the largely rural population of Trosia. It was a shame, as in Tadok's opinion–knowledge was a gift. The fact that Dalton and Sima would invest in such an education for their daughter spoke volumes of their character and love for their child. He wondered if Layla knew how privileged she was.

Layla suddenly grabbed his sleeve and pointed at a word in the book she was reading–"*The Art of Footland farming*", and looked up it him, her little face screwed up in puzzlement.

"It says, 'sickle'," he told her smiling.

She cocked her head to one side, so Tadok pointed at a long-handled sickle which sat in a box of tools at the front of the wagon and tried to mimic reaping wheat with the sickle.

He must have looked comical because she covered her mouth and giggled. Tadok smiled back at her.

She pointed to another word, and Tadok leaned in to look.

"Ah, that means 'milking'." Once again, he mimed milking a cow and she burst out laughing louder this time.

"Layla," called Dalton from the front of the wagon. "We're approaching the bridge; if there be water in the brook, I'll fetch us a nice trout for dinner. Hand me the fishin' rod, luv."

Tadok grinned at her and mimicked fishing. She laughed as she reached over towards the fishing pole.

There was a dull thud, and the wagon slowed to a halt. Suddenly, a scream erupted from Sima.

Three more thuds sounded as arrows ripped through the canvas above Layla. She shrieked, and Tadok pulled her down to the floor of the wagon.

"Stay down, little one!" he commanded.

Grabbing the long-handled sickle, Tadok hopped out of the back of the wagon and dropped to the ground the moment he landed. Crawling over to the low wall of the stone bridge, he assessed the situation. Sima crouched low on the other side of the wagon. Her eyes were wide, but she appeared unhurt. The same couldn't be said for Dalton. With dull, dead eyes, he was slumped over in the driver's bench, the shaft of the crossbow bolt which had ended his life jutted out of his chest.

Stay low! He mouthed to the terrified woman.

He dared a glance over his cover and immediately dropped back down as two bolts clattered against the stone wall. But he had seen them.

He had counted four of them, armed with crossbows. Dread gripped his heart as he realized these were no mere bandits. They weren't even humans. The jutting foreheads, the protruding incisors, the grayish skin...this was an orc raiding party.

Tadok wondered what they were doing so far south, but had no time to reflect on it. Two more bolts whisked over his head, one hitting the wooden wagon and the other ripping through the tarp. Tadok realized he couldn't stay like that. He crawled on his hands and knees a couple feet. It would take them a second to readjust their aim, but it may be enough.

He took a deep breath and dipped into his Flow. He started casting his spell while he was still behind cover, popping up like a jack-in-the-box as he completed the final hand gesture. His aim didn't have to be accurate; it was a diversion anyway.

Before the orcs could loose another bolt at him, the air behind them erupted in a cacophony of light and sound as colorful fireworks exploded behind them. The spell couldn't harm them, but the orcs didn't know that, and they turned to this new threat.

But the true threat was behind them. Tadok's forehead glowed red, and Dorkah was suddenly there. She didn't need to review the battle; he infused the knowledge into her the moment she popped into this reality. She charged growling at the orcs. The sound of the fireworks masked her advance, and the first orc died without even knowing why, as Dorkah slashed the back of his meaty neck, severing his spine from his brain stem.

The other three turned towards her, but it was too late for the next orc as the Eith'lin lunged at his throat, taking him to the ground.

Tadok rose to his feet and started sprinting to join the fight, his newly chosen weapon ready. Dorkah may have taken two of them down, but two orc fighters could still be dangerous, even for an Eith'lin.

He'd taken two steps off the bridge when he heard Sima's second scream. He turned around, intent on reassuring her that this demon was on their side, but his eyes widened when he realized what the real cause of Sima's terror was.

Behind them, three orcs charged across the bridge. They had laid in ambush from both sides of it.

He twisted to a skidding halt and began running back to the wagon.

Sima tried to run to him, but one of the creatures overran her, lopping off her head in one fell swoop of his cleaver. As her body fell, her headless neck sprayed blood all over the side of the wagon.

The orc didn't even stop, instead rushing at Tadok, his bloody cleaver held high.

Tadok drew upon his magic again just in time to raise a magical sheild. The spell hadn't fully encompassed him, when the orc brought his cleaver down. The strike would have slashed the half-elf's throat open, but to the orc's shock, his blade bounced off the invisible barrier and skipped off to the side, cutting a long red gash under his right armpit.

Ignoring the pain, Tadok slashed his sickle, hooking it around the orc's neck. He was shocked at how keen it was, as it cut through flesh, muscle and bone, sending the orc's head flying off his shoulders, as the creature had sent Sima's off her shoulder's moments earlier.

"Dorkah, I need you!" he shouted, as the next two orcs charged him. He had no time to look around to see the state of the Eith'lin, but knew that had she been injured he would have known.

The first brute to reach him had a large wooden mallet, which he swung at him. Tadok tried to bring his weapon up to block the attack, but wasn't fast enough. The wood connected with his shoulder, and he heard or felt a sickening crunch as his shoulder dislocated from its place. He howled in agony, dropping the scythe to the cobblestones. Backing away, it was all he could do not to pass out from the pain.

He managed to draw upon the Flow and shot his left hand forward, slamming it into the Orc's chest. The Orc roared as his gray flesh smoked and charred. Tadok allowed him no respite, shifting his hand from the creature's chest to his throat and squeezing with all his strength. Fused with electricity, Tadok's fingers seared into his flesh like butter, crackling with energy. The Orc wrenched the half-elf's hand off his throat, took a step back and fell to the ground, writhing and twitching as he tried to draw breath from his ruined larynx.

The last Orc had reached him, brandishing a wicked-looking spiked mace. Before he could split the half-elf's head open like a ripe melon, the dark shape of Dorkah leaped over him, jaws wide. The Orc swung at her, but she was too fast. Jaws snapped down on the orc's shoulder. As it fell to the ground. The Eith'lin slashed at its face and chest with daggerlike claws, spattering dark blood left and right.

Tadok nodded at her thankfully and turned to check on the other two crossbow wielders she'd been fighting before he'd called her. He was relieved to see them running up the hill, electing not to take a chance with the terrifying creature who had so easily dispatched three of their comrades.

Good, he thought. He didn't have the energy to fend them off.

Layla! He trotted over to the wagon, his useless right arm swinging at his side. His mind was racing on how to get her out without her seeing her two dead parents. He threw the wagon flap open with his left hand, and his heart sank.

In the wagon, Layla lay serenely, like she was sleeping. Only she wasn't. The black shaft of a crossbow bolt protruded from her back.

"No, no, no!" he cried.

He grunted painfully as he pulled himself up and into the wagon. He reached her and took her in his arm. She was as light as a feather. The wooden floor of the wagon, the books she'd been reading, the pillows and quilts they'd rested on as the wagon rocked on along the Triumph Road—all stained red with her blood. She was hugging her small doll to her chest.

Tears streaming unbidden down his cheeks, Tadok screamed at the heavens.

***

It had taken him two hours to bury Dalton and his family. There was no way he could dig proper graves, but with Dorkah's help he was able to find enough rocks for cairns.

He was no priest and didn't know what gods they even followed. Instead, he stood in silence, staring at the shallow graves of the family which had shown him compassion in a compassionless land. Dorkah was his only witness.

"I'm sorry," he said, laying Layla's doll at the head of her small cairn.

After another few moments, he turned his eyes west. To where the last two orcs had fled. He set the horses loose, and armed with his sickle and a salvaged crossbow, set off on the hunt.

But as the light began to fail, so did his strength. The pain in his shoulder had turned into a dull numbing ache. He wondered if he'd ever have use of the arm again.

But the real threat came from the slash in his side.

He heard Sellwyn's voice in his head. *It's important to take care of an injury first thing. Little cuts and bruises may seem small, but sometimes hold unseen dangers to our bodies.* Well, this was no mere scrape.

By the end of the hour, he could barely walk, and he slumped down under the branches of a pine tree. Blood was now flowing freely from the wound, soaking the breeches he'd been given by Dalton.

"I'm sorry, Layla," he whispered as tears came unbidden to his eyes. "I tried."

When he opened his eyes, a figure stood before him. A woman. She wasn't very tall, but the colorful headdress covering her head made her seem so.

"Sellwyn?" asked Tadok in confusion.

"I couldn't stop them," he sighed. "Gods know, I tried."

"I bet you did."

"There were too many. Even for Dorkah."

"Is she alive?", asked the shadowtouched.

"Aye."

Sellwyn nodded sagely. "Dorkah will live as long as you draw breath."

A thought dawned on Tadok, yet it didn't fill him with the dread it should have.

"Am I...dead?" he asked timidly.

"Not yet. But near to it, it appears."

"Oh," he said simply, not sure what he should say to that.

"But you won't die here, Sage's Rock. You still have a destiny to fulfil."

"What does that mean?" he asked impatiently. Now that he wasn't dying, he remembered how angry he was with her. "And where have you been? Why did you go? You discarded me like the shell of a walnut, with no explanation. Did I not deserve that much?"

She had the decency to look ashamed.

"I left to protect you, Tadok. You and Dorkah."

He stared at her with skepticism.

"Boy, you think you know, but you *don't*. There are entities in your world and in others which would seek you and your Eith'lin. Entities who are *not* your friends. If they can't find you, they'll find me. And the longer I stayed in your company, the more they were likely to."

Cryptic as always, he thought.

"They killed the child," he said, fresh tears leaking from his eyes.

Sellwyn stayed silent for a moment, lost in her thought. When she spoke again, her voice was grave.

"Many more children will die, unless you act. Terrible powers are clawing out of their prisons as we speak, and it is time for you and for Dorkah to join the fight."

"What—" he began, but she cut him off.

"Listen to me carefully," she cautioned, and Tadok noticed he could see the mountains through her face. She was becoming transparent. Her voice seemed to be receding.

"You must go east. Seek out the Old Tower. I have tried to shield you from the wars of your ancestors, but they are coming for you."

She looked behind her, and her face which was now like mist, looked afraid.

"Someone is coming. You must go east, Tadok," she said, her voice seeming far away. "I love you..."

"Sellwyn wait! What Old Tower?" he tried to rise to her, but he was in too much pain. "Sellwyn!"

A new face suddenly swam into his vision. This one hardened with darker skin and a black beard.

"Easy," said the face, "You're safe. Seirn has healed all your

237

wounds."

Tadok's head slumped back down.

23 DEFENSIBLE POSITIONS

The sun was rising up over the Suldan mountains, washing the landscape in a honey glow. A mist hugged the ground, allowing only the treetops and the hills to peak through the lake of grayness.

Robin, Tadok and Bunda emerged from the broken guard tower into the light. In his arms, Bunda carried the boy, Christopher Murley, gently.

Bunda couldn't estimate the amount of relief he felt to feel the sun on his face, and he whispered another blessing to Seirn. For being alive, for being out of that cursed place and for finding the boy.

Alive.

He'd lost hope, as had his companions. He assumed the boy had been devoured by the deep eel or had drowned in the underground waters below the village. He'd thought knowing where he'd died would be all the comfort they would have from this tragic tale.

But there he was, alive and breathing. He recalled Swegan's lecture on the underground honeycomb of tunnels which connected everything. One such must have led from the well to the pool in Malaketh's throne room. Probably brought on when Malaketh fought the champions who'd killed him and brought down the temple in his wrath.

Christopher had swum in darkness, finally emerging in the underground tomb, where he'd lived in the dark for four days and nights. He wasn't dehydrated, thanks to the water, but he was weak and tired.

"I'll check the stables," said Robin. "Hopefully we can overtake the villagers and return the boy to his mother's arms before we lose too much ground."

"I don't think that will be needed," said Bunda, staring at the broken main gate of the curtain wall.

Robin followed his gaze, and found an unexpected site. There they were; Marven and Odetta, Tilly, Swegan and Diggericut, Hanlan and his son, the Argun's with Theia supporting Aldeira and finally Onlan bringing up the rear with Yorgen, whose hands were bound in front of him. Ren and Mara lead the way. They all looked tired and frightened, but each held a weapon, either salvaged from the bandits or one of their own ownerships, like in the case of Swegan's ax.

"Ren," began Robin confused. "Why are you all here? You should be on the road to Berin's Inn."

Before the one-eyed half-elf could answer, a scream erupted from behind him.

Aldeira stared at her lost son, limp in Bunda's arms. Bunda knew that scream. It was the sound a person made when their life was shattered. Aldeira had screamed it twice in less than a week. It was one thing knowing her son wouldn't come back, but quite another to unexpectedly see his body.

But then Christopher raised his head and looked at her.

"Mummy?" the boy asked sleepily.

The scream cut short. Her eyes widened in disbelief, and then tears rushed unbidden down her cheeks. Leaving Theia Argun's side, she sprinted towards Bunda and her boy.

Bunda lowered the boy to his feet, still keeping his hand on his shoulder for support. He was very weak.

But it didn't matter; within moments, his mother crushed him in her arms, and his own sobs joined hers. They stood like that for a minute as the village folk milled around them. The looks ranged from shock to open grins. Even sour Yorgen seemed moved with emotion.

"I'm sorry mummy. I tried to swim back, but the monster..." the boy broke down in fresh sobs, as the gravity of his ordeal came rushing back to him.

"Hush now, my love," she whispered through her tears, "I have you again. Praise the gods!"

She shot a tearful look at Bunda and mouthed, *Thank you.*

"Why are you all celebrating, you fools?" asked Tadok harshly, dousing their merriment like ice water. "After all we went through to save the boy, you've doomed him and the rest of you!"

"Tadok has a point," said Bunda. "You shouldn't be here. Dell will be here by nightfall, and while *we* may be able to outrun him–you won't."

"I'm afraid, my friend, the time for outrunning has come and gone," said Ren gravely.

"What are you on about?" asked Tadok, squinting.

It was Mara who spoke. "As dawn broke on our way down, we saw them. They were coming around Broken Axle Bend. I couldn't count them from that distance, but it was definitely riders."

"'Tis true," said Ren in agreement. "I may have lost one eye, but my other is better than the two most people have in their skulls. It's definitely Dell, and he'll be here within an hour or two. Maybe three if he stops at the village first."

"Fuck!" cursed Tadok.

Looking at the broken fort whose courtyard they were all standing in, Bunda understood.

"And you thought that this was the best place to make a stand."

Marven and Ren nodded.

"Look at this place! It's in ruins," shouted Tadok in exasperation. "You could have rolled the dice. If Trin favored you, perhaps Hayek would dawdle to bury his men or try and find his prize. Perhaps he would stay here for days, giving you a chance!"

"Aye, lad," said the dwarf, his tone surprisingly gentle. "But perhaps he wouldn't. So we *did* roll the dice. And it settled on standing our ground."

"And how will those dice land? Will they magically help sixteen villagers–two-thirds of which are women, children, and elderly, defeat Hayek and at least twenty of his men?"

"No Tadok. That's not what they thought." That was Robin's voice, which, despite its calmness, cut the conversation like a hot knife. "They thought that sixteen villagers, a Seal Shore barbarian, a former thief and a half-elven sorcerer, would defeat Hayek and his men."

Tadok locked eyes with Robin. Bunda knew his rage. This was the exact thing Robin had promised him they would avoid. But that conversation now seemed so long ago. Before, they had fought mad priests, zombies, wolves, deep eels, bandits, wizards, and whatever the hell that horrifying thing in the tomb was. Now it looked like a reality, and Tadok knew it.

"Fuck!" cursed the half-elf again.

Then his shoulders slumped in resignation, and he shook his head, and under his breath, he muttered something in the form of, "You'll just have to pick another one, Sellwyn..."

Robin nodded at his friend in silence, not pressing for further information about his cryptic words. He then turned to the people of Suldan's Bluff.

"The woman, the children, the elderly and the prisoner—get into the tower and head down below. There is a room with cells there—Mara knows it all too well. Find whatever you can to barricade the door. The rest of you, stay up here—we need to form a plan."

"And avoid the door at the back of the corridor," added Tadok. "There's a nasty bone monster only Bunda can vanquish down there."

If anyone had questions about anything the three of them had encountered that night, they stayed their curiosity. There would be time to share stories later. Maybe.

As they milled about, hugging each other and praying to see another dawn, Diggericut stopped suddenly pulling Swegan's sleeve and pointing.

"Is that what I think it is?"

"Aye. I'm surprised you dinna know it was here. There used to be at least one in every garrison in the days before the war. But 'tis clearly broken."

"Perhaps not..."

Bunda smiled when he thought no one was looking and shot a glance up at the sun peaking over the Suldan Mountains.

Today was a good day to meet Seirn.

24 BANDITS

Dell Hayek wasn't a tall man. His five feet and four inches of height were emphasized as he swung off his saddle beside the hangman tree. His followers remained in their saddles.

The sun had already dried up all the mist, removing all concealment these men would have had from prying eyes. Not that they were trying to conceal themselves. Nothing in the pass or between Sebin and Berin's Inn would hold any threat to them. *They* were the mountain wolves, and woe to any unfortunate enough to be picked up by their scent.

Tadok wondered where Dell had found such a large warband. Were they all Shadder Hands? Were they perhaps hired muscle? Or other road bandits and raiders who'd been subdued and absorbed into his band? It wasn't clear. But one thing *was* clear…

"Twenty men, my ass," muttered the half-elf.

"What do you see, Tadok?" asked Robin, standing beside him on the wall.

Tadok turned to the Heartlander and blinked to adjust his eyes. The magical magnification spell narrowed his vision up close, disorienting him for a moment until his eyes focused for the range of the man standing right next to him.

"I'm counting around forty men and horses. They're as armed as a Tundrial raiding band, too."

"Trin be damned," swore Robin.

Tadok turned back towards the village. Any other watcher would have just seen the horses and could barely make out the men riding them. But with his magical vision, he was able to see swords, axs, and bows slung across their backs or hanging from belts and baldrics.

Hayek bent down between the freshly made cairns. He seems calm and composed. It was hard to make out his expression. At this distance all he could see was the beard which covered the lower half of his face.

Another rider dismounted and walked up to the bandit lord. There seemed to be some exchange between them. It didn't seem heated, which made Hayek's sudden outburst even more surprising.

Tadok couldn't hear what was being said, but suddenly Hayek slapped the man hard enough to knock him to the ground. Before he could rise, Hayek straddled him, striking him repeatedly in the face. The man seemed to try and fend off his commander's rage, but his hands were swatted aside as Hayek's fists rose and fell. After nearly a minute, the man's hands fell limp to his sides. What was most unsettling about the whole exchange was that none of Hayek's other men intervened. Even at this distance, Tadok could feel the fear that held Hayek's men in check.

Hayek finally stood, wiping his fists on the fallen man's cloak. He issued a command, and the riders turned their horses to the village, charging into Suldan's Bluff, each of them not wanting to be the last man to carry out their master's orders.

They washed over the village like a torrent. Splitting up between the houses. He could see them kicking down doors, weapons drawn. Had they found a living person in any of the houses they would have taken out their master's psychotic wrath out on them, be it a man, woman or child. Tadok could now understand the terror in Marven and Swegan's eyes when they learned that it was Robin, Bunda and he who had buried the sheriff and his boys. On the green, Hayek trotted in calmly astride his charger like a pebble in a disrupted anthill.

"They're heading into the village," Tadok said to Robin, without breaking eye contact with the bandits.

"At least that should give us a little more time," said Robin, looking over his shoulders at the preparations conducted in the courtyard.

"What little good *that* will do."

Tadok's concern at what was about to transpire wasn't unfounded. Beyond the misjudgment of the band's size, there were other concerns. He was tired. He hadn't slept for two days, and he'd not been sparing with his spells either. His Flow felt like a weak trickle, and not the powerful rush with which it flooded him when he used it after a good night's sleep. It meant he would need to rely on his crossbow and sickle in a fight, and that wasn't nearly enough. He only hoped he could buy enough time for Dorkah to heal fully from their skirmish with the half-orc the night before.

He was using the last of his energy for surveillance, which he supposed was as good a use as any.

That reminded him.

"We're going to need to prepare the other's for Dorkah," he said to Robin. "The last they'd seen her you'd told them she was a 'Dorkah Demon' who existed to devour the souls of liars. We want them to know she's fighting under our banner."

"Aye. We will. Once Hayek turns his men and horses to the tower, we'll set their minds and spirits to the battle to come. They'll know of Dorkah, and see her as a friend."

"While I would wish that to be so, I wouldn't rely on it," answered Tadok.

"Why is that?"

Tadok sighed. Aside from Sellwyn and his new companions, few had seen Dorkah and not headed off screaming in fright or lived long enough to do so.

"She's not of this world. Men fear what's not of their world."

To his surprise, Robin chuckled.

"What's amusing, Sandisan?" he asked suspiciously, thinking Robin may be ridiculing his fear over Dorkah's exposure to the world.

"Nothing. You've given me a solution for two hard truths I needed to tell them. If I were about to lock swords with forty blood-crazed brigands, I'd be happy to have my side bolstered by a *demon*."

Despite starting off the sentence smiling, his smile faded as he completed it. His eyes turned down, as did his smile. Tadok knew exactly what he was thinking. In a world filled with magic and monsters, demons were yet a thing of myth. Placed in the same category as dragons and bogymen. Tadok knew they existed somewhere in other realms, Sellwyn had told him as much, but they were there to represent the ultimate evil, in his mind. Used to frighten children into following their mothers' instructions. *'Go into the woods without my permission and a demon will get you. Demons eat children who don't eat their greens'*. But now, having actually seen a real one and read about its terrible exploits, Tadok would never again use the word flippantly.

"What are they doing now?" asked Robin, changing the subject.

Tadok turned back to the village and readjusted his magnified vision. The bandits were exiting the houses in confusion and disappointment that no villager had remained to be zealously tortured. As they gathered around Hayek, he suddenly turned and looked directly at the half-elf.

Fear gripped Tadok's heart. Could Hayek see him? He found himself crouching, despite knowing it was too far for humans to see anything more than the form of the lonely, ruined tower nestled in the mountains. Still, Tadok felt he could feel the bandit lord's eyes boring into him from afar, even if the half-elf couldn't actually see him.

"He's figured it out. He knows we are at the tower."

"Well then. I suppose there is no turning back now," said the Heartlander in calm resignation.

It was Tadok's turn to chuckle. "I don't think there was any turning back since you announced we would search for the child. You can be stubborn Sandisan."

Robin smiled at him. "You won't be the first to say it, half-elf." His smile shifted, and he looked at him solemnly. "But I'm glad you're here at my side, friend."

Robin began climbing down the broken steps to the courtyard where the rest were preparing.

"Robin," Tadok called after him. Robin halted, turning back.

"I'm glad you're at mine. *Friend.*"

***

"Hold still, friend," said Nick, trying to steady the half-elf as he took to his feet shakily. "You've been badly wounded. I gather it was you who slew those orcs at the bridge?"

The man looked at Nick in confusion, still trying to take in his surroundings. He began to try and push Nick aside but suddenly cried out in pain as his dislocated shoulder protested. His knees buckled, and Bunda rushed to catch him.

"Easy," said Bunda, "That shoulder isn't right."

His lord's magic could close wounds, repair tissue and even knit bones back together, but with a dislocated limb there was nothing to repair. Luckily, he needed no magic to fix that.

"Hold still, and count with me to three. One...two..." he didn't wait for three.

The half-elf cried out as Bunda yanked his arm back then pushed it into its socket in a fluid motion.

"There you go, friend. But you should keep the arm—"

"I'm not your friend," spat the half-elf and pushed him aside now that both his arms were functioning. "Where are they?" he asked, trying to focus his bleary eyes on the hills behind them.

Nick and Bunda glanced at each other in confusion.

"The orcs?" asked Nick.

"Yes, the orcs!"

"They're dead. We found their bodies on the bridge next to the wagon."

"That wasn't all of them," he said, picking up the crossbow which had rested beside him with his good arm. "Two escaped."

Nick began scanning the horizon, which had turned dark by now, his own bow ready.

"We haven't seen any sign of them, but if there are orcs wandering these parts, I suggest we set up a watch tonight. You need to rest, but Nick and I can split up the— where are you going?" he asked as the man started striding purposefully towards the foothills.

The half-elf paused, looking back at them. He seemed to take them in for the first time.

"I thank you for healing me, barbarian. May whatever god you follow bless you. Stay safe." And with that, he turned to leave.

"Are you daft, man, or just Trin-touched?" asked Nick in disbelief. "We just saved your life. You're in no shape to fight a dazed gopher, let alone a band of orcs."

"Don't you worry about me, I'm better off alone," he replied stubbornly.

"Clearly," he answered sarcastically.

The half-elf stared angrily at the Heartlander for a moment.

"What do you want? Coin?"

"Do you believe the balls on this one?" asked Nick, his own anger rising.

"We want nothing from you, half-elf, beyond not having to heal you again," said Bunda evenly.

"In that case, stay out of my way, and I of yours. Don't follow me," he called out over his shoulder as he strode off.

Bunda was about to follow him, but Nick put a hand on his shoulder.

"These parts are dangerous enough for those who aren't idiots. If this one chooses to get himself killed, then that's a death of his own making."

Bunda stared uncertainly at the man's back as he crested the hill, but decided not to insist on it. Besides, if they were going to split the night between them, it may be best to get some rest.

"This is as good a spot as any, but perhaps we should forgo the fire. How shall we keep watch? Four by four?"

Bunda finally turned back from the man and removed his travel pack.

"Aye. I'll take second watch, if you don't mind."

***

As Dawn broke, Bunda was ready to receive it, as he had every day since he'd been initiated into the order of Seirn. Kneeling, with his face to the rising sun, he raised his muscular arms and begun to chant.

"*Kutain adas gurd Seirn laktani raith. Kutain adas gurd raith silath dumari.*" *I welcome thee, Seirn Lord of the Morning. I welcome the sun, giver of life.*

He repeated the phrase in *Alan-Nemtang* six times.

"Do you do this every morning, Tundrial?" asked Nick in a slurred voice from under his cloak.

Bunda smiled at him as he rose to retrieve his shirt from the tree branch it hung on.

"I do. Didn't sleep well?" he asked.

Nick sat up and yawned sleepily. "I'm not much of a morning person."

"Why is that? All those who dwell in the light should give thanks that the sun rises and gives its warmth."

"Let's just say, I'm fine with the night." He began rummaging in his nap sack for something to eat.

"Only predators and criminals sleep by day and wake by night," said the cleric cheerfully, tossing him a loaf of hardtack from his own pack.

Despite his sleepiness, Nick caught it effortlessly and smiled to himself.

"It's good you're awake. We should try and make it past the foothills today. And I think we should not be on the road. Not until we're sure we've past those orcs."

Nick nodded. "I'm thinking the same thing," he said in between mouthfuls. "If my memory is as sturdy as *this*," he said indicating to the bread grimacing, "there is an abandoned farmhouse a few miles off the road which we could camp in tonight. No one's lived there for years, and those clouds don't look too friendly."

He was right. Bunda could see the dark clouds gathering to the east. They looked like bruises in the sky and were too plump and laden with rain to climb over the Suldan Mountain range. Bunda expected them to unload their contents by noon, and he would be happy to make it to shelter before he was too soaked. An old barn house could provide shelter and conceal a small fire if they kept it modest.

***

As the day stretched on, the two of them kept the Triumph Road to their south. They made sure that they were far enough from the road to avoid any ambush set for anyone traveling along it, but still in their sights so they didn't get turned around or lost. The open fields gave way to rising foothills as they neared the mountains, and the sky kept getting darker.

All around him, Bunda could see the remains of civilization. Low crumbling walls which had marked orchards or fields, burnt husks of houses and barns. From time to time, he could see bones of animals or humans littered near them.

"Who lived here?" he asked as they made their way around a shallow gully.

Nick shrugged. "Families. Communities. These lands were once rather populated, they say."

"What drove them out? Orcs and bandits?" He kneeled next to the tree and brushed off an old rusty arrowhead, turning it over in his hand.

Nick stopped and looked back at him, raising his eyebrow.

"You don't know?"

"Know what?" asked Bunda.

"You really don't," he mused. "Well, it was *your* people. Two and a half decades ago, during the War of the Broken Crown."

Bunda stood up tossing the arrow away as if it was poisonous. The *Tundrial* called that war, the *Ineil'tha.* Which translated as 'Overthrowing' in *Alan-Nemtang.* For his countrymen, it was a great moment in their history, when they had rid themselves of the tyranny of the Nemirian empire. His people had then crossed the Thunder Straits and cut a great swath of destruction all across the continent. He knew that they had turned back after being unable to take Sebin. Their ferocity and battle skill useless against the high walls and battlements of the fortified city. The Tundrial horde was ten thousand strong. The problem was that ten thousand warriors needed to eat, and during a lengthy siege, they would need to eat a lot. Any strategist knew that armies were only as strong as their logistic channels. The Tundrial had no such concepts. Their logistics boiled down to whatever they could carry on their backs or their saddles. The lands west of the Suldan were verdant and plentiful. However, as irony would have it, the horde had pillaged it like a plague of locust, leaving nothing that wasn't nailed down. In some of the wilder raids, bands of warriors had even set fire to the fields and the granaries, which worsened the situation.

Yet, unlike the Mainlanders, the Tundrial had no interest in subjugating other nations. Taking slaves was acceptable, as were the realities of war. But enslaving a whole people? It wasn't that the Tundrial had any compassion, especially not for those who'd taxd and dominated them for centuries. It was simply that ruling others seemed like such a bother. It meant they would have to actually govern the day-to-day lives of their subjects, which they had no interest in doing. You could buy a fish and eat for a day, or you could learn to fish. But you could also wait for the fisherman to return with his haul, then steal that haul whenever you like and rough up the fisherman, so he knows better than to protest. That was the way of the Tundrial.

But the stories told around campfires in Shard or in Tarthen always spoke of daring raids and great victories. No one mentioned the desolation left in their wake. As a boy, he'd assumed that the people went back to their lives once the warriors from the sea returned to their longboats. He hadn't envisioned that there was no life to return to. Even for those who survived the ax or the arrow, and didn't end up bound and dragged off to the isles, the odds of surviving through the next winter were small. Homesteads and whole villages would be simply abandoned, as those who survived tried to make it to the safety of the cities.

He now felt foolish for romanticizing it before. Foolish, and a little ashamed. He'd never taken part in raids. He had been too young when his father and his brothers would, and then he'd joined Seirn's order. In fact, the exile which Iron Tooth had imposed on him was the first time he'd actually set foot on the mainland of Trosia.

Had his mother come from a farmstead like the one they had passed? Had she been a young maid milking a cow or gathering firewood when his father and his warband had risen like demons from the hills around them and brought death to everyone she knew? Had his father raped her in the aftermath of the battle, or had he the decency to bring her home before he enforced marriage on her? There was simply so much he didn't know. He hated the fact that he couldn't talk to her.

This new outlook made her escape evermore justified. It also raised a longing in his heart to see her again if she lived.

"I'm sorry, mother. I'm sorry they did this to you," he whispered under his breath.

"What was that?" asked Nick, walking a few paces ahead of him.

"Nothing," he replied. "We'd best make it to that barn you mentioned. I gather it has a roof?"

***

The dark clouds didn't disappoint, and by afternoon a sheer vertical torrent fell from the sky and drenched everything. Bunda was grateful to Seirn when Nick suddenly pointed to a meadow as they crested one of the hills.

There was the farm. When people had lived there, there had been a number of buildings erected around it, and a stone well centered between them. But now it was clearly abandoned. Two of the buildings, which may have been houses, were burned black, and in the third, the roof had collapsed as the rotting wood beneath could no longer support its weight.

But the barn was still intact, with only a hole or two in the thatch. To Bunda's eyes, it looked very inviting.

They trudged down the muddy hill, the rain abating temporarily, thank Seirn. As they neared the base, he noticed Nick was picking up the pace.

A childhood memory of his brothers and him, racing up to the cliff during summers in Tarthen, where they would spend the day diving off it into the ocean below, came out of nowhere. The more elaborate and acrobatic the dive, the more prestige was gained.

Bunda picked his pace up to match Nick's, and the moment he caught the Mainlander's eyes, he grinned and set off down the hill at a sprint.

"Really?" asked the Heartlander. But it didn't stop him from launching after him.

As they raced, Bunda found himself laughing despite himself, and a quick glance backward showed that Nick was grinning, too.

While Bunda had the head start, Nick was clearly a better sprinter and he managed to overtake him near the finish line - less than twenty feet before the partially open barn door. Nick darted inside, and Bunda slowed himself down to catch his breath.

Just as he reached the door, it flew open and Nick was propelled backwards, through it, crashing into the larger man, and sending them both into the mud.

A tall, imposing figure emerged from the door, flanked by three of his companions.

As Bunda rolled over, trying to get back to his feet in the slippery mud, he glanced at Nick. He was covering his face where the orc had punched him, and blood was dripping from between his fingers.

The orc was now the only one grinning.

Other orcs emerged out of the darkness of the barn door. Had they seen them running down the hill like two idiots? They'd been so careful to avoid an orc ambush that they walked right into one. Had they kept up their caution, they may have been able to surprise the creatures, but it was too late for that now.

"Get up, Nick!" he called to his friend harshly.

Nick tried to rise, but only slipped and fell to his knees. Bunda could see the blood running from the cut above his eyebrow. The rain was making it look worse than it probably was, and the orcs simply laughed at his friend's plight.

Bunda turned back to them, and drew his saber.

"*Sues Kashik!*" he cried in the Divine, and suddenly his saber burst into flame.

The orcs ended their laughter abruptly, and drew their own weapons. The lead orc brandished a flail with a wicked-looking spiked head at the end of the chain. As for his companions, one brandished a loaded crossbow, another wielded two hand axs and the third wielded a large wooden club ending with nails hammered into it in one hand, and a javelin in his other hand. They fanned out, aiming to flank him.

Bunda backed up, protectively shielding Nick as he tried to regain his feet again. If his friend couldn't fight, there was little chance he could hold them off.

"Come on, you bastards. What are you waiting for!" he growled at them.

There was a twang as a crossbow let loose its bolt.

25 THE BRAVE

It was noon by the time Hayek and his men made it up the winding path to the tower. They halted when they saw Mendel's cart turned on its side, blocking the entrance where the gate had fallen off its hinges years ago. It didn't really barricade the portal, not being as long as the gate was wide. A man could easily walk around it, but it prevented them from charging in on their horses, three abreast.

Robin risked a glance from his hiding spot, atop of the wall, behind a broken merlon. The wall's merlons and crenels had crumbled into a jagged mass years ago. There wasn't much cover that hadn't crumbled or collapsed when the tower fell, but there was enough of it to conceal himself, Ren, Mara, and Trace–the blacksmith's sixteen-year-old son. Each was armed with a bow, knocked with an arrow. Robin had impressed on them the importance of staying concealed to mask their numbers until the fight began.

Dell was looking at the gate in contemplation. His men, not daring to disturb him, waited anxiously for orders, holding their position forty yards away from the wall.

"You there in the tower!" shouted the bandit lord, cupping his mouth with his hands so his voice would carry. His voice was like gravel, yet clear and confident. "You've done something very rare. *Stupid*, but very rare."

Robin resisted the urge to answer.

"Few men impress me. Yet you somehow managed to kill or capture my men, and now you've taken my tower. That's no small feat for a seasoned killer, let alone a sheep-fucking farmer."

His voice was cool as ice, but Robin could detect the hint of explosive rage bubbling beneath. But as long as he was talking...

Robin rose from his vantage point, putting himself in plain view of the bandits.

"Those were *your* men?" he asked innocently. "I hope you didn't pay much for them. They did mention that they took orders from a craven gnome-sized man with a pig's face and a goblin's brain."

Short men always seemed touchy on their height, and Robin was hoping that the humiliation in front of his men would send him over the edge, making him rash. Rash men made mistakes. While they had the tower, Dell had a force nearly four times their size, not to mention the experience gap in their fighting prowess. So it was down to dwindling his force until they could handle it in a melee. That meant it was a number's game, and any mistake Hayek made now would cost him men.

Hayek laughed at the insult, as if they were two old friends throwing good-natured jibes at each other over pints of ale.

"You're no farmer, son. And you talk like you come from Sandisan. Did the villagers hire you to fight me?"

"Hire me? No," he replied, matching Hayek's grin. A thought came to him, and he improvised. "Gale the Boon did. He's fed up with your blundering and sent us to find the treasure beneath the tower. Your men, now serve *me*. Well, the ones we didn't make examples of, that is."

Dell's men looked at each other uneasily. Mentioning the head of the Shadder Hands obviously unsettled them. But Dell only laughed again.

"*You're* a Hand?" he asked in disbelief.

"Aye. It was I who ran Reigar through, while you were sucking back-alley cocks in Sebin for bits," he retorted. "You don't believe me? You can ask your friend." He tossed the bloody head of the half-orc they had killed the night before. The one he assumed was Sledder—Hayek's second in command. The half-orc was hopefully Hayek's fiercest fighter, and showing his men that they had slain him may demoralize them somewhat.

Hayek made no move to examine the head. If the loss of his second in command had any effect on him—he never showed it.

"What about the wizard? Is he dead?"

"As a doorknob," answered Robin matter-of-factly. "Not much of a wizard, if you ask me. My man burned him to charcoal while he was looking for his spell book. You really should get better men. Speaking of men," he turned to Dell's henchmen and raised his voice.

"I'm under orders from the Shadow Master to slit all your throats. But I value good men, and I'll spare you all if you bring me that gobbo-ass's head," he said pointing to Hayek.

They looked at each other, but none moved to obey. *Well, it was worth a roll of the dice,* he thought silently.

Dell didn't even look back at his men. His confidence in their loyalty wasn't mere bravado either. The only thing Dell Hayek's men truly feared, was Dell Hayek.

"You see, boy; the problem with your tale is that the Boon is hundreds of miles away, in Sandisan. He doesn't even know of Delona's plans. But me, I'm *here*. And the last thing you'll see today before you die is your throat in my hands as I choke the shit-kicking grin off your face.

"But I'll make *you* an offer." The smile on his face and his jovial tone contrasted jarringly with his words. "Surrender the fort and come down here, and I'll not kill the villagers hiding in there with you. Otherwise, we'll butcher every man, woman, and child who were foolish enough to think you could protect them."

He's trying the same tactic I used, Robin thought. He wondered if any of the citizens of Suldan's Bluff were foolish enough to consider Dell's offer.

Well, he wasn't about to find out.

"Enough talk," he grunted, and made a gesture with his hand. Ren, Mara and Trace rose from their hiding spots on the wall flanking the gate, picked their targets and let their arrows loose in a heartbeat.

Ren's arrow struck one of the riders in the throat, dropping him off his saddle. Trace's arrow missed the mark, but hit a rider's horse, which whinnied, sending its rider rolling off to the ground. Mara's arrow was directed at Hayek, but the bandit lord simply twisted aside in his saddle and the arrow stuck in the tree behind him.

God's he's fast! thought Robin as he loosed his own arrow. He didn't aim at Hayek, as he was huddled low in his saddle. The original plan was for him to take out the leader, but Mara was proving to be terrible at following orders, apparently. Instead, he aimed at one of the men behind him, hitting him squarely in the chest. The man screamed and clutched the shaft before he fell to the ground.

The parley was over.

"Kill them!" commanded Hayek, and ten men swiftly dismounted, drawing their bows.

"Take cover!" shouted Robin, and dropped low behind the merlon. He didn't have time to check if the others did the same as arrows shrieked over his head or clattered against the stone wall.

Knocking another arrow, he waited for the volley to end. He rose quickly and picked another target - one of the archers, and let loose. The man fell with an arrow in his throat, and another screamed as Ren's arrow buried itself in his thigh. Fortunately, the loss of an eye didn't hamper the half-elf's archery skills.

Twenty riders, charged at the gate, hooves kicking up mud and dust. Luckily, they needed to slow down as they neared the upturned cart.

"Aim at the men at the gate! Mind the archers!" he shouted to his fellow archers.

He managed to take the lead one out, and Mara's arrow took down a horse when it pierced it through its neck. Trace finally hit a target, sinking his arrow to the shaft in a rider's gut. Ren missed as he had to duck under the next volley of arrows to avoid being pin-cushioned.

Robin shot a glance back into the courtyard. Everyone was in position, and no arrow passing over the wall had hit any of them. Good, but it was clear that this tower wouldn't be protected by four archers. Time for the next part of the defense plan.

He heard the whistle of the arrow less than a second before it hit him. It felt like an ogre flicked his earlobe. He raised a hand to the side of his head and felt warm wetness running down his neck. His ear was ringing. He turned to the man who's shot him and let loose his own arrow, which stuck in the man's hand, ending his archery days.

Hayek motioned to the other men he'd left in reserve. "Circle around them. Scale the walls!" he ordered them. The men leaped off their horses and split into two groups, each flanking the tower from the east and west.

Damn! He hadn't counted on them scaling the walls. The rough and broken curtain wall, overgrown with vines, would make scaling it easy. Hell, they'd used the same entrance the night before.

Below, the riders had dismounted and were dragging the cart out of the way. So much for that obstacle.

"Ren, Trace–they're scaling the walls!"

Ren, who was positioned with the youth on the east side of the wall, understood immediately. Dragging the boy by his collar, he ran down the wall, ducking under arrows as they sailed over his head. As he ran, he took a shot at the climbers below. If his arrow struck true, Robin couldn't tell from his vantage point.

"Focus on the archers," he commanded Mara, who was positioned with him on the west side, as he bolted along the wall to repel the climbers. "Don't get killed!"

Not staying to see if his command had been followed, he drew another arrow and shot one of the men circling the wall in the back, just as the riders who'd attacked the gate broke through, charging into the courtyard.

***

"Aim at the men at the gate! Mind the archers!"

Bunda heard Robin shout out the command as arrows continued to sail over the wall into the courtyard.

He muttered a prayer to Seirn, and his sword burst into flame. He'd done his best to meditate and conduct his morning ritual, but he still felt drained from the day before. All living things needed rest, even clerics of the Dawn Father. Without it, he didn't believe he had much more holy juice running through his blood.

Looking at the back of the wagon, which was now being jolted repeatedly by Hayek's men, he muttered, "We should have set it afire.

That would have slowed them down."

"Perhaps you're right lad, but 'tis too late for that," replied Swegan. The dwarf had donned a mail shirt which must have been ancient, but clearly well kept. The riveting was well-oiled, and missing links had been replaced over the years. "Don't you worry, we've got other surprises planned for them."

He looked at the other defenders. They formed a line in the center of the courtyard, ready to charge at the first attacker to pass by the gate. To his left and right stood Hanlan and Onlan. The smith was armed with a well-made steel longsword and a round wooden shield. While he watched the gate in anticipation, he couldn't help shooting sideways glances at his son on the wall with Ren. Bunda wondered how much it would be a problem for the gate-defenders if Trace was killed or wounded. Would Hanlan be able to execute his duties in such an eventuality?

Onlan stared at the gate in a battle-hardened veteran's grim determination, holding the long-shafted war ax salvaged from the half-orc who they'd killed the night before. Bunda recalled that the grizzled old half-orc had been a soldier in the War of the Broken Crown, so he had experience. On the other hand, he'd spent the last two weeks half-starved and tortured by Sheilagh.

After Onlan and Hanlan, stood Swegan and Mendel. Swegan was clearly no stranger to battle, but Mendel was visibly shaking as he held his long sword.

"It's easy lad," said Swegan, noticing Mendel as well. "Simply stick 'em with the pointy end, and whack whatever comes at you."

The wagon was suddenly pulled out of the way, and six attackers charged into the gate on foot. The first wave suddenly fell to the ground as screams of pain erupted from them. As they rolled on the ground clutching at their feet, one of them pulled out a two-inch iron caltrop from his left heel and stared at it in horror. Hanlan smiled in grim satisfaction. Trace and he had spent the morning twisting nails into the nasty caltrops that Hayek's men were now fishing out of their feet.

Behind the fallen men, the remaining attackers began surging through the gate.

It was time.

"Now!" he shouted, both for the men standing next to him and for Tadok, Diggericut and Marven positioned behind them.

The line of defenders suddenly parted down the middle, leaping to the side as the scorpion spit a volley of bolts directly at the gate.

The first line of men and horses fell to the ground in a spray of blood and screams.

Diggericut had been able to repair the scorpion. They had been able to load it with a dozen bolts, which now had found their marks, taking down a total of six men. The odds had been better evened, and it was all the clerics could hope for.

"Seirn!" he cried and charged the attackers as they were still trying to sort themselves out. He heard a cacophony of different war cries as the men with him followed suit.

***

"Now!"

Tadok heard the command, and a moment later, Diggericut pulled the trigger. The twelve-barrel siege engine simultaneously released every one of its tightly pressed springs, which in turn propelled the three-foot bolts through their tubes. Twelve deadly bolts were spit out directly at the gate.

A weapon like this was designed for shock attacks at ranks of soldiers. And Hayek's men definitely looked shocked.

Not wanting to miss an opportunity, Tadok, released his own bolt into the mass of men at the gates. While his single bolt looked like a puppy chasing at the heels of a pack of dogs, it still found its mark. Between the men who'd fallen on the caltrops, and the new wave of attackers skewered by the scorpion's projectiles, it was hard to miss. His bolt hit one of the caltrop victims squarely in the forehead as he tried to rise.

"Reload!" he commanded Marven and Diggericut. The innkeeper, who carried a large basket of bolts, started setting them into the tubes while the gnome started resetting each spring. An experienced artillery crew would probably be able to reload the thing in under a minute. But neither the gnome or the innkeeper were such. And while the gnome had understood the mechanics of the scorpion well enough to repair it, operating the thing took a different set of skills.

Tadok anticipated it would take them at least three minutes to make the thing operational again. Three minutes on the battlefield seemed like an eternity. Soon, the defender's line would break, and the courtyard would erupt into hand-to-hand combat. Each man's fate determined at the end of a sword point or an ax blade.

Bunda and his team managed to box the attackers into the twelve-foot-wide gate, using their surprise element and the fact that the bodies of bandits were piling up, hampering the advancement of their companions. But that didn't last long.

As he loaded another bolt into his crossbow, he suddenly looked up at the wall. He could see that on both sides, the defenders were fighting to keep the Hayek's men from climbing over it the way they themselves had the night before.

He then realized the arrows had stopped raining over the wall.

"Bunda!" he cried, "The rest of them are coming!"

Whether the cleric heard him or not, he couldn't tell. But suddenly, the wall of defenders seemed to fall back as a fresh surge of attackers pushed forwards.

The first to fall was Onlan. The large half-orc slashed wide with his ax severing the head of one of the attackers, then spun it over his head, crashing it down through the shield of another. He suddenly jerked back as an arrow embedded itself in his scarred stomach. He took a step back, trying to bring his ax up as a shield, but two bandits leaped through the gap he'd left in the defense. The first stabbed him through the knee, and as he fell forwards, the second stabbed him repeatedly through the back with his short sword, until he collapsed to the ground.

Then, the defensive line shattered as Swegan and Bunda turned to avoid being flanked by the two men who'd broken through.

Swegan managed to bury his ax into the ribs of the man who'd stabbed Onlan in the knee but had to roll to the ground as a man behind him slashed at his head with a long sword. The old dwarf kept his head but lost his weapon.

Bunda stabbed his flaming saber at the man who'd killed the half-orc. The man managed to block the thrust sending sparks and flames everywhere, but Bunda stepped forward, twisting around the parry and pressed the burning steel to the bandit's face. The man fell back screaming as his clothes and beard caught fire.

To his side, Hanlan went to help the fallen dwarf, but only got far enough to impose himself between him and the next attacker who rained blow after blow from his hand ax, splintering the blacksmith's shield.

Mendel was doing surprisingly well. He was screaming incomprehensively at the attackers, swinging his sword around like a madman. What he lacked in skill - he made up for in pure berserk ferocity. The first attacker lost his hand and the dagger in it, falling to his knees, screaming in shock. Another one tried to flank the villager but ended up losing half his jaw from a wild upward slash. The third one tried to get in for a quick stab, but Mendel slammed his forehead into the man's nose and as he fell back, he thrust his sword into his groin.

Still, more attackers were pouring in as Tadok watched. To add to his problem, he was fresh out of magic. Drawing upon his Flow, after he'd exerted it so much with no rest to rejuvenate was like trying to grasp smoke.

An attacker charged at him with a long sword. He raised his crossbow and let the bolt fly. It hit the attacker in the shoulder, but the man didn't even slow down. He took a step back and drew his sickle, but only as a distraction.

A dark shadow leaped at the bandit from his flank altering the charging man's trajectory instantly. The man tried to turn to this new menace, but Dorkah slashed his leg out from under him. As the man began to topple forward, the Eith'lin's jaws clamped shut on his face with a nauseating crunch.

Two bandits paused as the Eith'lin raised her head and growled at them menacingly, blood dripping from the row of needle-sharp teeth which lined her maw, her eyes black as coals.

She didn't give them a chance to act, pouncing on the first, claws extended forward, like daggers. The man tried to raise his sword, but Dorkah was faster. Her claws slashed, opening wide gashes in his gut and chest.

As the men fell, the second turned to flee, but Dorkah was on him in an instant, launching onto his back and pinning him to the ground.

"No! Please-" he began, but the Eith'lin mercilessly raked her claws across his back and neck, sending streaks of blood spattering across the courtyard.

Feeling a surge of confidence now that Dorkah had joined the fight, he turned to check on Marven and Diggericut. They had almost completed loading the scorpion. He was about to help them adjust the large machine's aim, when Marven cried out and fell to the

261

courtyard's stone floor, a dagger sticking out of his back.

Tadok looked up at the bandit who'd hurled the dagger. He and two of his companions leaped off the wall into the courtyard. He swallowed and put himself between the gnome and the new attackers.

***

Robin raced along the walls as arrows zipped past his head. The remaining four climbers split up into two groups. The piles of rubble which had served them for concealment now hampered his movement as he had to climb or leap over them.

He reached the first man to scale the wall and slammed into him with his shoulder as the man was getting to his feet. The bandit, dagger still clenched between his teeth, was shoved off and fell to the ground below. The second man managed to make it all the way up and block Robin's sword thrust. He wielded two short swords and slashed outward with both. Robin skipped backwards to avoid being disemboweled.

He drew his dagger, the one salvaged from the demon's ribcage, and faced off the enemy, rapier in one hand and dagger in the other. The man grinned at him savagely from behind a gray beard and lunged forwards, both swords poised at his chest. Robin twisted, narrowly avoiding the blades. He slammed his rapier down on both blades, pinning them to a crumbling merlon, and stabbed the man repeatedly below his armpit with the dagger. The bandit desperately tried to wrench his swords out from under Robin's blade, but by the time he managed it, he was already spurting blood from four dagger stabs in his ribs. He stumbled back, spitting blood, and fell to the courtyard below.

The next team was already on the wall and preparing to leap down into the courtyard and attack Bunda and his team from behind.

Robin had no time. He dashed towards them and hurled the dagger in an overhead throw at the first one. The dagger stuck the man's chest and sank all the way to the hilt. He dropped silently back over the wall as the other man prepared for Robin's charge.

This one clasped a war ax in both hands, and took a defensive stance. Robin had the faster weapon, so speed was his tactic. But as he neared the ax wielder, his foot slipped on a patch of loose gravel, and instead of the feint he'd been planning he stumbled clumsily, right into the man's mighty swing. It was all he could do to bring up his rapier in time to block the blow. The heavy ax crashed into the thin blade, sundering it near the basket hilt, cutting into his bicep. Despite the pain, he realized that had he not sacrificed his weapon, he'd have lost his arm. Using the man's momentum, he brought his dagger straight up into his throat, burying it all the way to the hilt and piercing his brain. The man's eyes rolled back in his head, and blood gushed over Robin's hand.

As the bandit slid off the blade, Robin stared at his dagger in amazement. How was it in his hand? He'd flung it at the man's companion, who'd fallen off the wall. He risked a glance at the fallen man at the base of the wall. The man was lying on his back in a pool of blood which was still fountaining out of his chest, but no dagger was there, because it was in his hand. Still bloody.

It hadn't flown back into his hand, or popped into existence with a puff of smoke; it was simply there. As if he'd been holding it all along.

His puzzled thoughts were interrupted as he heard Mara's scream, cut short into a gurgle. Her back to one of the merlons, she had both hands around a large bandit's wrists, trying to pry them off as he choked the life out of her. Her eyes began rolling back into her head and her feet were jerking and kicking up loose stones in desperation.

Let's try this again, he thought and took aim.

He launched the dagger at the man's back, but his aim was too low. It hit the man, hilt first in the buttocks. Even so, the man turned towards him, and seeing a new threat charging at him, he hurled the girl off the wall and drew his knife.

Robin had no time to see if Mara was all right. The man realized Robin was weaponless and grinned.

"Time to die, boy!" he snarled at the unarmed Robin.

Accept that he *wasn't* unarmed.

The man's eyes widened. One moment, Robin was about to punch him with an empty fist—the next moment, that fist suddenly clenched a dagger, which pierced through his leather armor, sinking into his stomach. He bowled over, dropping his own dagger, and Robin plunged his miraculous weapon into his back to finish him off.

Robin didn't spend any more time on the dying man and looked over the wall. Mara was crawling out of the branches and brambles of the bushes she had fallen into. She was scratched in a dozen places, but the cuts didn't look deep, and nothing seemed broken. She glanced up at him, nodding that she was ok.

It was lucky that the majority of the attackers were now at the gate, he thought. Otherwise, Mara would be on the wrong side of the line. Perhaps her wisest course of action was to run as far away as she could.

Robin dared to look around the battlefield.

The archers had stopped peppering them with arrows and had surged in to help the men at the gate who were being held off by Suldan's Bluff's defenders lead by Bunda in the courtyard below.

The half-orc and the dwarf were down, and Bunda and Mendel had been pushed left, and were losing ground, slowly backing up to the wall. Hanlan was also not doing very well. His shield was already in splinters, and he was doing all he could to keep two attackers at bay.

The rest of bandits surged into the tower courtyard but luckily were being held off by Dorkah and Tadok. They had agreed to keep the Eith'lin as a secondary line to improve the chances of protecting the women and children if they were overrun.

Robin shifted his gaze across the courtyard to the eastern curtain wall, where Trace and Ren were back-to-back fighting off two attackers.

Ren's teeth were clenched in grim determination as he blocked and parried a one-eyed bandit who wielded a curved cutlass. Behind him, Trace was fighting another man who hacked at him mercilessly with an ax. The terrified boy was armed only with his bow, and he skipped back as the attacker slashed his weapon, splitting the wooden bow in two. As he did, he smashed into Ren, shoving him forward–directly onto his opponent's sword. Ren's one eye widened, and his knees buckled. The bandit cried out triumphantly and swung his cutlass again, slashing the half-elf's throat. Ren spun around and fell to the ground. Dead.

"Ren!" Robin cried out, but he was too far to do anything about it.

Trace, realizing he was flanked by two attackers, fell to his knees, begging for mercy. But none of Dell's men would give any of them any such curtesy. The man with the ax grasped a handful of the youth's hair and yanked his head to the side. His ax rose and fell.

***

Diggericut was the only combatant who'd refused to arm himself. Between the weapons brought from the village, the ones taken from their would-be assassins in the inn and the bandits they'd dispatched the night before, there was no shortage of weapons to choose from. But the gnome was stubborn about *not* being a fighter. Still, gnomes had a natural affinity to machinery, and he was the one to fix the scorpion which had proved much more useful than a gnome with a sword in hand would have.

But now, with Marven lying face down with a dagger in his back, and two thugs wearing mail shirts and clutching swords in hands closing in, he may have been regretting that decision.

Tadok didn't have time to ask him. Three men had scaled the wall from the east side. The first, the one who'd planted a dagger in Marven's back faced him wielding a rapier. He gave a sidelong glance to the entrance to the tower. The door was hanging off one hinge, and somewhere behind it, huddling in fear, were the rest of the citizens of Suldan's Bluff. The women and children. The bandits must have figured this out.

"Go," commanded the rapier wielding bandit. "Kill the children. Keep the women alive." He commanded turning to face Tadok.

Dorkah, don't let them get to the women and children! He commanded her mentally, but didn't get a chance to see how she reacted as his attacker lunged at him. Tadok brought his sickle up to block the bandit's stab. He instinctively took a step back, and tripped over Diggericut, who was wide-eyed and frozen in place.

He fell to the ground as his attacker laughed and advanced. Before he could get to his feet, the bandit stamped his boot down on Tadok's wrist, pinning his sword hand painfully against the cracked cobblestones. The man pointed the tip of his blade at Tadok's throat, and the half-elf froze, readying himself for the final strike. But before he could end Tadok's life, he groaned in pain and carefully turned. A three-foot scorpion bolt was sticking out of his back, an inch from his spine. Behind him, Marven was on his knees, panting from pain and exertion.

"I killed you!" croaked the bandit in disbelief.

"Ye didn't do a very good job of it," growled the old innkeeper.

Making the most of the distraction, Tadok rolled left and kicked the bandit in the back of both knees as he did. The surprised man's knees buckled forwards causing him to fall backwards and skewer himself as the bolt was pushed all the way into his back, finally erupting from his ribcage.

Suddenly, he heard Robin scream Ren's name. He looked up to the east wall and saw the half-elf hunter fall. He watched in dread as the two bandits prepared to execute the cowering blacksmith's boy.

Something snapped in him. He reached down into his center, his effort fueled by his fear and desperation. He grasped at the last bit of his flow and shaped it into a spell he'd never cast before. It was dangerously beyond his experience. Mimicking the hand gestures he'd seen the mage use the night before, he formed two crackling balls of red energy which hovered for an instance in front of his face. Staring at the two bandits on the wall fifty yards away from him, he released the two magical projectiles. The energy globes sprung forward like angry cats being let out of a box. They spiraled around each other in a mesmerizing pattern as they sailed at the bandits on the wall, finally splitting up at the last moment.

The bandit who'd been about to sever Trace's head didn't see it coming. The magical bolt hit him squarely in the ear, and before he could scream, his head burst into flames. Dropping his weapon, he stumbled around for a moment, finally falling off the wall to the courtyard below. The second man managed to duck just in time, but it did him no good. Just as the wizard's spell had worked, the energy globe wouldn't abandon its purpose and its mark. It circled around the bandit in a wide arc and slammed into the astonished man's chest. The man screamed in pain as the flames began consuming him from within. His screams were replaced by thick greasy smoke, which bloomed out of his mouth and nostrils as his lungs were consumed, and he fell to the ground.

Trace, still on knees, but was looking at Tadok with a mix of astonishment and horror.

Tadok's knees buckled. He'd been running on empty before this advanced spell, and now he was truly depleted. His vision narrowed and the sounds of the battlefield around him were muted.

Before he could lose consciousness, a sharp pain brought him back to his senses. It wasn't his pain. It was Dorkah's.

He whipped his head around to look at the Eith'lin. She stood on her haunches positioned between the two bandits and the door. Her earless head was low, and her black eyes narrowed to slits. Her wide mouth was partially open, and bloody foam was dripping from it. A short spear protruded out of her back like a lopsided sign-post and one of her front legs was twisted in a way Tadok had never seen it before. Dark blood ran freely down it from a deep wound in her shoulder.

As Tadok watched, one of the attackers darted forward with a sword slash. Dorkah tried to dodge backwards, but her wounded leg wouldn't carry her weight, and the sword slashed her face, splitting her upper lip and spraying her dark blood up in the air in thick beads. She jerked her head from side to side, sending droplets of blood across the courtyard. Her attacker, thinking she was in her death throes, tried to stab her through her neck, but the Eith'lin dodged aside and clamped her ruined maw down on his arm. Despite her wounds, she clamped down tightly and jerked her head so violently that the man's arm was torn off from his elbow. His triumphant face contorted in pain and bewilderment as he stared at his bloody stump of an arm. He was so shocked that he didn't even try to move when Dorkah slashed with her good front leg, her claws disemboweling the man. But that was when the other bandit struck.

Wielding another short spear, he leaped on Dorkah's back, using the spear he'd lodged in it before as a handhold. The Eith'lin shrieked in agony, a sound that made Tadok's stomach churn, even if he hadn't dimly felt the pain himself. Then, her shriek was cut short as the man plunged his spear into Dorkah's head, splitting through her skull.

Dorkah collapsed like a marionette with cut strings.

Tadok screamed wordlessly. He tried to run to her side, but his legs wouldn't carry him. As he fell to the ground, he saw the bandit savagely tear out his weapon from her skull. He didn't feel it. The Eith'lin was no longer in pain. The man silently proceeded into the tower. Tadok's eyes locked on to the dull black eyes of the creature that had been his friend, his protector, and his family for most of his life. As his own vision dimmed, Dorkah vanished for the last time.

26 BROTHERS IN ARMS

"This is the definition of futile," muttered Tadok in frustration.

He had spent the day trying to track the orcs. He'd seen a few tracks which looked like they could be orc made, but he wasn't sure, and they didn't seem to lead him in any particular direction. The bleak truth of it was—he was no tracker.

"What about that?" he asked Dorkah, pointing at a patch of ruffled grass. "That could be an orc print, right?"

"*Right?*" the Eith'lin replied in her alien voice, but she didn't sound too sure.

He frowned. It was just as likely a wild boar which had crossed here the night before.

"Dorkah, you can accomplish so many extraordinary feats, yet you can't sniff out the trail of a pack of rancid orcs," he accused her in exasperation.

"*Can't sniff,*" she replied with the equivalence of a shrug.

To be fair, the Eith'lin had no nostrils. Her face was smooth and black, aside from her wide mouth and black eyes. Tadok often wondered about that. Despite the lack of ears, Dorkah still heard the world around her. She didn't seem to breath at all but could push enough air out of her mouth to make words. She would purr like a cat when she was calm, though her chest never moved. She could bite and swallow, but did so mostly in combat. He wondered how she disposed of whatever she consumed, as he'd never seen her expel any demonic excrement. Come to think of it, she never seemed hungry. She never slept, for that matter. He supposed she may receive rest and nourishment (and perhaps relieve herself) when she returned to her home after he dismissed her. He'd heard there were animals that could go for weeks without food or water, and he knew that some mammals hibernated during the winter, but the

268

comparison seemed forced in his mind. All in all, Dorkah was a conundrum.

A year ago, he'd delivered a letter from a Lady Ethelred of Culidge to her son, Lord Chester of Westerwick. Lord Chester had been on a hunt and was scheduled to return in a fortnight. Since he was under orders to give the letter directly to the lord, much to his man-servant's dismay, the staff had offered lodging at the lord's villa as he awaited his lordship's return. He'd had free reign of the household and discovered the lord had an extensive library. It was an unexpected delight, and he spent much of that rainy weekend pouring over old tomes and manuscripts.

In the library he'd found a copy of Chaulin's *Compendium of Creatures*, Volume II. Despite the fact that old Chaulin had documented over two hundred animals and monsters, he'd found no mention of Eith'lins or anything resembling them. Chaulin had been very clear on the fact that all natural land animals needed food, drink, and air to survive. But a short chapter at the end of the book mentioned creatures from beyond the realms of man. Chaulin called them '*Weirds*' and said they defied all rules of common living creatures. Some were pure elemental energy, made of water, earth, fire or air, and some were even stranger things. There was another short essay on constructs conducted by a gnome named Clundinta. These beings were made by men but infused with magic, such as the great Golems of Doar Keirn, which legend said protected the dwarven kingdom long after its fall. Those silent sentinels needed no sleep, food, or drink, and could even stand still for centuries until a threat rose to them or their dwarven charges. They were more items than living creatures.

Tadok concluded that Dorkah was something in between. A thing of the outer realms, like Chaulin's Weirds, but also like a construct as described in Clundinta's work.

He'd even tried discussing it once with Dorkah herself. But whether the Eith'lin understood her origins and chose not to share the information with him, or if she was oblivious to her uniqueness in his world, she offered no answer.

"This is futile," he muttered in frustration. "Perhaps I should have stayed with the two men from last night. Maybe *they* could track."

"*Two men*," agreed the Eith'lin.

"Oh, you think so? I can only imagine what they'd have done if they had seen you. That cleric would have probably sacrificed you to his god or tried to banish you."

Dorkah didn't seem troubled by the threat. Instead, she raised her head to the eastern horizon.

Tadok followed her gaze. The sky was darkening, and faint flashes of lightning cast a foreboding visage across the endless Suldan mountain range.

"Let's try something else," he suggested.

He climbed to the top of a hill. As he did, the winds picked up and cold, large droplets of rain began pelting him, and he pulled his thick wool hood over his head. When Tadok was standing on its grassy peak, he dipped into his Flow and magically enhanced his vision. Once his eyes could see three times as far as that of any normal man, he scanned the horizon.

Despite the lack of human settlements, or perhaps because of it, he had to marvel at the beauty of the land - the rolling hills, the small patches of woods, and the streams which crisscrossed the valleys. The lands of Suldan-Karr may have been wild and dangerous, but they clearly had their majesty.

There!

Two figures walked about fifty yards north of the Triumph Road. Their choice to walk parallel to the road and not on it was odd. The only explanation was that they were either trying to ambush someone or that they feared an ambush themselves.

"I think those are our saviors from last night," he mused loudly. "Perhaps I was too hasty in dismissing them."

He'd been thinking it over in his head all morning. The truth was that while he was set on avenging the murder of Dalton and his family, the more he sought out their killers, the more he feared he'd bitten off more than he could chew. Orcs were known to raid in warbands. A typical warband ran between ten and twenty-five warriors. There were only two explanations to why he had encountered only a few of them at the bridge. Either they had lost some of their members to other battles, or they were a smaller party splintered off from the larger band. If this were true, it would mean that the orcs who'd survived the fight at the bridge were on their way to rejoin their fellows. Thus, his quest could pit him against twenty blood-thirsty orc marauders. In that case, he and Dorkah wouldn't stand a chance. But perhaps with the aid of another two...

"Where are you going?" he muttered when they turned sharply to the north. He followed their trajectory and saw what looked like an abandoned farmhouse.

Wait, *was* it abandoned?

He could see figures standing near the entrance to the building, and it appeared there was one who was on the roof. A lookout, perhaps.

From this distance, it was nearly impossible to make out any details, but it was clear that whoever they were kept vigilant.

The lookout must have seen the two men, as he ran to the edge of the roof and seemed to be yelling to the men below. The faraway figures began scuttling about like ants. Heavily armed ants.

"Oh no..." he whispered when realization dawned upon him.

He'd found his orcs. And they seemed more numerous than they'd been when they retreated at the bridge. To make matters worse, the cleric and the Heartlander were headed right for them. Probably intent on seeking sanctuary from the storm. They were headed right into their trap.

"I suppose I *do* owe them my life," he said to the Eith'lin. Plus, he'd already established that he had better chances of fighting the orcs with them at his side. But none of that mattered if they were killed in a trap.

The barn house was closer to him than they were, so if he hurried, he just may be able to reach them in time.

"Let's go, girl," he said, setting off in a trot.

***

It took him little under half an hour to reach the barn, and he was sprinting by the time he did. It didn't help that the fools chose to charge into their trap. At first, he'd thought they'd seen the orcs and were charging *at* them, but he quickly realized by their demeanor that they were oblivious to the threat ahead.

He reached the outskirts of the farm as the Heartlander was ejected violently through the barn door. The orcs circled the two of them as the big barbarian, the cleric, lit his sword on fire. It was a useful trick, but he was still outnumbered and one of the orcs was wielding a crossbow.

"Damn!" he cursed breathlessly. It was clear he wouldn't reach them in time.

He halted and dropped to one knee, taking aim with his crossbow as cold rain pelted him again. Tadok wasn't a marksman, but he'd owned a crossbow before and had mostly used it for hunting. In the north, possibly due to elven influence, bows were the more common missile weapon employed by hunters and soldiers. But Tadok learned that his weaker physique wasn't a disadvantage with a crossbow the way it was with a bow. He'd heard that in warfare, a trained marksman could hit a target at nearly one hundred and forty yards away with a crossbow, but he'd never attempted shooting at anything farther than fifty or sixty yards away. The orc with the crossbow was nearly one hundred yards away. And it was raining, to boot.

He held his breath—not an easy task after he'd been running—and used all of his concentration to steady the missile weapon. Tadok pulled the steel trigger just as the crossbow-wielding orc took aim at the cleric.

The bolt struck true, hitting the orc in his right shoulder. The creature grunted in pain and jerked the crossbow down, sending its bolt into the ground.

Neither the orcs nor the humans realized what had happened for a moment. So, as they looked around in confusion, Tadok dropped his crossbow and drew his sickle. He was bent on killing at least one of the brutes with it. If he sent one of them to hell with Dalton's own tool, it would be a fitting revenge.

Both he and Dorkah charged, building up speed as they ran through the barren field. The Eith'lin's four legs quickly left him behind as she closed the distance, splashing muddy water from the puddles around her.

The orcs, finally identifying their new threat, turned to face them. One of them hefted a four-foot javelin and hurled it at Dorkah. The Eith'lin dodged the projectile easily, continuing to gallop at a mad pace at the lead Orc. The one with the flail.

The two large combatants collided into each other in a crash of black and gray. Dorkah's charge knocked him three feet back, but he managed to retain his footing, even flipping the Eith'lin in the air and hurling her away. As she sailed through the air, Dorkah twisted like a cat, landing on all four paws and growling.

The orc turned to her, only then noticing the three diagonal slashes which ran from his armpit to his hip. He tried to advance towards Dorkah, but the slashes widened at his midsection as his intestines began to spilled out of his belly. Dorkah leaped at him again; this time, her claw-studded paw tore at his kneecap, and the orc fell to the ground, bellowing in pain and rage.

Both the second orc and Tadok reached the melee at the same time. This one wielded a spiked club that he swung at Tadok's head in force. Tadok brought his sickle up in time to intercept the weapon, which lodged itself in the club. He yanked it to try and free it, but the larger weapon was stuck squarely inside the crescent of the sickle.

The orc clenched his teeth and yanked back. He was a muscular thug, and Tadok's smaller form held little resistance. Paying the price for not letting go of his weapon, the half-elf was yanked off his feet. He crashed into the weeds to his left, rolling a couple times. He scrambled to his feet, weaponless as both his sickle and the club rested where they had been dropped on the ground.

Suddenly, Dorkah was on the orc's back, slashing at his head with her deadly claws. The orc tried to buck the Eith'lin off his back, but Dorkah snapped her jaws around the back of his neck, latching on even stronger. She would have severed his spinal column but suddenly had to leap aside as the orc with the two axs arrived, hacking and slashing at her.

Tadok wasted no time and lunged forward to grab his weapon, trying desperately to dislodge it from the orc's fallen club. The orc came at him, massaging his bleeding neck, where he bled from a dozen small puncture wounds. He reached Tadok as he frantically tried to release his sickle, which had bitten an inch into the wood. The orc grabbed Tadok by the shoulder, painfully lifting the half-elf off the ground. He batted the two locked weapons aside and growled menacingly at Tadok. Up close, Tadok could see that the orc's lips and cheeks were ritually scarred, and his teeth had been filed to points. His mouth opened in a low growl, and Tadok almost gagged from the stench of his breath. He didn't wish to think about what the thing had eaten lately. The orc raised his other hand to clasp the half-elf's throat. He could probably snap his neck with one hand. But he didn't get a chance.

Tadok whispered something in the Arcane and shot his open palm at the orc's eyes. The orc howled in pain as his skin sizzled, and the horrible odor of burning flesh and melting eyes filled the space between them.

He hurled the half-elf to the ground, covering his face with both hands. Tadok got to his knees and chose his next spot, grasping the orc's groin beneath his loin cloth with his crackling hand and crushing it with all the strength he could muster in his fist. He didn't want to think of what part of the orc's anatomy he was clasping, but the orc's howl grew in intensity and pitch, finally waning into a pathetic moan as he sank to his knees.

The fourth orc, the one he'd shot with the crossbow, had drawn a curved, wicked-looking sword with a serrated edge and was locked in battle with the barbarian cleric. Aside from the crossbow bolt jutting out of his shoulder, the orc had a number of burns across his flank, and the cleric was bleeding from a cut above is knee. But the cleric seemed to have the upper hand as he advanced and pressed the sword-wielding orc backwards. The orc suddenly made a feint to the right, and as the barbarian raised his sword, he kicked at his stomach with his left foot. That proved to be a mistake. The barbarian took the blow squarely in the gut but leaned into it. Encircling the orc's foot with his left arm, he cleanly chopped it off below the knee. The orc's stump managed to spray blood and emit greasy smoke simultaneously. He fell to the wet ground, and the barbarian stabbed him in the chest.

Tadok looked around him. Dorkah was dispatching the last orc ferociously. He was lying on his back with the Eith'lin on top of him. He feebly tried to push her off as her jaws locked around his throat. With a quick jerk of her head, Dorkah tore out his jugular, and the orc's frantic attempts to push the Eith'lin off him were replaced with weak twitches.

The battle was over. The barbarian nodded to Tadok, who nodded back. They were now even. No need to discuss the topic. That settled, the barbarian then went to tend to his friend.

Tadok grunted as he freed his weapon and turned to the orc, moaning at his feet. Rain was now falling in force all around them. The orc's face was a mess. His eyelids were fused together, and the bold ridge of his nose had exposed bone peeking out where some of the flesh melted off. Both his hands were covering his groin.

Tadok leaned down.

"I know you can hear me," he said. The orc froze. "You and your friends shouldn't have come out of the Barrens. That was your first mistake, orc. I personally wouldn't care, but you made a bigger mistake yesterday when you killed Dalton, Sima, and Layla. But your biggest mistake wasn't killing them—it was leaving *me* alive."

"*Suth'rei katchi si kopast, elev!*" spat the orc.

Orcish wasn't one of Tadok's strong languages, but it was close enough to elven for him to get the general gist of it. *Suck cock, elf!*

"I don't think so," he replied softly, and drew Dalton's sickle across his throat. The orc died soundlessly in the mud.

***

The fire crackled as Bunda added another log, stoking it carefully. Nick sat on the far side, gingerly prodding the bandage the cleric had bound over his forehead.

"Stop touching it, Mainlander," commanded the cleric without even looking at him. He seemed to have a sixth sense when it came to the patients he treated. He drew the small pot of soup from the fire and carefully pored a steaming mug of it, which he handed to Tadok.

Tadok nodded thankfully but said nothing as Bunda returned to his seat opposite him. Outside, the storm raged, and Tadok was more grateful than he would admit for the roof above his head and the warmth the small fire had to offer. The soup was also welcome. It was savory with chunks of salted meat, which he assumed was rabbit, in addition to onions. He slurped it, careful not to scald his tongue, but paused when he noticed Bunda wasn't eating his. The barbarian cleric stared at Dorkah intently. The Eith'lin was curled up beside Tadok, purring happily with her eyes closed.

"Is it asleep?" asked the barbarian.

Tadok narrowed his eyes and focused his other senses on the stew. Was this a ploy? Were they trying to drug or poison him? Was the cleric testing the awareness of Dorkah in preparation to leap at him with his flaming saber?

"Dorkah doesn't sleep. *She* doesn't eat either. She's here to guard my back and kill any who would do me harm," he replied evenly sniffing at his mug.

The cleric's bushy brow darkened, but his companion, the one called Nick, chuckled.

"He thinks we're trying to poison him, Bunda." He smiled and took a big slurp of his soup to prove they weren't.

Bunda looked surprised. He pointed at Dorkah. "You're worried about *us*, sorcerer? If we wished you harm, we wouldn't have spent the time and effort dragging you back from Hell's gate when we saw you by the tree."

"Which Trin rewarded you for when I came to your aid today," he retorted. "Had I not, it would be a band of orcs sitting by this fire, making a stew out of the two of you and not of rabbits."

Nick cut in, trying to lower tension. "In that case, let's assume neither you nor we are here to slit each other's throats in the night. But you must agree that it's one thing to share a fire with a half-elven sorcerer, quite another to share it with a...*Dorkah*," he said, trying to twist his mouth around the Eith'lin's alien name.

The Heartlander's clumsy attempt to name the Eith'lin actually amused Tadok, and he smiled slightly.

"All right. What do you wish to know?"

"For one—is that a demon? Is it evil?"

"No. It isn't evil," interrupted Bunda before Tadok could answer. As he looked, he saw the cleric's eyes flash a deeper blue. Only for a fraction of a moment. He recalled Sellwyn mentioning something like that once.

They'd been chased out of a town near Port Keil a few years earlier by a mob led by a cleric. One of the patrons of an inn had caught a glimpse of Sellwyn's antlers when she'd not been careful. The next morning, a crowd had gathered outside the inn, and they had fled hastily before the townsfolk got to the lynching part of the event. The crowd had been led by a priest of The Four, claiming Sellwyn was a wicked demon-spawn and it was their duty to cleanse Trosia of foul things such as her. For the good of the children, of course.

Tadok had complained that all men of faith were the same and that they saw everything in black and white. Sellwyn had laughed and said that they actually see things in many colors. When he pressed her for what she'd meant, she explained that within the magical capabilities of the divine was the ability to see the auras of men, magical creatures, and even some objects. It allowed the *good* ones to discern the righteous from the wicked and the good from the evil. This must have been what the cleric sitting before him now had done.

To be honest, Tadok felt uncomfortable with this stranger

examining his aura. It was like being scrutinized naked.

"She comes at my summon and attacks who I tell her to attack. She won't harm a soul unless it harms me first or unless I tell her to. As for me, *Shard*," he said, turning to Bunda. *Tundrial came from Shard, right?* "I'm many things, but I wouldn't consider myself evil."

"The funny bit about that is that few evil men ever do," said Nick, taking another slurp from his bowl.

"No, *you* are not evil either, half-elf," confirmed Bunda. "And your companion is no demon. Whatever she is." With that, he blinked and began eating, as if the conversation had never happened.

"If that is settled, it is time I asked some questions of my own," said Tadok, setting his empty mug aside. "The two of you are heading west. It seems a perilous season to brave the Suldan pass."

"It is," agreed Nick and rose to his feet to collect the dishes. "But we both have a necessity which will be unmet if we wait for spring. I believe we have time to make it before the snows settle."

"Snow isn't the only danger in those mountains. What of bandits?" Gods know *he'd* had his share of ambushes on the road.

"Nick knows of a less trodden road which runs parallel to the Triumph Road," said Bunda. He'd quickly finished his meal and was kicking dry straw into a pile and placing his seal fur cloak on top of it.

"Aye," agreed the Heartlander, "it will add a couple days to the journey, but there're fewer pickings for robbers on this road than on old Triumph."

"And what of those that don't care about your possessions? What of wolves? I'm from the north, *Sandisan*. The more Agreina's wintery hand caresses the land, the more desperate they are and more willing to hunt humans."

"Of that you are right," began Nick, who spread out his own bedroll close enough to the fire to pleasantly toast one side of him, but not too close that a rogue ember would set him aflame in the night. "But I believe the three of us can handle wolves."

"The three of us?" asked Tadok in confusion. Were they offering him to join them? Truth be told, he'd never traveled for a significant amount of time with anyone since Sellwyn.

"Apologies," said Nick, confusing the reason for Tadok's surprise. "The *four* of us," he said, nodding at Dorkah.

"Who said I was—"

"Well, the wagon on the bridge was headed east. I suppose that was your direction when the orcs interrupted you."

Tadok said nothing but nodded silently after a few moments.

Bunda began snoring softly as Tadok looked up at the stars through the hole in the rafters. The clouds had temporarily parted, showing a brilliant night sky, leaving only the howling wind outside to remind him of the storm.

It wasn't such a bad idea, thought the half-elf as he lay down his head on Dorkah's smooth flank, and curled up in the cloak he'd received from Dalton. The journey to Sebin would take about a month if the weather favored them. And all events since he'd left Berin's Inn proved that having able companions at his side could prove safer than traveling alone. In addition, these two seemed to be the only people except for Sellwyn who ever accepted Dorkah without attacking or running in fear.

"Sandisan," he asked quietly, not sure if Nick was still awake.

"Hmm?" asked the Heartlander after a moment.

"Are there any villages or settlements along this 'less trodden road' you speak of?"

Nick yawned. "Well, if memory serves, there is one."

27 KILLING BLOWS

Bunda saw Onlan go down, but he could do nothing about it. Hayek's men pushed back their line of defense with renewed vigor as their companions, who'd been pelting arrows at Robin and his team, joined the melee. They had initially successfully held them back, boxing them into the gatehouse. But now, with Onlan dead, their line was broken, and it was every man for himself.

Bunda saw the dwarf take out one of Onlan's killers but fall himself. Bunda couldn't pay any more attention to the right flank as a bandit charged him. He managed to dance around the bandit's thrust and press his flaming saber to his face, lighting the man's beard and hair on fire.

As the bandit withdrew, screaming wildly, he stepped hard on one of the caltrops and fell to the ground, twisted and wiggling like fish out of water as his face burned. Bunda looked around and saw that Hanlan was protecting the dwarf, but his shield had been splintered to bits. Bunda leaped at the man attacking him, slashing his saber at the man's unprotected flank. He screamed and fell to the ground, blood pooling quickly around him, as his clothes began to burn.

He made it to Hanlan in time to block a new attacker's thrust. The smith used the bandit's distraction to slam the remaining bit of his shield in the man's throat, where the splinters left a jagged gash, severing his artery. The man was able to raise his hand to his throat but was losing so much blood that he was dead before he hit the ground.

All around him, the courtyard was in pandemonium of pitched individual battles, and life or death was determined by personal skill and luck. Bodies were strewn everywhere. They hadn't even had much time to remove the bodies from the night before, adding many more to the blood-soaked cobblestones. Smoke was beginning to rise from the men who'd died by his own flaming sword, partially obscuring the gate. And everywhere, the sounds of fighting and dying rang. He could see that Mara and Robin were fighting bandits who had scaled the west wall, and Ren and Trace were back-to-back doing the same on the east battlements. Dorkah was causing mayhem with the men who'd first broken through their line, but it appeared Tadok was facing off bandits who'd somehow gotten behind them.

Mendel was holding his own for now, ferociously hacking away at anything that came near him. He reminded Bunda of the famed Thunder Warriors of the isle of Northern Song, an island in the Seal Shore archipelago, who were said to rile themselves into a frenzied berserk in battle, fighting long after they should be dead. As much as he wanted to aid the man, he had a good chance of being run through by Mendel himself when he was in such a state. The mild-mannered farmer with five children was no more. Instead stood a crazed beast of a warrior, and woe befell those who underestimated him.

"Ren!"

He heard Robin scream and swung around to look at the eastern wall just in time to see the half-elf they'd saved from the wolves fall. But now Trace was in trouble, and he could do nothing to make it in time. He turned to glance at Hanlan, but luckily the smith wasn't watching his son's beheading. He was wide-eyed and focused on a figure that strode like death on two legs through the smoke of the gatehouse.

Dell Hayek.

Hayek wielded a rapier and a long dagger, which could hardly be called such as it was closer to a short sword. Under his tunic, Bunda could see mail glinting, but Dell wore it with the ease of a man used to carrying the extra thirty pounds of steel. Up close, Bunda could see he had a scar that ran from his lip all the way up to his forehead, splitting his left brow. His face was a mask of grim rage and hatred. These villagers and the strangers who fought with them had cost him too much time and too many men, and he would make them pay for it tenfold.

Mendel, empowered by adrenaline, charged the bandit lord with his sword held high. Dell easily sidestepped the wild swing and sank his dagger into the Mendel's sword arm while at the same time slamming the hilt of his sword into his face. Mendel collapsed like a felled tree. Hayek stabbed downward at his head and would have pierced his skull were it not for Bunda, who charged into him, leaping at him with a flying kick.

The Tundrial's boot should have struck Hayek in the head, but at the last moment, the bandit lord dipped backwards like a limbo dancer, and Bunda sailed over him. Before Bunda could realize what had happened, Hayek brought his rapier to bare, slashing Bunda in the lower back as he passed over.

Bunda groaned as a hot flash of pain raked his back. He landed, stumbling forward, and immediately started coughing as the smoke of burning flesh filled his lungs. He leaned heavily on the uneven stone wall with his sword held up, pointing at Hayek, who was smiling coldly at him.

As he panted, trying to catch his breath, he could feel warm blood running down his back. Dell was the better fighter by far, and Hanlan and Swegan couldn't help him as they were already embroiled in another fight against two more of Hayek's men who'd come through the gate.

Seirn, give me strength, he prayed silently. He was fresh out of spells to cast. The gifts of his deity were limited without rest and meditation. It was an odd rule, but one the faithful followed, well, religiously.

Bunda wanted to survey his surroundings. To call for his friends' aid. But he dared not take his eyes from the dangerous man that stood before him.

Hayek struck like an adder, his rapier slicing through Bunda's shirt and nearly penetrating his shoulder if he hadn't dodged at the last moment—only to feel the bite of Hayek's dagger as he raked it across his knee.

Bunda backed away, fully exiting the tower's gatehouse, keeping his sword between Hayek and him. *He's toying with me,* he thought. And it was working. He felt his strength fading as blood ran from his back and leg. He focused on the pain, willing himself not to lose consciousness.

Dell advanced again; this time he danced around Bunda's stab and swept his leg out from under him with his rapier. As Bunda bent and teetered, trying to regain his balance, Dell brought his knee up right into the cleric's chin, sending him flying backward. Stars exploded into Bunda's vision, and he felt a tooth detach from its place in his mouth. Next, he was on his back, shaking his head to clear it as Dell stood over him, dark and terrible.

Dell Hayek raised his rapier to end Bunda's life, and the Tundrial knew there was nothing he could do. He had no fight left in him.

But as Dell was about bring his weapon down, he suddenly twisted around, batting a projectile that somersaulted through the air at his head. It was too fast for Bunda to see what it was, but he clearly heard the ring of steel against steel. A split-second later, Robin collided with the bandit lord, sending the two of them rolling to the ground.

***

Robin breathed a sigh of relief when Tadok's spell took out the two bandits on the east wall a fraction of a second before Trace was beheaded. Suldan's Bluff had buried enough children this week.

He turned his attention to the men at the gate. Onlan was down, and Bunda, Swegan, and Hanlan were huddled together against more bandits who were pouring in. He suddenly heard a scream and turned his head to Tadok. The half-elf didn't seem hurt but was on the ground reaching out towards the tower. Robin followed his gaze in time to see the death of Dorkah. He stared for a moment in utter shock.

Dorkah was a pure killing machine. She'd been pivotal in every battle they'd had since they met. Robin didn't even think she *could* be killed. But there she was, sprawled on the blood-soaked cobblestones with her eyes closed. She looked so vulnerable. And then she vanished.

Then he saw the bandit who'd killed her slip through the door of the tower. Tadok was on the ground—perhaps dead—and Marven was lying face down with a dagger in his back. The gnome was huddling next to them, trying to revive them, while Bunda and the men who had stood with him had their own problems.

Robin ran along the wall, getting as close to the entrance as possible before leaping off the old stable's collapsed roof. He landed on his feet and rolled over his shoulder to break the fall. Scrambling back up to his feet, he sprinted as fast as his legs would carry him to the tower and bolted inside.

In the tower, he paused for a moment to catch his breath and allow his eyes to adjust to the dimness. Ahead of him, the corridor was empty all the way to the stairs which led down to the prison. That was where the women and children of the village would make their stand should the defenders fail.

He heard a scream from that direction, followed by a yell. He launched into a run down the corridor and down the stairwell, leaping the final four steps. He burst through the door, ready for the grisly sight of dead women and children.

To his surprise, the bandit was lying on the ground, choking on his own blood. He was surrounded by Aldeira, Tilly, Odetta, and Theia, all of whom held bloody daggers. Christopher, along with Mendel's children, was huddled in one of the cells, crying and shaking. The only other figure on the ground was Yorgen, whose unseeing eyes stared blankly at the ceiling. He still had both his bound hands clasped around the bandit's spear, which was lodged in his sternum. Aldeira looked up at him and sighed in relief. She then looked at Yorgen. A look of pity in her eyes.

Since they'd learned of Yorgen's betrayal, the only expression Aldeira had ever graced the old drunk with was loathing. Robin was confident that she would have had no reservations about allowing the village to lynch him if that was the group decision. But now she stared at him with a different air. She noticed Robin staring at the dead man and cleared her throat.

"When the man came through the door, Yorgen charged him. He had no weapon, and his hands were tied, but it didn't matter. Even when the man ran him through, he held the spear and wouldn't let him have it back. He knew he would die, but this way, we had a chance of killing him."

"He saved us," added Tilly in a shaky voice. Her own resolve broke into wracking sobs.

"Hush now, woman. What's yer news from up top?" asked Odetta, obviously more concerned with her husband and the others than with the fate of Yorgen.

Robin hesitated, unsure of what to say. He couldn't tell her about Marven, not right now.

"We're holding our own, but I need to get back out there," he said quickly. "Stay here!" he called over his shoulder as he ran back up the stairs.

As he exited the tower, he was blinded by the noon sun. When his eyes adjusted, he could see Dell Hayek push Bunda through the gate. Ignoring everything else, he sprinted towards him. This would end *now.*

As he arrived at the gatehouse, he could see Hayek poised over Bunda, ready to end his life. Robin hurled his magical dagger straight at Hayek's back.

"Die, bastard!" he yelled.

The dagger somersaulted blade over the hilt, a shining disk of steel and death. But just as it was about to strike Hayek, the bandit lord swung around and slapped it out of the air with his rapier.

It didn't matter because following the dagger came Robin himself. He was charging at such speed that his collision with the bandit lord knocked Hayek off his feet, but unfortunately, he, too, lost his footing.

Both men rolled away from each other, and both men quickly regained their feet. Robin felt the dagger return to his hand magically and crouched low, locking eyes with Hayek.

Hayek smiled coldly, matching Robin's battle stance.

"Time to die, son," he said coolly.

"Not your fucking son!" Robin growled and lunged forward.

Robin was at a disadvantage as Dell wielded two weapons, both with better reach, and he was armed only with a dagger. But Robin was a street fighter. Growing up in Shadder Street, he was never taught professional warfare or trained to duel like a noble. In the docks of Sandisan, few fights were ever fair, and Garian had taught him how to turn a disadvantage into an asset.

He's overconfident. He expects you to be on the defensive, coached the ghost of his brother.

Robin's lunge caught Hayek by surprise, which allowed the younger man to get within the guard of his sword. He stabbed at Hayek's chest, but his dagger was parried by Hayek's own knife. Not missing a beat, he slammed his left palm into Hayek's face, hoping to crush his nose. Hayek jerked his head back, and Robin's palm smacked him in the forehead.

Hayek took a step back, thrusting at him with his knife even as he tried to bring his rapier up. Robin pinned the rapier with his dagger, catching Hayek's left wrist in his hand.

They stood frozen that way for a few seconds, locked in a deadly embrace. But the fight now boiled down to a test of strength, and

Hayek clearly had the physical advantage. Robin's right arm began to shake as Hayek inched his blade closer to Robin's ribcage. Robin suddenly reversed his tactic, and instead of forcing Hayek's wrist away, he pulled into it, narrowly avoiding the dagger tip, which scraped the back of his shirt, and slamming his forehead into the man's face, stunning him.

Now Hayek's nose was broken, as apparent from the two rivers of blood that gushed out over his mustache. But the move had left Robin dazed, and he reeled backwards, blinking away the stars that flashed in his vision.

Hayek was no longer smirking. His rage was clearly visible. His mouth was open and panting since it was his only operational orifice for oxygen now. He took a moment to spit blood on the ground and wipe his mouth with his sleeve.

Well, it looks like you got him mad, he thought in Garian's voice.

It was now Hayek's turn to press the attack, and he wouldn't be blindsided again.

"You'll—" he began but suddenly froze. His eyes bulged in surprise as he stared down at his midsection. The long shaft of a feathered arrow had grown out of his navel.

Robin turned his head and stared at Mara with bleary eyes. Her hair was disheveled, her neck was red where the bandit had tried to choke her earlier, and she had a dozen small cuts and bruises from falling off the wall. But she stood there, staring at Hayek with cool eyes. Gone was the impetuous girl they'd rescued from the prison last night. Before him stood a grim goddess of death. She was already calmly knocking another arrow.

Robin wondered if Hayek's look of disbelief was due to being shot or the fact that a sixteen-year-old girl was the one to shoot him. But before he could say another word, Mara's second arrow pierced him again, inches away from the first. His knees buckled, and he fell to the ground.

Robin calmly stepped over to the fallen man. Dell tried to raise his sword, but Robin simply kicked it out of the way.

Dell looked into Robin's eyes with hate. But after a second, he sighed and let his head fall back to the ground.

"Enjoy your victory, boy," he said weakly. "Know that you've angered powerful people. Delona Ravin will end you horribly." He chuckled, but his grin turned into a grimace of pain.

"Maybe. But that's no longer your problem," he answered and plunged his dagger into Dell Hayek's heart.

28 FAREWELLS

"In my village, there is a saying," began Bunda solemnly, his eyes searching the small crowd. "We owe a debt to the sea for its bounty. And sometimes the sea gives, and sometimes it takes."

The sun had set over the weastern part of the Suldan mountains, covering the valley in shadow. The wind had soothed and was gently rustling the last leaves of the great sycamore tree, which was poised silently at the entrance to the village like a grizzled old sentry. The same tree where they had buried Sheriff Murley and his sons four days ago. Before him gathered all the living residents of Suldan's Bluff. The living residents who had come to bid farewell to the dead.

The hastily erected cairns of Jenathy, John and Dreith Murley had been replaced by proper graves, with wooden posts as markers. They would be replaced within a year by permanent headstone, as was the custom of the land. Next to them, three fresh graves had been dug for Onlan the half-orc, Ren O' the River, and Yorgen. There had been a debate about the last, whether he deserved to be buried with the heroes of Suldan's Bluff, but Aldeira herself had put the argument to rest, saying that while he may have betrayed the memory of her husband and two sons, his sacrifice had saved her last son and the rest of the children of Suldan's Bluff. Whatever his crimes had been, the old sour drunk had redeemed himself in the end and deserved the hero's funeral with the rest of them.

"Perhaps we all live in debt to the gods. For every triumph we achieve, we suffer failure. For every moment of joy shared with friends, we shed tears at times of sadness. And for every new life we celebrate, we must mourn lives taken.

"We choose not when the debt is paid, and its burden is not carried by those who've passed on to their makers, but it is a weight carried by those who must go on. And go on, we must."

He looked into the eyes of all who were present. Aldeira held tightly to the shoulders of Christopher as if she would never let him out of her sight again, which she very well may not. Her eyes shed tears freely, but his eyes were dry. While he had been reclaimed from the darkness of Malaketh's tomb, he would never be truly free of all he had seen and experienced that week. Perhaps one day the boy would find peace, but Bunda knew the Sheriff's son's journey would be long, and not without hardship. Still, to survive what he had...the boy was strong. And that gave the Tundrial cleric hope.

"The road before us is hard, especially now, when our anguish is too much to bear. Yet, this is the way of life. A mother who carries her born for nine months must suffer in the last moments before she can hear the joyous cries of her child. And Seirn's warming rays of light come only after the darkest hours of night."

Tilly had her arm around Mara, who was sobbing uncontrollably. Was she crying for John? Perhaps the gravity of what she'd endured and achieved had sunk in. The girl who was not yet a woman had been braver than most seasoned warriors Bunda had met in his life.

Bunda was mildly amused to find Hanlan and Trace standing beside the two women, the blacksmith's burley hand holding the seamstress' openly. Robin had told him that the village talk was about a secret courtship between the two widowers. Perhaps the hardship of the last few days had pushed them to be less secretive about their relationship. Bunda was surprised at how much the thought warmed his heart.

Next to them stood Mendel, his hand bandaged, gathering his own family in his arms. Beside them stood Odetta, tears flowing freely down her weathered cheeks. While Marven had survived the battle, his wounds had been considerable, and despite his objections about missing the funeral, he was resting in his bed at Odetta's strict orders, which left no room for argument. Many men with such wounds died following battles, succumbing to their injuries. Yet, with Aldeira's talented care, he may survive.

Beside them stood the shorter figures of the dwarf and the gnome. Diggericut was dabbing his eyes with his cap, and Swegan's sad eyes revealed his age. How many tragedies had this old dwarf seen since the fall of his homeland Doar Keirn.

"But the balance set by the gods must be observed in the world. The moon waxs and wanes, the tides ebb and flows and the nights chase the days. The debt is paid by all things, and the balance is maintained."

Standing last, a little removed from the crowd, was his friend Robin. The man who he'd known as Nick when they'd first met. Bunda had brothers, and apparently so did Robin. Yet, over the last month they had saved each other's lives so many times and had shared so many moments of fear, pain, and triumph that the brotherly bond which had developed was as strong in Bunda's heart as any he shared with his own blood. And he was sure Robin felt the same way.

He lifted his eyes to the hill overlooking the village. It was too dark to see, but he could imagine his other friend, Tadok, standing there alone, overlooking the valley and the funeral. Perhaps he was using his enhanced vision to see them.

To say Tadok had been crushed by Dorkah's death was a blatant understatement. The bond between the sorcerer and the strange creature was stronger than any bond between mortals. She was part of his soul. Bunda wasn't sure the half-elf would ever know how to live without her. Yet, he would do everything in his power to offer comfort and companionship to the lonely man. He, too, was now a brother in Bunda's eyes.

"So tonight, we write a new pact with our fallen. A pact and promise to remember them always. Remember the pain of their deaths along with the joys of their lives, and when the Dawn Father sends his rays of light come morning, shut your eyes, friends, and feel their touch, for they are watching over us."

He closed his eyes solemnly, and his voice and heart sang in *Alan-Nemtang*. An old prayer to the gods to watch over the souls of the fallen. As he did, candles were lit by the mourners and set in earthen grooves around each grave, lighting the cool night with a flickering warm glow.

When he was finished, silence washed over the grassy clearing. Only the wind whistled lightly through the branches of the old tree. The last leaves would soon fall, covering the new cemetery of Suldan's Bluff.

A place where heroes rested.

***

Despite Bunda's imagination, Tadok wasn't staring at the funeral from his place on the hill overlooking the village. His eyes gazed at the night sky. The storm clouds which had accompanied them since they'd met at the foothills had cleared, revealing a spectacular canopy of millions of endless stars.

Tadok knew many myths about the stars. They were the souls of the dead, holes poked in the blanket of night by some god or the torches of the hosts of heaven guarding against the hordes of hell. Tadok didn't truly believe any of them. This was because, in his experience, when men didn't know the reasons nature did what it did; they made them up.

Yet, if he was wrong, and they *were* souls of the dead, perhaps one of those shining pinpoints was Dorkah. Or maybe her soul would shine in the alien sky of her own world. The thought made him sad and lonely.

His mind wandered to his mother's funeral all those years ago. Standing in the fallen snow as the clerics shrouded her in white, he'd been so alone. But when Dorkah had first come to him, the little boy who he'd been had known in all certainty the universe had made a vow to him. He would never be alone again.

Tadok Starkin wasn't ready to release the universe of its vow just yet. Not tonight.

And thus, he sat on the grass and closed his eyes. He allowed his mind to return to that day in the woods when she'd first come to his aid. He channeled all the fear he'd felt as a boy desperately trying to escape his tormentors. He added to it all the terrifying experiences he'd shared with her since. It wasn't enough. And try as he might, his mind kept slipping into happier memories. Memories of them playing in the woods when he was a child with a new friend. His only friend. Of racing across meadows or unsuccessfully trying to hunt. He could feel in his mind the smooth touch of her skin as he'd laid his head on her warm flank countless nights by roadside fires. Just the two of them. Two minds. One soul.

Had his eyes been open, he would have seen the glow blooming in his forehead like a beacon. The glow intensified with his memories until it was so bright that had any of the villagers looked up at the hill that moment, they would have seen another star shining in the night.

Dorkah will live as long as you draw breath, Sellwyn had said. Tadok prayed for the first time since the death of his mother. He prayed to any god who would listen that Sellwyn had been right.

The light from his forehead slowly faded, and the hilltop was washed in darkness. The wind blowing through the grass was the only sound.

The corner of Tadok's mouth twisted into a smile. He carefully opened his half-elven eyes and gazed into Dorkah's black ones. She cocked her smooth head and allowed her long tongue to loll between the pointy teeth of her wide maw.

"There you are!" he said softly, tears of joy flowing down his cheeks.

"*Ta-dok*," purred the Eith'lin, who sidled up to him, pushing her snout against his face.

He threw his arms around her.

***

"All settled?" asked Odetta.

"I believe we are," answered Robin, fastening the pack saddle to the horse's flank. He checked the composition of supplies for their journey. Dried meats, cheeses and hard-tack bread, oats for the horses, warm wool and fur blankets and a satchel with salves and medicine provided by Aldeira. Thanks to Hayek, horses were abundant, and they had chosen the hardiest-looking ones for the journey to Sebin.

Robin leaned back, resting his hand on Hayek's rapier, which he'd claimed for himself. Robin would never know where the bandit lord had acquired it, but it was clearly the work of a master smith. It was perfectly weighted, and the basket hilt was gilded. A fine weapon. Across from it, on his other hip, was the strange dagger that had ended both Hayek's life two days ago and Malaketh's two millennia ago. He'd tested it out several times since the battle and even showed Bunda and Tadok its magical properties. Tadok had mentioned that the Enlightened Academy in Sebin may have magical scholars who could tell him more about the hidden properties of the ancient blade.

"Are you not concerned about riding into Sebin with Hayek's horses?" asked Hanlan, standing beside Aldeira on the green. He was now wearing the sheriff's badge as the new protector of Suldan's Bluff.

"No," answered the Heartlander, shaking his head. "These horses are unbranded. I'll wager Hayek and his men spent no coin for them anyway."

He looked eastwards to the rising sun. There were other dangers awaiting them at their destination. During the last two days since the battle, he'd thought more and more about Tommy and Dilal. What would await him when he finally made it to the capital of Nemir? But first they needed to make it to— and then out of— Sebin. There, Delona Ravin, who'd spurred Gale the Boon when he'd murdered his brother, reigned supreme over the Hands.

"What of you?" he asked, changing the subject. "Dell Hayek was answering to a master. That master may send others to pick up his errand."

Hanlan nodded solemnly. "Aye, they may. And we have decisions to make. But thanks to you three, we have choices where we had none before."

"You could still take the road to Berin's Inn. It may yet be perilous, but you'll have no bandits at your back."

Odetta shook her head and smiled. "This be our home, Robin Hugh. We've shed too much blood and tears over it, to abandon it now."

Hanlan nodded thoughtfully, then turned his head to the lonely tower on the hills east of the city. "The armies of Nemir were generous enough to leave us a, more or less, standing fort. I think that the winter snows blocking the pass may grace us with enough time to rebuild it, and make use of it, if a new Hayek chooses to bring trouble to our door."

It was an interesting thought. The tower would afford them road surveillance for miles in every direction. If a consistent watch was kept, the village would have ample time to reach its safety should a threat rise. Then his thoughts were drawn to the haunting memory of what lay beneath the tower.

"Hanlan," he began, thinking carefully about how to continue his sentence. "Below that tower. In the prison…"

"I'm sure Swegan and Diggery can think of a way to bury it." He smiled and then became solemn. "I swear to you, Robin, No one will find it."

They hadn't shared with the people of Suldan's Bluff what they had found below, beyond delivering Christopher Murley to his mother. He wasn't sure how much of it the boy had seen in the darkness he'd endured during his imprisonment there. They'd decided it was best for the villagers not to know about Malaketh and the Journal or anything they took from the tomb. Even so, their unwillingness to speak of it had spurred a few rumors in the town, and the general understanding was that whatever they found beyond the door would remain sealed and concealed.

Robin nodded uneasily.

"Well, whatever you do, I think Suldan's Bluff would do good to have another priest or cleric. A proper one this time."

"Aye, we will. Once things are settled, Mendel will head on down to Berin's Inn or Sebin and proposition the houses of worship there. I'm sure a holy man of one god or another would like to have his own parish. Perhaps we could welcome a cleric of Seirn?" he suggested hopefully, his eyes wandering to eastwards along the road to the place where Bunda and Tadok would meet him.

Odetta enforced the hint. "My boy, there be a home for all three of ye here, should ye wish to stay. I hope that be clear to ye..."

"True. I'm sure you'd make a better sheriff than I," said Hanlan.

Robin couldn't help the laughter that erupted from his gut as he mounted his horse. In his mind he heard Garian's ghost laughing too.

"Master Smith. *Sheriff,* that is. Better chance of me becoming your priest than me becoming a lawman."

***

The fire crackled in the small campsite, illuminating three men and one Eith'lin. It reminded Robin of the night they'd spent in the barn after their battle with the orcs. An event that seemed to have taken place ages ago even though a month had barely passed since.

"So she can't die?" asked Bunda from his seat on a fallen tree.

"It's not exactly as such," explained Tadok. "She *can* die, and she did. But our souls are connected as if with a tether. And while I live, she can be drawn back. At least I think that's the way it works," he said as he stroked the Eith'lin's smooth head.

Despite the joy Robin felt when Bunda and he had learned of the Eith'lin's return—more for Tadok than for himself, a sense of unease filled him when he stared at her.

Dorkah had visibly changed. She was still obviously Dorkah, but she'd grown larger. The muscles in her shoulder were more prominent, and nubs, which could have been small horns or ears, rose from her head where none had been. Wagging behind her was a new long black whip like tail which ended in a flat bony nub. Her mouth, which was previously lined with small needle-like teeth, now had two canine fangs, which hung lower than the rest of her teeth.

Yet, she was the same Dorkah. They'd asked, but Tadok had been unable to say why this strange evolution had occurred. The Eith'lin was a mystery to all of them. Even to the half-elf. Perhaps that's what made Robin most uneasy. Dorkah was evolving. But into what?

Yet, his friend was happier than Robin had ever seen him, and he didn't want to darken his mood. Instead, he changed the subject.

"If Trin favors us, our journey will continue as it is now, with no storms or snow."

"Trin doesn't control the weather. That is the business of other gods," answered Bunda sagely, sucking on a tobacco pipe.

The pipe had been a gift from Marven. All the villagers had tried to find ways to repay them. But the three of them had agreed among themselves that they would take no gold from the people of Suldan's Bluff. Hayek may be dead, but the winter was still perilous, and the loss of so many of their able-bodied men would pose many challenges in the next few months. Besides, Hayek's riders had left them horses to choose from, and they'd collected a fair share of corins and sorins from the dead bandits, enough to allow them to indulge themselves in a comfortable inn for at least a week when they reached Sebin.

Looking at his friend, Robin kept a secret opinion that the pipe made Bunda look comical. The broad-shouldered barbarian puffing on the stem of the pipe reminded him of one of the characters from "The Unsensible Elf," a comedy which was one of the Lion Theater's favorites. What had been the name of the befuddled old wizard who always seemed to misplace his pipe or spectacles? Was it Shiogen? He couldn't remember.

"Trin doesn't control the weather, but he does watch over travelers," he said wistfully.

"Oh, let's not start a theology debate before bed, please," said Tadok, rolling his eyes. "Pray to whomever you need to that the snows politely await our descent from the mountains."

Bunda frowned, but Robin smiled, clapping the large man on the back. He rose to his feet and stepped over to his blankets, which he'd placed near the fire, as was his habit. His back was aching from hours of being seated on the saddle, and he was grateful that Dorkah would keep watch tonight as she did every night. Having a member of the party that didn't sleep was proving itself very useful.

Suddenly, Tadok laughed loudly. A sound that Robin was unsure he'd ever heard before.

"What is it?" he asked as Bunda and he stared at the half-elf.

Tadok's laughter died down to a chuckle.

"Your name," he said between chuckles.

"What about it?"

"Your name is Robin Hugh."

"Aye, we've been through this," said Robin in confusion. Was this another argument about him lying to them? He'd thought they had gotten over each other's initial secrecy.

"You were a thief, and your name is 'Robin Hugh'."

"And?"

Bunda began laughing too.

"What are you two on about?" asked Robin, losing patience.

"Never mind, Sandisan, go to sleep."

Robin was about to argue, but he was simply too tired to do so. He would find a way to wring the punchline of this joke out from Tadok or Bunda tomorrow.

The blankets given to them by Tilly were soft and welcoming. And the fire had slightly toasted the wool, which was the perfect remedy for the chilly night air.

"Robin," began Tadok as Robin wormed his way into his bedroll and closed his eyes.

"Hmmm?" he asked sleepily.

"How dangerous will Sebin be? Won't Hayek's mistress, this Delona Ravin, seek revenge?"

"Aye, there is that chance. Although chances are that none who escaped the battle managed to make it through the pass horseless and wounded."

"Seems like a dangerous thing to leave to fate," said Bunda from his own bedroll.

Robin shrugged. "Feel free to pray if you wish," he began, pausing to yawn. "In any case, I don't plan for us to be there much. Perhaps a day. No more."

"I have an errand at the Enlightened Academy which I need to attend to," stated the half-elf.

"Oh?" asked Robin, lifting his head to look at Tadok. It was the first he'd mentioned it.

Tadok paused before answering. "I wish to present them with the necromantic wand Sheilagh possessed. The crazed priest and his dark mistress must have a connection to the demon's tomb."

"It could be a coincidence," suggested Bunda.

"Perhaps," said the half-elf, but it seemed unlikely to all of them.

Robin didn't want to think of the torture chamber in the undercroft of the church, or of Malaketh's tomb. Not so close to sleep. He'd been having strange dreams of being suffocated in the darkness, of dying buried alive under mountains of rock. He assumed it was natural, considering the ordeal they'd emerged from.

"I suppose we'll have enough time for it in the city, but we should try not to dawdle there. Peddling dark artifacts may draw prying eyes, which are best avoided."

"And where from there?" asked Tadok after a pause.

"East. Sandisan," he replied curtly. "A place with answers, I hope."

He lay awake thinking of Tommy and Dilal. But imagining his brother's plight didn't bring on sleep either. So, he gazed up at the stars and called upon the memory of little Christopher and Aldeira locked in a loving embrace in the tower courtyard. So many things in his life had gone so horribly wrong. Yet here, in the middle of nowhere, he'd made a difference, and a little boy had returned home to his mother. In a world wracked by wars, bandits, and chaos, it was a tiny thing. But it was a start.

As sleep overtook him, Robin's heart found hope.

EPILOGUE

I wait. I wait and I dream. I dream of return to my realm and my city. To my throne. I dream of revenge on those that had deposed me. But before this, I dream of escape. Of release. The agony of my death is frozen in time, tormenting me for eternity. The hours become days, the days become years, and the years become centuries. All the while, my pain is unending.

I am substance without form. Purpose without shape. My conscious floats in darkness, with nothing and no one to touch, and nothing to consume. This is my existence, now and for all time.

But then, a shift. A change in my endless prison. I sense something new. It is just a sliver, but it is there.

Another consciousness. Another soul touches my prison. There is a crack. An infinitely small crack, but a crack, nonetheless.

I am nothing. I am smoke and shadow. Still, my will is endless. I focus on the crack, and the gap widens. It is still too small for escape, but now I sense the world beyond.

I feel...hope.

I will put my essence into a word. A single word spoken by a voice with no owner.

Robin.

In the small clearing in the middle of a lonely mountain pass, under a star-filled night, Robin's eyes shot open.

THE END

ABOUT THE AUTHOR

E.Y Bluestein lives in northern Israel with his wife and three boys. When he isn't dreaming of demons and sorcerers he's a business development director for a large tech firm. It's not as glamorous as the intrigues of Trosia, but it pays the mortgage and he's pretty good at it.

Demonic is his first published book and is the first step in the wonderous Soul Trade Saga - an Epic tale of adventure, sacrifice and a whole lot of hack-and-slash.

Made in the USA
Columbia, SC
04 November 2024

44986667R00167